# MARRIAGE
# AT THE COWBOY'S
# COMMAND

BY
ANN MAJOR

AND

# HOW TO SEDUCE
# A BILLIONAIRE

BY
KATE CARLISLE

MILLS & BOON

## "This isn't happening," she whispered.

"Something sure as hell is," he muttered, sounding angry and lost too all of a sudden. "I should have stood my ground and stayed in London."

"You could always just go."

"No, it's too late now. The damage is done." His eyes devoured hers, and she thought he stared straight into her soul, which had always belonged only to him. "I've seen you. I've touched you. And I'm curious…about a lot of things."

She didn't understand the stillness that possessed her, held her and him. Was she in a trance? Was he? Clasped tightly against his tall, muscular body, his heat flooding her, she could barely think, barely breathe.

"I'm going to hate you for this," she whispered, and then she kissed him.

Dear Reader,

While I grew up in a city in south Texas, the rest of my family lived in a small Texas ranching town near the Panhandle. One of the highlights of my summers back then was visiting my cousins up north and riding their horse, Gypsy, bareback…all day long. Maybe Gypsy didn't enjoy this as much as we did because she regularly bucked us off.

Stories about independent women who love horses became a part of me early on. I've always liked reunion romances too. So, why not a reunion romance about a horse woman and the cowboy who left her behind to become a billionaire in London?

Six years later, when Luke returns home, Caitlyn is a widow with a son. Her ranch is heavily mortgaged and she is in danger of losing her horses.

Luke is the last man Caitlyn wants to have anything to do with. When Luke learns her son is his, he offers to help her…for a price. Of course, the price they will both have to pay for their new life together is love.

Enjoy,

*Ann Major*

P.S. Visit me at www.annmajor.com!

# MARRIAGE
# AT THE COWBOY'S
# COMMAND

BY
ANN MAJOR

Published in Great Britain 2012
by Mills & Boon, an imprint of Harlequin (UK) Limited,
Eton House, 18-24 Paradise Road, Richmond, Surrey TW9 1SR

© Ann Major 2011

ISBN: 978 0 263 89135 5

51-0312

Harlequin (UK) policy is to use papers that are natural, renewable and recyclable products and made from wood grown in sustainable forests. The logging and manufacturing processes conform to the legal environmental regulations of the country of origin.

Printed and bound in Spain
by Blackprint CPI, Barcelona

**Ann Major** lives in Texas with her husband of many years and is the mother of three grown children. She has a master's degree from Texas A&M at Kingsville, Texas, and is a former English teacher. She is a founding board member of the Romance Writers of America and a frequent speaker at writers' groups.

Ann loves to write; she considers her ability to do so a gift. Her hobbies include hiking in the mountains, sailing, ocean kayaking, traveling and playing the piano. But most of all she enjoys her family. Visit her website at www.annmajor.com.

This book is dedicated to Stacy Boyd and Shana Smith and the Desire team. Their names do not appear on the cover, but they worked very hard to improve this story, and I am deeply in their debt.

# One

Desperation mounting, Caitlyn Wakefield stared at her accounting ledgers. There was no way she could make her next mortgage payment to Sheik Hassan Bin Najjar. No way.

So, what would she say to Hassan's mysterious honorary son, Raffi Bin Najjar, when he showed up today to check on her operation?

She had no clue.

She'd gone over the books numerous times, hoping she'd figure out how to make her next payment and get her ranch on a viable financial footing, but all she saw were too many fixed expenses without enough income.

Even if she asked Hassan for more time, which she believed he would give her, she needed to make some serious and painful adjustments or she'd just be deeper in debt down the line. She couldn't expect Hassan to bankroll her forever.

The awful numbers began to blur and her head to pound.

She hated disappointing Hassan. She wanted to make him proud of her. But the sales she'd counted on hadn't materialized. And she was again on the verge of losing her ranch, just as she'd been six months ago when Hassan had helped her by buying her mortgage.

It was nothing short of a miracle that Hassan, one of the world's richest sheiks, had become her friend, benefactor and banker. The fact that he was wealthy and she was not and that he spent most of his time in the Middle East and Europe while she lived in Texas would have been more than enough to keep them from ever knowing one another but for their mutual passion for Thoroughbreds.

They'd met by chance at the September yearling sales in Keeneland, Virginia, more than a year ago. Her timely advice had saved Hassan from buying an overpriced animal that had gone lame a mere four months later during a race, causing a jockey's death. The animal had been destroyed. The sheik had written her a note, thanking her, saying he would have hated being involved in a tragedy of that magnitude.

Then, six months ago, he'd phoned her again when Sahara, one of his most promising Thoroughbreds, developed a problem with starting gates. Caitlyn had been stunned by the sheik's offer to come to his stables in Deauville to work with the animal—for three times her normal fee.

It was just after her success with Sahara that he'd gotten to the bottom of her financial distress over a dinner they'd shared. Soon after, he bought her note from the bank.

Considering how much Hassan had done for her,

she hated disappointing him. What could she say to his honorary son that would reassure Hassan?

Frustrated, she slammed the books shut. Only when her gaze fell to the small snapshot of her son, Daniel, riding bareback did her expression soften.

He'd been forbidden to ride the horse by himself, of course. Smiling, she picked up the picture and stared at his slim, dark likeness. Even when he was driving her crazy by being too curious or foolhardy, he filled her long days with joy. He was five, all boy and way too big for his britches a lot of the time, but she remembered how proud she'd been of him at Keeneland last year. Hassan, too, had been impressed with Daniel. So much so that he'd told her about his only biological son, Kalil, whom he'd nearly lost to a kidnapping in Paris a few years earlier.

"That's when I made Raffi, the man who rescued Kalil, my honorary son," Hassan had said.

She had smiled politely, her mind on the animals in the various pens and on Daniel, who'd been darting about under their feet.

"Your son reminds me of Raffi. So much energy. Once that energy is harnessed, he will be formidable."

"Really?" she'd replied, not paying much attention to Hassan's remark.

"Yes, even Daniel's eyes resemble Raffi's. They are the same shade of green. It's an unusual color in my part of the world."

"In ours, too," she'd said absently. "His father had green eyes."

They'd talked more, about Texas and her ranch. He'd asked for a card.

"Raffi once lived in Texas…in your vicinity, I

believe." Hassan's gaze, more intent than before, had been on Daniel.

Ever since that first meeting at Keeneland, in all his calls and notes, Hassan always asked about Daniel. His grandfatherly interest in her son had become one of the chief reasons she liked the sheik so much.

Setting down Daniel's picture, she tried to refocus on the problem at hand. She hated that she could think of nothing that would turn Wild Horse Ranch around. Not that she wasn't used to being broke. When she was a child, her parents had constantly worried about bills and creditors. Never would she forget the day her father had told her and her mother that he'd lost their ranch. When they'd been forced to move into town and lease land for their ranching operation, she'd felt shattered. Nearly as shattered as she'd be if she couldn't win Raffi Bin Najjar's sympathy.

Chewing a fingernail, she went to the window and stared out at the sea of brown grasses. The early December air had been cool and crisp an hour before dawn, when she'd arisen. Her only indulgence before coming to her office was a single cup of strong black coffee.

*To give me strength,* she thought as she circled the cold cup with her fingertips.

What could she say to a stranger who probably knew little about ranching, even if he'd spent time in Texas? How could he—a wealthy, sophisticated man, who lived in London—possibly appreciate the calamity the worst drought in decades had wrought on her ranch and horse farm? How could a bachelor sympathize when she told him she'd been distracted and unfocused after her husband's death, when she'd had her grief, his work and hers and her son to take care of? How could a billionaire understand the effect of an entire country mired in recession? Everybody wanted to sell their horses, not buy hers. Her income had diminished while her expenses had continued to mount. Business was picking up. But not quickly enough.

Swigging back the last of her cold coffee, she tried not to think about being the second Cooper to lose the ranch despite all her sacrifices to save it. The biggest sacrifice being her marriage to Robert, when she'd found herself pregnant and alone nearly six years ago. Not wanting to remember what had led to her wedding day, she fled to the stalls to feed her beloved horses.

Sensing her anxiety from the rapid ring of her boot heels on the concrete floor of the barn, Angel and the other horses swung their necks around and watched her with their concerned brown eyes. Their tails lifted and swished expectantly while the barn cats swirled at her feet.

Odd, the profound comfort she always felt when alone in the barn with these huge animals. Their soulful silence as she stroked them brought her peace during times of stress.

Angel nuzzled Caitlyn's hand with her whiskery muzzle, searching for a treat. "Robert was a bad manager," Caitlyn whispered to the horse, "and I'm no better. I spend too much money on all of you, my precious darlings." Angel nickered softly as if she understood. "I need a miracle, and soon."

Angel snorted.

"Well, it's possible! Hassan says his son is a billionaire, that there's nothing he can't fix. Raffi made his fortune in a mere five years, you see, by buying distressed companies."

Perhaps she could convince him that a distressed

ranch wasn't that different from a company in trouble. She felt a faint twinge of hope as she remembered what Hassan had said when he'd shamelessly bragged about his son.

In a recent phone conversation, when she'd complained of her escalating expenses, Hassan had told her she was a woman of talent who shouldn't have to worry about money.

"I will send my son to devise a plan to put you on sound footing. He will know just what to do once he takes a look at your operation. He is a brilliant businessman."

She'd been scheduled to meet this brilliant businessman six months ago, when the sheik had flown her to Deauville to work with Sahara. Hassan had told her that Raffi would dine with them, but his son had been unexpectedly called away on business.

To prepare for their meeting today, she'd researched Raffi, but there hadn't been many articles about him or a single good photograph. Most of the stories rehashed the event that had brought Hassan and Raffi together, a tale she'd heard from Hassan.

Five years earlier, after Raffi had single-handedly confronted three terrorists to rescue Kalil, Hassan had hired him. Raffi advanced rapidly and, with the sheik's money behind him, had soon branched out on his own. The sheik had sealed their bond by making Raffi his honorary son. During their shared dinner in Deauville, Hassan had confided that he would like to see Raffi settle down and raise a family.

From what she'd gleaned on the internet about the younger Mr. Bin Najjar's private life, he went through women the way some men ran through cigars. But a woman like her—a horse trainer who wore old jeans and rarely bothered with makeup—wouldn't interest him.

"What do you think, Angel? Should I go the extra mile and put on lipstick?"

Angel whinnied enthusiastically, probably because Caitlyn was holding a carrot.

"Lipstick it is, then. Maybe Mr. Raffi Bin Najjar will give us our very own miracle."

As Caitlyn stroked the mare, she relaxed.

Only later would she wonder why she hadn't had the slightest premonition that Raffi Bin Najjar was no stranger to Wild Horse Ranch—or to her.

By the afternoon, Caitlyn had forgotten all about the need for lipstick. All it had taken for her day to spin hopelessly out of control was one phone call.

Lisa, her best friend and owner of the neighboring ranch, had sounded so desperate. "You know bees stung Ramblin' Man in his trailer last week, and he hasn't been himself. I have to move him to Mom's stud barn to cover a couple of mares, but he simply will not load. I don't know what to do. Can you help me?"

"Only if you can ride him over here, and get someone to drive the trailer to my round pen," Caitlyn had said. "Daniel's ridden off somewhere with Manuel, and I've got an important business meeting in a couple of hours with Mr. Bin Najjar's son."

"Oh, right—about your mortgage."

"Bin Najjar's driver just phoned and said they're on their way from the airport. So, I'm stuck here."

"Oh. Okay. I guess I can make that work."

So now, instead of going over her accounts, preparing for her meeting or bothering with lipstick, Caitlyn was standing in Ramblin' Man's shadowy horse trailer, holding a lead rope attached to the stallion's halter. Wild-eyed Ramblin' Man had only put a single hoof in the trailer and was staring at her as if she were a giant.

"It's okay, baby. Nothing to be scared of," Caitlyn said gently. Snapping the lead line, she backed Ramblin' Man out of the trailer before he grew more alarmed. "You were so brave to put a foot into the trailer."

When she gave the command to retreat, a relieved Ramblin' Man jerked backward and raced away. Caitlyn jumped out of the trailer and watched him run. She'd bring him back in a minute or two. He needed to build up his courage to work on what they'd already accomplished.

"Caitlyn!" Lisa squealed from the far side of the round pen. "Why didn't you tell me Luke Kilgore was your mysterious appointment?"

Caitlyn recoiled, the name of her former lover slicing her heart like a knife.

*Luke? Luke, who'd left her pregnant at twenty-one? No... Why would he show up today, of all days?*

She jerked her head around and saw the tall, dark man in the flawlessly cut business suit lounging against the rail beside Lisa. The sight of him looking so virile and smolderingly masculine made her mouth go dry. Once, she had longed for Luke's return, dreamed of it. But now her dream felt like a nightmare!

Those gorgeous green eyes, the high forehead, the chiseled cheek and jaw, that classically straight nose and those mocking, sensual lips that had once kissed every inch of her body—they could belong to no one but Luke. The shock of recognition made her shiver with torrid memories.

He was as handsome as ever, but this elegantly

dressed man couldn't possibly be the same bitterly ambitious cowboy she'd loved.

"What are *you* doing here?" she demanded.

"My driver said he called and confirmed. You and I have an appointment."

"*You're* Raffi Bin Najjar?"

He nodded. "I've been known to answer to that."

"What kind of man changes his name?"

"I have two names. The one I was born with and the one Hassan gave me when he asked me to be his honorary son. Hassan prefers to call me Raffi. So I let him. One of my weaknesses is indulging those I love."

"You're too old to be adopted," she said, lashing out with her words.

"Who said anything about adoption?" His lips smiled, but his eyes didn't. Obviously, he was a man of the world now.

"What exactly does it mean, then, to be an honorary son?"

"Ask Hassan. He probably made it up. Hell, for all I know I'm the only honorary son in the world." He moved away from the rail. "Sorry my showing up here is such a shock," he said.

"No, you aren't. You deliberately tricked me!"

"Think what you like."

"I don't *like* anything about this situation!"

"Maybe neither the hell do I."

Still, despite her fear and the nameless dark emotions engulfing her, his taunting, all-too-familiar, husky voice drew her, just like it had that first day when he'd stood on her porch asking if he could see her daddy because he'd needed a job and nobody else in the county would even talk to Bubba Kilgore's son. She'd been a teenager and highly susceptible to the lure of the forbidden. Her crush had lasted several years—right up until he'd gotten her pregnant and left the county for good.

Well, at twenty-six, knowing what he was and what he'd done, she should be immune to his charms.

*Right.* If she was so grown-up and mature, why had the pace of her heart accelerated?

Her gaze darted past him to the house. *Where was Daniel?* She hoped, *prayed* he'd stay out of sight until she got rid of Luke.

"You're looking good, Caitlyn," Luke said, but his lips didn't curve into the sexy smile that used to follow her name.

Not that she wanted it to.

"You, too," she said reluctantly. The last thing she wanted to do was flatter him. "How is this possible?" she said, motioning to him, standing in her yard.

"What? The son of the county's no-account drunk making good?"

Lisa's sudden burst of flirtatious laughter was awkward. "Don't run yourself down. You've come a long way since then, Luke. You never were anything like Bubba."

"Thanks."

"Caitlyn's told me how rich your honorary father is! And how rich *you* are!" She moistened her lips and glanced at him slyly through her long, dark eyelashes.

Luke looked away.

Caitlyn winced. Her friend's excessive interest in Luke bothered her. As did her words.

She remembered how Luke had once had a habit of making self-deprecating remarks. People laughed, as he'd intended, but she'd known his jokes had covered soul-deep shame for having Bubba as a father. Luke had always wanted to be more than he'd been. Well, now he was rich and powerful, but was he any happier?

Quickly she reminded herself that his happiness wasn't her problem. He'd jilted her and moved on to better things, more beautiful women. He'd probably never hungered for her—as she'd hungered for him.

Or had he? He did seem as keenly aware of her as she was of him, which was hatefully gratifying.

As Lisa leaned closer to him, Caitlyn insinuated herself between them. "So, you really are Raffi Bin Najjar? I did some research, but couldn't find much."

Luke pushed away from the railing and stood taller. He'd filled out, but on him, the extra weight looked good. She was sure he was made of hot, solid muscle. The thought of touching him now made her own skin heat.

"I pay people to remove stuff I don't want on the web," Luke said.

"You can do that?"

"Most of the time. I'm not a movie star, so I'm not hounded by the paparazzi unless I'm out with somebody famous."

"Like your supermodel girlfriends?"

His mouth twisted. "Jealous?"

"Of course not! But you should have told me who you were, you know."

"Why? I'm here as a favor to Hassan. Not because I want to make your life easier. For some reason, he's become fascinated by you and your affairs."

"He's been extremely helpful."

"Yes, and I want to know why. I couldn't find out if I'd tipped you off."

"He told me you once lived here, but, of course, since

I didn't know who you really were, I thought nothing of it."

"I'm as curious about his motivations as you are. Did you two talk about me the night you went to dinner in France?"

"Not much."

"Did he tell you he invited me to come that night?"

"Yes, but I didn't know who you were, so I didn't pursue it."

"I watched you through binoculars when you were working with Sahara and decided to bow out."

So, Luke had been in Deauville, too, and had deliberately rejected her. Again.

This whole situation felt like a setup. She remembered Hassan's comments at Keeneland about the color of Daniel's eyes. She remembered Hassan asking her about Daniel over dinner in Deauville. When he'd asked questions about her son, she'd thought he was merely being polite. She'd been so proud of Daniel. She'd talked way too much about him, given away too much. She'd shown Hassan pictures, and he'd stared at them for a long time, even asking if he could keep one.

Had Hassan figured out who Daniel's father was? As one of the world's richest men, he could probably find out anything he wanted to know. Of course he would be curious about his protégé's past. Had he sent Luke here to discover Daniel?

Maybe this reunion could have been avoided if she'd been more clever. But no, she'd taken Hassan's actions at face value. He'd written her a note after Keeneland, and fool that she'd been, she'd felt flattered that such a man had remembered her name. When he'd called and asked her to help with Sahara, she'd been flattered again. And she'd needed the money too badly to question his motives. Then, once she was in France, she'd been too impressed by the glamour of his château and stables to think rationally.

"We stuck to small talk mostly," she said now, without mentioning their conservation about Daniel.

"But after taking you to dinner, he bought your mortgage. Anything happen…*after* dinner?" Luke's hot gaze slid over her slowly, causing her nerves to sizzle. Did he think she was easy because she'd been easy with him?

"Don't you dare insinuate that your…'father' and I had an affair, because we didn't. He was nice to me. That's all."

The intensity of Luke's gaze unnerved her. "Half a million dollars nice?"

"During dinner, I told him about my ranch. We got into finances, and I was frank about my problems. I was afraid I was about to lose the ranch. He said he appreciated what I had done for Sahara and that he wanted to help me. He stunned me by saying he'd buy the mortgage and help me get back onto my feet."

"That was all there was to it? Hassan doesn't make a habit of befriending people and rescuing them."

"He calls *you* his son!"

"I saved his kid's life. Took a bullet, too. You work with Sahara an hour or two—and he buys your mortgage? I don't get it."

She hadn't, either—although she now had a few suspicions.

"I needed the money, so I took what he offered. Wouldn't anybody in my position have done the same thing? Didn't *you?*"

"He taught me a lot when I went to work for him," Luke agreed. "He opened a lot of doors."

"I'll say. Those doors must have been made of solid gold. Five years later you're a billionaire."

Ramblin' Man walked over to the trailer and stuck his nose inside. She noted his behavior, but couldn't take any satisfaction in his progress, so long as Luke was here.

"It's true. I owe him everything. And I think the only reason Hassan helped you was because of me," Luke said.

"You? I don't get it."

"Somehow he must have figured out we'd been involved. There's nothing he wouldn't do for family, and if you claimed some tie to me…"

"But I didn't."

She again remembered Hassan's comments about Daniel's eyes and she felt afraid. Still, with an air of bravado, she said, "Why don't you ask him why he helped me?"

"I did ask him. He was evasive. So, I came here to satisfy my curiosity, and because Hassan forced the issue. The fact is, this ranch is the last place I'd willingly return to. Just as you are the last person I'd help, if I had a choice. But Hassan wants to help you, and he asked me to figure out how to do it, so here we are—stuck with each other."

"Why don't you just leave?"

"And tell Hassan to keep bailing you out? No, I'm going to get to the bottom of this. I'm here to protect Hassan."

His narrowed green eyes pierced her. His sharp words stung. *She was the last person he'd help, if he had a choice.*

He was angry. Why? He'd betrayed her family, jilted her and left her pregnant, with unattractive options, while he'd reinvented himself as this arrogant, world-class businessman. What did he have to be mad about? Unless he knew about Daniel…which he didn't. At least, not yet.

Again her gaze strayed to the house, searching for Daniel.

*Don't panic. Be polite. Just send him on his way—fast.* How hard could it be to get rid of a man who didn't want to be here?

So much for her miracle. She was in worse trouble than before.

Caitlyn turned to Lisa. "Look, I need to talk to Luke. In private. You can work with Ramblin' Man on your own until I get back. Do a little groundwork…like I showed you before he put his foot into the trailer."

"Okay," Lisa said reluctantly, glancing at Luke.

"Follow me," Caitlyn said curtly as she unlatched a gate and headed out of the round pen. She was tired of Lisa hanging on to their every word, and there was the added danger that Lisa might blurt out something about Daniel.

Luke nodded casually to Lisa before loping after Caitlyn. "Look, if you need to get her stallion in the trailer before we talk, go ahead. I have a report from one of my CEOs that I need to read. Our meeting can wait a half hour. Lisa told me about the bees."

He'd had time for a private chitchat with Lisa before Caitlyn had seen him. Her sudden burst of jealousy infuriated her.

Caitlyn stopped in the shadow of the barn and whirled to face him. "I'm canceling our meeting."

"The hell you are. I flew all the way from London."

"I don't care if you flew in from another galaxy. You had no right to come here under false pretenses."

"I promised Hassan I'd figure out a solution to your problems."

"I don't want your help. You're too late, Luke Kilgore. Six years too late. I've made it this long without you. I can keep on making it without you."

His green eyes flamed with surprise, and fresh suspicion. "What the hell do you mean by that?"

Her hand flew to her lips and she took a step backward. She'd almost said too much. Maybe she *had* said too much. Notching her chin higher, she held her ground. "Nothing," she said. "I want you to leave! Now! You haven't been welcome here for a very long time."

"Is that so?" He glanced upward to the barn. "I remember a time when things were very different between us."

She remembered, too. They'd made wild, sweet, unforgettable love in the hayloft. Ever since, he'd haunted her dreams. Even after he'd abandoned her, he'd cast a long shadow over her marriage.

"When you were a teenager, you followed me everywhere. I couldn't load a bale of hay without finding you watching me," he said. "You damn near threw yourself at me."

"I was a young, stupid fool!" she cried, hating that she'd once made no secret of how intensely she'd felt about him.

"I was the fool. Hell, maybe I still am." He grabbed her by the waist, pulled her close. "If it's the last thing I do, I'll figure out why Hassan really sent me here. I thought he wanted me to marry the woman I'm dating, Teresa. Then suddenly he sends me here. Why?"

She jerked free of his grip because she couldn't concentrate when in his arms. "I thought he sent you to solve my money problems."

"There's another reason. I'm sure of it. You made him think we're still connected."

She shook her head in denial. "I didn't." Frantic to distract Luke, she said, "Teresa? Is she another of your gorgeous supermodels?"

"No. A countess."

In spite of the fact that his love life was no concern of hers, Caitlyn was suddenly crushingly aware of how plain and unappealing she must seem in her dusty jeans. He'd become a mega-success while she was on the verge of bankruptcy.

Only by biting her tongue until she tasted the coppery flavor of blood was she able to remain silent. Too bad that the minute she quit biting it, she lost the battle to prove she could behave like a lady.

"If she's so perfect, you'd be a fool not to propose to her!"

"She's a little young. Nineteen. I was actually considering asking her to marry me, when Hassan started in on me about coming here. Ever since he met you at Keeneland, he's asked questions about my life in Texas. He won't say why, but I think he's decided I'm still hung up on you. Well, I'm not! I don't believe in rehashing or whining about the past, and I'll do whatever it takes to convince him—even work with you on your finances."

She caught a whiff of his musky scent mingling with minty cologne, and her feminine hormones flared. "So marry your precious Teresa and prove you and I are ancient history!"

His eyes slid over her. "You don't look much like ancient history. You look as sassy as ever. So, no man's tamed you yet? Not even your husband?"

"Leave him out of this! He's dead, you know."

"I'm sorry." There was genuine regret in his deep tone. "This is a big place. In the middle of nowhere. It must get lonely out here."

Unimaginably lonely, especially at night, when the wind blew and the eaves groaned and the coyotes howled as she lay in the dark, her head spinning with money worries.

She'd lain awake, alone, for too long. But she had a ranch to run, son to raise, hence little time for fun.

Too aware of the hunger that sparked in Luke's green eyes and her own vulnerability, she took a step backward.

When he reached out and took her by the hand, she fought to pull it free. He held on tight, lifting her palm and inspecting it closely.

"You've been working hard. Too hard." The sympathy in his voice surprised her and temporarily lessened her anger. Without thinking, she quit tugging and leaned closer to him.

What was she doing? Softening toward him? She should fight him harder, yank her hand free, but her emotions were escalating too fast to control. His tall, powerful body and his understanding intoxicated her. She'd done without a man's passion for too long. Done without *him*. If only she'd had an inkling she'd see him today, she could have steeled herself.

Instead of trying to run, she froze. His beautiful green eyes—eyes she had so adored—stared straight into hers, igniting her soul, burning away the years and the hurt and the hatred, and melting her resistance.

He lifted her callused palm to his lips and kissed it. Only then did she jerk her hand from his. "You probably prefer women with soft hands."

"I thought I did. These days I don't meet many

women who work outside with animals the way you do. When I left Texas, I dated lots of women. Until I saw you working with Ramblin' Man, I thought I'd put you totally behind me.

"You were so good with him. I respect that. You looked so beautiful and wild. I wish I'd come back, at least once, to check on you. I suddenly realized I never…said goodbye."

"No…you didn't." She caught herself. "This isn't happening," she whispered, feeling shattered by his admission, by the sweetness of his kiss on her poor battered hand.

"Something sure as hell is," he muttered, sounding angry and lost. "I should have stood my ground and stayed in London."

"You could always just go."

"It's too late now. The damage is done." His eyes devoured hers. He stared straight into her soul, which had always belonged only to him. "I've seen you. I've touched you. And now I'm curious…about a lot of things."

She didn't understand the stillness that possessed her, held her. Was she in a trance? Clasped tightly against his tall, muscular body, his heat flooding her, she could barely think, barely breathe.

It was as if she were in a dream, as if she was again caught in the vortex of the youthful passion that had nearly destroyed her. For years she'd told herself she'd do it differently if she was ever faced with such temptation again.

Now, here he was.

*Time to smarten up, Caitlyn.*

But she lifted her head, parted her lips invitingly. Her nipples tightened into pert berries, throbbing where they brushed his shirt and felt his heat. Slowly he lowered his mouth to hers, nibbling her top lip as he'd done in the past, sucking on it, tasting it. Then she melted against him.

"Oh, God," he muttered.

Instantly, nerves tingled in her tummy. Where he was concerned, she'd always been easy. Why did he have to make her feel so good, so fast?

Sighing, she wrapped her arms around his neck, threaded her fingers in his silky hair, stood on her tiptoes and kissed him right back. He was simply too delicious to resist.

"I'm going to hate you for this," she whispered, her voice thick. "Most of all, I'm going to hate me."

"I hear you, sweetheart."

Then his tongue invaded her mouth, and sweet, urgent needs made her arch her body into his hardness. Like a mare showing heat, excitement blazed through her. She ached with needs she'd never felt for any other man, not even her husband.

She knew what she was doing was wrong. Luke had hurt her, rejected her, hurt Daniel without even knowing Daniel existed. She hated him for all the lost years since he'd left.

And yet there were other emotions alongside the hate. Kissing him now was like coming home after living for too many years with strangers. She couldn't get enough. She wanted him to tear off her jeans, throw her over his shoulder and carry her into the barn. She wanted to open her legs and lie down in the hay with him again.

She wanted too much. She always had.

For another long second she was alone in the universe with him. Then Ramblin' Man exploded in the trailer and Lisa yelled.

As if he suddenly realized where he was and what he was doing, Luke's hands fell away. He jumped free of her with an abruptness that startled her.

Distantly, she heard Lisa soothing Ramblin' Man in the round pen.

Luke's eyes hardened, and he cursed low under his breath.

In a bewildered daze, she stared at him. More than anything, she had wanted to stay in his arms, to cling to his strength, to enjoy feeling like a woman for the first time in years.

But that was impossible now.

"Take your hands off me! Let me go!" Caitlyn whispered needlessly. The humiliating truth was that Luke had already moved away and was no longer touching her.

He was silent for what seemed an eternity.

What was he thinking? Did he have demons she knew nothing about?

"You kiss like a woman who hasn't had any in six years," he growled, glaring at her.

She stared down at the scuffed toe of her roper boots. As always, he was uncannily perceptive. The last thing she wanted him to suspect was how she'd longed for him all through the lonely years of her marriage.

"If you want it that bad, we'd better go inside," he said. "Or do you still prefer the loft? Frankly, it doesn't matter to me. All I want is to get you out of my system—permanently."

Feeling ashamed of her reaction to him, she lashed out at him, too. "Ditto! I don't want you touching me again—ever! I want you gone! That's what I want."

"You didn't kiss me like a woman who wants me gone, sweetheart."

"I don't know what came over me, but believe me, I want you gone."

"Well, while I figure out your finances and Hassan's motives, I'll figure out our chemistry, as well."

"No! You're going to forget that stupid kiss and go— now."

"And if I go, how will you solve your money problems?"

"I'm too upset to think about that."

"Well, you'd better think about it."

"I can't work with you."

"You'd better adjust your attitude, because you don't have a choice."

Looking every bit as upset as she felt, he shoved a lock of thick black hair back from his brow. "Tell you what. I'll leave…for tonight, so you can adjust to the idea of me being around. But I'll be gone for one night only. Then I'm moving in until we get this mystery solved and your mess figured out. You're fifty miles from town, and, after tonight, I don't want to waste time commuting. You'll need to make up a spare bedroom for me."

"The hell you say! Do you think I would let you move into my house after what just happened? I don't want you in this state!"

"Do you really want me to tell Hassan you won't work with me?"

Of course not. And Luke knew it.

"Because I will," he said. "If I tell him to pull the plug on you, he'll do it."

She shook her head, not wanting to believe that.

"The ranch and your horse operation will be history. I could convince him to sell everything at auction. You know what that means."

Yes. She knew. There was such a weak market for her horses, that several would be euthanized or sold to meat packers.

"Hassan would never…"

"I think I know him better than you do. He wants to help you, but if you refuse his help you will leave him no choice but to make unpleasant decisions. Do you want to lose the ranch again, like your daddy did?" he continued. "Only, this time there won't be a rich idiot like Robert Wakefield to marry and give it back to you."

"I haven't lost it yet, thank you very much! You're only rich because of your connections to Hassan. Well, I know the real you, and maybe I don't think you're so great. My mother warned me that you were just like Bubba."

Her mother had fired Luke because he was a thief. Cait hadn't wanted to believe he'd stolen cash out of her father's truck, but when Luke had never returned or contacted her to contradict her mother's claim, the truth of his betrayal had seemed self-evident.

"So, you believed her?" Something flashed in his eyes. Was it pain? Or rage? "You're wrong," he said. "You don't know me at all. You never did. And I didn't know you, either, or I would never have been fool enough to mistake you for a sweet, innocent girl and fall in love with you."

His startling admission flashed through her like lightning. He'd never admitted he loved her, and she wasn't about to believe him now. Believing him would only soften her heart toward him.

*Love.* He didn't know the meaning of the word.

"Leave," she whispered.

Much to her surprise, he nodded. "Like I said…I'm going…for now. I intend to spend the afternoon talking to your accountant. I had hoped to take you with me, but it seems our new business arrangement is going to take some getting used to."

He spun on his heel and strode toward the long black limo parked in front of her house.

If only this would be the last she'd ever see of him. But he'd be back tomorrow, and while he was in town there was no telling what people might tell him about Daniel, especially if he asked the right questions. There had been talk at the time of her marriage—talk that had never completely died.

Even if no one talked, if Luke moved in, he'd see Daniel on a daily basis. There was no way she could keep the truth a secret for long.

Better that she control how he found out.

She shut her eyes and sucked in a breath. She had to tell him the truth herself.

"Wait!" She ran after his tall, broad-shouldered figure.

He turned and regarded her so coldly, a chill traced down her spine. How would she ever find the courage to tell him he had a son? But she had to. Period.

"I'll meet you in town…a little later…after I finish working with Ramblin' Man," she said. "What time's your appointment?"

He told her.

She licked her lips and said she'd be there thirty minutes late. "After we get through talking with Bruce, there's something I need to tell you. Something personal," she whispered awkwardly, staring anywhere but at him. "It's very important. Maybe we could have coffee at Jean's Butterchurn. We can talk privately there."

His eyes narrowed. "This isn't going to be good news, is it?"

"I guess that will depend on how you take it," she said. "It's not altogether bad news, but it's certainly not something I relish telling you."

Then she shook herself and stood straighter. No matter how much she dreaded her hour of confession, she wasn't going to give him the satisfaction of seeing how afraid she was.

"Well, I've got a stallion to load," she said briskly.

"Later, then." He turned and headed to his limo.

# Two

What the hell did she have to tell him that was so important?

It wasn't the first time she'd fed him that line. On the day he'd left for good, nearly six years ago, she'd told him she had something important to tell him. But when he'd gone to meet her in their secret place, her mother had showed up instead. Her mother had fired him and set him straight about a lot of other things, too. Caitlin planned to marry someone else.

Luke had left, but later when he'd calmed down, he'd called Caitlyn. She'd never answered his calls, so he'd written. She'd never written back. Clearly, she'd wanted him out of her life but had lacked the courage to break up with him in person.

Who cared what she had to say today? Quit thinking about it, he told himself.

As if he could. Her brown eyes had been huge,

fear-filled dark orbs, her shaky tone ominous. He'd wanted to reach out and pull her close. Thank goodness he hadn't acted on that rash impulse. She didn't deserve his kindness, nor his compassion. She never had.

*They say you can never go home.*

As he'd told Caitlyn, Luke damn sure wouldn't have come here if he'd had a choice. He belonged in London, in his office, sitting at the helm of his many businesses.

But Hassan, to whom he owed everything, had prevailed.

For nearly six years, Luke Kilgore had avoided all things Texan, especially its women. He wanted no one with dark hair or fiery dark eyes that held a hint of vulnerability; he wanted no one with a soft drawl that sounded too much like a cat's purr.

Now, sprawled in the back of his leased stretch limo on this fool's errand, trying to pretend he was relaxed, Luke's fingers clenched, wrinkling the latest of his CEO's reports about Kommstarr's disgruntled employees. Luke thrust it aside impatiently. Steve's figures in defense of his out-of-control expenditures at Kommstarr made no sense. Luke didn't like firing people any better than Steve did, but some cuts had to be made.

Hell, Luke had hardly been able to concentrate since he'd landed in San Antonio last night and felt the warmth, even in winter, of the vast, starlit Texas sky. So different from London's gray, damp chill that all he'd been able to think about was *her*. In his hotel in downtown San Antonio he'd even dreamed of her.

Why was she scared?

Caitlyn Cooper Wakefield.

Now that he'd seen her, touched her, tasted her, she'd

scrambled his brain just like she'd done in the past. How could she still get to him?

Six years ago she'd merely been Caitlyn Cooper. A respected rancher's only daughter. She should have been off-limits to the motherless son of the county's number one drunk, Bubba Kilgore. She would have been—if she'd obeyed her daddy or if Luke had had enough sense to keep his hands off her.

Luke compared the woman she was now to the slim girl she'd been back then. She'd been more cute than beautiful, with a freckled nose and wide, dark, innocent eyes that had sparkled with curiosity and laughter. And she'd laughed a lot. At least, in his company.

She hadn't laughed today.

Back then she'd seemed to find him as exciting as he'd found her. From that first afternoon, when he'd stomped onto her daddy's porch, desperate for a job, and she'd refused to invite him in, there had been vital chemistry between them.

She wasn't nearly as beautiful as the women he dated now, and she didn't dress as fashionably. She'd never cared about those things. Deep down he admired her because she wasn't vain. Her face was narrow and angular, her thick black hair unruly. She hadn't worn any makeup. Did it matter? There was something real, something genuine about her, and she sure as hell knew how to kiss.

He wished he could forget how seductively soft and warm her lips had felt beneath his own, forget how good she'd tasted, forget how hard he'd become even before he'd grabbed her this afternoon. Lacking polish, she was all fire and sass, making him burn.

Her hands had climbed his chest and wrapped around his neck as if she knew she belonged to him and no one else. When she'd leaned into him and pulled him close, he'd felt the heat of every female curve.

She'd been hotter than ever, maybe because she'd known exactly what she wanted. Or maybe she'd missed him…really missed him, as he'd missed her.

Like the kiss today, the memory of the long-ago evening when he'd made love to her still had the power to sear him. He hadn't gone looking for trouble that evening, but it sure as hell found him.

He'd knocked on her door, looking for her daddy. He'd needed an advance against his wages since Bubba had drunk up the rent. She'd come to the door in tight shorts that skimmed her curvy bottom and said, "Maybe he's in the barn."

Only, she'd known he wasn't when she'd followed Luke out there, closing the big, heavy doors behind her, calling to him across the dark in that raspy purr of hers. Then she'd undone her hair so that it tumbled around her shoulders. When she'd held out her arms and told him she loved him, he'd tried to talk some sense into her, even as his heart thundered.

"You don't know what you're doing, girl," he'd warned.

"But I've always known how I feel," she whispered, "ever since I first saw you."

"You're too young to know anything. Folks around here think I'm nothing."

"I don't care. I don't want to go my whole life wanting you like this…and never having had you." She moved toward him. "Just once. That's all I'm asking for."

"No one can know," he said.

"Nobody but us," she'd whispered, sliding into his arms, her soft curves melting against his hard muscles.

She'd felt right, perfect.

"Just us," he'd murmured, kissing her passionately.

For him, that time with her had been special. No other woman had ever come close to mattering so much. But then, no other woman had used her mother to throw him out like he was nothing. That had been equally hard to forget.

Had she just wanted to scratch an itch? Had she known then she would have to marry Wakefield if she wanted to get her precious ranch back? For years Luke had tormented himself with those questions.

She'd been the first girl he'd loved—and she'd be the last. She'd taught him love held a dark power. She'd taught him there were worse things than having a mean old man for a father. She'd taught him there were worse things than being born poor. She'd taken a hatchet to his heart and soul.

Swearing she loved him, she'd given herself to him on a bed of hay that night in the barn. Then, as soon as she could, she'd married Robert Wakefield, no doubt because he was the son of the banker who'd repossessed her family's ranch.

But life had a way of being messy, and nothing had worked out as she'd planned. Robert had died. The ranch was in trouble again, and she was a struggling widow with a son.

A son. Funny that he hadn't seen the kid. Not that he wanted to see Wakefield's kid, who was living proof that she'd been with another man these past six years.

Some people were good at letting go. Luke envied them. Not that he didn't go through the motions of a man who'd moved on. He owned a glamorous penthouse in London. Invitations to his parties were sought after. He dated the most beautiful women in Europe. Except for his friend Nico Romano, an Italian prince with an independent wife from Texas, his married male business associates said they envied Luke his carefree life.

Although he didn't pick up the report again, Luke barely spared a glance out the tinted windows. He didn't have to. The harsh brown scrubland was deeply engraved into his consciousness.

He'd accomplish this errand for Hassan as quickly as possible. Then he'd figure out once and for all what was behind Hassan's obsessive interest in Caitlyn.

Not that he hadn't tried to find out after Hassan had met her at Keeneland. When Luke hadn't reacted to the Wakefield name, Hassan had pressed, asking him if he'd known Caitlyn Wakefield personally.

"Yes, I worked for her father."

"And? Did you care for her?"

"It doesn't matter. Her mother fired me. I left Texas and never saw any of them again. Why do you want to know?"

"You don't talk about Texas much."

"I'm not all that proud of who I was in Texas, or of how people treated me. It's something I've tried to put behind me."

He'd thought that was the end of it. Then Hassan had asked Caitlyn to help him with Sahara and had invited Luke to Deauville without telling him he'd hired Caitlyn as Sahara's trainer. When Luke had seen her working with the stallion, he'd asked Hassan again why he was so interested in her. It would have been so much easier to use a world-class French trainer instead of bringing Caitlyn from the States.

Again, Hassan had been evasive, saying only that her advice had saved him from making a particularly disastrous purchase.

"Why did you invite me to dine with the two of you?"

Luke had asked. "It's as if you are determined to get us together."

"Sometimes we are rash in our youth. Sometimes it's a mistake to lose touch with old friends."

"Not in this case."

"You could be wrong, my son."

"Well, I won't come for dinner if you insist on including her."

"I do insist on her presence tonight."

"Then I'll pass."

"You shall be missed, my son."

Hassan's stubborn behavior and fascination with Caitlyn made no sense, but Luke would get to the bottom of it. Then, hopefully, within the week, he'd be home with Teresa.

Luke saw a flash of movement out the window. A handsome blood bay horse, ridden by a small figure, sprang across the road right in front of the limo. The driver honked and hit the brakes too fast and too hard. The bay spooked and started bucking.

Tires squealing, the limo fishtailed in a swirl of gravel, sliding to a standstill in front of a prickly pear cactus. The pages of Steve's report came loose and flew all over the limo's plush interior.

The riderless red horse plunged wildly away from the veils of dust near the car, racing across the depopulated landscape. Then he stopped and circled back, staring at something on the ground. When the dust settled, Luke saw a small boy lying still and lifeless on the road.

Luke leaped out of the limo at the same moment as his driver.

"I didn't see him, sir! Not until it was nearly too late!"

"It wasn't your fault," Luke assured the man.

"He came out of nowhere."

"See to the car." Luke strode toward the prostrate boy, who'd stirred at the sound of their voices.

A cowboy came running from the pasture. "The boy, he got away from me, señor."

When the kid moaned, Luke felt some of his tension ease. The car hadn't hit the boy. He'd just been bucked. Maybe he was okay. At the same age, Luke had ridden just as recklessly and had taken many a hard fall without doing permanent damage. In some ways, kids were tougher than adults.

Careless of the fine wool and silk blend of his custom-made suit, Luke knelt on the ground beside the boy.

The kid groaned and sat up, blinking at him suspiciously. The boy's red-checked cowboy shirt was torn in two places. He raised a quick, thin hand to shade his tanned brow, squinting at the brilliant afternoon sun coming from behind Luke. The boy's lips parted in a gap-toothed grin.

"You okay…?" Luke began, feeling a jolt of recognition.

"Sorry, mister. I…"

The kid had jet black hair and green eyes—green eyes that were the exact same shade as his own.

Luke's gut twisted. Emerald eyes stared straight into his for an endless moment, during which Luke felt something near his heart shift.

Luke didn't believe in coincidences, and Hassan placed an inordinate value on sons. Was this boy the answer? Did Hassan think…?

Had Hassan seen Caitlyn's son and noticed the resemblance to Luke? Had Hassan met the boy at Keeneland?

Suddenly Luke couldn't breathe. It was as if a band had wrapped around his chest and squeezed. In a weird panic—he never panicked—he fought to ignore dozens of questions that bombarded his stunned mind.

"I asked you if you're okay?" Luke's voice was hard and strange, unrecognizable. "Anything hurt? Broken? Are you dizzy?"

The kid felt real. The rest of his life—London, Teresa, his businesses, his unstoppable ambition, even Hassan—belonged to a dream that had nothing to do with his life, which was here.

"I'm fine, but I've got to catch that damn Demon before he bolts for the barn and I have to walk all the way back."

"Don't cuss."

"Sorry!"

The kid didn't look the least bit sorry as he sat up and got ready to spring to his feet.

Luke put a hand on his shoulder. "Not so fast. Why don't you sit here a minute or two, catch your breath."

"I said I'm okay," the boy protested impatiently, looking defiant.

*Just as Luke would have done at the same age.*

"Right. And I say it's too soon to be so sure. What's your name?"

"Daniel." His bottom lip curling, the kid stared at the ground.

"You got a last name?"

"'Course I do! Wakefield." There was fierce pride in his low tone, the kind of pride Luke had never felt for his biological father. When the kid tried unsuccessfully to shake loose from Luke's iron grip, his bottom lip grew even more prominent.

"My name's Luke Kilgore."

"Glad to meet you, Mr. Kilgore," Daniel said automatically.

"Glad to meet you, too."

The boy on the ground didn't look a thing like the blond, blue-eyed Wakefield bunch. Luke's mind raced backward.

"How old are you, Daniel?" Luke asked slowly, as unwanted pressure pounded in his temples.

This couldn't be happening. But it was. The angry kid looked just like *he'd* looked at the same age.

"Five."

The number was a sucker punch in the gut.

*Damn her.* Was this why she had married Wakefield so quickly? Had she been pregnant? Had she slept with them both and hoped to pass off his baby as the wealthier Wakefield's to get the ranch back? Had she despised the thought she might be carrying a Kilgore?

Luke clenched and unclenched his fists. When one speculated, one was usually wrong. What mattered now was finding out the truth.

"Does your mother know where you are?" Luke asked in a low, even tone. "That you were riding Demon bareback?"

The kid tensed and then lowered his eyes guiltily. "Sure. I was with Manuel, so it's okay."

"Right," Luke said softly. "What do you say we catch Demon so the two of you can run along home, back to the ranch, so your mother won't worry?"

"She's not worrying. She's too busy getting ready for her meeting with some guy."

"That would be me."

"Oh. Are you rich? Some car, huh? Long." His eyes lit up. "Like a bus."

"Not exactly. It's called a limousine. Limo for short. What do you say we catch your horse?"

Luke and Daniel stood up together, and Manuel joined them. Demon's ears shot forward and he whinnied. As Luke and the boy dusted themselves off, the blood bay gelding hung his head and licked his lips.

Good sign, Luke thought as Manuel slowly approached the horse.

The well-proportioned gelding didn't run away. He stood docilely, allowing Manuel to retrieve the reins. Manuel swung himself onto the horse. Then Luke lifted Daniel up to the mounted man.

A shadow passed over Daniel's face as he looked down. "I got you all dirty. You're gonna tell Mom on me."

"I'm not sure what I'll say to her. But I'll catch up to you two at the house," Luke said, his tone hard as he dusted himself off again.

"Did you come to buy a horse or something?" the kid asked.

"Or something."

"Good, 'cause me and Mom could sure use the money."

Money—had she married Wakefield because his daddy had been a banker and he'd owned Wild Horse Ranch? Or to give her baby a name?

When had she learned she was pregnant? Was her pregnancy the reason she hadn't taken his calls or answered his letters?

"See you," Daniel said, dismissing Luke casually.

Then the boy leaned forward with the ease of a natural rider. Soon boy, man and horse were cantering down the shoulder of the road while Luke stood still and silent, watching them.

Luke identified with that half-wild kid. Almost as if Luke was riding Demon himself, he felt the calves of those thin legs gripping the powerful animal. They were his legs, his knees squeezing tight, his lean body leaning forward, his hands lightly holding the reins. It was him urging the great creature faster, faster, until the ride became exhilarating.

"Breathe, Daniel. Don't forget to breathe," Luke whispered.

Then horse, boy and man were flying, airborne, united, and Luke's own soul rushed after them. He hadn't felt this alive in years.

What if the kid was his son?

No sooner had the trio melted into the haze of the horizon than a knot of longing formed in Luke's throat. Should he have let Daniel back on the beast so soon? The boy had said he was fine, and he was with Manuel. But was the boy okay? What if he had a concussion?

Acute parental anxiety was new to him and made him feel foolish. The kid probably wasn't even his. But whether he was or he wasn't, Luke's concern caused beads of sweat to break out on his brow.

Had Caitlyn wanted him gone so he wouldn't find out about Daniel? Was that why she'd been afraid? If so, she was far more deceptive than he'd believed.

Luke wanted answers, and he wanted them now. Grabbing his cell, he punched in Hassan's number. It was probably midnight Hassan's time, but Luke didn't give a damn.

As always, Hassan's voice was warm with paternal interest in a way that Luke's biological father's never had been.

"Raffi. You had a safe journey? No problems?"

"Only one. I just met Daniel."

There was a long silence before Hassan finally spoke. "I saw him at Keeneland. He looked so much like you."

"Why didn't you tell me?"

"I was right? He *is* yours, then?"

# Three

As soon as his limo had returned to Caitlyn's ranch and braked in front of the house, Luke flung open his door. He felt torn by the conflicting emotions raging inside him. He wished he'd never come to Texas; he was glad he'd come. He wished Hassan had leveled with him from the beginning; he was glad he'd seen the boy with his own eyes. He was furious at Caitlyn and yet filled with tenderness for her bravely defiant little son. He was in such an irrational state, he knew she was the last person he needed to talk to, but he wanted her to know that if the kid was theirs, he wouldn't walk away from her or Daniel.

"The boy looked so much like you," Hassan had said over the phone. "I couldn't forget about him and do nothing. That is why I helped her. That is why I sent you and nobody else. If you are family, so are they."

"You could have told me."

"I was so struck by him when I saw him, I knew you would be, too. I know what it is…to nearly lose a son. I wanted you to see him for yourself. To be struck by him as I was."

Oh, Luke felt struck, all right.

"There are some things a man must see and feel for himself, decide for himself," Hassan had said.

Fisting his hands, Luke stormed toward the round pen and frowned when he found Lisa instead of Caitlyn. The young woman leaned against a railing, watching and listening to the commotion in her gooseneck trailer.

"Where's Caitlyn?" he demanded.

"Ah, back so soon." Lisa batted her long eyelashes boldly as she fingered the falls at the end of her quirt.

"Caitlyn better not be in that trailer with your horse!"

Her brows snapped together. Sucking in a miffed breath, she quit fiddling with her quirt. "Why not? She knows what she's doing. Why, she's almost got Ramblin' Man loaded. And in record time. He can be a brute, that one."

Luke's fury and impatience vanished. The thought of Caitlyn in that tiny trailer with a huge, unpredictable stallion that had to weigh well over a thousand pounds made his gut clench. Was she suicidal? He wanted to scream at her to get the hell out of there, but of course he couldn't do that without endangering her even more. So, instead, he moved soundlessly around the pen, taking a circuitous route so as not to spook the stallion. He'd wait behind the trailer until she'd safely loaded the horse.

When he reached his destination and she still hadn't come out, his heart began to thud more forcefully. Then he heard her soothing voice, along with the nervous clatter of Ramblin' Man's hooves.

Why couldn't the beast just load?

"No bees today," she was saying in that feather-soft purr. "Nothing for a big boy like you to be scared of. Come on, baby, just one more step and you can go home. Don't you want to go home?"

And then Luke's cell phone rang.

Before Luke could shut it off, the horse had exploded, his head banging into the roof, which caused him to react even more wildly. Hooves banged. Caitlyn screamed. Ramblin' Man, his eyes round, burst from the trailer faster than a rocket off a launchpad, dragging Caitlyn behind him by a slender foot. Somehow she'd gotten tangled in the longe line.

Easy to do in such tight, dimly lit quarters, he thought grimly.

With a cry of sheer terror, Lisa leaped out of the round pen so she could watch the drama from the other side of the railing without risking her own neck.

It had been a while since Luke had dealt directly with horses, but he remembered that when a fifteen-hundred-pound horse wanted to take one step, five men against his chest couldn't stop him. Ramblin' Man wanted out of the pen, and if somebody didn't get him under control, he'd trample Caitlyn or drag her to death first.

Without a thought for his own hide, Luke placed both hands on the railing and threw himself into the pen. Yelling to Lisa to throw him her quirt, he caught it on the run and raced toward the horse.

Thankfully, Manuel sprang into the pen alongside him. With the other man's expert help, Luke soon grabbed the double-braided marine rope Caitlyn had been using as a longe line. With it and the quirt, he took charge. Applying pressure, he soon had Ramblin' Man's attention and respect.

"Stay where you are," he ordered Manuel. Ramblin'

Man had heeded a few commands and had stopped to stare at them, so Luke handed Manuel the heavy, webbed line. "Keep his attention focused on you while I free her."

Manuel nodded grimly and clucked to the horse.

Not wanting to spook Ramblin' Man further, Luke walked slowly to Caitlyn. She was sitting up by the time he reached her, tugging fiercely at the line around her ankle.

Before he could hunker down beside her, she'd snatched the line loose and was glaring at him as if everything was his fault—which, unfortunately, it was.

"Were you trying to kill me? Is that your idea of a solution, Kilgore? There was a time when you knew a thing or two about horses."

He still did. He owned a stable, and several of its horses were champions.

"I'm sorry," he muttered. "I was upset about something else and I forgot about my damn cell phone."

"City slicker!"

"I said I was sorry."

"Well, don't just stand there gaping at me, give me a hand up before somebody else calls you and Ramblin' Man finishes what he started."

Luke pulled her to her feet, but no sooner had she put her weight on her ankle than she gave a cry that pierced his heart. Damn it. Against his will, he cared about this woman.

Crumpling against him, she cursed under her breath, coupling his name with several colorful invectives that would have made him laugh under different circumstances.

"Let me go!" she yelled.

"If I do, you'll fall on your delectable ass!"

"Anything's preferable to being in your arms!"

"Hey, you jumped me this time," he said, grabbing her.

"Did not!"

Pulling her closer, he swung her into his arms. "You're not walking on that foot till we figure out what's wrong with it."

"You can't tell me what to do."

"Just you watch me."

When she began pushing at his wide shoulders, he ignored her puny struggles and carried her toward the gate with long, even strides.

"Open it," he commanded.

"The hell you say. Put me down this minute."

"In the house. On your bed. Not until. Unless you enjoy lounging around in my arms, you'll open the damn gate."

When she hesitated, he whispered against her earlobe, "Your choice. I can stand here all day. Hell, I'm beginning to think you're stalling so I'll kiss you again."

As his mouth descended toward hers, she moved her head away from his. Unloosing more highly creative curses, she grumpily lifted the catch. Then she crossed her arms over her breasts and endured his carrying her to the house in stony silence. This time, when he'd climbed the stairs to her porch and stopped at the front door, she reached out and twisted the doorknob.

"Where's your bedroom?" he asked. They stood in the living room, which was filled with pictures of her parents and Daniel. As usual, her dominating mother was frowning in every shot. Funny, there wasn't a single shot of Robert, Cait's beloved, belated husband. Again, Luke wondered why she'd married the other man so quickly after Luke had left. She'd seemed so madly in love with him, Luke was no longer sure he believed her mother's version of the story.

"Just put me on the sofa and go."

"Don't make me ask again."

"Down the hall. First door on the right."

When he finally laid her down on her rumpled bed, she moaned—maybe from the pain in her ankle, maybe from exasperation that she had to deal with him—and he felt an unwanted twinge of sympathy.

"I'd better take a look at that ankle," he whispered, his deep tone uncustomarily gentle.

To his surprise she didn't object, although she did wince when he unzipped her boot and removed it. Taking great care not to hurt her any more than he had to, he examined her ankle, slowly moving it in circles, first one way and then the other.

She grimaced. "You know, this foot play isn't my idea of fun!"

"Nor mine."

Pearly dots of perspiration dotted her brow. "So, how much longer are you going to do this?" she said through gritted teeth.

"You have full range of motion. I think we should ice it."

"There's a bag of peas in the freezer. Bottom shelf."

"Okay. Can I get you anything else? A glass of water?"

She shook her head. "After you get me that sack of peas, I'd like for you to go back to London."

"You're going to need some help around here."

"Not from the likes of you."

Ignoring that dig, he went to the kitchen, returning swiftly with the peas, which he pressed against her ankle. "Now, if you'll give me the name of your doctor, I'll call him for you. You need to have your ankle checked out by a medical professional as soon as possible."

"Haven't you done enough damage for one day? I want you gone. Lisa can help me with the rest."

As if on cue, the front door banged open, and Lisa called out to her.

"Lisa!" Caitlyn yelled, sounding panicky. "Back here."

"Mom?" Daniel cried. The boy's flying footsteps resounded in the hall as he raced ahead of Lisa and slammed into the bedroom. "Mom!" he began breathlessly. "Oh, Mr. Kilgore? You're still here." He suddenly looked doubly anxious.

Daniel had changed into a white shirt, so there was no evidence of his fall.

When Luke's knowing gaze locked on Caitlyn's face, she whitened. Noticing that she was fisting and unfisting the top edge of her sheet, Luke sank down onto the bed beside her. He couldn't believe it, but he almost felt sorry for her.

Leaning closer, he whispered, "You and I have a lot more to talk about than your financial mess, don't we? Or am I wrong about Daniel being the real reason you're so anxious to get rid of me?"

"How did you know his name?"

"I met him a while ago. He's the reason I came back so fast."

She closed her eyes and swallowed hard. "This isn't happening."

"So, is he mine?" Luke murmured even more softly against her ear.

Her eyes widened with guilty alarm.

"Is he?" Luke repeated, determined to make her answer.

She closed her eyes, and lifted her chin up and down ever so slightly.

"Thought so," he whispered. "You've got a lot of explaining to do...when we're alone."

She stiffened. "I was going to tell you," she said in a voice too low for Lisa to overhear. "This afternoon."

"Right."

"I was!"

He stared through her.

"This doesn't have to change anything," she murmured tightly.

"Are you out of your mind?" he whispered.

"You said this was the last place you wanted to be."

"That was before my little run-in with Daniel. Now, I want to know how this happened, and why you never bothered to inform me."

"You were gone, remember? Robert was here. And now? A man like you couldn't possibly want any permanent ties to me or him or this place."

Luke remembered his mother leaving and how awful he'd felt without her. It was unacceptable to think of Daniel growing up without both his parents, if possible.

"You don't know a damn thing about what I want. Apparently you never did. But I'll give you a real big clue—Daniel changes everything."

Lisa was frowning, her intent gaze never leaving their faces.

Curious as well, Daniel tiptoed nearer. "Why are you in bed when it's daytime? Are you hurt, Mom? Or sick...like Daddy?" His voice thinned. "Why is Mr. Kilgore still here? Why are you both whispering?"

Forcing a weak smile, Caitlyn reached out and

smoothed Daniel's dark, tousled hair. "It's just my ankle. I got tangled up in the longe line. I'll be fine in no time."

"Since it's all my fault that your mother was hurt, I'm going to stay here to help you all out till she's better," Luke said.

"No…" Caitlyn sputtered.

"Don't be ridiculous, Cait! Why, I think that's real generous of you, Luke," Lisa said. "It'll be a pleasure having you around."

"The pleasure's all mine," Luke drawled.

Daniel's face relaxed. Sighing heavily, he agreed, "Good. 'Cause I was really, really scared. I fell off Demon today, and Mr. Kilgore helped me remount. Did he tell you about it, Mom?"

"No. Not yet," Caitlyn said.

"Good, 'cause I thought maybe I was in trouble. That's why I was hiding."

"He fell off that horse, and you knew it!" Her eyes flew to Luke. "Why didn't you tell me?"

"Believe me, I would have, if Ramblin' Man hadn't exploded the way he did. Meeting Daniel was weighing heavily on my mind. That's why I didn't think about my phone when I was waiting for you to finish in the trailer."

Her slim hand froze in Daniel's. "I see," she whispered. "Honey, could you go out into the living room for a second with Miss Lisa while I talk to Mr. Kilgore privately?"

"But can't I just stay while you talk—"

"No."

"Please. Just for a second."

"He and I have some business to discuss."

"But I won't listen!" Refusing to budge, Daniel

crossed his arms over his thin chest and curled his lip. Luke could see that the kid did as he pleased a lot of the time. Not always a good thing.

"Daniel!" she said sharply.

"You're not going to sell Demon to him, are you?"

"No. Just some big-people talk that would bore you."

"I won't interrupt," he said, inching closer to her.

"You heard her, so don't argue. Just go," Luke said in a voice that was both firm and kind. "We'll be through in no time. Then you can stay with your mom for as long as you like."

Daniel nodded and got up. "Can I have a cookie?"

"Lisa, do you think maybe you could find a snack for Daniel?" Luke asked.

Lisa, who had been hanging on to every word, reluctantly took Daniel's arm and led him down the hall. "Sure thing. Daniel, how about some milk and cookies?"

"Only one, Lisa," Caitlyn said. "Sugar makes him hyper."

"Can I have chocolate chip...?"

"If you have any," Lisa said.

"In the freezer," Cait said.

Forgetting his mother, Daniel ran down the hall to check the cookie jar.

Luke got up and closed the door. When he went back to her bed, Caitlyn grabbed his wrist and pulled him closer. Warmth flashed through him. Then, realizing she was touching him, she yanked her hand away as if she, too, felt the burn.

He held his breath for a charged second, far from unscathed by the feral need she still aroused in him so easily. He wasn't over her. He wanted her. He'd never wanted another more than he wanted her.

"Don't tell him who you are. Do you hear me? Because you're not his father. Not in any way that matters."

*Because of you!*

He was angry, but it was still all too easy to imagine her at nineteen, pregnant with his child and enduring her strict, critical mother's censure. Had she been afraid to confess the baby was his? If she'd made some bad decisions, so had he. He should have returned to check on her. Maybe she would have told him about the baby. Well, it was too late to change the past, but that didn't mean he couldn't change the future.

"Let's get something straight. If he's mine, I intend to be a father to him in the future—whether you like it or not."

"He's yours, I guess, but only biologically," she snapped.

"Then he's mine. Period. I can see he needs a father, too. He has way too much freedom to do as he pleases."

"Don't you judge me! There's a lot you don't under-stand. Daniel is upset because the man he believed to be his father is dead. There's no way he could handle discovering who you really are."

"Maybe not right now.... I have no intention of telling him until he's more accustomed to me. I'll know when the time is right."

"He blames himself for Robert's death. He'd run off and had all of us scared to death. Robert had been ill for a while, and I was overwrought about that. When Daniel finally showed up that afternoon, I'm afraid I said some things that really upset him. Then Robert died suddenly, before any of us thought he would, and Daniel blamed himself. I've told Daniel it was Robert's illness that killed him, not anything Daniel did. But I don't think he believes me."

"Poor little guy. That's a heavy load for a young kid," Luke said. "I can see he's had a rough time."

"Yes, he has—thanks in part to you."

"That from the woman who never bothered to inform me of his existence."

"You were supposed to meet me that afternoon. You left without even bothering to say goodbye."

"Had I done that, I would deserve your anger. But that's not the way it was, and you damn well—"

She interrupted him. "You were already gone when I found out for sure!"

"I wrote and told you where I was. I called. You never answered. You married Wakefield!"

"You called?" She scowled at him in confusion, probably for reminding her of how badly she'd treated him. No doubt once she'd made up her mind to marry for the ranch, she'd decided never to look back. She'd considered him collateral damage and nothing more.

Casting blame for the past accomplished nothing. What he did to resolve their present problem was all that mattered. He heaved in a breath. "I don't like remembering you or what happened between us any better than you do. So, okay, hate my guts to your heart's content, and let me hate yours. But there's something you need to understand. A simple DNA test will prove he's mine. As his father, I could fight for custody. With my money I could make your life a living hell. I intend to know my son—with or without your permission. So we can work together, or you can fight me. It's your choice."

"Don't you dare use your money to threaten me! Just because I'm a woman who's temporarily down on her luck, you think you hold all the cards. Well, you don't! He's mine, and I love him. And he loves me."

"I know that. I respect that. But I want to be part of his life, too. Is that so unreasonable?"

"Under the circumstances, yes! You live in London, and we live here."

"Geography."

"I have a ranch—here."

"You could relocate…nearer to me. You can raise Thoroughbreds anywhere."

"Why would I do that? I read about the shallow, materialistic life you lead, the beautiful women, the wealth…. I don't want Daniel influenced by a man who'll teach him that women are disposable playthings."

"That's not what I'll teach him. And for the record, I'm too busy *working* to see all the women the gossips say I see. You don't know me well enough to pass judgment."

Maybe he hadn't really known *himself* until this moment. Although his life was filled with all the so-called right people and things, his loneliness was profound. It was as if long ago he'd lost some vital piece of himself. At times when he thought he should be content, he felt restless instead. In such moments he always wondered what it was that he could possibly need to complete his life.

Coming back here—seeing Caitlyn and then Daniel—had changed him. For the first time in a long time, he felt driven by something true rather than by anger or the ambition to prove himself. He had a son. He was determined to be a father. He'd been hasty when he'd let Caitlyn's mother speak for her.

"I'm going to change my lifestyle," he said. "This has made me realize it's time I settled down."

"All because of Daniel?"

"Absolutely."

"Why should I believe you?"

"I don't care what you believe. All you need to know is that I intend to get to know him and be his father. Thus, I'll be staying here, with you, indefinitely. Like I said before—if I were you, I'd cooperate."

"What about your work, your life, your countess in London?"

"Much as I appreciate your concern, I'll figure out a way to make my plan work."

"But nobody's invited you to stay. Nobody wants you."

Her words sent a chill through him as he remembered his loveless childhood. He'd had no mother, a trashed house and a father who'd been almost worse than no father. The whole county, including Caitlyn's mother, had called Bubba Kilgore trash and thought that Luke was no better.

Well, he had money and prestige now, lots of it, and he had Hassan's paternal love. Teresa, who had the pedigree and the polish he lacked, wanted to marry him. All he had to do was ask her. Had he hesitated to propose because she was too young, or because, deep down, even with Teresa at his side, he often felt alienated in this luxurious life he'd built?

Strangely, he felt more grounded with Caitlyn. Was it because they shared the same roots? Or because his feelings for her went deeper than he'd let himself believe?

He would stay here and help Caitlyn. He didn't care what he had to do or say to get his way. Since he'd been born in the gutter, he could sink to her level no matter how low she went.

Thus, his voice was very hard when he spoke to her again. "Would you really send your son's biological father away when he's the only man who can pull your sweet little ass out of the financial mess you've made? If you're destitute, what will happen to Daniel? The day might come, sooner than you think, when you'll beg me to take him."

"Never!"

"You'd prefer him to starve? I always thought mothers wanted what's best for their children."

"Of course I want what's best! I just don't think you're it!" She lunged at him, but the movement was ill considered and it twisted her ankle in the sheets. She cried out in pain and collapsed against her pillow, her thin face ashen.

His fury forgotten, he sank down beside her again, hating himself for having made such unreasonable threats in the heat of anger. "Are you okay?"

"Yes," she whispered, shaking, closing her eyes to shut out the pain. Or maybe to shut him out.

"I'd better call your doctor," he said, as he gently replaced the frozen peas on her foot. "What's his name?"

In that same weak, pitiable voice she told him. "But I don't want you staying here...helping me," she said defiantly.

"You don't have a choice. The sooner you accept my decision, the sooner you'll realize you might as well make the best of it."

She bit her lower lip and released it. Probably because she was weakened with pain, she sat very still. Finally, she nodded.

Maybe she wouldn't continue to be impossible. Maybe he was making headway toward his goal.

Or maybe after a night's sleep she'd rally and fight harder than ever.

He didn't care one way or the other. He wasn't leaving Daniel.

Or her.

# Four

Luke sat on the couch as Daniel struggled to phonetically sound out the word *dog*.

How hard could it be to read that word?

Holding on to his patience, Luke caught his breath. Fortunately, Daniel got it and then read the rest of the sentence without any more problems.

Daniel had started kindergarten in the fall, and Caitlyn had told Luke the boy had to be helped with his reading every night. So Luke had volunteered.

Earlier, when she'd finally realized no amount of discussion would make Luke change his mind about staying, she'd taken a new tack. With a crafty smile, she'd said, "Well, if I'm stuck with you, we might as well find a way to make you useful."

"I'm sure I'll have plenty to do, fixing your finances."

"You know how it is on a ranch. There's always lots of hard, physical work to do, and with my ankle..."

"You win," he'd said with a smile.

She'd grabbed a pen and had dashed off a long list of chores. She'd probably chosen some of them, like mucking out stalls, because she remembered he'd thought they were unpleasant as hell.

Since he suspected the real purpose of her requests was to drive him away, he'd read the list and beamed as if in delight.

Except for the stall mucking, he'd charged through her tasks with an enthusiasm and competence that had irritated her to the extreme.

"Now, I have a list of my own, you know," he'd said when he'd finished. "On it are things you can do to please me. First thing is for you to cooperate. The second is that you need to let my chauffeur drive us both to your doctor and home again."

"You have so many stables to clean and horses to bathe, you have no time to waste on a trip to town with me," she'd said as he led her to the limo.

"Is grocery shopping in the number one position on your list or not, sweetheart? How can I do that if I don't go into town? I see right here that I'm supposed to buy feed. Where exactly is the feed store?" He'd got into the limo.

Sulkily she'd turned her back on him and stared out the window in gloomy silence, but he'd ignored her snit, using the quiet time in the limo to return several pressing international phone calls.

In the end, because he'd needed to make still more calls, including one to Teresa, he'd sent his driver to shop for groceries while he'd stayed with Caitlyn at her doctor's office.

The doctor diagnosed a sprained ankle. He'd put her

in a boot, gave her crutches and told her to rest a couple of days before she started hobbling around outside.

"Do you have anybody who can help you, besides Manuel?" he'd asked. "I mean at night. In the house."

"Me," Luke had volunteered, slinging a possessive arm around her. "I'm staying at the house."

When she had flushed and tried to shrug free of his offending arm, the doctor cocked his eyebrows. "I see."

"It's not what you think," she'd muttered.

The doctor had smiled knowingly. "Then it's settled. Wonderful. You must rely on him for everything these first few days."

"Surely that's not necessary," she'd argued, trying to make light of her injury.

"Unfortunately, it is." The doctor had been adamant that if she was to get a full recovery, she needed to stay off her ankle for a good two weeks.

Smugly, Luke had taken charge. "You must be a good patient and do everything I say, sweetheart," he'd teased. "Doctor's orders."

The doctor had nodded conspiratorially while she'd silently fumed.

Luke had cooked their first shared supper—an omelet and toast—and washed dishes and supervised Daniel's bath. Then he'd played with various action figures with the kid on the floor of his room until she'd hobbled down the hall and reminded them Daniel still needed to practice his reading.

"Isn't it time for you to call it a day and forget about issuing more commands?" Luke had asked her after leading her to her bedroom. "You're not getting rid of me, you know. The doctor put me in charge. I run international corporations. I think I can take care of one woman, one little boy and a few horses and cows. Hell, cows feed themselves."

Her brows had flown together at that. "You know better than that."

"That I do," he'd said with a smile.

"I imagine in a day or two you'll be so bored you'll be longing for London and your lavish lifestyle, not to mention your countess."

"That doesn't mean I'll leave Daniel. Then there's Hassan. I promised him I'd help you."

Ignoring her pout, he'd poured her a glass of water. When she'd dutifully swallowed her pain pill, he said, "Good night. I'll say a prayer to whoever's listening that a night's sleep improves your attitude. You really are an incredibly difficult patient."

"Because of you! The only thing that could possibly improve my attitude is for you to—"

He'd leaned closer and touched her lips with a blunt fingertip. "Hush, before you say more mean things about the father of your son. You were in trouble long before I showed up. I'm here to help. So, good night. And that's final…unless you want me to tuck you in and kiss you good night." He'd said that only because she'd looked so cute frowning at him, that he'd forgotten they were at war.

Caught by surprise by his last comment, she'd glanced at his mouth and blushed most becomingly, her lips parting slightly, as if in invitation, before she'd caught herself.

Heat washed through him.

"Would you get out?"

"My pleasure," he'd whispered, smiling at her as he'd closed her door softly. "Sweet dreams."

Her eyes, deep and dark in her flushed face, had shot sparks at him.

Ten minutes later, Luke was still thinking about her brilliant, intelligent eyes and how they made her thin face even lovelier than the elegant Teresa's. Caitlyn's eyes warmed him, made him feel young and eager again, as he had when he'd been in love with her. Indeed, the memory of her brilliant eyes was still distracting him as Daniel labored through the story about a wise owl and an idiot mouse in need of a lesson.

Then the phone rang. Daniel, no doubt anxious for any excuse to stop reading, asked, "Can I quit now?"

"Yes. That was very good."

Not about to wait for Luke to change his mind, Daniel shot off the couch and ran down the hall to his room.

Damn, Luke thought, when the phone didn't ring again. Caitlyn, who was supposed to be asleep, must have answered the call. He was wondering what the caller wanted, when he heard a crash in her bedroom.

Afraid she'd gotten up and fallen, Luke rushed down the hall and flung open her door.

Bathed in the golden glow of the bedside lamp, she wore nothing but a pair of skimpy red lace bikini panties. Leaning against one crutch, her arms were outstretched as she bent to put on a red bra. When the door banged open, she'd frozen, staring up at him with huge dark eyes.

Erotic longing surged through him in a warm tide. She blushed but made no move to cover herself. The moment went on and on. Why did she stand there in shock and let him devour the sight of her lush figure?

Hell, why didn't he have the sense to look away? But he couldn't. She was too beautiful. His heart pounded violently, and his avid gaze remained fixed on the voluptuous curves of her hips and the globes of her firm, high breasts. He couldn't have looked away had his life depended on it.

Didn't she guess how powerfully she affected him? Or did she? Was she doing this to seduce him?

Feeling short of breath, he fought to control himself. God help him, he wanted to pull her into his arms. He wanted to touch her more than he'd ever wanted to touch any woman.

He knew just how she'd feel if he were to lave her pink-tipped breasts with his tongue—as sweet and velvety and warmly luscious as the most luxurious dessert.

He wanted her, and what he felt wasn't casual. Her hold on his heart wasn't logical. In fact it was stupid. But it was a reality; and the reality irritated him.

"Didn't anyone teach you to knock?" she said in a furious whisper.

"Bubba never did put much stock in manners."

Hooking her bra, she grabbed her blouse and pulled it on.

"I heard something crash," he muttered. "I thought maybe you'd fallen…hurt yourself."

"I'm fine, as you can see. So you can go."

When she bent to pick up her jeans, he finally got a grip and turned his back on her. "What the hell do you think you're doing? Out of bed? You're hurt and on pain meds."

"I'm dressing. Manuel needs help. He's in the brood-mare barn."

"You're not going out there!"

"I have to."

"No, I'll go."

"What good would you be?"

"Some things you don't forget."

"You could've fooled me when you spooked Ramblin' Man with your cell phone."

Her reminder about the phone rankled.

"I'm through dressing, so you can turn around now," she said.

He pivoted angrily. "I said I'll go. And that's the end of it. You're on crutches. Now get back in bed and stay there. Or I'll stay here, too—to watch over you." His voice softened dangerously on that last threat.

They gazed into each others' eyes, each wary. What was this force that drew them, bound them no matter how hard they both fought it?

Luke told himself to seize her crutches and go, but he couldn't.

"All right," she whispered. "You win."

She sank back down on the bed, causing the mattress to groan and the sheets to rustle. Lying down again, she pulled the sheets up to her neck, but her eyes threw flames at him.

What was her game? If she truly wanted him gone, why had she stood there nearly naked, deliberately inviting his gaze?

She was the mother of his son and virtually alone out here. He felt responsible for her and the boy in ways he'd never felt responsible for anyone but himself. And whether she knew it or not, the one thing Luke had become very good at was living up to his responsibilities. He wasn't turning his back on his son or her.

Luke felt proud as he watched the mare and her newborn foal. At the end of the birth, the baby's legs had been tangled up and coming out wrong. Luke was glad the ordeal was over.

The foal had been gulping for every breath as they'd pulled him out. Luke had been so worried he'd wished he'd let Manuel call the vet, but by that point it had been too late. If they'd gone another few seconds without pulling out the colt, they would have lost him. Caitlyn had been right to doubt his abilities.

"Nice work," a woman's voice purred from behind him.

Luke turned and saw Caitlyn, looking almost as wobbly on her crutches as the foal did on his new legs. But her eyes were radiant as she studied him and the colt. Then she shook her dark hair back so that it slid over her shoulders like a heavy curtain of mussed silk.

"Didn't trust me, did you?" he mused.

"I'm afraid you're right. Couldn't sleep for imagining the worst," she whispered, "although I feel a bit groggy now."

"You shouldn't have come out here. You should be resting."

"It's hard to do what you should do sometimes, isn't it?" Her eyes burned him in the shadowy light. "At least you did one thing right today. But now you're a mess because of it—city slicker."

For the first time, he realized that the white shirt and jeans he'd put on before the afternoon's chores were covered in blood. "Right. Okay, show's over. I need a shower, and Manuel can finish up in here. You," he said to Caitlyn, "are going back to bed. Am I going to have to carry out my threat and move into your bedroom to keep you there?"

Again, her warm gaze locked with his in a way that made his stomach tighten with need.

"That won't be necessary," she whispered huskily, as he came out of the stall.

"Too bad."

"Don't start."

In spite of himself, he smiled. He felt proud of his work with the foal, and the approving light in her eyes made his heart leap. He was even hungrier to have her. Was she remembering how she'd stood in the lamplight, wearing nothing but her red panties, inviting his gaze?

He sure was.

And his desire for her was growing fiercer by the moment.

# Five

Despite the pain medication she'd taken, Caitlyn drowsed fitfully for no more than an hour or two before bolting up from another all-too-familiar nightmare about her parents' car wreck. She always woke up just as the car veered off the bridge into the arroyo. Unlike Robert's death, which had occurred a mere month after theirs, their deaths had been unexpected.

After she caught her breath and quit sobbing, she heard what sounded like her door closing gently.

"Luke?" she cried softly.

He didn't answer.

Had he come to check on her? She heard a heavy footfall in the hall. Then his door opened and closed.

Why hadn't he answered her? Not that she wanted a repeat of earlier when he'd caught her dressing. Still, she felt vaguely disappointed that he'd ignored her when she'd called out to him.

Usually, when she woke up after one of her night-mares, she was all alone with Daniel. Sometimes knowing that her parents and Robert were gone and that the entire weight of Wild Horse Ranch's fate rested on her inadequate shoulders made her feel so desolate she wouldn't sleep for the rest of the night. In the mornings, she would face whatever challenge confronted her. But at night, she always felt vulnerable.

Growing up on the ranch, the place hadn't felt lonely. Her father and mother had been alive, and there'd been more hired hands. Of late, she hadn't been able to afford the skilled help she needed. When Daniel was at school, it was just her and Manuel.

For the first time since Luke's arrival she didn't mind so much that he was right down the hall, promising to help her sort out her affairs. She hadn't asked him here, and she hadn't wanted him. But his presence felt oddly comforting. He'd certainly made himself useful tonight in the barn, which was surprising considering his lavish lifestyle in London.

He'd taken charge of her recovery and had been unfailingly kind as well, not to mention resourceful. He'd been unexpectedly good with Daniel, too, and the boy had taken to him. As she'd listened to them read together, she'd realized Robert had rarely spent any time with the boy. Not that she'd blamed him. All Robert had ever promised Daniel was his name.

What if Luke really took a long-term interest in her son? That might be just what Daniel needed after losing Robert.... No, she couldn't let herself think about that. In all probability, Luke would tire of ranch life and the novelty of a son, as he'd tired of her so quickly all those years ago. And when he left again, he'd break her son's heart.

How could she prevent that? She risked havoc if she fought Luke. Hassan had sent him to help her, and now he'd found out about Daniel. There were too many reasons why she had to work with him.

The pain in her ankle sharpened. Thinking to get her pain medication, she threw off the sheets and grabbed her crutches, but then she heard the sound of Luke's low voice on the porch. When he continued talking, curiosity got the best of her. Hobbling over to her window, she lifted the drape. She gasped at the sight of Luke leaning against a porch post with his phone pressed against his ear. He'd found the exact spot where the signal was best.

Who had he called after he'd left her? She strained to hear, but his deep voice was so low she couldn't catch a single word.

Pulling her robe over her thin nightgown, she laboriously swung herself down the hall. She opened the front door and soundlessly let herself outside.

"Hi, there," she called out, shivering in the chill breeze.

He whirled. Quickly he bit out a goodbye, saying words something to the effect of, "Gotta go, call you later." Then he slid his phone into his pocket.

"Talking to your girlfriend?" she asked, feeling a little put out at the thought of his beautiful countess. Not that his love life was any of her business, she reminded herself.

He neither confirmed nor denied who he had called as he walked toward her, which made her crankier. "It's 9:00 a.m. in London. I couldn't get a signal in the house, so I came outside."

"I'll take that as a yes."

"Think what you like."

He'd showered since she'd last seen him. Vaguely she remembered falling asleep to the sound of the water running while he'd sung a bawdy Western ballad off-key.

He smelled sexily of minty cologne and soap.

"Did you even go to bed?" she asked.

"Couldn't sleep. Jet lag. Problems with one of my newly acquired companies. I worked on my laptop awhile. What's your excuse?"

His white shirt was open at the throat, revealing tanned skin. His jeans molded to his muscular thighs. But it was the intensity of his dark, hooded gaze that challenged her and sent a trill of sensation up her spine. Suddenly it was very difficult to breathe.

*You are the reason I can't sleep,* she thought, praying he was unaware of her powerful reaction to him. How was she supposed to doze with such a virile hunk showering right down the hall, especially if he was the very man who triggered all the erotic memories and hot longings she'd fought for years?

*How could he have left her back then, without even saying goodbye?*

For a second longer his eyes remained as turbulent as her own wayward emotions and then he seemed to master some beast inside himself. Turning away, he picked up a glass from the railing, swirled it and drained it.

*Did he have regrets, too?*

With a sigh, she moistened her lip with her tongue.

He groaned and looked up at the sky. "Pretty night," he said. "I've missed stars." Then he turned and studied her. "Apparently, I've missed a lot of things I didn't know I missed." His heated gaze left her mouth and ran up and down her length, lingering in such a way as to stir her.

"My ankle hurt." She hoped her tone was matter-of-fact even though she felt a little breathless.

"Take more pain medication."

"I heard you out here. I was curious."

He leaned closer. "You know what they say? Curiosity leads little girls into big trouble. Especially if it involves a man."

She tossed her head back. "I can take care of myself."

"That being the case, I'd offer you a drink," he said smoothly, "but whiskey doesn't mix with those pain pills you're on."

He lifted a bottle of Robert's best whiskey off the floor and poured himself a second drink. "Hope you don't mind me raiding your liquor closet. I'll replace it."

"Drink all you want. It was Robert's. Just remember alcohol's not good for jet leg," she said rather primly. "You should be drinking water instead."

"Oh, really?" He chuckled, his green eyes flashing teasingly in the moonlight. "I remember a time when you weren't such a Goody Two-shoes. A time when you liked to live dangerously."

"I'm no Goody Two-shoes now," she snapped.

"And that is the gist of our problem." He stepped closer to her, so close she could smell the whiskey with the cologne, so close she could feel the heat of his body, fierce despite the cool night air.

Her nipples tightened against her thin cotton nightgown in reaction to him. Instead of backing away, fool that she was, she stood her ground, shivering a little, and not from the chill air.

"I know just how wild you are, sweetheart, and just

how good you still taste. That's what's torturing the hell out of me. Being in the house with you, knowing you were right down the hall…was getting to me. So, I came out here. But being out here with the smell of grass and hay and dust in the air brings it all back—especially memories of you. Being here makes me feel almost like I never left. Why is that? What are you doing to me?"

"But you *did* leave. And you wouldn't have come back now of your own accord."

"You know why I left!"

She glared at him, remembering that her mother had said cash was missing from the truck when she'd explained why she'd had to let Luke go.

Still, he should have said goodbye.

"But I don't want to talk about all the bitter stuff. Not when this whiskey is so good. Not when you're standing out here looking so damn beautiful you make a grown man want to cry."

"As if you ever cry."

He laughed. "So why did *you* come out here on the porch? What do *you* want?" he demanded. "Are you chasing me, girl, like you used to? Because this time I don't aim to run."

"Of course not!" When he laughed again, she caught her lower lip in her teeth and stared at him uncertainly. Was he right? Had she been chasing him? Just a little?

No! But he did look uncompromisingly masculine and devastatingly attractive.

"I'd better go back inside," she whispered raggedly.

"Too late, sweetheart. You should have thought about that before you came out here to tempt me."

"I did not come out here for that reason!"

"I think you did. And I think I know exactly what

you want. I'll give it to you, sweetheart, anytime. Just say the word."

"Not in this lifetime."

"Really?" He laughed again. "This is only our first night. We're both exhausted, and you're injured. Even so, neither of us can sleep because we know what we want. Because we know how good it would be."

Afraid of him, and the feelings and memories he aroused, she turned to go, but he seized her by the arm. His hands gripped her waist, snugging her against his long, lean body. At such close range she could see the curve of his thick black lashes and the tiny lines fanning beneath his glittering eyes. His sensual mouth was full and much too kissable.

He frowned down at her, staring at her in a fierce way that made her blood fire and her willpower dissolve.

"You shouldn't have come back," she said. "Hassan should have sent someone else."

"If it weren't for Daniel, I'd agree. But we have a son, and Hassan suspected Daniel was mine right from the first."

"How do you know that?"

"He told me. On the phone. Right after I saw Daniel. So I came back. And discovered we still have this…"

"This…this what?" A wild, tender sweetness filled her. For a second she was in the past, when she was in love with him. Back then he'd made it easy to believe that his feelings for her had run as deep as hers for him.

She wanted him to kiss her again, to feel his tongue in her mouth. She wanted his large hands on her body, their fingertips blistering her through her thin nightgown.

"Don't pretend you don't feel it, too. This insane, completely self-destructive need," he growled, lowering his mouth to the throbbing hollow of her throat where her pulse beat madly. "I thought it was dead. I willed it to be dead. But it's stronger than ever."

Hissing in a breath, she swallowed tightly as his warm lips devoured her neck, nibbling her soft flesh, flooding her body with hot melting sensations.

"Let me go! You're just a long way from home and feeling horny."

His smile was grim. "I wish to hell that was all this was. I wish to hell..."

Her heart fluttered at the desperate passion in his tone. Did he feel more?

He plunged his fingers into her hair. "I used to love your hair. I loved the way you smelled—like Texas wildflowers in the spring. Nothing's changed. You smell just as sweet, and you're just as soft—underneath your thorny exterior. You're sexier than ever, and I still want you. I told myself for years I hated you. Maybe I do. But right now I want you so much I don't care how the hell you used me."

She wanted his mouth on her lips, wanted to lie under him, but the savage anger in his passion-drugged voice brought her up short.

He had some nerve to accuse *her* of using *him*. She was not about to take such abuse from a man who'd stolen money from her parents, a man whose abandonment had nearly destroyed her.

What had she ever done to him except adore him? Nothing. He was to blame for everything that had gone wrong between them. He'd taken everything she'd given and had let her parents down, as well. Then he'd trashed the most beautiful moment in her life by walking out on her without even a goodbye or an explanation.

With a final lust-filled glance at his sensual mouth,

she placed her hand against Luke's hard-muscled chest and pushed with all her strength.

"You're right. I shouldn't have come out here. I'm tired. My ankle hurts. I need my pain meds. And the last thing I need is you, a skilled seducer of women, pressing yourself on me."

"What?" With eyes that were dazed with desire, he stared at her hard, trying to focus. Finally, the thin set of her lips and slitted gaze must have convinced him she meant what she said. He sucked in a hard breath and loosened his grip.

"Okay. I forgot your low opinion of me when it comes to women." His voice was curt. "But for future reference, don't go following me around in the middle of the night now that you know what I want. I've made myself plain, so I'll think you're bloody well asking for it."

"Well, I won't be!" she lied. "This is my house and I'm used to having the run of it! I won't be told what to do or where to go in my own home!" She wanted to snap out more sharp, stinging lines, but she was too upset—and too needy for the same things he'd said he wanted. She didn't want to leave him, but she had to.

Her knees felt weak, and her hands were shaking. No telling what despicable thing she might still be capable of doing with him if she didn't put some distance between them. Besides, he had the look of a man who was barely holding himself in check.

"Whether you like it or not, you're not living out here alone anymore," he growled. "I'm a man with a man's inclinations."

"I got it the first time," she said in a low tone that sounded much calmer. But she wasn't calm. She was furious. "I don't like you giving orders in my house."

"Your house? It won't be for long—unless you work with me! You and I have to figure out a way to rein in expenses, sell acreage or..."

"I don't want to talk about money tonight."

"You're right. It's premature."

Notching her chin up proudly, she turned to go. Then, as quickly as she could while hampered by her crutches and the knowledge that his gaze burned her backside, she walked to the front door. Once inside she made her way down the hall, stopping to check on Daniel before returning to her own room.

Long after she took more pain meds, she lay in bed feeling hot and needy. Her skin burned with the memory of him watching her dress and the blistering warmth she'd felt when he'd stared at her with such longing. Even now, some wayward part of her reveled in how urgently he'd clasped her to him on the porch.

Part of her wanted to walk down the hall to his room, slide into his bed and wait for him to come inside so she could melt against his body and beg him to take her. She wanted him to kiss her endlessly. She wanted him inside her. She wanted sex, fast and hard, the kind of sex she hadn't had since he'd left. Not that she'd had *any* sex—period. Maybe if she had him again, she would wake up free of his dark spell once and for all.

But she wasn't a man. She wasn't as comfortable owning her true sexual feelings and needs as he obviously was. She was overly emotional about sex with Luke and had most likely romanticized it.

When he'd made love to her in the barn that long-ago evening, he'd been infinitely gentle. He'd kissed her, held her, took the time to pleasure her, said sweet things that had made her feel special.

"I've never been with a virgin before. I want it to be

perfect for you," he'd said in an awed tone, pulling her close.

And it had been. Maybe because she'd been so madly in love with him, and he'd seemed equally in love.

The second time he'd made love to her, he'd been driven. Yet nothing had ever made her feel so adored and complete as his shattering climax.

Now, an hour or so after leaving the porch, she was still awake, when she finally heard him come back inside.

Holding her breath, she listened as he shot the bolt. Then she counted his footsteps as he walked down the hall to his room. She heard him come out and go into the hall bathroom and take another long shower.

A cold one, to quell his desire? Or a steamy one to relax him?

How could even the sound of the tap arouse her, making her imagine him tall and naked? But it did. She felt wet and oh so achingly hot. Then he shut off the water, and that was worse. She imagined him warm and solid, his hard body wrapped in a white towel that would be so easy to remove, if only she had the nerve to admit all the things he'd accused her of.

Fisting her sheets, she told herself she had to be strong.

After his bedroom door closed a second time, she couldn't stop thinking about him lying in his bed alone. She relaxed her hands, but her heart continued to race. More than anything, she wanted to go to him.

She threw off the sheets and sat up. Tearing off her nightgown, she lay down again and stretched out in the dark. With fingertips that trembled she began to touch herself, imagining Luke's hands on her body, bestowing all the forbidden caresses she craved.

# Six

The next morning when Caitlyn woke up an hour later than usual, she was shivering because she was nude and her covers had fallen off. Leaning forward, she pulled the sheets and blankets over her and lay nestled in a plump pile of feather pillows. She was glad she didn't have to do chores or get Daniel off to school. Feeling groggy and disoriented from her injuries and the pain medication, she lay there for some time, savoring the pleasant sensation of warmth and quiet in her semidarkened bedroom. How nice it was that Luke was here to shoulder a few of her responsibilities.

With a sigh, she remembered dreaming of Luke making love to her. For a moment or two she savored those dreams, but as she grew more alert, she became unhappily aware that he was the last man she should be fantasizing about. He'd abandoned her. He was a billionaire with a beautiful countess for a girlfriend. No way could he ever be seriously interested in someone like her again. Not that she would want him to be. No—most definitely not. He was only here for Hassan and Daniel.

Annoyed now, she sat up straighter and switched on the light. Immediately her gaze fell to the silky folds of her peach nightgown, which lay neatly on top of her bedside table. On top of her gown was a slip of paper, which she greedily seized.

It was a note from Luke saying he'd fed Daniel and had gone down to the main road with him to wait until the school bus came. She wadded up the note and then unwadded it and reread the boldly flowing black script.

Luke had come in here and seen her naked!

As she imagined him standing over her, she felt a mixture of embarrassing emotions—desire, shame, tenderness. She imagined his gaze feasting on the sight of her body as she lay nude. She really should hate this almost pleasurable reaction to what was really an uncalled-for invasion of her privacy. What had he thought when he'd found her twisted nightgown on the floor and her covers thrown off?

He certainly hadn't seized the opportunity to awaken her and take advantage. No, instead he'd made himself useful by getting Daniel fed and off to school. In spite of herself, she was impressed that a shallow, wealthy bachelor would have known what to do without waking her and asking for her expert advice.

The thought of him caring enough to put himself out, even that little bit, for their son—and for her—touched her heart in ways that it shouldn't.

*It doesn't mean anything. Daniel's a novelty to him right now. And he did it for his son, not to please me.*

She was *not* falling under his spell again! He'd

betrayed her family's trust and left as if she'd meant nothing.

She got up and dressed. Her routine took much longer than usual—the crutches made every step slower, and she normally didn't waste time on makeup or finding her most flattering pair of jeans.

When she finally reached the kitchen in jeans so tight she wanted to scream, she found Luke's rinsed cup in the sink along with a fresh pot of coffee.

Breathless from dragging herself around, she poured herself a steaming cup and sat down at the table. She already ached under her arms from the crutches. On a normal morning she would have been up and out hours ago. She'd taken her good health for granted. Now that she was helpless and dependent on Luke, not to mention so attracted to him she was torturing herself by wearing skin-tight jeans, she felt confused and out of sorts.

She wanted him gone before he knew his full power over her, but hampered by her ankle, she couldn't go about her usual chores without him. Horses needed to be fed, watered, exercised, clocked, bred, inoculated and prepared for shipping. Someone had to deal with drivers, who needed documents signed. Stalls had to be cleaned.

If only she had a larger staff, she could avoid Luke. But with Daniel away at school, and Manuel being her only full-time employee, she would have to spend a lot of time with her ex-lover. Luke had dismissed his driver, so he'd be driving her to town for a follow-up with the doctor and the rescheduled appointment with her accountant.

So much togetherness was not good. She seemed to be becoming obsessed with the man. But what could she do other than endure him until she was better?

The most hateful question of all: what would she have done without him?

Lost in a circle of worries, she heard the unfamiliar ringtone of a phone coming from the living room. Thinking the call might be important, she slid her crutches under her aching armpits and hobbled toward Luke's phone.

A name stood out in bold black on the screen: Teresa Wellsley.

Caitlyn bit her lip. No matter how dependent on him she was, she had to remember Luke had a life that included a beautiful countess named Teresa. He might desire Caitlyn, but that was probably because she was the only woman available at the moment.

She couldn't let herself forget about Teresa. Not for a minute.

"So when did they die?" Luke asked softly from behind her.

A shiver of excitement coursed through her at the nearness of Luke's soft voice. All morning she'd fought to remain emotionally aloof, but that was proving difficult. He was being so nice.

She hadn't wanted him to accompany her on this errand. Using a garden hose, Caitlyn splashed water on the green lawn and flowers surrounding her parents' immaculately kept graves, which were located in the cowboy cemetery half a mile from the ranch house.

"Nearly a year ago. In a car wreck. There was a violent thunderstorm. Mother was driving. You know how she always had to be in charge."

When he nodded grimly, she remembered that her mother had never liked him. Her mother had even

seemed to relish firing him for stealing, because she'd
been proven right.

"Nobody knows what happened. Maybe she was
avoiding an animal. Their car skidded off that bridge
just outside of town."

"Into the arroyo?" His low, sympathetic tone made
her heart catch.

She nodded. "The car rolled and caught fire. The
sheriff said they died instantly."

"I liked your father. Before Hassan, he was the only
man who saw the good in me."

Caitlyn appreciated the fact that he admired her
father and didn't run her mother down. He could have
held a grudge, despite his own guilt. Her mother had
never been one to keep her opinions to herself, and
her opinion of Luke, from the first, had been that her
husband never should have hired Bubba Kilgore's trashy
son. She'd never let her father forget how Luke had
betrayed him by taking the much-needed cash from the
truck.

"Dad liked you a lot, too," Caitlyn said, suddenly
recalling that her father had been an excellent judge
of character while her mother had always been more
impressed by wealth and show. As Bubba's boy, Luke
had had nothing to recommend him to her mother back
then. After she'd fired him, her mother had been quick
to point out it was a blessing in disguise in that it freed
Caitlyn to marry Robert.

"Maybe your mother would have liked me better if
you hadn't chased me so boldly."

It probably wouldn't have mattered. Her mother
had wanted Caitlyn to end up with Robert Wakefield
because his daddy owned Wild Horse Ranch at the time.
But there were hard truths about Robert that might have

made her mother think differently. She'd definitely have a change of opinion about Luke, if she could see him now. What was a little missing cash compared to an income in the billions?

"I enjoyed defying my mother by flirting with you. I couldn't stand the way she always tried to run my life, even after I was an adult, but I miss her. I miss both of them. I felt so alone after their accident, which happened a few weeks before Robert died. Now that they are all gone, I have no one I can talk to."

Was that why she was talking to Luke as if they were friends? Was that why her resistance to him was dissolving so quickly?

"I felt all alone after my mother died, too," he said. "Dad was so far gone. It was because of your father that I began to see a way out."

She wanted to ask why he'd taken the money when he could have asked for a loan, but she didn't.

"In a way, I owe your dad as much as I owe Hassan. Which means I owe his daughter, as well."

"You owe me nothing! Daddy always said you were an incredible worker."

"It's the trait that made Hassan take a chance on me. Money can be very destructive in the wrong hands. For a man with no self-discipline, no goals, there are many temptations. Hassan wouldn't have backed me had I lacked the determination to withstand corruption."

Those weren't the words of a thief. Was he speaking the truth? She hadn't asked him about the money or why he'd left. She'd believed her mother.

Did she have a false opinion of him and his life in London? Was he really a wealthy man who used his money to attract and then discard beautiful women? He didn't act like he was. From the moment he'd found out about Daniel, he'd put his son first. Not only that, he'd gone out of his way to help her. He'd been sent here to work on her finances, but he'd done so much more.

No! She would be a fool to reverse her poor opinion of him so easily. He'd left her! Her mother had sworn he'd stolen money. He'd left *Daniel*. Why should she give him the benefit of the doubt just because he was so sexy, just because he listened and paid attention?

Luke's silence made her nervous.

Caitlyn hated suspense. As a child she'd hated counting the days until Christmas. When her parents had taken her on trips, she'd pestered them every five minutes with, "Are we there yet?"

This was more suspense than she could handle.

It was late in the afternoon of their first full day together. He'd arrived only yesterday, but it seemed longer.

Rosy sunlight slanted across the pasture as she stood outside her barn watching Luke shave Angel's whiskers with an electric razor. What she wanted was for him to give her some clue as to his plans for her ranch's future.

Besides taking her to the doctor and the accountant, he'd spent most of the day studying her operation, yet he hadn't said anything. Now, his attention was maddeningly focused on her big darlings, who were flirting with him like a pair of shameless hussies. He was laughing as Lilly inserted her nose between his hand and Angel's head.

"Lilly wants her turn," he said. "I think she's jealous."

"Indeed."

Luke smiled. "Maybe she isn't the only one."

"Lilly's superaffectionate with everybody!" It ran-kled that her big babies had taken such a fancy to Luke and were vying for his attention while ignoring her. But, he'd always been as good with horses as he was with women.

He turned the razor back on. When he finished with Lilly, he stroked both horses and gave them carrots to munch. They neighed and nudged his shirt pocket with their noses.

"Like women, they love attention and presents," he said. "I'm not above carrying around a few carrots to win their favor."

As he stroked Lilly, she felt like she would burst if he didn't tell her what he thought.

After getting Daniel off to school and taking her to her parents' graves, he'd driven her into town to see the doctor and Bruce, her accountant. The three of them had gone over the books, and during a quick business lunch Luke had asked Bruce lots of probing questions. Although Luke had taken a few notes, he'd said little, thus revealing none of his thoughts on the subject.

Bruce's grim listing of the bare facts and his obvious relief that a man as successful as Luke was here to help had unsettled her stomach so much she'd left most of her sandwich on her plate. She didn't like being dependent on anyone, much less Luke Kilgore. But what choice did she have?

Luke had insisted they have a conference call with Al Johnson, a ranch manager in between jobs, a man with numerous successes in turning around ranching operations like hers.

"But I can't afford a manager, and I don't want some stranger telling me what to do," she'd said.

Upon returning to the ranch, Luke had insisted she rest, while he'd driven her ATV to the various barns and paddocks and pastures, inspecting everything. When he'd returned, he'd still offered nothing.

She couldn't take his silence anymore!

"Okay! So, you've spent the whole day thinking about Wild Horse Ranch. Did you come up with a financial solution or not?"

"Don't worry. These things take time," he murmured, not looking at her as he stroked Lilly's muzzle. "You need to concentrate on healing."

She heaved in a breath. Under different circumstances, she might have enjoyed hanging out with him and her horses, since he was being so pleasant. But not today. Not when she wanted to know what he was thinking.

"Surely you could give me some hint as to what you think, what you'll tell Hassan. What was his attitude when you last talked to him? Is he worried enough to shut me down?"

"Hassan could afford to bankroll you indefinitely. So could I, for that matter."

"You? Why would I want that? I want Wild Horse Ranch to be a solid business."

"There's always more than one way to skin a cat," he said. "The ranching part of your operation is in the black. It's the horse business that's jeopardizing everything."

As if she didn't already know that. The horses were her passion.

"Like Al said over the phone, you need to raise capital and lower your debt. You could sell some of your bloodstock. I wrote down my thoughts on what I'd sell if I took that route. I called Al back and we discussed—"

"No. I've been building my breeding stock for years."

"Building too fast, it would seem. With horses that haven't always panned out."

"I had a run of bad luck."

"A run you couldn't afford. Surely you understand that you can't keep borrowing without jeopardizing the entire ranch—again. It wasn't so long ago that your father lost it to the bank during that terrible drought. Remember? When I lived here, your father had just moved your family back to the ranch, but he was leasing it from the Wakefields."

"Of course I remember! Who could forget such a thing?"

"Any rich boyfriends like Wakefield waiting in the wings to save you this time?" There was an odd predatory glint in his eyes.

"Don't joke about something like that."

His expression hardened. He didn't look like he was joking. "So, you're not dating anyone seriously?" he asked in a lower tone.

A little gasp escaped her throat. "That is none of your business!"

"Well, are you?"

"No!" she snapped before she had time to think of a clever lie. "And the only reason I'd ever marry again is for love!"

"I wonder—were your motivations equally noble when you married Wakefield?"

She almost choked. "Of course they were!" she sputtered indignantly. "I loved Robert! We grew up together!"

"How reassuring. But if you did marry for money, there's no shame in it. How do you think the aristocratic families in England have kept their estates intact for hundreds of years?"

"How would I know?"

"All too often, marrying well is the only practical thing to do."

Was that why he considered his countess so perfect? Or maybe that was why the countess considered *him* so perfect.

Caitlyn wasn't about to admit she'd learned her lesson about marrying for the wrong reasons, so she bit her tongue and gloomily watched him stroke Lilly with his long, tanned fingers.

"I don't care about aristocratic families in your precious England," she said.

"Well, if you don't like the idea of marrying for money, maybe you could take in a rich partner."

"Someone with a big ego like yours, who'd want to call all the shots?"

"Okay. You could syndicate some of your mares."

"That would mean even more male egos to deal with."

"You could lease Wild Horse Ranch and work here on a salary."

"And lose all control? No! I don't like any of your so-called solutions."

"I could hire Al Johnson to run the place for a while. He could make the brutal cuts that are necessary, get things running smoothly and then teach you how—"

"No! I was afraid of that...."

"Look, you can't keep doing what you're doing. Why don't you sleep on these ideas, and we'll talk again tomorrow morning. There's nothing like a good night's sleep to make one more amenable to practicalities."

"I'm not changing my mind."

"All right, sweetheart, if you're sure—I do have another solution."

"What?"

"Since you've been so negative about all my other suggestions, I think I'll keep it to myself for now."

"It's my life and my ranch you're playing God with. Just tell me!"

"When I'm ready. Remember, you played God with my son for five years."

She heaved in a breath. His response infuriated her, but he did have a point about Daniel. Then something hot and dark flashed in his eyes, causing her to shiver.

"What?" she whispered.

His gaze fell to her lips and then lower, raking over her figure in the skin-tight jeans that she'd worn just to provoke him.

Heat consumed her. Her skin felt raw. Hating the wild flare of her rampaging emotions, she wished she'd worn something baggy. She was a fool to have dressed to entice him, when his glance left her breathless and made her sizzle.

"Sorry to upset you," he said dryly. "That's not my intention."

"I wish I could believe you." She frowned at him. "I don't like waiting," she whispered. "That's all."

His hungry gaze slid over her a second time. "What could possibly be more enjoyable than…anticipation?"

"Lots of things…when it comes to dealing with you."

He laughed.

Suddenly, because of his nearness, she was restless.

When she stamped her boot, his laughter deepened into something bolder. "Enjoy," he whispered in a low, seductive voice before turning and leading her big darlings to their stalls.

Knotting her hands around her crutches, she watched him disappear with her horses into the shadowy barn.

Being in Luke's power was unendurable. How could he force her to consider all those unpleasant business options while keeping her in the dark about his true intentions? She had no doubt that his final solution would be worse than anything he'd mentioned so far. Otherwise he would simply tell her. If he was any other man, she'd think he was afraid.

She wanted to call him a coward. She wanted to kick him. But as long as he had financial control over Wild Horse Ranch, she had to restrain herself and put up with him.

# Seven

A red sun stained the twisting branches of the live oaks as Luke and Daniel stirred the coals of their fire. Caitlyn stood apart from them, feeling increasingly uneasy as she watched the blaze.

The copse had once been his private refuge, but after she'd followed him here, it had become their special meeting place. He'd even carved their names in the center of a heart on a tree trunk.

She didn't like it one bit that he'd picked this particular oak motte for their supper tonight. It stirred way too many unwanted memories.

Earlier she'd pleaded with him. "Why can't we just eat a quick meal in the house?"

"Because a picnic in the oak motte would be much more fun."

"Not for me. Besides, you're not here for fun. You're here to solve my problems. And then leave."

His quick, knowing glance had reminded her that she had no clue as to his true intentions.

"I meant more fun for Daniel," he'd said as he'd thrown hamburger buns, bananas, marshmallows and a pair of rusty tongs into a bag.

"Yes! I want to go, Mom!"

When Daniel had smiled at her, there had been no way for her to argue further.

And Daniel was having the time of his life. Luke had let him build the fire. Now, as he stirred the flames a bit too aggressively with a long stick, he sent brilliant sparks popping into the dry leaves.

"Why can't we cook the marshmallows now?" he demanded, as more sparks flew.

Luke jumped over the ring of rocks surrounding the fire and stamped on the burning leaves with his boots. "After supper," Luke replied for the third time without the slightest trace of annoyance.

In spite of her misgivings, Caitlyn smiled. Luke, who'd waited at the bus stop for Daniel to return from school, was extremely patient and attentive with the boy in a way that Robert never had been. Daniel's noise, constant demands and clutter had driven Robert crazy, especially after he'd become ill.

"Mom never likes me to come here," Daniel said.

"As if that's ever stopped you," Caitlyn said. "This copse is your favorite hiding place, isn't it?"

"Because I know you won't follow me here."

For her, the shady grove was haunted by her memories. Here, Luke had imprisoned her against a tree trunk with his hands and kissed her until her toes had curled.

"It used to be my favorite place on the ranch, too," Luke said, his gleaming eyes meeting hers in a challenge. "Some of my fondest memories happened in this oak motte." He stared at Caitlyn. "I even carved my name on a tree to stake my claim on something precious that once belonged to me."

She gasped. "That tree was cut down a long time ago!"

"You've been here before, Luke?" Daniel whispered.

"I used to work for your grandfather," he said, releasing her from his gaze to look at Daniel.

"For Paw Paw? You did? Wow! When was that?"

"A long, long time ago."

"How come Mom didn't tell me? Mom?"

When Luke's sardonic gaze flew to hers along with Daniel's searching one, her heart skittered wildly. "You'd have to ask her," he said.

"Mom just told me you were a rich guy who buys horses."

"Well, she was right…as far as it goes. But your mom and I, we're old friends."

"Not anymore," she inserted quickly. "That was another lifetime."

Strange, but suddenly it felt like yesterday. The past seemed all too vivid beneath the sheltering shade of these familiar trees.

"But once—we were very good friends," Luke insisted. "The best friends ever."

When she shot him a warning glance, Daniel looked from her to Luke in confusion.

"Are y'all keeping a secret or something?"

Her heart thudded violently.

"We were friends—before she married your father," Luke added.

"But I didn't know Luke was coming here yesterday," she blurted out. "He just showed up out of the blue."

"Well, I'm glad he did. And I'm glad he's going to help us," Daniel said, looking both innocent and pleased. "'Cause now you won't have anything to worry about anymore. Luke's great at just about everything, isn't he, Mom?"

If only she were still as innocent as her son and could believe in Luke's inherent goodness. Once, she'd seen Luke as her very own hero cowboy, riding in to save the day. She hadn't believed him capable of the low things her mother had warned her about and later accused him of.

"He's Bubba's son," her mother had said. "Oh, he's handsome, I'll give you that, girl. But he can't be faithful, and he'll prove what he is soon enough."

Caitlyn, who'd felt the sting of his betrayal on all levels and knew the pain of innocence lost, felt increasingly threatened by him, both personally and financially.

How would he use his power over her and her son?

It didn't matter that Caitlyn knew what Luke was capable of. Her sexy house guest had her thinking about him day and night.

Luke, with his silky black hair. Luke, with his powerful shoulders and lean body. Luke, with the devil's own grin.

Last night had been particularly sleepless. Thus, on the third morning of his stay, as she watched his tanned hand stab a thick slab of ham in the too-intimate confines of her tiny kitchen, she felt too near her breaking point. Slamming her coffee cup down on the table, she leaned toward him.

When he tensed and jumped back from his eggs,

she smiled triumphantly. Maybe she wasn't the only one on edge.

For the last two nights she'd barely slept. Not that she'd stripped off her nightgown again or touched herself—even though she'd wanted to. No, instead, she'd lain awake for hours, listening to every creak of the house, thinking about Luke lying in his bed down the hall. She'd ached for him.

"You've been here two full days."

"Don't forget the nights," he murmured in a low tone.

At the mention of those nights, which she'd deliberately avoided saying anything about, warm color crawled up her neck.

"I want to get this over with! So what's your mysterious solution to my problem?" she demanded. "What is it? You have to tell me!"

He set his fork on his plate with a clatter and stood up. "Do I, now?"

Was he as nervous around her as she was around him? Did he feel ensnared by the sensual tension that had her emotions so tangled? She might think he was simply afraid to answer her question, but she knew Luke wasn't afraid of anything.

After placing his dishes in the sink, his lean, broad-shouldered back was to her. He called down the hall to remind Daniel it was time for them to wait for the school bus.

Refusing to be ignored in such a high-handed manner in her own home, she shot out of her chair, only to wince when her ankle touched the floor. Blinking back tears and taking a quick breath to clear the pain, she carefully hobbled to the sink. Leaning on one crutch, she said, "Surely you have things to do in London."

"Many things."

"Teresa being one of them?"

He turned. The lean, bronzed face that had haunted her dreams was taut with mockery. "For someone who claims she is utterly indifferent, you do take an inordinate interest in my love life. I can't help but wonder why."

That he saw through her so easily galled. "Why can't you just cut to the chase, so we can get this over with and go on with our lives?" she snapped.

"Since I know about Daniel, 'going on with our lives' is not possible any longer." He stared down at her, studying her too intently through his long, sooty lashes. "Is that what you really want—me gone and out of your life?"

"Of course. But I can't help but wonder what my life here will be like if you change the way the ranch is run. I heard you talking to Al Johnson again yesterday. Why did you call him? Is he coming here? In what capacity? Why? What are you planning? The suspense is killing me."

"I can see that, and I'm sorry."

"Tell me what you plan to do."

"All in good time," he repeated. "Much as I enjoy your company and the possibility of a spirited argument, we don't want Daniel to be late to school, do we?"

Mutely, she shook her head. Without another word on the subject, he turned and stomped down the hall to hurry their son along—a necessary chore, since Daniel was so easily distracted. He was probably playing with an action figure instead of putting on his shoes at this very moment.

Still, she wanted to run or, rather, hobble after Luke and badger him into telling her. But she knew him well enough to realize she would humiliate herself to no purpose. No doubt her curiosity amused him. The wiser course was to wait him out. Otherwise, he'd simply dig in his heels and put off telling her for even longer.

Thus, several more days passed without him referring to the matter at hand and with her biting her tongue to keep from drilling him. Even after she threw away her crutches and was able to resume her full routine, never once did he allude to his mysterious solution other than to ask if she'd reconsidered any of his other options.

When she'd said no, he'd seemed almost content to settle down to ranch life. When he wasn't making international calls or working on his laptop, he made himself useful by helping with Daniel and assisting Manuel with the heavier work. He didn't complain, either.

But with the passing of more days and nights—interminable, sleepless nights—she felt the raw, too-intimate, highly charged sensual cravings between them build.

Last night when he'd come out of the hall bathroom, shirtless, he'd nearly bumped into her. She'd caught her breath and barely managed the willpower to skitter down the hall into her own room and bolt the door.

This morning when she'd caught a glimpse of him through the cracked bathroom door as he'd shaved, his dark head cocked to one side and his white shirt unbuttoned, the mere sight of so much tanned muscle had sent tingles through every nerve in her body. She'd known the sensual joy of his body. The man lured her, as only the drug of choice can lure an addict who knows its pleasure full well and has been forced to do without for too long.

That evening after supper, she was grumpy as she

faced still another sleepless night brooding over a man she did not *want* to want. He'd had another conversation with Al Johnson without telling her what they'd talked about. She wanted to know what he was up to, but some crisis had erupted in London. For more than an hour, he'd been holed up in her dining room behind closed doors, engaged in a tense overseas conference call with several of his top London executives.

She didn't want to eavesdrop, but his deep, hard voice carried. Apparently, the employees at Kommstarr, his most recently acquired company, didn't like the massive changes he was instigating. Never had he sounded more ruthless than he did when he insisted his executives slash jobs and budgets and make lists of assets to be sold.

These were people's lives he was dealing with! She couldn't help but wonder what chance her horse farm had. Would he coldly demand that she sell her darlings? After all, they were mere horses.

He had to think his solution would upset her, or he'd tell her what it was. How could she lie awake longing for such a tough, arrogant brute? Maybe she was better off not knowing what he intended for Wild Horse Ranch.

She had to tune out his impending decision or she would go crazy dwelling on all the scenarios she could dream up. Summoning her willpower, she marched to Daniel's room, thinking she'd read her son a chapter of *Harry Potter,* only to find her precious darling curled up on his bed, with his blanket pulled up to his chin. She didn't like the way his green eyes burned in his thin, flushed face.

"Mommy, I'm c-cold," he said through teeth that chattered.

"Honey! What's the matter?" When she leaned down

and felt him, his forehead was hot. "We'd better take your temperature," she said before rushing to the bathroom to find the thermometer.

Luke was closing his phone and stepping out of the dining room when she dashed back into Daniel's room with the thermometer.

"What's wrong?"

"I think Daniel's got a fever."

Luke stood over her as she took Daniel's temperature.

"He's got a fever. I'll give him a cool bath and some medicine," she said. "If he's not better in the morning, we'll call Dr. Williams."

After bathing him, she gave Daniel a hug and put him to bed early with a great many toys to comfort him. Later, as she lay awake in her bed, her thoughts were on Daniel rather than on Luke's mysterious solution. Still, she was aware of Luke getting up during the night to check on Daniel.

Around midnight, when she hadn't heard Luke in a while, she decided to check on Daniel herself. But when she tiptoed to his room, Daniel's door opened and Luke stepped out into the hall wearing only his black pajama bottoms.

As soon as she saw him, the hair on her nape pricked with sensual awareness. "How is he?" she whispered, pulling the edges of her thin robe together with shaking fingertips.

"His fever broke. He's fine—now."

"Is he?" She attempted to make her voice casual as she slipped past him and went inside to make sure. Their bodies brushed, and the heat of his skin set off jitters at all her pleasure points.

After sliding her palm across her son's cool forehead, she adjusted his blankets and his favorite stuffed animals. Immensely reassured that he would probably be perfectly well by morning, she came back out into the hall, clutching a stuffed brown bear, only to start when Luke called her name from the dark.

She turned. He stood beside their son's open door, his feet planted wide apart.

Their gazes met. At the sight of all that muscle and the black hair on his wide chest, she clenched the bear protectively to her breasts.

"You're right," she said in a breathy voice. "He's fine. Just had to make sure."

Luke's fine bone structure looked even tauter than usual in the dimly lit hall. What was it about the dark that made her blood run wilder?

Despite the danger Luke posed, she was terribly glad she wasn't on the ranch alone with a sick child. Luke cared about Daniel, as she did. He seemed to feel the same profound responsibility, which amazed her since he'd known his son for only a few days. But because he did feel so strongly about Daniel, she felt linked to him by more than mere desire.

Why, fool that she was, she was beginning to believe in him again, as she had when she'd been in love with him. It seemed impossible that such a man would rob an employer he'd respected and abandon a woman he'd loved. He didn't seem capable of such unsavory behavior now, and she wondered if he ever had been.

Suddenly, as she continued to stare at him hungrily, she remembered Luke's warning that first night when she'd followed him out to the porch. So, what was she doing—standing in the hall, ogling him?

It was always a mistake to mix business with pleasure. The fate of Wild Horse Ranch was in his hands. If for no other reason, she should fight her attraction.

If she didn't want to send the wrong message to this man who held such power over her, she should say a curt good-night and march into her bedroom and shut the door.

Instead, she continued to stare at him, her heart pounding and her breath fluttering.

When he took a step toward her, an electric shock went through her. Even then, she remained where she was, shivering from the thrill of what might happen next. He took another soundless, heart-thudding step. And then another. And another.

"Caitlyn?" The bold challenge in his emerald eyes set off a pulsing excitement that sizzled through her even before he reached out to touch her.

"Luke?" Torn, she backed away from him.

"Come to me," he whispered thickly. "Just let me hold you."

She should run. She knew that. His past betrayal stood between them. The role he intended to play in Daniel's life was still uncertain. He had the beautiful, perfect Teresa waiting for him in London. Teresa, the countess who probably had soft hands and a softer life. But right now, London and Hassan and all their unresolved issues seemed so far away.

Feeling strange and excited, Caitlyn took a tremulous step toward him, and then another, until she stood close enough to touch him. She trembled with the need to slide her hands over his body. Still, she hesitated.

"Luke," she breathed.

He touched her first, causing her to shudder. Wasting no more time, he gently framed her face with his blunt fingers and plundered her mouth in a long, hard kiss. His tongue plunged inside, taking possession of her.

Her heartbeat quickened. Rising on her tiptoes, she kissed him back for all she was worth.

A fierce laugh erupted from his throat as he caught her closer and aligned their bodies, so she was all too aware of how powerfully aroused he was. Another kiss sent her world spinning out of control until she was limp and clinging to him. That was when he stunned her by ending the kiss with the same startling abruptness with which he'd begun it.

Breathing in savage bursts, his hands fell to his sides and clenched.

"What?" she whispered. "What's wrong?"

"That's for you to say. I don't want you to regret this tomorrow."

"Don't you want me?"

In the deep shadows his eyes glittered. "Yes, I want you," he growled. "How can you even ask?"

When he didn't touch her again, she knew he must be giving her the chance to change her mind.

But for the life of her, she was helpless against the tide of desire that swept her. From the first moment he'd returned to the ranch, some force had taken over. It possessed her utterly now. She'd always wanted him. She'd measured all other men by him, even after her mother had convinced her he was no good.

She'd wanted him more each day he'd been here. She'd been lonely for this, for him, for too many years. She was only human. How long could she fight the inevitable? If he'd gone that first day without ever finding out about Daniel, then maybe she would have been safe. But now that he knew the truth and she saw how much Daniel needed him, she couldn't regret that he'd found out.

She knew Luke didn't love her and that almost

certainly he never had. But in this moment all that mattered was the sexual joy she'd know if she slept with him again, if only for one night.

She hurled herself into his arms, and he caught her against his naked chest, crushing her close. "Darling," he whispered in a low, raw tone that thrilled her. "Sweetheart. I want you so much. But I won't pressure you."

"I can't fight what I feel for you any longer."

He pushed her against the wall, kissing her until her heart raced and she could barely breathe. She knew he was wrong for her. Still, she clung to him, never wanting to let him go…because she knew too well the loneliness of being without him. Six long years she'd lived here without this man's love. "I want you more than anything," she whispered. *Despite everything.*

"Okay, then…."

Lifting her into his arms, he carried her to his bedroom. He kicked the door shut and threw the bolt. Then he swept her down onto his bed.

"Take off your clothes," he ordered in a deep, hoarse voice that caused her to shiver.

She tore off her robe. Then she lifted her nightgown and flung it away. "Beautiful," he rasped. His eyes devoured her as he ripped off his pajama bottoms.

"You're beautiful, too," she whispered as she studied his broad shoulders, rippling torso and huge erection. "So beautiful."

He lay down beside her and stroked her breasts, and tongued her navel. Her nipples hardened and goose bumps pricked all over her belly. "When I left you that note and found you in bed naked and looking so adorably sexy, it was all I could do not to kiss you awake."

*Adorably sexy.* With a shy smile that probably gave too much away, she turned her face fully toward his. She had hoped he'd felt something like that for her.

"Adorable," he repeated. Gathering her closer, he kissed her passionately.

At the contact with his hard lips and naked skin, she trembled. His body was warm and muscular. His obvious desire made her feel loved and safe, but, of course, that was an illusion.

*Something to worry about tomorrow...*

Better to focus on the burning thrill of his hands and mouth, better to abandon herself to this soul-deep need he had taught her to want, better not to worry about the consequences.

But they would come eventually.

In no time, his mouth and hands took her beyond anything she'd ever experienced or imagined, even with him. As his tongue laved her, she arched her body into his. Soon she was lost in the white heat of a passion that left her shattered. Afterward, all she could do was lie limply in his arms, her fingertips splayed across his chest feeling every beat of his heart.

Their first night together, so long ago, she'd been limited by her shyness and inexperience. Now she knew that no one else could ever make her feel like he did—rapturous, ravaged, cherished and utterly satisfied.

She loved him. Fool that she was—she always had. Not that she'd been proud of loving him, after the way they'd parted. Still, he'd been sweet to her when she'd been a girl, and ever since he'd come back, he'd taken care of her and Daniel, amazing her with the depth of his feelings for his son.

Even so, being older, she should know that gratitude and sexual attraction and having a son together were not enough for a solid relationship. She should have resisted temptation.

Easy to say, when not faced with Luke and her own needs. When he again kissed her lips as hungrily as he had out in the hall, she did not resist. The second time was even better than the first.

When it was over, she lay beside him, feeling faint and shaken. Wrapped by the darkness and their body heat, neither spoke. She could only wonder what he thought and felt. She didn't ask, since she feared the worst.

Why had he slept with her? Would he be finished with her now? Would he announce his solution and then leave? Did he now feel free to marry the perfect Teresa?

A strange desolation stole over her heart. She was such an idiot to want him, and then to sleep with him, especially when he had final say over the fate of Wild Horse Ranch. But could one control one's feelings?

She closed her eyes, willing herself to sleep and forget, but such peace did not come easily. This night in his arms had heightened his power over her. She knew she would want him again, and again. She wanted him to love her, to stay with her, to be an ordinary rancher rather than a glamorous billionaire.

But that was not possible. So somehow, when he informed her of his plans to get her ranch on sound footing, she would find the strength to let him go.

# Eight

This was one of those moments in life that was so perfect she wanted to seize it and make it last forever.

Cool air seeped through the ancient wooden windowpanes, bringing with it the sound of morning doves. Soon it would be time to get up and get Daniel ready to catch his bus.

Drowsily Caitlyn lay still, savoring this fleeting moment. It was delicious to just remain under the covers, nestled close to Luke's blistering warmth. All too quickly his watch alarm went off.

He rolled over and kissed her lips. "Time to get up, sweetheart," he drawled in a lazy voice, his heated breath tickling her earlobe.

"Hmm," she murmured. For another long, delightful moment Caitlyn lay where she was, her eyes closed, not wanting to face the day or its realities. She hadn't slept so blissfully in years.

"If you don't get up, Daniel will find you here in my bed," Luke whispered. "Is that what you want?"

"Of course not." Not that she liked being reminded that her presence in his bed might be a shameful thing in other people's opinions. Her eyes snapped open and she forced herself to sit up and focus.

He seemed so cool and businesslike this morning. Leaning down, he picked up her nightgown and handed it to her.

Feeling uncertain, she pulled it over her head. Then she stood up and grabbed her robe, tying the sash.

"We'll talk later," he said.

"About your mysterious solution?"

His expression darkened. "Did you sleep with me thinking I'd go easier on you when it came to sorting out your ranch's problems?"

"No!"

His green eyes seared her.

"No!" she whispered, feeling guilty even though she didn't have a reason to. "How can you ask me that?"

"Easy."

"Maybe you're like that, but I'm not."

"Okay. I'll take your word for it. Let's leave it at that."

She hated the distance he was deliberately putting between them.

"When are you planning to go back to London?" she asked.

He frowned. "Sooner than I'd like. There's a crisis brewing in one of my more recently acquired companies."

At the thought of him leaving for good, a raw, aching loneliness swamped her. So she played dumb. "Oh, that's what that phone call last night was about?"

"Yes. Although, I would have sworn you were hovering right outside the door, hanging on to every word. I hope I didn't sound too tough."

She blushed. "Maybe I did glean that some of your new employees see you as a tyrant."

He exhaled a sharp breath. "There are necessary adjustments that must be made for that company to be viable and competitive in the global marketplace. I'll explain later."

She nodded. Without a word, she crossed the room and opened the door to leave him.

He touched her shoulder and pulled her back for a spontaneous kiss. When she jerked away, he said, "Caitlyn, I'm sorry we seem to have gotten off on the wrong foot this morning. Is something else the matter?"

"Like you said...I'd better go before Daniel wakes up and finds me with you."

"Right."

She scampered down the hall on her tiptoes, but stopped short in her own room at the sight of her reflection in her mirror. Her dark hair was wildly matted; her eyes looked bruised. Fighting tears of humiliation, she swallowed. She was sure last night hadn't meant much to Luke, and she felt ashamed that he might suspect the depth of her feelings for him.

Despite the problems with the ranch, she'd seen herself as a strong person. She'd survived Luke's betrayal, a marriage of convenience to a man who hadn't been able to love her as a real husband, her parents' deaths and then Robert's illness and death. She'd lived with pressing financial burdens as a single mother. But once Luke reappeared she'd realized just how vulnerable she'd always been...alone out here with no family other than Daniel. And needy, at least where Luke was concerned.

Last night in his arms she'd felt a rush of joy such as she hadn't felt since her parents' and Robert's deaths. But what was such foolish happiness based on if all he'd felt was lust?

Soon, he'd issue some unpleasant ultimatum concerning her ranch and darling horses. Then he would leave her to deal with her options. Luke would leave and be glad to be gone, and she would go on, alone. Still, the sooner the business between them was over, the better. Because every day and every night that she spent with him, she would only fall more deeply under his spell.

Moving slowly, she showered and dressed. Vaguely she was aware of Luke telling her through the door that he'd made coffee and would see to Daniel. Thinking how nice it was to have him do fatherly things for Daniel, her attitude toward him softened even more.

Still, because she was determined to avoid him, she tarried so long in her room that when she finally came out, the house was empty.

Somehow she had to make him tell her the solution to her business problems so she could end this—before it got any more complex.


He shouldn't have slept with her.

But how could he have stopped himself?

Maybe sex was a basic mammalian function, but it always complicated the hell out of everything.

After dropping off Daniel at the bus stop, Luke drove Caitlyn's truck up to the house and braked in a whirl of dust. Reluctant to face her for reasons he didn't analyze, he cut the ignition. Out of the corner of his eye he saw furtive movement at the kitchen window, but when he turned his head the curtains snapped together.

Clearly, she was in no mood to face him, either. The sex had been so great last night, he'd thought their connection might help his case. But as usual, Caitlyn hadn't reacted as he'd expected. She'd been so moody and unpredictable this morning, he now wished he hadn't lost control.

He was in a bind. Because of the crisis in London, he had to get back. He'd run out of time to woo her or cajole and explain. But because of Daniel he wasn't about to go away without clarifying their situation. Daniel needed a man in his life. Her business was going under. She needed Luke's skills, his money and his support, with Daniel and in her business.

He'd decided to offer her marriage in exchange for such help.

No doubt Hassan had bankrolled her ranch primarily because he was sure Luke would help her once he knew about Daniel. So, knowing Hassan would support whatever decision he made, Luke wanted to step in and take over as soon as possible.

When the thought of marrying her had first occurred to him, he'd been stunned to realize how old-fashioned he was. Why bind himself to a woman who'd treated him so badly?

But there was Daniel, who needed a father, and Luke, who knew too well what it was to be fatherless. His childhood had been bleak after his mother had left. Maybe for that reason he'd always idealized families where both parents stayed together and raised their children.

He'd already missed five years of Daniel's life, and he didn't want to miss any more or to divide Daniel between them in a custody arrangement.

Still—marriage? In this modern time surely there

was a better, easier way for him to help her and become a part of his son's life? But he had to admit that this wasn't a logical decision. From the moment he'd seen Caitlyn, a widow now and free to marry, he'd known his powerful feelings for her were far from dead.

For years, jealousy over her marriage had consumed him. That emotion and the love he'd felt had eaten at him for so long it had separated him from all other women, including Teresa. He wished he didn't feel so strongly for Caitlyn, but against all logic he wanted her by his side.

He didn't know why he felt so deeply. Maybe it was because they were linked by this land and culture. In London he always felt edgy and alienated. Here, with her, he was his true self. He'd always been ashamed of being Bubba's son, of not being good enough for Caitlyn, according to her mother.

Well, he was rich now, and proud of it. He was in a position to solve all of Caitlyn's problems.

Daniel might be the catalyst behind his proposal, but Luke wanted to share his life and wealth with Caitlyn. He knew his proposal would be ill-timed and ill-received, but the fact that he'd once loved her and that he was still so strongly attracted to her made him hope that he could forget how poorly she and her family had treated him. Perhaps she would see him as the man he'd become instead of the man her mother had thrown off the ranch.

For six years, the memory of Mrs. Cooper's gloating had taunted him.

"She's with Robert Wakefield, who can offer her way more than you ever could. If you love her as you say you do, you'll collect your pay and leave. All you'll do if you stay is ruin her life, and ours, too. Your own mother ran away. Do you want to make Caitlyn so miserable she'll do the same?"

Hurt by Mrs. Cooper's words, hurt that Caitlyn preferred Robert Wakefield, he'd left in a rage. A few weeks later, he'd decided to hear Caitlyn's side, so he'd called. Her mother had answered with the news that Caitlyn was happily married to Wakefield.

Jealousy had torn through him. Luke had slammed the phone down, believing he'd lost Caitlyn because he'd been poor. Ambition born from that pain had driven him to great heights. He vowed to become more than the nothing Mrs. Cooper believed him to be.

Well, he wasn't nothing anymore.

Now he frowned, hating wanting Caitlyn so much but clear about what he had to do. He headed up the stairs, into the house. Crossing the living room, he strode into the kitchen.

Her back was to him when he banged open the door.

When she stiffened instead of turning to greet him with a smile, his stomach clenched.

After last night he felt like wrapping her in his arms and kissing her endlessly, but her coldness stopped him.

"The bus was right on time." What an inane thing to say, he thought, but how should he begin when she was clearly in a snit?

"Was it?" she replied indifferently.

"About last night," he began, warmth stealing into his voice as erotic visions swamped him.

"Right! Last night!" She jumped back as if he'd struck her. Then she whirled around and placed both hands on her hips. "Don't worry. I know it was just sex...and that all we have is Daniel and that you have your Teresa and your real life in London."

"Hey. Wait a minute—"

"No, you wait! I know last night didn't mean anything. You said you wanted to get me out of your system."

"That's not how I feel."

"I'm a big girl! You don't owe me anything. I told you from the first all I want is for you to leave! I think last night proves we should finish our business and get back to living our own lives, before we drive each other even crazier."

His heart pounded with astounding violence. How could she dismiss him and what they'd shared last night so carelessly? He'd never felt half so much for any woman, and he'd come in here to ask her to marry him. Where was the passionate woman who'd come alive in his arms last night?

Suddenly he hated all those tender emotions and craven feelings that woman had aroused in him. His gaze narrowed. With extreme difficulty he masked his anger and fierce hurt and fought to appear as indifferent and cold as she believed him to be.

"I understand how you feel," he said. "But unfortunately we have a son."

"Yes, well, I don't find his existence as unfortunate as you do," she snapped.

"You know what I mean. I'm thrilled with Daniel. I love him. I'm only sorry I didn't know about him sooner."

She tilted her chin defiantly. "So you mean now that you're so high and mighty, you hate feeling connected to me, just as much as I hate feeling connected to you."

Last night was beginning to feel like a dream. Was he a fool to care so much for her? To want to give her another chance?

Her face and lips were bloodless. But her eyes, which

for a moment reminded him of her mother's, blazed with what he took for passionate dislike.

Hell, no, he didn't hate being connected to her, but her harsh words and look made him mask his pain with cruelty. Pride made him swallow any tender confession he might have made. She'd just become the last woman on earth he'd ever reveal his true feelings to.

After investigating her situation here, he'd admired her hard work and the gambles she'd taken to make Wild Horse Ranch succeed. She'd worked herself to the bone. Why, her palms were as rough as Manuel's. But she had pluck and more determination than most of his executives. She was a good mother to Daniel, too. Sure, she'd had a run of bad luck with some of the mares she'd bought, but she had a fighting spirit and a determination to succeed. That went a long way with him.

It didn't bother him one bit that she wasn't rich. He hadn't started off with money, either.

The past was a negative he didn't like revisiting. But she'd been young and probably easily persuaded by her mother and by her family's need to get the ranch back. Caitlyn's courage and passion for horses and her accomplishments since her parents' deaths were heroic.

Bottom line: he'd admired her—immensely—until two seconds ago. Now, raging anger momentarily consumed every positive feeling he'd had when he first walked into the kitchen.

"I may hate the connection every bit as much as you do, but I'm asking you to marry me anyway. And in case you don't realize it, since you don't like the other choices we already discussed, you have no better option. Daniel is my son. Because I owe him, I'll bail you out of your financial mess."

"What?"

"You heard me. I'm asking you to marry me."

"Well, for your information, I don't want your charity."

"Maybe I don't want to give it. Neither of us has a choice."

"Surely we could work out something else."

"I think Daniel would be better off if his parents didn't live on opposite sides of the ocean."

"What about your glamorous Teresa?"

"Collateral damage."

"Just like that you'd dismiss a woman who's perfect for you to marry a woman you dislike?"

"Just like that," he growled.

"Daniel's in school."

"Kindergarten."

"Well, I won't marry you! You're the last man on earth I'd ever willingly choose!"

"And you're the last woman I'd choose." *Liar,* he thought even as he said it. "But you will marry me. Or eventually, you'll lose Wild Horse Ranch and everything else you've worked so hard for—just like your father did."

When she whitened, he hated himself for that empty threat. The reality was he'd probably save her horses when it came to that—for Daniel's sake. But he didn't stop.

"Your precious horses simply are not worth the cost of such care. As I said, you have no better option than marriage to me. You do hold the trump card—Daniel! Think about that! You're good in bed, too, and that's a talent that means something to a man like me."

"Good in bed." She hissed in a breath.

He hated himself in that moment. He hadn't meant

to propose like this, angrily, tastelessly and without any gentleness, but it was done. Maybe it was just as well. Knowing how she felt, he was damn glad he hadn't groveled.

Outside, a car door slammed. Luke and Caitlyn were too busy mulling over their anger and hurt feelings while glaring at each other to pay any attention.

Light footsteps ran up the stairs outside. A fist banged on the door. Then Lisa cried jauntily, "Caitlyn?"

"Damn," Luke growled under his breath.

The front door opened and Lisa stepped into the living room as only a good friend who was very sure of her welcome would. "Caitlyn?"

"She's in the kitchen," Luke yelled stonily.

"Oh, hi there, handsome." Lisa was all smiles as she simpered into the kitchen, carrying a sheaf of papers under one arm. "You're just the man I was looking for."

She was dressed in a tight white sweater and an even tighter pair of jeans. Her long-lashed glance darted from his drawn face to Caitlyn's. "Hey, am I interrupting something?"

"Nothing important," Caitlyn said in a tone that further infuriated Luke. "*He's* through saying what he came here to say."

"You sure you're doing okay, girlfriend?" Lisa asked. "You don't look so hot."

"Doing great," Caitlyn replied.

"Good. I'm glad to hear that. But I really came over to see Luke." She batted her lashes up at him. "It's about these old papers my bank sent me. It's business stuff. I thought maybe Luke, being so smart and all, could help me."

"Sure," he said. "Anytime. Helping a woman in distress is my special calling."

"Did you hear that, Caitlyn? Sounds like your banker sheik pal sent the right man to help you out of your jam."

Luke beamed. Caitlyn gave them both a scorching look and turned away haughtily.

"Just a minute, Lisa," Luke said as he strode over to Caitlyn.

Putting his mouth close to Caitlyn's ear, he murmured, "You think about my proposal, sweetheart. Al Johnson and the team he's assembled can be here to take over for you in a heartbeat. They'll take good care of your horses and cattle operation until we can make some other arrangement."

"He's already assembled a team? You let him do that behind my back?"

"I want an answer by tonight to my proposal. Because tomorrow I'm returning to London with or without you. Marry me, and this place you love will be free and clear. Your horses will be fine."

"But I won't be here with them!"

"I said we'll work something out on that score! Look at it this way. If you don't marry me, you'll only go deeper into debt until you strain Hassan's patience to the breaking point. Eventually, unless someone like me gifts you with a lot of cash, which is unlikely, you'll have to sell land, or horses, or your entire operation. Every month that passes, your bargaining position weakens. Trust me—without my help, or drastic cuts, you will lose this place that you love so much. And you'll force a custody arrangement that will be difficult for Daniel. None of that has to happen. If you marry me, Daniel will have a father, and you will have Wild Horse Ranch. Your horses can move to the U.K."

"And what will you get out of the bargain?"

"Daniel. *And you.* Don't ever underestimate the value

of your appeal to me, sweetheart." When he stroked her cheek with a caressing fingertip, his blood pumped much too violently for his liking. "You were my first love, remember. I want you very much."

She shook her head. "I'll never believe that!"

"Then think about last night. I wanted you, and if you didn't want me just as much, you put on a damn good act."

"Luke!" Lisa called from the door in a husky, flirtatious tone. "I'm waiting, sweetie!"

Caitlyn hissed under her breath, "You'd better go, *sweetie*. Your admirer's getting impatient."

# Nine

Marriage to Luke? Why had he asked *her* to marry him when he'd hesitated about marrying Teresa, who was supposedly so perfect for him?

Because of Daniel, of course. Because he felt obligated.

His proposal had Caitlyn's emotions in such a snarl that she could do nothing but think about what he'd said.

The day got worse. Lisa stayed all morning, flirting with Luke outrageously while he helped her fill out her papers at the kitchen table. Caitlyn was furious that she felt jealous. A man who was as rich and handsome as Luke was could have any woman. It increased her irritation that, no matter what he said, the only reason she could possibly find for him to ask her to be his wife was because of Daniel. His desire for her would be no reason to propose.

The sound of his deep, kind voice as he explained

the papers to Lisa so annoyed Caitlyn she slammed out of the house to work in the broodmare barn.

Not that she could concentrate on her beloved broodmares once she got there. She was so mad she almost wanted him to go and live his perfect life with his perfect girlfriend so maybe someday she could forget him. Too bad his relationship with Teresa wasn't her only problem. There was also Daniel and his need for his father. And the future of Wild Horse Ranch. She couldn't go on as before, even if she didn't marry Luke.

And she didn't want to marry Luke under these circumstances. She knew too well how easily a marriage of convenience could falter. But what better choice did she have? She didn't find the idea of selling land and livestock and figuring out a new career all that appealing, either. And what about Daniel? Would she be able to make enough to take care of him, or have the time to give him all the right opportunities? He needed a mother and a father, and she was beginning to believe Luke really wanted to fill the parental role.

Still, she wanted a loving marriage, and Luke hadn't mentioned love. Loving him made her vulnerable where he was concerned. How could she live with him as his wife and survive emotionally?

Later that afternoon Luke was on the phone with his executives in London when it was time to meet Daniel's bus, so Caitlyn went.

"Where's Luke?" Daniel demanded as he piled into her battered truck with his backpack. "I like his limo a lot better than this old truck. He's got neat stuff—water and colas and real nice seats."

"You know he gave up the limo, and besides, he's on the phone. He's got a problem with one of his businesses."

Daniel kicked his backpack onto the floorboard. In no hurry to return to the house or Luke, she opened Daniel's folder to see what his homework might be. The page that fell out was a drawing of a man and a woman and a little boy under which his teacher had written the word *family*. The man had green eyes. The woman had long black hair. In between them was a kid with green eyes the exact same shade as the man's.

Caitlyn's stomach knotted as she examined the picture, which was obviously of Luke, Daniel and herself.

"Did you do this today?" she asked.

"I was s'posed to draw a family."

"Who are these people?"

"That's Luke," he said in exasperation, jamming a finger at the stick figure with the green eyes.

"And the mother?"

"You! Mom, do you think Luke could ever be my new daddy?"

Desperately, she swallowed. Then, without thinking, she wadded the paper up and threw it on the floorboard. "No! Not in a million years!"

"But Mom!"

"Buckle your seat belt!"

"But you tore up my picture!"

"I'm sorry! I truly am. I-I'll straighten it out." She leaned down, picked it up and began smoothing it. Then she handed it to Daniel.

"You ruined it! It's all wrinkled!"

"I'm sorry," she said again. "Maybe you could draw another one," she whispered in a low, choked tone.

When he didn't say anything, she turned on the ignition and drove home much faster than usual.

"Why couldn't you marry him?"

"I don't want to talk about Luke! We were doing just fine before he showed up!"

"Well…I wouldn't mind if you did…marry him," he said with equal force. "'Cause I like him. A lot! The bus driver says we look alike. And Luke said that if he had a little boy of his own, he'd want him to be just like me."

"He said that?" Her voice sounded scratchy.

"He said he couldn't ever like any boy better than me. Not even his own kid."

Her stomach felt tight. This was all Luke's fault, she thought irrationally. He should never have come back!

Knowing that she was being unfair, she shut her eyes. In her heart she knew Luke and Daniel belonged together. Luke would make a wonderful father. She didn't want to remember how Daniel used to follow Robert around only to be rebuffed most of the time.

Perhaps it would have been simpler if Luke had never kissed her, or made love to her. Or shown her the truth—that she was still in love with him. He belonged in his glamorous world in London with an equally glamorous wife. She couldn't be that wife—no matter how much some secret part of her longed to be at his side. Luke had risen to heights that made a true marriage between them impossible.

How would she get through this?

By living one hour at a time, one day at time, until finally the pain dulled.

She brushed away the single tear that slid down her cheek.

Oh, what a mess she'd made of everything!

"Are you two mad at each other?" Daniel asked too brightly.

At the dining room table, Caitlyn sat stiffly across

from Luke and a platter of fried chicken and mashed potatoes.

Silence.

"Of course not," Caitlyn finally managed, since Luke refused to answer.

"Then why won't you talk to each other? And why'd she tear up the picture I drew of you?"

Luke's hard gaze slid across the table to her. "Maybe because I've asked your mother to marry me," he said quietly.

"What?" she gasped, glaring at him.

"This is great! Are you going to, Mom? Are you going to?" Daniel cried eagerly.

"I can't believe you would do a thing like that! You have no right to involve him," Caitlyn cried.

"Why not?"

"Why not? How can you ask me that? He's a small child, that's why! It's unfair to involve him!"

"It's a family matter, and he's a very important part of the family."

"But Mom, I already told you I want him to be my new daddy."

"There," Luke said, "it's settled. The vote is two against one."

"It is not settled," Caitlyn said. "Not by a long shot. This is not a democracy. I decide who I'll marry. Or, in this case, who I won't marry."

Luke grabbed her hand and reached for Daniel's. "So, will you marry me?"

Twin pairs of green eyes burned her.

"Do it, Mom! Please!" Daniel whispered.

It seemed unfair, the two of them working together this way.

"All right." She finally relented, unable to say no to the pleading in Daniel's gaze. "I'll marry you."

Daniel threw himself in her arms, and she hugged him tightly. Not that she dared so much as glance at Luke.

So, it was settled. Because she'd made such a tangle of her life; because Luke wanted to be a full-time father and would be good at it; because Daniel, who'd always craved a father, wanted Luke to be his father so much.

And because she loved Luke and couldn't bear to see him go away to London, knowing she would never see him again.

Maybe he didn't love her. Maybe she couldn't measure up to the perfect Teresa or be the wife a man like him needed, but if she didn't try, she'd never forgive herself.

No sooner had he gotten Daniel into bed than Luke knocked on Caitlyn's bedroom door.

She cracked the door half an inch. Her eyes were wet looking. Had she been crying? Because of him?

"You can change your mind," he said when she refused to meet his eyes.

"No. I mean…yes," she whispered in a tone that betrayed her utter misery.

"Yes?"

"Yes! I'll marry you! Like I told both of you earlier!"

"You remember what I said about you being good in bed? You know this will not be a marriage in name only?"

"Yes, I understand what marriage means."

"Then you'll share my bed? Willingly?"

His heart sped up. After a long moment she nodded. "If you insist."

"I insist. So—prove it."

"Now?" She let out a breath.

"Kiss me. Show me that you belong to me," he said.

"But we're not married."

"After last night, does that matter?"

She closed her eyes, curled her fingers tightly.

Did she dread his touch? Maybe, but when he pushed the door wider and reached for her, she did not resist him.

"Touch me," he whispered, trying to hide his eagerness. He stepped further into her bedroom and shut the door. "Touch me everywhere."

When her chin notched up an inch, he thought she would defy him. But she didn't.

As her rough hands roamed gently over his body, his anger began to subside. In its place came that loathsome tenderness he'd felt last night, showing him how deeply he desired her good opinion. This was the girl who'd followed him around in his youth, the girl who'd given him her virginity, the girl he'd adored. When she was his wife, he would take care of her. If their marriage worked out, she would have to move her horse operation to the U.K. and visit Wild Horse Ranch only a few times a year, but he did not intend to let her work so brutally that she ruined her hands. He would buy her pretty things.

But right now, he refused to think about the future or the power she held over him. Instead, he drew her to the bed and laid her beneath him. He would think about her warm hands undressing him, stroking and caressing and circling him. Then, much to his surprise and delight, she placed her wet mouth where her hands had been and sucked deeply.

He groaned in ecstasy. Placing his hands in her hair,

he spoke words he'd never intended to say, but because he felt so much for her, he could not stop himself.

When he was close to the edge, he pulled her beneath him and plunged deeply inside her, claiming her as his own.

When her arms tightened around him and she clung to him mindlessly, pleasure such as he had never known filled him. He swelled even bigger against her velvet warmth until he thought he'd die.

He didn't want her to feel this good; he didn't want to desire her this much. But treacherous feelings mushroomed inside him. She was slick and hot and tight. With every stroke, his tumultuous, conflicted feelings grew until they all but overwhelmed him. Maybe he and Caitlyn could find a way to make their marriage work.

"Caitlyn."

Tilting her head back, she stared into his eyes. Whatever she saw in their depths made her heart stampede. With a sigh, she fused her mouth to his and kissed him deeply. As he exploded inside her, he whispered her name over and over again.

At least in the bedroom, if nowhere else, she was his.

Caitlyn stared moodily out the window at the glittering Las Vegas strip. Vegas was the last place she'd ever thought she'd marry.

After making love to her last night Luke had held her close and said they should get married in Vegas before going to London.

"Why Vegas?" she'd whispered uneasily.

"Because it's fast and easy. Because we can obtain a license and marry the same day with very few questions asked. We have enough problems, don't you think? The first one being you and Daniel moving away from your home on very short notice."

"And leaving my horses."

"Temporarily. We'll figure out something. All the more reason why we don't need the stress of planning a wedding."

"But none of our friends or family will be there to celebrate with us."

He'd shot her a quick, dark look, and she'd remembered he didn't consider their marriage a celebration. For him, it was an obligation.

"Okay, since you hate the idea of such a wedding, I'll make all the arrangements," he'd said. "We'll have to delay our trip to London by a day or so."

"But how can I leave the ranch? It doesn't run itself, you know. I have to pack."

"I hired Al Johnson and his team. They'll be here first thing in the morning."

"You were that sure I'd say yes."

"Yes was your best option."

So here she was in Vegas, alone in one of the fanciest hotels on the strip, waiting for Luke and Daniel to return from buying a wedding license. Making use of her time, she'd dressed in a stunning off-the-shoulder black dress that Luke had bought for her. As gorgeous and practical as the dress was, she couldn't help remembering the white gown she'd worn when she'd married Robert. Because of her mother, her first wedding had been completely traditional.

Eyeing the bottle of champagne Luke had placed on ice for later, she paced restlessly.

Where was he? Was he losing his nerve?

Finally, when another half hour passed and he still

didn't arrive, she went over to the chilled bottle and popped the cork.

Why wait when she needed to fortify herself for a ceremony that would probably be in some tawdry Vegas chapel?

Pouring herself a glass, she lifted it and made a silent toast to love and luck. Then she sipped slowly. Maybe, by some miracle, things would work out and they'd be happy. She imagined Luke coming home and sharing his day, preparing an evening meal together, making love. They'd do things with Daniel, have friends over like a normal couple. Maybe they'd go to parties, and to children's birthday parties, and take family vacations. She hoped so.

Somehow it was easier to imagine him working all hours while she struggled with loneliness and homesickness. Luke would prefer his glittering crowd to a simple evening with her and Daniel.

As the bubbly liquid slid down her throat, she stalked the lavish penthouse suite, stopping to stare out the tall windows, where the sight of the gaudy city slammed her again. This city with its glittering lights and glittering women was all about easy money and easy virtue, not true love. What chance did their marriage have?

Suddenly Caitlyn heard a key and then the door opened. Luke was back with Daniel, who bounded inside shouting her name. No sooner had her little boy hugged her than he pushed free of her clinging arms, anxious to show her a new toy Luke had bought him at the children's museum.

"Look. It's a propeller on a stick. If you twirl the stick in your hands, it flies. See!"

Indeed it did, skittering into a chandelier and then plummeting. For the next five minutes, the three of them chased the thing about, finding it under a red velvet couch, behind a gold curtain and on the pink marble counter of the bar. Then Luke, who was elegantly clad in a dark suit, clapped his hands and put a stop to the mayhem.

"Enough. I've got the limo waiting. It's time to get this show on the road. We leave for London very early tomorrow morning."

Daniel, who was wearing a new suit Luke had bought for him, puffed out his chest importantly and grinned from ear to ear. "Luke says I can be his best man! And ring bearer! He says I'm everything!"

Over their son's black head, Luke's gaze locked with hers. She willed him to smile or say even one kind word that would give her a ray of hope.

He said, "You wanted family to play an important role at our wedding."

She smiled wistfully, liking that he'd listened, that he'd remembered. "Come here, best man, so your mother can tuck your shirttail back in your pants."

Luke laughed.

Their wedding was small. Two chapel employees served as the only witnesses in a gold-tinted sanctuary adorned with too many angels and artificial flowers. The reverend said his words in a mechanical rush.

Despite the champagne, Caitlyn felt tense and shaky. Beside her, Luke seemed aloof and cold. Daniel, however, appeared to be bursting with joy and pride. He clutched the wedding band, twisting it round and round his finger as he bounced from one foot to the other.

When the moment for the ring came, Daniel became so excited he dropped it and had to crawl under two pews to get it. When he emerged, his shirttails hung loose and his hair was rumpled. Luke knelt down to take the ring from Daniel.

"Do you want to help me slide it on your mom's finger?" he asked.

Beaming with pride and pleasure, Daniel nodded. Then their two hands, Luke's so much darker and larger, slid the gleaming band of diamonds on to her slim finger. Before she had time to get used to the first ring, Luke slid on an immense solitaire engagement ring.

"You didn't have to," she began. "It's too much."

The man officiating said in a deep, glum tone, "You may kiss the bride."

Still holding Daniel's hand, Luke turned to her and lifted her chin with a fingertip. His nearness made her catch her breath. Pulling her against his long body, his lips brushed hers briefly, yet so tenderly her heart sped up. Strange, how even the lightest of kisses was charged with heat. For one sparkling second, she thought that maybe someday all her dreams would come true.

After that gently searing kiss, Luke squeezed his thumb against her palm and smiled down at her, a warm smile that told her he remembered all their other kisses. Then he let her go and leaned down, his attention on Daniel.

"You can open your eyes now," he said to their son, who'd been hiding his eyes while they'd kissed.

"Is it over? Are we married now?" Daniel asked.

"Yes," Luke said, his eyes burning her. "Yes. We're married."

# Ten

Marriage to a billionaire.

From the moment their jet set down at Heathrow, Caitlyn's life changed so suddenly and irrevocably, she felt thrown off balance. At their hangar, two stretch limos awaited them, one to take her and Daniel to their flat and the other to take Luke to his office.

Even though she talked to Al Johnson or one of his men on a daily basis, she missed the ranch and her horses unbearably. Technically the ranch was still hers, and Luke had promised they could move the horses to the U.K. when their lives settled down in London. Still, she felt like she'd lost a big part of herself.

Their first week together passed in a breathless blur. She was dazed from jet lag, and Luke was swamped by the ongoing crisis at Kommstarr and the resulting media frenzy. At least that was his excuse for spending so little time with her and Daniel.

The phone rang all the time. Luke was constantly defending himself in interviews and convening with his PR people. She saw his face splashed across the scandal sheets and television more than she saw it at home. Somehow he found the time to hire a tutor for Daniel so that their son could keep up with his studies until he was enrolled in a new school.

During that stressful time when they were both getting their bearings, Hassan arrived in London to welcome her. He called, issuing an invitation for dinner at his suite in two nights' time.

"I have nothing to wear," Caitlyn said to Luke the morning before they were to meet Hassan. She'd learned at their first party how inadequate her wardrobe was for her glamorous new life. The paparazzi had taken several unflattering photos and made the most of their coup. One headline read The Billionaire Marries Cinderella.

"I'll have my secretary recommend a personal shopper," Luke said.

"I don't like feeling so helpless."

"You'll soon learn all that is required. If I did it, you can. Give yourself time. Meanwhile, don't forget to enjoy London with Daniel while you do. I want you both to be happy. As soon as we select a school and get him registered, he'll be in classes all day." Having said that, he'd dressed quickly and left for work even earlier than usual.

Her new personal shopper, a Mrs. Grayson, called her an hour later to set up an appointment for that afternoon. When Caitlyn hung up, the rest of the day loomed before her, empty and devoid of any responsibilities. She'd always worked. So much freedom wasn't easy. With a butler, a housekeeper, a tutor and maids, with only the long-distance management of her ranch and horse operation to occupy her once Daniel was in school, how would she make herself useful?

Maybe Caitlyn would have found London more enjoyable if she'd been a normal bride on her honeymoon. Or even if she'd been a normal tourist who knew that after her vacation she'd be returning to Texas.

She tried to make the best of it. She took Daniel on long, lovely walks through the city.

They saw world-class museums; the city's public parks filled with nannies, children, skaters, walkers, bikers and all sorts of people sitting on benches reading or eating their lunches. But what she liked best was riding with Daniel in Hyde Park.

Daniel, however, proved to have a small boy's taste for the macabre, preferring the torture chambers of the ghoulish London Dungeon. Its squealing caged rats and dripping water beneath the rumbling trains thrilled him. He was almost equally mesmerized by the Egyptian mummies in the British Museum.

Such delights aside, the more familiar she became with Luke's lavish, over-the-top lifestyle, the more difficult it was for her to pretend she could ever fit into it. His A-list friends included celebrities, lords and their ladies, his superwealthy business associates and their bejeweled wives.

Luke had even instructed her to leave the flat by a back exit and to wear sunglasses and a wide-brimmed hat to help elude the paparazzi.

Initially, she'd protested. She didn't want to hide or to have Luke's security team accompanying her throughout the city. But Luke had made her understand that his wealth made them targets.

"If the paparazzi discover you, it's best to say nothing," he warned. "Not always easy. But just remember they try to use your words to hang you."

And then there were Luke's offices, vast and sophisticated. He didn't drive much, but his cars were numerous and luxurious. He preferred being whisked about by his chauffeurs or helicopter pilots so he could work and return phone calls. At night she and Luke were expected to attend glamorous fundraisers and business functions. But even when they were home, his penthouse flat on the Thames with its minimalist décor and view of Chelsea Harbour was not the kind of home where she and Daniel could kick back and relax. The flat brimmed with museum-quality art, and she had to watch Daniel every second for fear his curiosity would get the best of him.

She longed for trees and birds. For the vast stillness and silence of the ranch. For unobstructed views and opulent sunsets. For privacy, a commodity she'd never realized she cherished.

She thought constantly of her big darlings back home, but all too often, her daily phone calls to Al and her vet only increased her anxiety. Yesterday, the driver who'd come to pick up three two-year-olds being shipped to California had demanded that accession numbers be written on the health certificates. She'd tried to help Al locate the certificates in her disorderly files to no avail.

Then he'd put her in a real panic when he'd told her that Angel, who'd been vaccinated against strep equi, had an abscess and was being quarantined and tested for the dreaded strangles bacteria.

Terrified, she'd called her vet.

"Don't you worry," Dr. Morrow had assured her. "We're just taking precautions. I'm ninety-nine percent sure she doesn't have it."

If only she weren't so far away, she'd thought. "Only ninety-nine percent? Not worry? The horse business has not been a gentle teacher."

"It never is, my dear. But you enjoy your honeymoon and your handsome husband."

If only she were a normal bride and life with her handsome husband was that simple.

Much to her surprise, Hassan was not alone when they were ushered into his immense suite at The Savoy. Its green marble floors, walnut wainscoting and twelve-foot ceilings were complemented by plush white couches lit softly by lamps with pale, rosy shades. Hassan sat on one of the couches with a stunning couple. The man, who was tall and dark, had eyes only for his wife. She, a slim brunette in a floating white muslin dress, wore a white gardenia in her hair. They sat so near each other, they looked like teenage lovers.

When Hassan stood up, his dark face alight with pleasure, he embraced Caitlyn and told her she looked beautiful in her sparkling red dress.

"It is so good that you are now my honorary daughter."

She nodded as he knelt to engulf Daniel's hand in his much larger ones.

Hassan arose after a lengthy private conversation with Daniel about something the child was holding. "I must congratulate you, my son," he said to Luke. "Your wife is even more beautiful than I remembered, and Daniel is everything a man could wish for in a son. I should know."

"I owe you," Luke said. "For giving me my son."

"I never thought that in this life I could repay my debt to you."

"But you did."

"When I saw him at Keeneland I knew," Hassan said.

As the men shook hands, Daniel set a pair of plastic dragons on his plate and beamed at everybody. Caitlyn, who had specifically told him to leave the dragons in the limousine, ignored this infraction.

"Do you like London, my little friend?" Hassan asked Daniel.

"My favorite is the dungeon! It's really creepy!"

Hassan laughed. "And that's a recommendation?"

"He's five, so yes." Caitlyn smiled.

"And you? How do you like London, Caitlyn?"

"Who could not enjoy such a city? But it is very different from the life I'm used to."

"In a good way, I'm sure."

"Yes, but I miss the ranch."

"Of course you do, but you will have a long, happy life in which you will visit the ranch often." Hassan turned to Luke. "I am pleased with your solution," he said. "Very pleased. I'm just sorry you have to be distracted by business problems when you should be enjoying your beautiful bride."

"I am enjoying her," Luke said, drawing her into his arms. "Having her and Daniel here puts business into perspective."

"But I forget my manners," Hassan said, indicating the attractive couple on the sofa. Quickly, Hassan introduced everybody.

"Principe Nico Romano and his lovely Principessa Regina Carina," Hassan said. "Nico stopped by my office today and I told him about Raffi's marriage. He's an old friend of Raffi's, you see. He couldn't wait to be introduced to you."

"I met Nico when I first went to work for Hassan," Luke said. "We hit it off immediately."

"By the way, Hassan, you can cut the titles," Nico said.

"Especially mine," Regina said. "After all, I was born in America."

"But I thought all you Americans loved titles," Hassan said.

"Not so much," Regina said. "I found them quite intimidating when I first came here. In fact, I still do. I prefer not to use mine—although it does come in handy if I run into a problem making a reservation for lunch."

"Where are you from?" Caitlyn asked.

"Austin, Texas."

"I'm from Texas, too."

Regina smiled at her, radiating friendliness, warmth and acceptance.

"I'm afraid I led a very ordinary life…until I decided to vacation in Italy and fell in love with Nico. I didn't know he was a prince at first," Regina said.

"How romantic."

"Yes, it was, but in the beginning there were problems. He was a prince. I wasn't rich. Certain people in his family didn't think I was…suitable."

"That would be my mother," Nico supplied, chuckling. "She can be formidable."

"In her defense, our worlds were so different, even Nico and I thought marriage was impossible."

"What was impossible was living without each other," Nico said in a deep, husky tone, drawing Regina even closer.

"We live in London because, frankly, I like living where people speak English," Regina said.

"And it is better for us if we don't live too close to my mother," Nico explained. "She's very old-fashioned."

"I'm an immigration lawyer," Regina said.

"You work? That doesn't sound like the life of a princess."

"My mother-in-law would love you for agreeing with her, wouldn't she, darling? We have a child, a little girl. Gloriana. She's three and our precious little whirlwind. But I have to do something besides chase her around drafty palaces and attend royal functions."

"I understand," Caitlyn said.

"Nico didn't at first. I'm afraid it was up to me to bring the Romanos into the modern world."

Nico smiled indulgently, not in the least perturbed by his wife's comments.

"Where is Gloriana?" Caitlyn asked.

"She has an early bedtime, so she's home with her nanny," Nico replied.

Strangely, despite the elegance of Hassan's white-and-gold suite, the extravagance of the numerous tasseled sofas, plump chairs and hassocks, the richness of the many courses of food and wines, Caitlyn found herself relaxing long before the men were offered port. She liked these people and felt comfortable with them—even if Hassan was the richest sheik in the world and the Romanos were royalty. She especially liked Regina, who'd transformed herself from an ordinary Texas girl into an Italian princess.

Maybe there was hope for Caitlyn, too.

"You are remarkably beautiful," Luke said when at last they were alone in their bedroom with all of London twinkling below them. At his husky voice and hot glance, her tummy flipped.

It took immense self-discipline to keep her gaze glued to a workboat making its way up the Thames. "Thanks to the help of your personal shopper, the eminently talented Mrs. Grayson," she said modestly.

His gaze slid over her in such a lingering way she blushed in anticipation of the carnal delights he was teaching her to crave.

"I wouldn't give her undue credit. Although the red and the stylish cut certainly become you, you would be just as breathtaking without them. I was proud of you tonight."

"Thank you."

"You seemed happy. All evening I found myself regretting that I haven't been able to pay you enough attention since I got home. You know how it is when you leave—everything piles up so that you're swamped doubly when you return. I will figure out how to change that."

Ripping his tie through his collar, he crossed the room and took her in his arms. All week, she'd lived for moments when they were alone. Closing her eyes so she could savor his clean, male smell, she parted her lips as he gathered her close.

"But beautiful as you are in red silk, I prefer you naked," he whispered against her ear. When he lowered his mouth to her lips, heat washed through her.

Deftly, his hand found the zipper at the back of her dress. Within an instant the fiery silk had pooled at her feet and he was carrying her to his bed. When his tongue entered her lips, her hands around his neck tightened.

"Oh, Luke…" Arching her slim body against his heavy erection, she sighed. "I need you so much."

Suddenly, she was in a bigger hurry than he was.

Finding his waistband, she undid his belt. He groaned when she unbuttoned his slacks and then slid her hand inside to explore his bare skin. When she squeezed him and moaned, he inhaled a sharp breath.

"We should slow it down, make it last." Kneeling, he positioned himself above her but didn't lower his body to hers. "You are exquisite."

"No!" she whispered, arching upward, frantic to join her body to his in the most primal way.

"If you insist," he murmured.

When he finally slid inside her, she circled his waist with her hands, tugging him closer. "Yes! Yes!"

Within seconds they were moving together, up and down, faster and faster, his hard flesh plunging inside her.

The priceless paintings in the room blurred. She couldn't breathe fast enough. Her fingertips climbed his spine and dug into his neck. She wanted him desperately. All too soon she was clinging, exploding, screaming. Only after her pleasure did he find his own, and when he did, she climaxed again. For a long, shuddering moment he held her perspiring body against his own, his blunt fingertips caressing her gently.

She felt so shattered, she wept. He smoothed her hair and kissed her forehead. "Don't cry, sweetheart."

"It scares me the way the sex keeps getting better and better."

"I rather like it," he murmured. "We can do it again if you like."

"I don't like needing you so much."

"Why not? We're married, aren't we?"

Yes, but only because he'd felt obligated, she thought, wishing with all her heart that he could truly love her.

# Eleven

The next morning, Caitlyn awoke blushing. Her deliciously sensual dream had involved Luke making love to her while they rode Sahara across a moonlit desert. Sighing with fresh longing for Luke, she reached across the bed to touch him, but found only his empty pillow.

Sitting up, she opened her eyes. The bedroom was bathed with soft, gray sunlight. On her bedside table lay a crisp note.

*I'll make it a point to get home early, sweetheart.*

So, he'd left, and she wouldn't see him for hours.

Remembering his kisses and caresses, she shivered with yearning. Stretching, she ran her fingers through her silken hair. Then she grabbed his pillow and inhaled his clean, masculine scent.

She felt happy. Truly happy, for the first time since he'd come back into her life.

If he didn't love her, he was never unkind…unless,

she amended, she provoked him. The thought made her smile.

Maybe he cared a little. Maybe even more than a little. He'd said he was proud of her. He'd acted as if he adored her. There was no denying that the sex last night had been extraordinary.

But they never mentioned the past. He hadn't explained why he'd taken the money and run, why he'd walked out on her without saying goodbye or why he felt justified in being angry about the past. How could she trust him and build on that trust if they couldn't talk to each other about the things that mattered?

Despite her nagging doubts, she got up, humming to herself. Checking her cell, she saw a text from Dr. Morrow with the good news that Angel had tested negative.

Wonderful, she thought. Still humming, she showered and went to find Daniel so they could breakfast together.

She was still aglow an hour later when she and Daniel were riding in Hyde Park on the famous sand-covered bridleway, Rotten Row.

"Mom, is that great big bird a seagull?" Daniel cried as he pointed to a huge bird near a fountain. "I thought everything was s'posed to be bigger in Texas."

"Texans do brag, but no, I don't think that's a seagull…although it is some kind of seabird. Very good observation. Later, we'll have to get a bird book and look—"

Before she could complete her answer, a man yelled her name. When she twisted in her saddle, a dozen flashes went off in their faces. She gave a cry of despair when she saw the horde of reporters stampeding toward them from behind a tall hedge.

The paparazzi.

It was all the stable groom could do to hold on to Daniel's frantic horse. When Caitlyn's gelding reared, pawing the air wildly, she dealt with him in a firm, gentle manner that soon had him under control. Then Luke's security team surrounded them.

"We've got to get you both out of here," Thierry, the head of security said.

A man in ripped jeans with keen gray eyes and a long-lensed camera pushed closer and fired questions at her as he took dozens of pictures.

"Why did your husband buy Mullsley Abbey, the home he and Teresa Wellsley toured together, and then marry you?"

"No comment," Thierry said.

"Excuse me." Caitlyn blinked in confusion. "Mullsley Abbey? I don't know anything about that."

"Rumors said he intended it for Teresa as a wedding gift," the rude reporter said.

"I don't know anything about this!" she exclaimed.

"Why did he marry you?" another man in thick glasses demanded.

"What do you mean?"

"Mrs. Kilgore, did you marry him for his money?"

"No!" she said defensively. "It was his idea to marry me! Yes, I owed money. But he's the one who offered to help *me*."

"Isn't that another way of saying you married him for his money?"

"Is the kid Kilgore's?" another asked.

"None of your business!"

Their questions and condescension were making her too furious to think. Fortunately, Thierry got between her and Daniel and the clamoring herd.

"Is he Kilgore's?"

"No comment," Thierry growled.

Quickly, he helped her and Daniel dismount. Other members of the security team attended to their mounts while she and Daniel were hustled across the lawn to the safety of a black SUV. They sped away, only to be chased by a swarm of motorcycles. Big-eyed, Daniel pressed his face to the window.

Minutes later, after having been notified by Thierry of the ruckus, Luke called her on her cell. "Are you and Daniel okay?"

"Yes," she whispered, staring at the motorcycles. "They…they said you bought a house you'd intended to give Teresa. Is that true?"

He was silent for a long moment. "No."

"But were there rumors about it being intended as your wedding gift to her?"

"Look, I'll explain everything tonight when I get home."

"But…"

"You said you're both okay. That's all that matters. We can't worry about what the press dreams up to say about us every day for the rest of our lives. They always distort everything." He said a tense goodbye and hung up.

The story broke on television early in the afternoon, before Luke got home. Every talking head in Great Britain wanted to know who billionaire Luke Kilgore really loved—the English heiress or the Texan fortune hunter with the little boy.

"I'm not a fortune hunter," Caitlyn said to the television. "I'm not!"

There were clips of Teresa on Luke's arm, which must have been taken before he'd come to Texas. She was a young, ethereal blonde, who smiled at him as if she adored him. There were clips of their visit to Mullsley Abbey and its immense deer park. After these, a clip from today of Teresa in a white miniskirt, her cheeks tear-streaked as she dashed from Luke's office building, was aired repeatedly. She was equally beautiful in tears.

Why had Teresa gone to see Luke? Had she deliberately let the bloodhounds catch her there?

The worst clip of all, if she didn't count the ones of Daniel's pale face plastered against the SUV's window, was of an angry-looking Caitlyn defending herself by saying, "It was his idea to marry me! Yes, I owed money. But he's the one who offered to help *me*."

After seeing that clip for what had to be the tenth time, Caitlyn flipped the channel in disgust only to find another story about Luke.

"Billionaire Kilgore has been in the news because too many of his employees at Kommstarr see him as a rich CEO who wants to break up their company while firing talented people," a female newscaster brayed in an accusatory tone. "Here's what one single mother who lost her job this week has to say about him." She handed the microphone to a pretty young woman in tattered jeans, who was bouncing a crying blue-eyed baby in her arms.

"That's right. I'm a single mum, I am. Where will the likes of me go in this job market? Kilgore is filthy rich, but he's got no heart. I pity those two women, the countess and the gold digger, who are fighting over him. He may be Mr. Moneybags, but he'll break their hearts, same as he broke mine. And my little girl's. Just look at her—poor lamb. How am I going to feed her?"

Behind Caitlyn, the front door slammed. She whirled

just as a haggard Luke stepped into the room. His shoulders sagged as he leaned his briefcase against the wall.

"Nothing those people are saying is true. Not a word," he said quietly. She noted the dark circles under his eyes.

"Of course," she whispered. "I believe you."

The next clip was again that of the furious Caitlyn.

A muscle jerked in Luke's hard cheek.

"That's out of context," she whispered defensively.

"I'm sure it was. I told you they'd twist anything you said or did. Why did you talk to them?"

"Because they asked me questions."

He crossed the room, grabbed the remote and turned off the television.

"What about Mullsley Abbey? Is it true? Were you intending it for Teresa before you found out about Daniel?" she asked.

"No. I visited it with her once as a regular tourist, and then I found it was for sale and became interested in it. Caitlyn, I married you. Not Teresa. I want to forget the past. I want us to start over."

"For Daniel's sake?"

"Not just for his sake, but for ours, too."

"Did you buy Mullsley Abbey?"

"Yes. For us."

She swallowed. Not that the hard lump in her throat dissolved.

"And what about Teresa? Did she come to see you today?"

"Yes."

"Did you know she was coming?"

He nodded. "She called me yesterday."

Yesterday? So, last night when he'd held her in his

arms and made love to her, he'd known he would see Teresa today. Had he been trying to manipulate Caitlyn with sex?

"Did you tell her that you felt like you had to marry me...because of Daniel?"

"No, because that's not the only reason I married you. Look, I'm sorry that I'm getting so much negative publicity right now. The takeover makes me a hot news item, so that makes you...us...and Teresa...into a secondary story—an imaginary love triangle."

*Imaginary?*

"I'm sorry about it, but I can't help it," he continued. "Are they discussing the factory I'm opening in Bedfordshire and all the new jobs there? No. The networks are after ratings—period. If I were you, I wouldn't watch the so-called news for a while."

"How else can I know what they're saying? Or what you're doing?"

"It doesn't matter," he said.

"It matters to me."

"It isn't real."

"When I see myself being quoted and accused of being a gold digger, it feels real," she said.

"You said they distorted what you meant. Well, they twist my actions, too. You know you're not a gold digger."

"Do I? You said you'd finance Wild Horse Ranch if I married you, and you did."

"I wanted you to marry me. I would have said anything or done anything to achieve that."

"But the fact is, your wealth, your ability to save the ranch was a factor in my decision to marry you. So, in a sense, I am a gold digger."

"Okay. My money's an issue, then. But that doesn't

make you a gold digger. You can concentrate on the negative or the positive." He paused. "I would like to make our marriage work."

Was he telling the truth? she wondered.

"Those people are after one thing—salacious stories. They lie. They exaggerate. My fame and wealth will always make us vulnerable to this kind of attack. But fame is an illusion. It's just an opinion held by some people, all of them strangers, because I'm wealthy and own public companies. They don't know me, the man. Or you. Or what I feel about you. What they say doesn't need to have anything to do with us."

He'd bought the house he and Teresa had looked at together. He'd known she was dropping by the office. Those facts were real.

"I don't know what to believe anymore," she said slowly.

"I've been at this awhile. My advice is don't watch this stuff. What we need is time to ourselves to adjust to our new life together."

"But we don't have that luxury," she whispered. "We live in a fishbowl with the whole world judging us. What will that kind of life do to Daniel? What will he think of you and me?"

"You're right. I should have addressed the issue sooner. We need to take steps to protect him immediately."

"What do you mean?"

"We have to tell him the truth…about who I am."

"What?"

"We've got to tell him I'm his real father. Tonight. Now."

"No! I told you. He's all mixed up about Robert. He's not ready."

"Would you prefer that he hear lies and half-truths from the kids at school? Do you want him to feel all mixed up like you're feeling? No, you were right the first time. Telling him the truth is the only way we can protect him."

# Twelve

"That was one bite! Do I have to eat more?" Daniel glared at the spinach soufflé that was still on his plate as he set his fork down.

"No," said both his parents in low, icy voices.

Their cool glances met for a mere half second. Quickly, Caitlyn looked away, her eyes seeking the safety of Daniel.

"Can I leave, then?" he asked her. "Please. I want to play with my castle and dragons."

"Before dessert?" Caitlyn replied. "It's chocolate mousse."

"Okay. I'll stay."

Daniel stared at each of them and then at the crystal chandelier above the gleaming dining room table. Luke and Caitlyn continued to eat their soufflés, which had become tasteless in the suffocating silence.

"Why do we have such a big table?" Daniel asked.

Why couldn't he just sit quietly for once? Caitlyn thought, and then realized it was hardly Daniel's fault that she felt so tense and out of sorts.

"For dinner parties," Luke replied.

"But it's always just us," Daniel answered.

"We'll have parties in the future," Luke said.

"Who'll come?"

"Our friends."

"Do you have any kid friends who could bring more toys?"

"Some of my business associates have children."

"What are their names?"

"Daniel!" Caitlyn snapped.

"What?" Daniel asked. "What's wrong with asking questions?"

"Nothing," she whispered, chastened. "Mommy doesn't feel well, that's all."

Daniel sighed. Lapsing into a silence that was almost as glum as hers, he stared up at the ceiling again. For the next few minutes there were only the sounds of glasses being lifted and set down, of silverware clinking against china. Her nerves strained to the max, Caitlyn set down her fork.

"You're doing it again!" Daniel said.

"What?" Both adults eyed him guiltily as he glanced from one to the other.

"Not talking to each other. Not looking at each other. Y'all will only talk to me. How come? Are you mad at each other again?"

"No, we have a secret we're going to tell you after dinner, and it's making us nervous," Luke said.

Caitlyn looked up at him, aghast.

"I don't know about your mother," Luke said, reaching across the table and wrapping her clenched hand in his, "but it's sure making me edgy and none too talkative."

Caitlyn tried to yank her hand free, but Luke folded his hand over hers and held on tight.

"A secret! I can't wait! Tell me now!"

"And skip dessert?" Caitlyn said, still struggling to free her hand.

"Mom, can't you tell me now and then we'll have dessert after the secret?"

"We can do anything we want to," Luke said, smiling at Caitlyn. Letting her go, he stood up.

Taking the boy's hand, who clung to him happily, he led Daniel onto the balcony. Caitlyn followed them, nervously wrapping a cashmere pashmina around herself when she began to shiver in the damp, chill air.

Sitting down, Luke drew Daniel into his arms.

"Did you know that the minute I met you, I knew you were special?" Luke began.

Daniel's big, white smile flashed as he curled more snugly into Luke's arms.

"And you are special, much more special than I realized." He smoothed Daniel's hair behind his ear. "You know I told you that your mother and I are old friends, that we knew each other before she married your father."

"Yes," Daniel murmured.

"Well, the truth is, we were more than friends. We fell in love. You are our son."

Daniel sat up straighter, looking from one to the other. "For real?"

"For real," Luke said. "I am your real father. But I didn't know it until I saw you that day in the road."

"Why didn't you tell him about me, Mom?"

"Don't blame your mother. I went away. She didn't

know where I was. She married Mr. Wakefield, and you were told he was your father."

"But why? Why did you leave her and not tell her where you were going?"

"It's not that simple, but that's a story for another day."

"So that's why our eyes are just alike," Daniel said in a low, awed tone. "Everybody says so. And our hair's even the same color. But I'm not as tall as you."

"Yet. You're only five, so you'll probably grow."

"Really? So, I'll grow big and tall…just like you?"

"Maybe even taller. But only if you keep eating your spinach soufflé."

"Yuck."

"When I found out about you, I thought we should become a family. Your mother agreed. So here we are."

"And that's the secret?"

"That's it."

"Now can I eat my chocolate mousse?"

"You've been very patient. I believe you've earned it."

"Will chocolate mousse make me grow tall?"

"Not nearly so tall as spinach soufflé," Luke said, chuckling as he rumpled Daniel's hair.

"That's not fair!"

When Daniel sprinted ahead of them to the kitchen, Luke looked at Caitlyn, whose chest felt unbearably tight. So many things in life weren't fair, she thought.

"Well, I thought that went rather well," he said, sounding pleased.

"I suppose." Her voice was barely audible, and she couldn't meet his eyes.

"So, why the long face?" he whispered, concern in his low tone.

"I'm cold. Let's go in."

"Right. Let's not talk about all the elephants in the room."

She frowned. Why did she feel like her life was spinning out of control? Why couldn't she stop thinking about the beautiful house Luke had visited with Teresa?

Why couldn't she believe Luke when he said he wanted to make their marriage work? Why was it easier to believe the vicious taunts of strangers?

"Surprise!"

Caitlyn, who'd been expecting another intimate dinner party on Hassan's plump sofas, gasped. Rather than something sparkly, for a party, she wore the simple off-the-shoulder black sheath that had been her wedding dress with a string of pearls.

When the huge throng of well-wishers in black ties and evening gowns advanced, she froze in the doorway until Luke gently nudged her forward.

A man at the back of the crowd tapped his champagne glass. "Congratulations are in order!"

"A toast! Hassan! A toast to your son, the bridegroom, and his bride."

When dozens of people lifted their champagne glasses, Caitlyn swayed dizzily against Luke.

Hassan rushed forward, took her hand to steady her and said something in flowing Arabic that Caitlyn could only suppose was a toast. When he finished, he drained his glass and threw it at the marble fireplace, smashing it into gleaming shards that caught the light from the lamps and shot golden rays of fire. Everybody else drank to the toast and broke their glasses, too.

More crystal flutes were brought on silver trays, and

soon the glittering crowd surrounded them, clamoring to be introduced to Raffi's bride.

"So glad to meet you," each said in turn, pressing her hand until her fingers hurt. Thankfully, most of their conversation was directed toward Luke, whom they knew.

"So surprised when we heard Raffi got married."

"Wonderful of Hassan to throw this party so we could meet you, love."

"We thought he'd never—"

"So many different women. And all of them so beautiful," one man said into her ear. "But you are the fairest of all."

"I'm sure," Caitlyn whispered, wishing with all her heart that she was.

"Still, you'll need to keep an eye on him, young lady," the man's wife warned.

Finally, after she'd been introduced to everyone—lords, ladies, film people, businessmen and their wives—Luke left her with Hassan, saying he'd bring her a plate of food. But a bony, birdlike woman with a teased puff of red hair pounced on Hassan immediately, saying she had something very important she simply had to tell him.

"Just for a bit, my dear. I won't keep him long."

"Gossip, no doubt, knowing Marie." Hassan winked.

Caitlyn said she didn't mind in the least and was stranded alone on the edge of the party. For a second or two she felt conspicuous and uneasy, but she wasn't alone for long.

Arm in arm, both of them smiling at each other and then at her, Nico and Regina strolled over. Then Luke appeared with plates of sushi.

Immediately, Caitlyn relaxed. If Regina could transform herself into a princess and manage a difficult royal mother-in-law, there was hope for Caitlin, too.

"Where's Daniel tonight?" Regina asked.

"We have a new nanny."

Several pleasant moments of conversation about Glory's mischievous antics and the details of their meeting with the new teacher ensued. Caitlyn was laughing when the front door opened and a flash of shimmering white drew her attention to a lovely blonde.

A hush fell over the crowd. Beside her, Luke stiffened as if he'd been struck a blow.

"Oh, no," Regina whispered, touching Nico's arm. "It's Teresa. What's she doing here?"

The wild-eyed girl stared at Luke and then at Caitlyn for a moment that seemed to stretch endlessly. For that lifetime, it was as if they were the only three people in the room.

The girl was radiantly beautiful, but her lavender eyes held poignant desolation. Caitlyn felt both jealousy and sorrow as the girl took one faltering step toward Luke before losing her nerve. Perhaps she remembered that she hadn't been invited. She flushed. Then with a little cry, she turned and fled.

"Excuse me," Luke whispered before rushing to Teresa's side and ushering her back out the door, which closed behind them.

"Poor thing," a woman standing nearby said to her companion. "Everybody knows she's the one he really loves."

Pain stabbed Caitlyn like an ice pick to her heart. For a moment, she found it difficult to breathe.

"Why would you say that when he married Caitlyn?"

"Because I always thought they made a gorgeous

couple. Teresa is so refined. She comes from such wonderful people. He bought the house he intended for her."

Caitlyn's confidence drained away.

"You can't believe everything you read."

"Well, what could a horse trainer from Texas and a man like our Luke possibly have in common? And her dreadful accent." The woman laughed. "Did you speak to her?"

Caitlyn lifted her head and tried to pretend she hadn't heard.

"You mustn't worry what other people think. Or about Teresa showing up uninvited to attract Luke's attention," Regina said gently. "Sometimes it's difficult for the young and beautiful to accept the ending of a relationship they've set their hearts on. She was so sure of him."

*Because he'd made her feel secure in his love?*

Caitlyn nodded mutely. She understood Teresa's pain too well. At nineteen she'd felt sure of his love, too. Then he'd left without saying goodbye.

In less than five minutes, the door opened again, and Luke strode back inside—alone. He was pale and tense, but he caught Caitlyn's eye and went immediately to her side.

"Sorry about that," he whispered tightly against her ear. When he touched her arm, she stepped away from him.

"It's okay," she said. But she didn't feel okay. She felt unsure.

Even though she tried to avoid his touch, he tucked her hand into his and brought it to his lips. "I think she's on the road to accepting our marriage."

Caitlyn bit her lips. What about Luke? What did he feel? Even though he stayed at her side for most of the

evening and acted the part of a very devoted bridegroom, the party celebrating their marriage had been
spoiled. At least for Caitlyn, who kept seeing the beautiful, brokenhearted Teresa searching a sea of faces only
to find Caitlyn at Luke's side. Caitlyn kept seeing Luke
running after Teresa. He'd put his hand on the girl's
spine as he'd ushered her outside. The girl obviously
adored him and was so exquisitely beautiful.

Later, when Luke left her to talk to Hassan, Caitlyn
overheard snatches of furtively whispered conversations that tore her heart into more pieces.

"I hear he married her in Vegas. You can be sure his
wedding to Teresa would have been a grand affair."

Luke said the press coverage didn't matter, but
these people were his friends. It was obvious that they
believed Teresa was the right bride for Luke. They knew
him, didn't they?

Luke tried to talk to her on the way home, but she
turned away and kept her face pressed against the glass
of the limousine. When they had undressed and were
in bed, he tried to pull her close, but she shook him off,
saying she had a headache.

"That's the oldest excuse in the book," he teased,
running the pad of his thumb down her spine and causing her to shiver.

"Please—just leave me alone," she whispered even
as she began to ache for him.

The thumb followed the same tingling path back up
to her neck. "Are you upset because of Teresa?"

"No," she lied.

"Do you want to talk?"

"No! I don't want to talk! I want to go to sleep. I'm
tired. I'm not in the mood."

"Maybe I could persuade you to be in the mood," he said huskily. "I'm very good at that, you know."

His hand slid against her spine again, and she felt a familiar frisson of electricity.

"I said no," she whispered desperately.

She knew she was being unreasonable, but she couldn't stop herself. She wanted him to hold her and reassure her. She wanted him to make wild, passionate love to her, and yet…and yet she kept remembering Teresa, so she pushed him away.

Yes, she was jealous of the beautiful young girl who had loved and lost him. He'd once said Teresa was perfect, and those other women concurred. Such a woman would be better suited to the role of a billionaire's wife than she, who was homesick for her ranch and horses, who sometimes felt she would never fit in here.

Her mind raced in circles, repeating a constant refrain. She had Luke. Hadn't he said he wanted to make their marriage work? That meant he was trying to forget Teresa. She should be happy. But she wasn't. She wanted to possess his soul as he possessed hers.

He kissed her hair. "All right, then."

When he finally rolled over onto his side, she lay on hers. Crossing her arms over her breasts, she felt stiff and cold and proud and utterly miserable as she stared up at the ceiling.

He was soon asleep. She lay awake for hours, listening to his even breaths in the dark, loving the sound of them, loving him, knowing that she had to summon the courage to give him his life back.

Sometimes a woman, even a smart woman, could be her own worst enemy. Caitlyn hadn't slept well after she'd finally dozed off. She knew she shouldn't go looking for trouble so soon after waking. She should think her plan through. But riddled by her insecurities, she was in such an awful mood, she couldn't help herself.

She despised herself for craving him, hated the circumstances that had brought them back together. If only she could fit into his world as well as that lovely girl with the desolate lavender eyes.

Logically, Caitlyn knew that Luke was a grown man who had made his own choices. Fitting into his world would take time. Building a solid marriage required work and patience. But after last night, she wasn't feeling logical or patient.

When she stormed into the dining room, she found him sitting alone at the end of his long dining room table. He was reading his newspaper, eating eggs, mushrooms and bacon. He looked so tall and darkly handsome in black slacks, a white shirt and tie—so adorable.

Her heart lurched. She hated to interrupt him when he was enjoying a rare moment of solitude, but she couldn't stop herself.

"Luke."

He looked up. Did she only imagine that his eyes were shadowed with pain before he smiled pleasantly and tried to pretend nothing had gone wrong last night?

"Good morning," he said. "Feeling better, I hope?"

"This isn't working," she said, lashing into him with the fury of an unruly child. "You know it as well as I do, only I won't pretend any longer."

An edge of steel crept into his voice. "If you're still upset about last night—"

"I'm not. I'm talking about us. Our marriage. Living together. I don't belong here. In London. With you. I can't do this. I belong in Texas."

His mouth thinned. "Look, I understand it hasn't been easy. First, you had all your ranch problems. Then I show up and propose. You give up the only lifestyle you've ever known. Adjusting to life over here took me months, years. All we've had is two damn weeks while I've been up to my ears in business crises and paparazzi."

"You need a wife more like Teresa. You said she was perfect for you."

"Well, she isn't. I'm very sorry about that embarrassing episode last night, but Teresa and I are finished. She understands that now. I think she had to see us together to get closure. You will never have to meet her again. Nor will I. Unless by accident. She's young. She will fall in love with someone else, marry and be very happy."

"This isn't just about Teresa. It's about me. I know you rescued me, okay? That was very noble of you."

"Hell, I married you because I wanted to."

"You didn't act like you wanted to."

"Damn it! I was angry that morning, if you'll remember."

"No. The fact is, you didn't love me six years ago, and you don't love me now!"

"Don't tell me what I feel—then or now."

"You betrayed my family and walked out on me!"

"The hell I did."

"Nothing's changed other than that you learned we have a son."

A muscle in his jawline throbbed. "I'm not having this conversation now—when you're obviously over-wrought about last night."

"For the last time, this is not about last night! This is about us. We don't belong together anymore, if we ever did."

He crushed his newspaper and threw it down on the table.

"We have a child. We should think of him and what's good for his future instead of poking at old wounds."

"What I'm trying to tell you is that I'm going home—whether you like it or not."

"Just like that? What about the future of your ranch and your horses? How will you straighten out your finances if I fire Al and his team?" He stood up and was about to walk toward her when his cell phone rang.

"Do what you like. You don't own me," she cried. "Somehow I'll figure out my future on my own."

He grabbed his phone and punched a button, silencing it. "What about Daniel? Do his feelings matter?"

"Of course they matter. More than anything." She heard the loud, furious, chopping whir of his helicopter circling before it landed on the roof above them. Obviously, she'd used up what little time he had.

"He can stay here with you for a while. We'll work out a permanent custody solution later," she said. She'd never been separated from Daniel, nor he from her, for any significant length of time. But she'd kept him from Luke for five years, and the boy had just learned Luke was his real father. To be fair to them, she couldn't rip him away while she sorted out her emotions and problems.

"So, you have it all figured out. Daniel's life. Mine. And we have no say."

"That's right. You all but forced me to marry you. I told you we were doomed from the beginning. If I leave, you are free to live the life you choose."

Above them she heard the whoosh of helicopter blades. He was probably late for an important meeting.

"Am I?" His eyes darkened with cynicism. "What if I say—I choose you."

"I would know you made that choice out of obligation, and that's no basis for a marriage."

"Maybe it's true I would never have returned to Texas if Hassan hadn't seen Daniel, but once I saw you, you mattered to me, too."

"Not enough. You've never wanted me enough. Not now and not in the past."

"Damn it, if you can believe that, I won't force you to stay. But don't tell me I didn't love you six years ago. It was *you* who walked out on *me*—probably because you and your family thought I was nothing and Wakefield was a means to get your precious ranch back!"

"That's not what happened, and you know it."

"The hell it isn't! Why do you think I've worked my ass off ever since?—it's because I didn't want to be a nobody who couldn't even hold on to the woman I loved. What irony…"

Grabbing his jacket off the back of the chair, he slung it over his shoulder and strode out of the room.

"But I didn't think you were nothing," she whispered behind him. "That's ridiculous."

If he heard her, he never looked back.

"I didn't walk out on you," she whispered defensively. *But you're walking out on him now.*

She went to the window and watched the helicopter whir noisily before spiraling upward and disappearing into the thick gray clouds.

A single black carry-on stood beside the front door. There was only one thing left to do, and being a coward, she'd put it off until the last moment.

Walking down the hall, she heard Daniel in his room playing with his toys long before she reached him.

Hesitating outside his door, she listened to his action figures threatening each other with doom and destruction.

"Daniel?" She slowly pushed his door open.

He looked up eagerly. "Are you going to play with me?"

"Not today."

"Can we go see the mummies?"

"I can't, but maybe your new nanny can. I'm afraid Mommy's going home to Texas for a while."

He went still, his green eyes clouding. "Are you going to take me with you?"

"Only if you want to go. You're my little boy. You're always welcome wherever I am. But you're Daddy's little boy, too, now."

"What about Daddy? Where will he be?"

"He is going to stay here. He has to work."

"Who will be with him besides me if you're not here?"

Teresa, maybe, she thought.

"All his friends and fellow workers."

"They don't come home with him at night."

"No, they don't. But you'll be here with him. He'll read to you and play with you just like he does every night. And anytime you want to come to Texas to be with me, I'll come back to get you."

"You will?"

She nodded.

"Then I want to stay with him, for a little while, but I don't want you to go. I want you to stay here with us."

"I can't, honey."

"But I want you here!"

"I know. I want to be with you, too. But I have to go home. To figure out some grown-up things."

His bottom lip curled dangerously. He put his action figure down and came toward her, dragging his feet. Slowly, he put his arms around her and held on for a long time.

When he finally let go, he said, "I don't want you to leave."

"I know, honey." Guilt swamped her. Her throat tightened. "See you soon," she whispered. "Real soon."

"When?"

"In a few weeks," she said, realizing there was no way she could leave him for much longer. "I promise we'll be together soon."

"I just want us all to be together like the picture I drew," Daniel pleaded in a very small voice.

"I know, honey."

"I thought we were going to be a real family."

If only she felt like her marriage to Luke could work, but in reality their lives and tastes were so different now, she didn't think their marriage could prove viable in the long run.

She hugged Daniel fiercely and then let him go.

# Thirteen

Each day felt endless. She'd thought maybe the leaden pain in her heart would lessen in familiar surroundings, but without Daniel and Luke, the ranch felt like a prison cut off from the rest of the world by endless acres of grass and mesquite.

It was a struggle to get up in the mornings, a struggle to dress, to eat, to get through her work day, so she forced herself to follow a rigid schedule. In the evenings, when she finally came in from the barns, she would go to Daniel's room and sink onto his bed.

At night she would lie in his bed holding Daniel's stuffed bear, missing her son. And then she would tremble, dreaming of Luke, longing for his strong arms around her, his big body pressed against hers.

She had lied that night when she'd pushed him away. She had wanted him, ached for him, burned for him with a fever, but she couldn't believe he wanted her with the same ardor. He had married her for practical reasons, not romantic ones. He hadn't wanted to split Daniel between them. He'd said he desired her and that they could build on that. But could they, when she was so different from his glamorous friends? Wouldn't he be happier if she freed him to marry someone he loved?

When Lisa learned Caitlyn was home, she rushed over and found her in the barn brushing Angel.

"But how could you leave Luke when he's so rich and handsome? When he so obviously still loves you?"

Her last statement cut Caitlyn deeply. "I don't want to talk about it."

"Well, that's not much of a welcome," Lisa grumbled. "But I forgive you because your heart must be absolutely breaking. It's all over the internet. That Teresa he was so in love with is simply gorgeous."

Caitlyn sucked in a deep breath.

"What is she—a countess? What was it like to live the fairy tale?"

Hadn't Lisa noticed that Cinderella didn't end up with her prince?

Caitlyn brushed Angel's gleaming coat more furiously. "Lisa, I know you mean well, but don't come over here telling me what's on the internet. That's the last thing I need."

"Okay! But how could you leave Daniel? Why?"

"It's not forever. It's for a short visit. He's with his father. He needs to get to know Luke."

"Oh! Luke really is his father? Oh, my God! So, that's why you looked so sick when he first showed up! And *that's* why he married you so fast. I wondered why a rich guy like him would..."

"Thanks! I don't really want to talk about all this."

"I guess not—since you never said anything before," Lisa said huffily. "Not even to me, your best friend."

"If I'd told you, you'd have told everyone!"

"I would not!"

"Okay. You would have told one person who would have told one person.... I did what I thought was best for Daniel."

"But how could you leave Luke after he came back and acted so smitten and then did right by you and Daniel without wasting any time?"

Had he seemed smitten?

"And I don't see how leaving is best for Daniel. It seems to me Luke's the one who's trying to do what's best for everybody. Not you."

"Luke doesn't love me, okay?"

"His eyes followed you, and he married you, didn't he? He must care about you a little. In fact, my guess is he cared a lot."

"I don't know. All he said was that he was trying to make the marriage work."

"Well, that's good. Honey, that's great!"

"He felt obligated."

"Hey, a rich guy like him isn't going to do anything he doesn't want to do. You've always been way too independent. Honey, don't you know that something like thirty percent of all men marry women because of kids? You can't walk out on a good man for a dumb reason like that! He was doing the right thing!"

"It wasn't dumb to me. I want him to be happy."

"Oh, my God! This just gets worse! You really love him! And I'd bet money he loves you, too! Are you an idiot? You walked out on a billionaire, who's the father of your child, a man you love? Who probably loves you?

Girl, you're not going to get another chance like this! You've got to call him. Tell him you're sorry."

She felt so left out and alone. But she had to take this time for herself—for his sake as well as for hers.

"Girl, you don't look so good. Do you want me to get you a cola or something?"

"Yes, would you, please?"

Anything not to talk about Luke and their marriage.

Caitlyn sagged against the rough wall of Angel's stall. How would she live like this, alone—for the rest of her life—without him?

"I made it before when he betrayed my family and left me," she whispered fiercely to Angel, whose big brown eyes stared at her with understanding. "I can do it again. I just have to make up my mind and be disciplined."

Angel whinnied.

But she needed him on a more profound level than she'd ever needed anything—even the air she breathed.

Getting over him the second time was going to be much worse than the first. Back then she'd been so much younger and more resilient.

*Fool—who are you kidding? You never got over him. You were kissing him like you were starved for him the first chance you got.*

Feeling dazed after doing without Caitlyn for seven long days, Luke let himself into the flat. Daniel, who missed his mother unbearably during the day while Luke worked, was spending the night with Nico, Regina and Glory because the three of them were much better company than he was. Thus, Luke had the flat to himself.

The place felt drearier than a tomb. His footsteps

sounded hollow as he walked across the wooden floor to pour himself a gin and tonic.

All week he'd thought about what Caitlyn had said— that he'd betrayed her parents and left her six years ago because he hadn't really loved her. The truth was, when she'd discovered she was pregnant, she'd sold herself to the highest bidder. Since he'd been poor, that hadn't been him. The unfairness of her accusations infuriated him.

Damn it. He hadn't left her. What the hell did she mean he'd betrayed her parents? Her mother had fired him and thrown him off the place. Maybe Caitlyn had put her up to it, which meant that *she'd* left *him*. He'd worked long and hard to achieve his success so no woman would ever make him feel as small and worthless as she had again. But it hadn't made any difference. She'd walked out on him again as if he were nothing. Maybe she was right. Maybe he should never have married her.

But as he sat down a new thought formed. Maybe he'd been wrong to avoid talking about the past. He'd thought it was no use whining about the lousy things that couldn't be changed. He'd wanted to build a relationship starting from where they were now. He hadn't seen any point in arguing over what had happened. But maybe they hadn't been able to trust each other because they hadn't had a frank discussion. Maybe it didn't matter so much *what* had happened but simply that they both listen and try to understand. He'd been so intent on stabilizing their current situation, he'd been blind to the importance of acknowledging the pain of the past.

He was well into his second drink when Hassan called to invite him to dinner. Unable to face another night alone, he accepted, warning Hassan that he wouldn't be good company.

"You're right. You don't look so good, and you reek of gin," Hassan said as soon as Luke sat down at the restaurant table.

"Thanks."

"It wasn't a compliment."

"Thanks for your concern, then. Or whatever the hell it was."

"What are you going to do?"

"She left me because I made her miserable. I imagine that's why she had her mother run me off six years ago. She only married me because I practically forced her to, so I don't see a remedy. Do you?"

"Do you love her?"

"Unfortunately."

"Have you told her?"

"No."

"Well, damn it, why don't you?"

"She's gone."

"So, it's not like we live in the Dark Ages. Go after her."

"What's the point?"

"What if she loves you?"

"I almost told her I loved her...back in Texas, but she made it very clear that she didn't love me. Very clear. I was hoping to change her mind. Apparently, I failed."

"The question is, why did she leave? I say she's unsure. You come back—this big rich guy. She's having problems. Hell, she wasn't expecting you. You married so quickly, she probably didn't know what to think. Here in London she was out of her element with your glitzy lifestyle and friends. Then the press made it worse by saying you and Teresa should be together. You have to admit Teresa is beautiful. It would take a very confident woman to compete with a gorgeous countess, especially when some of your own friends seemed to think you preferred Teresa."

"But I don't. If I'd wanted Teresa, I would have married her."

"I know that, just as I know what you feel for Caitlyn and the boy. But does Caitlyn? What else have you two neglected to talk about? If this was a business deal, you wouldn't give up so easily. Go after her and get to the bottom of this. If not for your sake, for Daniel's. He needs to be part of a complete family. You and Caitlyn need to tell each other everything—the whole truth. You need to find out why she married Robert Wakefield. You need to tell her why you left her."

"She left me for Wakefield. That's why I left Texas."

"Have you discussed this with her? Once you've dealt with it openly and honestly, maybe then you can both forget."

"Until now, I preferred to forget about it without ever discussing it."

"Maybe she doesn't see it the same way. Communicating about what happens in our lives can be more important than the actual events."

"Maybe it's six years too late."

"Or maybe not. Forget your pride for once, before it costs you the thing you want most. Because of her, you've been a driven man for six years. What if neither of you can be as happy with other partners as you could be with each other? And then there's Daniel.... Put your pride aside and go to her—before it really is too late."

\* \* \*

The shadows were long against a golden glaze of sunlight as Caitlyn stepped out of the house after dinner. Not that she noticed the beauty surrounding her.

She carelessly let the screen door bang behind her. Pulling a sweater over her shoulders against the chill, she headed across the pasture for a late-afternoon walk. The house was too lonely without Luke and Daniel.

Angel snorted a greeting as she trotted up behind her.

"Hey, big girl." Caitlyn pressed her cheek against Angel's neck for a long, consoling hug.

"Okay, no tears. I promise. But no carrots, either. We're just going for a walk."

Angel nodded as if she understood. After a little while, the two set off in silence.

Thirty minutes later, as they passed the oak motte on their way back to the house, the sunset streaked the darkening sky in incandescent pink and violet rays.

"Pretty night, isn't it, girl?"

Apparently Angel thought silence was the best answer, because she lowered her head and nibbled the high lush grasses.

Somewhere in the distance Caitlyn heard a whiny, whirring sound. Straining her ears, she tried to place it, but a breeze stirred through the trees and rattled the dry leaves, and she heard nothing more. Still, the sound made her think of Luke coming home every night in his helicopter.

A sharp pain pierced her. She missed him so much, especially at night. And because he was suddenly on her mind, she decided to venture inside the oak motte that held so many memories.

Silently, she walked through the trees until she came

to the tree where Luke had carved their names. She'd
lied to him when she'd told him their tree had been cut
down. Placing her hand on the bark, she traced the rude
letters, remembering too well how she'd stood behind
him, watching breathlessly as he'd carved. Back then
she'd thought he would love her forever.

"Luke," she whispered. "Oh, Luke…."

Behind her, a boot crunched heavily on dry leaves.

She whirled as a tall, broad-shouldered man stepped
out of the shadows. His long, easy gait was achingly
familiar. So was his jet dark hair. Her heart raced. She
couldn't believe what she was seeing.

"Luke? What are you doing here?"

"You told me our tree was gone."

"I wasn't entirely truthful."

"No. You weren't."

"What are you doing here?" she whispered.

"I'm here because I love you. Because I've always
loved you. In the past. Now. Because I never stopped
loving you."

"But you left me six years ago without even saying
goodbye."

"Only because I thought you preferred Robert and
didn't want me."

"I didn't prefer Robert! And I don't believe you ever
thought I did! Why would you think that when I was
always chasing after you? I was wild about you. Besides,
I told you I had something important to tell you. I asked
you to meet me here. But you didn't come."

"I got here early. Your mother was here waiting for
me. Not you. She was standing right by this tree."

"My mother? How could she possibly have known
to come here at that exact hour?"

"Apparently, she'd been watching us for some time. She said you were with Robert."

"Only because there had been an accident at his university. A college friend of his had died. She'd sent me over there earlier in the day to console him."

"Well, that's not what she told me. She said you were with him because you loved him, because you'd always loved him."

"But why would she lie?"

"She explained how his father had bought your ranch after the Wakefield bank foreclosed on you, how your marriage to Robert was the family's only chance to get the ranch back and make things right. She said I was standing in the way of all that, that he could give you everything and that I could give you nothing. She fired me on the spot and told me to take my things and clear out."

"She said you stole money, and she had to fire you."

"She told you that? I never stole anything in my life."

"She said you were worthless and worse than irresponsible to steal from a man who'd trusted you."

"If I'd done what she accused me of, she would have been right. I guess that's the only way she could be sure she'd be rid of me without your dad trying to track me down. She knew you and I made love in that barn. She said she watched us go in together, and she saw you later when you came out. She said it made her sick that you were wasting yourself on me. She told me if I stayed, I'd ruin your life, the same as my father ruined my mother's."

"Robert and I were good friends. Always. But nothing more."

"You married him."

"It's not like you think."

"I knew how much you loved your parents. I knew your mother was harder on you than your father was, way harder, but I believed that in time she'd convince you Robert was the right man for you. From that moment, I vowed to prove myself as good as any man. I became ruthlessly ambitious and I got richer beyond anything I'd ever imagined. But by then it was too late. I'd lost you."

"How could you leave without talking to me? Without calling to at least say goodbye?"

"I did call! And I wrote! I left messages."

"Well, I never got any of them. Not a single one."

"That's not what your mother told me. The last time I called she answered and ordered me to stop harassing you. She said that if you wanted to talk to me, you'd call. That you'd gotten all my messages and you had my number. I said, 'Put her on the phone.' She replied, 'She's married—to Robert Wakefield. Happily married.' Then she asked if I still wanted to talk to you. I slammed the phone down. I'll never forgive myself for not coming back, even then, to ask what you felt. All these years I thought you didn't love me, I was in hell."

A crushing pain for what he'd suffered and for what she'd suffered suffused her chest. Her dominating mother could have done everything he accused her of. She would have justified it, thinking it was the best thing for the family and the ranch.

Caitlyn sighed. "I was in a hell of my own, too. When I found out I was pregnant and you were gone, I didn't know what to do. That's why, in the end, I married Robert. I wanted Daniel to have a name."

"Not to get the ranch back?"

"That was part of it, but I thought mostly of Daniel. Of course, I knew the marriage made my mother and father happy. I won't lie about that. I liked pleasing them. In the end, since you were gone, I just saw it as the best solution for all concerned."

"I shouldn't have left without talking to you, without hearing your side. I should have come back. I will never forgive myself for abandoning you the way I did. You were right to hate me."

"Well, I forgive you," she said softly. "My mother could be very determined. Now that I know the truth, I feel betrayed...by her. I can't believe she made those decisions for me so high-handedly. And yet I can. She would definitely choose you now. She'd probably give herself total credit for you turning so well."

He laughed, but there was a bitter edge to his humor.

"I've been grieving for her so fiercely. This twist is going to take some getting used to. I can't help feeling very angry at her."

"She did what she did because she loved you."

"No, she saw me as a child, and she wanted to control me as one controls a child. She didn't know that I was grown, with a woman's heart. She had no idea the torture she put me through. She misjudged you and Robert. His friend, the one who died...."

"What about him?"

"They were lovers. Robert was gay. His family didn't know. Nobody knew. Nobody except me. He'd come out to me when we were kids. When I told Robert I was pregnant, he told me about Joel. Robert married me because he couldn't imagine he'd ever love anybody else. But I think maybe he did. I think the marriage became an unendurable trap for him. I never told anybody until now...because in this county if you tell one person..."

Luke chuckled. "The whole county will know by dinnertime."

"And Teresa? What about Teresa?" she whispered.

"I love you."

"Why did you buy that house?"

"For you. For us. I bought it right after we got married. I couldn't see you running a horse farm in London, and I couldn't imagine you being happy for long without something more to do. Little boys need more space than my flat."

"What?"

"I know you'd rather live in Texas...."

"One thing I've learned since coming back is that I want to be with you and Daniel, all of us together, more than anything...especially if I have my precious horses, too."

He kissed her. "I bought Mullsley Abbey for us, sweetheart. We can spend our vacations here at your beloved ranch, but when we're in the U.K., Mullsley Abbey is a short commute to London by helicopter or limo for me. We'll have plenty of room for more children. Out there, the pace of life is a bit slower, more like life here. We won't have to go to so many parties. And I intend to make some changes in my work schedule so we can have more time to be together. In short, it was to be a surprise wedding gift for you."

"And I thought..."

"The worst of me...as usual."

"Never again."

"Let us hope. But the tendency does run in the family. Your mother definitely saw only the worst in me. Occasionally, you have been known to do the same."

"Don't tease."

He laughed. Reaching for her hands, he pulled her closer.

"You really don't love Teresa?" she whispered.

"I love you. Only you." He wrapped her in his arms and held her tightly. "If you want the truth, I think she was mainly after my money."

Staring into his eyes, Caitlyn circled his neck with her arms, ran her fingers through his silky black hair. Then she framed his face with her hands. "I'm so glad you came back for me."

Bending down, he pressed his mouth to hers.

"So am I."

He kissed her slowly as if to savor her taste and the silky texture of her lips. Warmth flooded her until she felt like she was overflowing with passion and happiness.

He loved her. He always had. Finally, she believed this miraculous truth.

Hand in hand they walked back to the house in the starlit darkness, Angel trailing them.

When they climbed the stairs to the porch, Luke pulled her into the shadows and kissed her again.

A chain squeaked noisily. "Does this mean I won't have to choose who to live with?" piped a treble voice from the swing at the end of the porch.

"Why, Daniel, honey!" she cried. "It's so good to see you! Where did you come from?"

"Daddy brought me. He told me to wait here at the house. Does this mean I can live with both of you? All the time?" he cried.

She went to him and touched his face just to make sure he was real.

"I'm sorry I went away." Threading her fingers

through his dark bangs, she brushed them out of his eyes. "I missed you so much."

"But are you going to live with Daddy and me?"

"She sure is," Luke said, scooping him up into his arms.

"So, are we a real family now?" Daniel asked.

"You bet! I think this calls for a group hug just to prove it," Luke said.

"But no more kissing!" Daniel ordered sternly.

Luke made no promise. Curving his hand around Caitlyn's nape, he brought her close enough so he could whisper into her ear. "Later. We'll kiss later. We have the whole night.

"No, we have the rest of our lives."

# Epilogue

*Three years later*

The rotor blades made a thunderous clap-clapping clamor as the helicopter whirred downward toward the lush, green countryside.

Luke loved coming home to Caitlyn and their children, but today, because of Caitlyn's news, his enthusiasm knew no bounds.

Another baby....

Lisa, their daughter, was two, so maybe it was time.

He leaned to one side and peered out of the helicopter. Usually he felt great pride when viewing Mullsley Abbey from the air. Up here he could see the ancient house in all its glory, its stately gardens, orchards, deer park and maze. But today his gaze was glued to the track where Caitlyn usually worked the horses she was training.

Strange. The track was empty. No sooner had the helicopter landed than he sprang out of it and ran toward the stables.

He thrust open a door and was about to enter the shadowy building when he heard her soft voice in the arena. Backtracking, he headed in that direction. All too soon he caught the pungent smell of sand flying from hooves.

Keeping to the shadows, so as not to interrupt the session, he watched her. Sasha, a temperamental stallion, had thrown back his head and was prancing sideways. Caitlyn was speaking to him calmly, waiting out his burst of temper. Finally, her stillness brought him to his senses, and they began to canter, moving like one.

She was magic on horseback. She was magic, period. The luckiest day of his life was the day he'd returned to Wild Horse Ranch.

All the pain of the past came screaming back through him, the years without Caitlyn and Daniel, his anguish and the fury that had fueled his fierce ambition.

He didn't regret any of it.

For better or for worse....

He loved it all, the good and the bad. Loved her. Loved every minute of their lives together.

When Sasha whirled, and Caitlyn saw him, she gave a cry of pure joy that made the sun burn brighter and the trees sparkle with a fierceness that nearly blinded him. Quickly, she dismounted and handed the reins to a groom before turning and flying into his arms.

Wrapping her hands around his neck, she clung— just as she had when she'd been a girl and he'd kissed her for the first time.

He remembered everything, every moment they'd ever shared.

"Why didn't you tell me you were taking off early? I would have stopped working, showered.… Maybe even put on some lipstick."

"I wanted to surprise you. I like you just as you are."

She smiled, longing to believe him, but being female, she didn't quite.

He kissed her long and hard in a manner that left no doubt about the truth of his statement, or his intentions. "After you told me about the baby, I wanted to be with you. Only with you. I resented my business associates. If I'd stayed at the office, I would have abused everyone."

"Shame on you, darling."

"What do you say we make the most of my playing hooky?"

"What exactly do you have in mind?"

"I think you know, but just in case…" He whispered hot and provocative words into her ear that made her flush and laugh merrily. Then he grabbed her hand and tugged her in the direction of the stables.

"But not in…a stall," she said under her breath, giggling. "I'm afraid I really do have to draw a line… since someone might catch us."

"All right. If you refuse to indulge my darkest fantasies, inspired by our first time in the barn…"

Inside the tack room behind Sasha's stall, which smelled of leather and soap, he bolted the door and shoved her against the rough wall.

"Is this any way to treat a pregnant lady?" she teased as she began to unthread his tie. Using the silken ends, she reeled him closer.

"Just say the word, and I'll stop."

"Kiss me," she begged. "And then do all those wild, dirty things you just promised me you'd do."

Closing her eyes, she lifted her lips to his and abandoned herself to the wild exultation of their passion that fused not only their mouths and their bodies but their souls.

He stripped her slowly, garment by garment. When she was naked, he fell to his knees before her and paid homage with his lips and tongue to this woman he'd always adored.

"I love you," he murmured huskily afterward.

She closed her eyes and took a long, shuddering breath. "I love it when you say it like that."

For three years his joy in this woman had grown. No longer did he feel that some vital piece of himself was missing. With her by his side and in his bed, he was complete.

Tugging her close, he whispered against her ear, "I love you. More than anything." Then he began to make love to her slowly as if they had all the time in the world. For once she didn't rush him.

\* \* \* \* \*

## "The idea that I would ever be stupid enough to fall for you is pretty funny."

"Stupid enough?"

"Yes, stupid enough. Let me count the ways." She held up one hand and began ticking off fingers. "First, you're a grouch in the morning. You leave newspapers lying around everywhere. You date a woman once and then never call back. You're a big baby when you're sick."

Brandon had heard enough. He placed the file on the chair in front of her desk and stalked closer. He brushed against her, then slipped his hand around her nape and urged her closer.

She moaned. "What are you doing?"

"What do you think I'm doing?"

"I'm not sure."

"I am."

And then he kissed her.

Dear Reader,

I grew up in California and always loved visiting the Napa Valley wine country. So it didn't take much arm-twisting for me to choose those romantic, grapevine-studded hills and valleys as the backdrop for Brandon Duke's story.

Confident, handsome Brandon is the third of the Duke men to face his comeuppance from his mother, Sally Duke. The most determined of the brothers to fend off his mum's matchmaking manoeuvrings, Brandon is nevertheless taken by complete surprise when his bespectacled, sensible secretary, Kelly, returns from vacation looking absolutely stunning. But then he finds out her true reason for getting a fashion makeover—and that's when he really gets into trouble!

I've always enjoyed the forbidden fantasy of the boss and secretary love affair. I suppose you might attribute it to the fact that I worked as a legal secretary for many years. But trust me on this: I never worked for such a gorgeous boss as Brandon Duke! I would've remembered!

I hope you love reading Brandon and Kelly's story as much as I loved writing it. Please stop by my website at http://katecarlisle.com and let me know. While there, you'll find pictures and links to some fantasy resorts I imagine the Duke men might've owned, as well as background stories and fun facts about me and my books.

Happy reading!

*Kate*

# HOW TO SEDUCE
# A BILLIONAIRE

BY
KATE CARLISLE

Published in Great Britain 2012
by Mills & Boon, an imprint of Harlequin (UK) Limited,
Eton House, 18-24 Paradise Road, Richmond, Surrey TW9 1SR

© Kathleen Beaver 2011

ISBN: 978 0 263 89135 5

51-0312

Harlequin (UK) policy is to use papers that are natural, renewable and recyclable products and made from wood grown in sustainable forests. The logging and manufacturing processes conform to the legal environmental regulations of the country of origin.

Printed and bound in Spain
by Blackprint CPI, Barcelona

*New York Times* bestselling author **Kate Carlisle** was born and raised by the beach in Southern California. After more than twenty years in television production, Kate turned to writing the types of mysteries and romance novels she always loved to read. She still lives by the beach in Southern California with her husband, and when they're not taking long walks in the sand or cooking or reading or painting or taking bookbinding classes or trying to learn a new language, they're traveling the world, visiting family and friends in the strangest places. Kate loves to hear from readers. Visit her website at www.katecarlisle.com.

Champagne, chocolate and many thanks go to my brilliant editor, Stacy Boyd, for helping me give Brandon and Kelly's romance a truly happy ending.

# One

"Memo to self: Cancel all employee vacations," Brandon Duke muttered as he reached for his coffee cup and realized it was empty. Yet another reminder that his invaluable assistant, Kelly Meredith, was still away on vacation. She'd been gone for the past two weeks, and that was fourteen days too long as far as he was concerned.

It wasn't like Brandon couldn't get his own cup of coffee. He wasn't that lame. It was just that Kelly always beat him to it, showing up with a piping hot refill at the right time, every time. She was a dynamo in every other way, too. Clients loved her. Spreadsheets didn't intimidate her. And she was an excellent judge of character, something he'd recognized early on. That was a quality worth its weight in gold and he'd taken advantage of it from the start by having Kelly accompany him to various business meetings all over the country.

Brandon's own instincts were spot on when it came

to judging a potential business partner or the motives of a competitor, but Kelly was a strong backup. Even his brothers had gotten into the habit of having Kelly vet new hires and solve problems in other departments. They called her the miracle worker, for good reason. If there was a thankless job that needed handling, Kelly grabbed it with both hands and worked her magic. Everything ran more smoothly because of her.

Taking advantage of the early morning quiet in the still empty office suite, Brandon grabbed a legal pad and began to scribble notes for a meeting with his brothers later today. Now that the Mansion at Silverado Trail, the Dukes' newest resort in Napa Valley and the jewel in the crown of the Duke hotel empire, was about to celebrate its grand opening, it was time to focus his energies on new properties and new challenges.

Reading what he'd written, he was reminded of another reason he needed his assistant to come back from vacation: she could decipher his handwriting.

In the middle of bullet-pointing several options for a takeover bid on a small chain of luxury hotels along the picturesque Oregon coast, Brandon checked his calendar. Every hour of the day was filled with appointments, conference calls and deadlines, many of them connected to the grand opening celebration. Good thing his assistant would be back today, and about damn time. The temp replacement had been competent, but Kelly was the only one who could handle the myriad pressures and scheduling conflicts involved in the upcoming festivities.

And speaking of pressures, his brother's wife was about to pop out a baby soon. This would be Mom's first grandkid, and you would've thought no other child had ever been born. Talk about a major celebration. But what in the world was Brandon supposed to buy the kid? Season tickets on the 49ers' fifty-yard line he could swing, but otherwise, he was clueless. Didn't matter. Kelly would know the perfect gift to buy and she'd probably wrap it, too.

Brandon heard rustling and the sound of drawers opening just outside his partly opened door.

"Good morning, Brandon," a cheery voice called out.

"About time you got back, Kelly," he said with relief. "Come see me after you've had a chance to settle in."

"You bet. I'll just make a pot of coffee first."

Brandon checked his watch. Sure enough, she was fifteen minutes early, one more indication that she was an ideal employee who deserved all the perks the job offered. But he still planned to outlaw vacations from now on.

"Ah, it's good to be back," Kelly murmured as she powered up her computer. Hard to believe, but she'd actually missed Brandon Duke while she was gone. The sound of his deep voice gave her a little thrill she attributed to the fact that she loved her job.

She stashed her tote bag and purse in the credenza behind her desk and quickly made coffee. Her hand shook as she filled the pot with water at the small kitchen kiosk across from her office and she forced herself to relax. She really was happy to be back at the job she loved, so why was she so nervous?

Okay, she'd made a few changes while on vacation, but nobody would notice, right? Nobody ever noticed anything about her except for her savvy business sense and can-do attitude, and that was just the way she wanted it. So if she happened to be wearing a dress today instead of one of her usual pantsuits, who would care? The fact that she'd never worn a dress to the office before wouldn't stand out to anyone here. Even if today's dress was a beautiful dark gray knit that buttoned up the front and clung subtly to her curves. And that was just fine and dandy.

And if she'd finally changed over to contact lenses, so what? She'd been wearing the same boring eyeglasses for the past five years. Change was a good thing.

"Kelly," Brandon called from his office. "Bring the Dream Coast file with you when you come in, will you?"

"Be right there."

The familiar sound of Brandon Duke's voice made Kelly smile. He should've intimidated her from day one. At six feet four inches tall, he towered over her, and she knew for a fact that he was rock-solid muscle underneath his designer suits. She knew, because she'd run into him more than once at the hotel gym and seen him in shorts and a T-shirt. A former NFL quarterback bench-pressing ridiculously heavy barbells was quite a sight. Sometimes, while watching him, she found it hard to breathe steadily, but she chalked up those moments to spending too much time on the treadmill.

She chuckled at the thought of some of her girlfriends, who'd told her they would kill for a chance to see the stunningly handsome Brandon Duke working out in gym shorts. Luckily for Kelly, she'd never been tempted by her boss.

Yes, he was gorgeous, almost unbelievably so, but to Kelly, having a great job meant a lot more than having a brief, meaningless affair with some superstar athlete. And yes, an affair with Brandon Duke would never be anything but brief and meaningless. She'd seen firsthand the women who lined up to date him, and she'd seen them flicked off without a backward glance within a couple of weeks. It wasn't pretty, and she never wanted to find herself in that line. Not that she would qualify to stand in that line, but—

"What are you thinking?" she whispered to herself.

She'd never thought of her boss in those terms before and she wouldn't start now. Shaking her head in disgust, she had to wonder if maybe she'd taken too many days off.

As the coffeepot filled, Kelly took a moment to glance out the wide bay window and felt both proud and lucky to be here in this job. Who wouldn't want to work on a hilltop in the heart of Napa Valley, overlooking lush fields of grapevines as far as the eye could see?

Brandon and his small corporate staff had been working on-site at the Mansion at Silverado Trail for the past four months. They would stay here another month or so, until the resort was up and running and the grape harvest was over. Then they would all relocate back to Duke headquarters in Dunsmuir Bay.

By then, Kelly's plan would be complete, and her life would settle down to normal. But until then, she would simply have to remind herself to relax and breathe.

"Do you hear me, self? Just relax," she murmured as she ran her hands over her dress to smooth away any wrinkles, then filled two large mugs with hot coffee. "Breathe."

She stopped at her desk to drop off her own mug and pick up a short stack of mail, then pushed her boss's door fully open.

"Good morning, Brandon," she said breezily, and placed the mail on his desk.

"Morning, Kelly," he said, as he wrote rapidly on a legal pad. "Great to have you back."

"Thank you, it's nice to be back." She placed his mug on his blotter. "Coffee for you."

"Thanks," he said absently, still writing. After a moment, he reached for his coffee and looked up. His eyes widened as he cautiously put the cup down. "Kelly?"

"Yes?" She gazed at him, then blinked. "Oh, sorry. You wanted the Dream Coast file. I'll be right back with it."

"Kelly?" His voice sounded strained.

She stopped and turned. "Yes, Brandon?"

He was staring at her in...disbelief? Shock? Horror? Oh, dear. Not a good sign. And the longer he stared, the more nervous she became.

"Oh, come on," she said. "I don't look bad enough to have stunned you into speechlessness." She fiddled with her dress collar as she felt heat moving up her neck and settling into her cheeks. No need to be embarrassed, she scolded herself.

"But, what did you do to..." His voice trailed off as he continued to stare at her face.

"Oh, you mean the contact lenses? Yeah. It was time for a change. Be right back with the file."

"Kelly." His tone was demanding.

She turned again. He was still staring, this time at her hair. With a sigh, she brushed a strand back from her cheek. "I had it lightened and shaped. No big deal." Then she waved him off and rushed to find the file.

Great. If Brandon was any example, people would be staring at her as if she were an alien. How was she supposed to relax and breathe and put her plan into action under those circumstances, darn it?

As she anxiously rifled through the file drawer, she heard the distinctive sound of Brandon's leather executive chair rolling back from his desk. Seconds later, he was standing in the doorway. Still staring.

"Kelly?" he said again.

She stared up at him from the files. "Why do you keep saying my name?"

"Just making sure it's you."

"Well, it is, so cut it out," she told him, then found what she was looking for. "Ah, here's that file."

"What did you do?"

"You asked me that already."

"And I'm still waiting for an answer."

Her shoulders drooped for a split second, then she straightened. There was no reason to feel self-conscious, especially not with Brandon. He'd given her glowing reviews and generous raises. He respected and admired her ability to work hard and solve problems. He was her employer, not her overlord, for goodness sake. "I got a little makeover."

*"Little?"*

She raised one shoulder in a casual shrug. "That's right. I lost a few pounds, got a haircut, some contact lenses. No big deal."

"It is from where I'm standing. You don't even look like you."

"Of course I look like me." She wasn't about to mention the week spent at the pricey spa or the private etiquette and speech lessons. He would think she'd gone insane. Maybe she had. She'd always been levelheaded, and rational to the point of being called a nerd back in college. Now she wasn't sure what they would call her.

"But you're wearing a dress," he said accusingly.

She looked down, then back at him. "Why, yes, I am. Is that a problem?"

It was his turn to look discomfited as he took a step back. "No. God, no. No problem at all. You look great. It's just that…" Scrubbing his jaw with his knuckles, he searched for the words. "You don't wear dresses."

He'd noticed? Color her surprised. With a resolute smile, she said, "I do now."

"I guess so," he said, searching her face, still looking doubtful. "Well, like I said, you look great. Really great."

"Thank you," she said, still smiling. "I feel great."

"Yeah. That's great." He nodded, then gritted his teeth and exhaled heavily.

If everything was *great,* why was he scowling?

"Oh!" she said, feeling ridiculous as she thrust the thick manila folder at him. "Here's the Dream Coast file."

His hand grazed hers as the file passed between them and she felt a buzz of awareness all the way up her arm.

Brandon's frown lines deepened. "Thanks."

"Sure thing."

He walked back into his office, then turned. "It's great to have you back."

And that was how many *greats* so far? she wondered.

"Thank you," she said. "And I'll have the month-end sales figures calculated for you in twenty minutes."

He closed the door and she sagged down into her chair. Grabbing her own cup of coffee, she took a big gulp. "Oh yeah, it's *great* to be back."

Brandon tossed the Dream Coast file onto his desk and continued walking across the plush office until he reached the floor-to-ceiling window that lined one long wall. He and his team were working out of the owner's suite on the penthouse level of the Mansion at Silverado Trail, and he never grew tired of the view. Normally, when he gazed out at the gently sloping hills of chardonnay grapevines, he relished the pride he felt when he saw such visible symbols of his family's success.

A hot air balloon drifted silently in the sky overhead and birds skittered from tree to tree across the hills. But he ignored all of it as he caught the barest whiff of flowers and spice drifting in the air. He wasn't used to his assistant wearing perfume, or maybe he'd never noticed that she did, but for the first time ever, the arresting scent conjured up visions of a cool hotel room and a hot blonde. Naked. Wrapped in sheets. Under him.

Kelly. He could still smell her. Damn it.

He'd made a fool of himself just now, gaping at her as though she were a juicy steak and he were a starved puppy. Hell, he hadn't even been able to speak. He'd sounded like a damn parrot, repeating her name over and over. But he would lay the blame for that solely at her feet. She'd succeeded in shocking the hell out of him and that never happened to Brandon Duke.

A makeover? He shook his head as he paced the length of the wall of glass. Who could fathom a woman's mind? Kelly didn't need a makeover. She'd been fine the way she was. All business, completely professional, smart, discreet. Never a distraction.

Brandon didn't like distractions in the workplace. In his office, it was all business, all the time. After ten years in the spotlight of the NFL, he was all too aware that distractions ruined your game. You took your eye off the ball and the next thing you knew, you were buried in a pile of tough, ugly defensive ends who would just as soon see you dead.

Brandon splayed one hand on the plate glass window. Talk about a distraction. Who knew his competent assistant had those amazing curves and world-class legs hidden beneath the boxy pantsuits she'd worn every day? And those eyes, so big and blue a man could get lost in them?

Most disturbing of all, she seemed to be wearing some kind of new, glossy lipstick. It had to be new, otherwise he would've noticed her incredibly sexy, bee-stung lips long before today. But he was noticing now. He'd almost spilled his coffee noticing.

Her new dress clung to every curve of her lush body. Curves he'd never known existed before. Even though he saw her in the hotel gym regularly, she always exercised in a big T-shirt and sweatpants. Who knew she'd been hiding a body like that under all those layers of sweaty workout clothes? She'd clearly been working here under false pretenses all this time.

"Now you just sound ridiculous," he groused. But who could blame him? His sedate, hard-working assistant was simply gorgeous. It was such a betrayal.

And what the hell had happened a minute ago when her hand touched his? He thought he'd felt something sizzling inside him. It had to be his imagination, but recalling that sensation of skin against skin caused his groin to leap to attention. He smacked the wall in disgust.

"Change is good," he grumbled sarcastically and he sat back down at his desk. No, change *wasn't* good. Not when he was used to Kelly's nondescript hair and the way she'd always worn it pulled back in a sensible ponytail or bun. Now it was the color of rich honey tumbling across her shoulders and down her back. It was the sort of color and style that begged a man to run his hands through the lustrous strands as he eased her down to feast on those luscious lips.

His body continued to stir to life and he squelched the feeling by slapping the file folder open and riffling through the papers to find the document he needed. It was useless.

"This is unacceptable." He refused to lose the careful sense of order and decorum he had always maintained in the workplace. The job was too demanding and Kelly was too important a part of his staff to allow her to suddenly become a distraction. Or more aptly, an *attraction*.

It was time to nip this in the bud. He reached across his desk and pressed the intercom button on his phone. "Kelly, please come in here."

"Be right there," she said briskly. Seven seconds later, she walked into his office carrying a notepad.

"Sit down," he said, standing up to pace some more. He didn't quite trust himself with taking another glance at her legs. Damn it, this just was not going to work. "We need to talk."

"What's wrong?" she asked in alarm.

"Look, we've always been honest with each other, haven't we?"

"Yes," she said carefully.

"I trust you completely, as you well know."

"I know, and I feel the same, Brandon."

"Good," he said, unsure of his next move. "Good."

Now what? He'd never been at a loss for words before. He glanced at her, then had to look away. How and when had she become so beautiful? He knew women. He loved women. And they loved him. Some might even say he had a sixth sense when it came to women. So why hadn't he known Kelly was this attractive? Was he blind?

"Brandon," she said slowly. "Are you unhappy with my work?"

"What? No."

"Did Jane do an okay job while I was gone?"

"Yeah, she was fine. That's not the problem."

"Oh good, because I would hate to—"

"Look, Kelly," he interrupted, tired of this cat and mouse game. "Did something happen to you on your vacation?"

She was taken aback. "No, why would you think—"

"Then what's with this makeover thing?" he blurted out. "Why'd you do it?"

"That's what you called me in here for?"

"Yeah." And he wouldn't go into how ridiculous he felt

for bringing it up, but he had to know. "Why do you think you have to get all dolled up to—"

Her eyes narrowed. "All dolled up?"

"Well, yeah. You know, all made up and…hell."

"There's something wrong in trying to look my best?"

"That's not what I said."

"Did I overdo it somehow? I mean, the makeup counter woman showed me what to do, but I'm new at this. I'm still practicing." She lifted her face to gaze at him and her lips seemed to glisten as they caught the light. "Tell the truth. Is my makeup too much?"

"God, no, it's just right." *Too damn right,* he thought, but didn't say.

"Now you're being nice, but I don't believe you. The way you looked at me when I came in this morning…"

"What? No." *Oh, crap,* he thought. She wasn't going to cry, was she? She'd never cried before.

"I thought I could do it. Other women do it, for heaven's sake, why shouldn't I?" She jumped up from the chair. It was her turn to pace as she pounded her fist into her palm. "I thought I was being subtle. Do I look like a fool?"

"No, you—"

"You can be honest."

"I'm being—"

"This was a crazy idea to begin with," she muttered and leaned back against the wall with a sigh. "I can figure out complex mathematical calculations in my head, but I don't know the first thing about seduction."

*Seduction?* Something hit him low in the solar plexus and he wasn't sure of his next move.

"This is so embarrassing," she moaned.

"No, it's not," he said, silently hoping he'd come up with something profound to say. He had nothing.

"What am I supposed to do now? I've only got a week

left to…oh, God." She covered her eyes for a moment, then stared up at the ceiling. Finally, she folded her arms across her chest and tapped one toe of her shiny new heels against the carpet. "How could I be so stupid?"

He walked up to her and grabbed her by the shoulders. "Stop that. You're one of the smartest people I know."

She glared up at him, her plump lips pouty now. "Maybe in business, but never in romance."

Okay, romance and seduction were definitely on her mind. And now he realized they were on his mind, too. The question was, why? In all the years he'd known Kelly, Brandon had never once heard her mention a name connected to any romantic interest. And now, all of a sudden, she was making herself over to attract some guy? Just who was she thinking of seducing? Did Brandon know the guy? Was he good enough for Kelly?

Brandon paused to carefully word his next question. "Who are you trying to seduce?"

Frowning now, she stared at her fingernails. "Roger. My old boyfriend. But I should've known it wouldn't work."

*Roger?* Who the hell was Roger? Brandon had to admit that the part of him that should have been relieved to hear she wasn't out to seduce *him* was surprisingly disappointed. Not that he would ever allow anything to happen between them. But still, who the hell was she talking about?

"Who's Roger?" he asked aloud.

"I just told you, he's my old boyfriend. His name is Roger Hempstead." She stepped away from Brandon's grip and moved back to her chair. "We broke up a few years ago and I haven't seen him since."

"How long ago did you break up?"

"It's been almost five years."

He made a quick calculation. "But that's about how long you've been working here."

"That's right." She leaned one elbow on the armrest and looked up at him with a valiant smile. "After Roger and I broke up, I couldn't stand living in the same small town where everyone I knew could dissect my every word and movement. I decided to relocate as far away from home as possible, so I looked for jobs in California and found this one."

"I'm glad you did, but it must've been quite a breakup."

"It wasn't fun," she said carefully, "but I've moved on."

"Have you?"

"Yes, of course." She nodded her head resolutely. "But then, last month I found out that Roger's company booked their corporate retreat here at the Mansion. He'll be here next week." She took a deep breath and exhaled. "And I wanted to knock his socks off."

"Ah, I see." And he did, sort of. Resting his hip on the edge of his desk, he said, "If it's any consolation, I can pretty much guarantee you'll knock his socks off."

She gazed at him skeptically. "You're just saying that to be nice."

"I'm not that nice. Trust me."

Her lips twisted into a frown. "I do. Usually."

"I never lie, remember?"

"True, you don't typically lie. To me, anyway," she allowed.

He chuckled. "So it's been about five years since you broke up with this Roger character, and now you want to make an impression."

She nodded with determination. "I really, really do."

"You will. I promise."

"Thanks." Her brief smile faded. "But I don't know what I'm doing. I'm fine at business, but the world of romance is beyond me."

"Tell me what I can do to help."

Kelly regarded him with interest. "You mean it?"

"Sure." He was willing to do almost anything to get things back on track. If Kelly felt secure, she'd be able to do her work and stop worrying about this clown Roger. Then, once Roger was gone, she'd go back to behaving like the Kelly he was comfortable with. His universe would once more be in alignment.

"That would be wonderful," she said with enthusiasm. "I could really use advice from someone like you."

"Someone like me?"

She smiled and he was struck again by how beautiful she was. Damn, how blind had he been all these years?

"It's just that the two of you are so much alike," she said. "You and Roger, I mean. It would really help to get your perspective on things."

"What do you mean, we're alike?"

"I mean, both of you are strong and handsome and arrogant and ruthless and, you know, type A all the way."

Huh. That was accurate enough, although he'd always thought he was fairly laid-back compared to his two brothers. He did appreciate the strong and handsome part of her description, though.

Kelly had stopped to ponder what she'd just said, then added softly, "Wow, no wonder Roger didn't think I was enough for him."

Brandon bristled. "*Enough* for him?"

She sighed. "You know what I mean. I wasn't attractive enough for him."

"What makes you say that?"

"He told me so when he broke up with me."

For some reason, Brandon felt an irresistible urge to pulverize something. Like Roger's face. "You're kidding."

"No," she said wryly. "I'm really not. But you saw what I looked like before the makeover, Brandon. Plain, wholesome, unremarkable. Not exactly supermodel material."

A twinge of guilt pinged inside him as he realized that was exactly how he'd always felt about her. But he'd considered that a good thing. Now he was just glad he'd never mentioned it out loud.

"But I understood where Roger was coming from," she continued. "He is very special, after all."

"Special? He sounds like a jackass."

She tried to stifle a giggle but didn't quite succeed. "Oh, he is, but he can't help it. His family has a very strong influence on him. His mother's ancestors came over on the *Mayflower,* you know."

"Members of the crew, were they?" Shaking his head, he said, "Listen, Kelly, do you want me to have him killed? Because I know someone who knows someone who could—"

Kelly laughed. "That's a sweet offer, but no. I just want to make him regret what he said when he broke things off, that's all."

He studied her for several moments. "He hurt you."

She shook her head. "No, no, he told me the truth and I have to be grateful for that."

"Grateful? Why?"

She smiled tightly. "Because he helped me see things more clearly."

"What kinds of things?" Brandon asked warily.

"My own shortcomings."

Once again, his fists were itching to punch something. Roger's stomach, maybe, since he'd already mentally broken the jerk's nose.

She smiled brightly. "So that's why I've decided to get him back."

"What? Get him back?" Why in the world would she

want that scumbag back? Hell, Brandon didn't even know Roger and he already hated him.

"Yes." She spread her arms out. "And that explains the makeover."

And with that, she made a show of checking her watch, effectively ending the conversation. Probably a good idea.

"So," she said, changing the subject, "do you want me to order lunch from catering?"

He wasn't finished talking about this, but clearly Kelly needed a time out. So he'd let it go. For now.

"Yeah, that would be great. I'll have the steak sandwich."

"Sounds good. I'll call it in."

He leaned forward in his chair. "Listen, Kelly, if you need any help or advice, anything at all, you'll come to me. Promise?"

"Really? You mean it?"

"Absolutely."

She studied his face as if she were weighing the depth of his sincerity. "You're sure?"

"I wouldn't have offered if I wasn't."

She seemed to carry on a short debate with herself, then said, "Okay, there is one tiny thing you could help me with. If you wouldn't mind."

"You name it," he said, reaching for his coffee mug.

"I'll be right back." She rushed out to her desk and was back in less than twenty seconds, holding a shopping bag from a well-known and expensive lingerie shop. Taking a deep, fortifying breath, she pulled some wispy scraps of sheer material from the bag and dangled them for him to see.

"Which do you like better, the black thong or the red panties?"

# Two

He choked on his coffee.

Dismayed, Kelly ran around and pounded his back. "Are you okay?"

"Fine," he managed to say. "I'm fine." He'd be even better once she backed off and her curvaceous breasts were no longer rubbing against his arm. He was only human, for God's sake. And hard as granite.

He'd been tackled by some of the biggest linebackers in football history, but nothing had ever rendered him apoplectic before now. As he took a deep breath and let it out, the thought entered his mind that maybe she was trying to kill him. Could Roger have treated her so badly that she was going to take it out on every man she knew?

It wasn't enough that she'd changed the playing field with her hot new look, but now she was shoving her panties at him. Didn't she know that those little scraps of silk would be forever imprinted on his fragile male psyche?

Now he would be forced to spend the next millennium imagining her in that black thong. Was she really that clueless?

"I didn't mean to shock you," she said. "But you said you would help."

"Didn't shock me," he insisted, his voice sounding as if a frog had taken up residence in his throat. "Coffee went down wrong. Just...give me a minute."

She finally moved back to her side of the desk and quickly shoved the bits of lace into the shopping bag.

"They'll work just fine," he said softly, not trusting his voice yet.

Her eyes glittered with hope. "Really?"

"Believe it," he said with a nod. "Any normal guy would be grateful to see you in either pair."

"You mean it?" Her eyes cleared and she smiled. "Thank you, Brandon. Oh, and I apologize again for springing them on you."

"No problem."

"To make this work, I really need to know what guys consider sexy." She frowned, then admitted, "Roger never thought I was."

"Never thought you were what?"

"Sexy."

Brandon sat forward in his chair. "Does Roger have some kind of learning disability or something?"

She laughed. "Thanks for that. I'll go order lunch now."

"Good idea," he said, thankful his voice had returned to full volume. "Oh, and Kelly?"

She stopped at the door. "Yes?"

"Go with the black thong."

Later that afternoon, Brandon hung up the phone from a two-hour teleconference with his brothers and their lawyer.

"That guy never stops talking," he said, shaking his head at the sheer immensity of the lawyer's convoluted vocabulary.

"I was thinking you must pay him by the word," Kelly said, flexing her fingers. She had taken notes during the entire meeting and now she stood and stretched her arms. The movement caused the knit fabric of her dress to stretch so tightly across her perfect round breasts that Brandon had to look the other way to stifle the first stages of another rock-hard erection.

"I'm getting more coffee," she said. "Would you like some?"

"No, thanks. Will you have a chance to type up your notes and analysis this afternoon?"

"Definitely. I'll get right on them."

"I appreciate it."

She closed the door and Brandon gritted his teeth. He needed Kelly to rethink this new wardrobe situation if he was going to survive the week. Hell, even her ankles were causing him palpitations. There was something about those high heels she was wearing that did awesome things to every inch of her legs.

An hour later, after the rest of his team had gone home, he walked out to Kelly's area to find a property file and caught her pouting at herself in her compact mirror.

"Oh." She blinked in surprise and quickly slapped the mirror closed and threw it in her drawer.

He rested one hand on the doorjamb. "I know I'm going to be sorry I asked, but what were you doing?"

"Nothing. What do you need? A file? Which one? I'll get it." She jumped up and pulled the top file drawer open.

"See, now you're just raising my curiosity level," he said, "so you might as well tell me."

She clenched her teeth together irately. "Fine. Roger

complained about the way I kissed, so I was practicing in the mirror. There. Are you happy?"

He shook his head. "Roger is a complete idiot. Why do you care what he thinks?"

She glared at him. "I told you, I want to get him back."

"Yeah, that's what I don't get." Disgusted with the subject of Roger, he moved to the file drawer and began to sift through the folders himself. "Where's the new Montclair Pavilion file?"

"I've got it right here." She picked up a thin folder and handed it to him. She looked so dejected, he couldn't help but feel sorry for teasing her.

"Look, I'm sure you kiss like a goddess," he said. "So stop worrying about what Roger thinks."

"I just wish I could practice on something besides a mirror," she said gloomily.

"Yeah," he agreed absently as he thumbed through the file. "It usually works better to go with a real-life target who'll actually kiss you back."

She shot him a hopeful look. "I don't suppose you'd be willing to help me out with that."

He glowered at her. "Get real, Kelly."

"What do you mean?" Realization dawned slowly. "Oh! No, no! I didn't mean for *you* to kiss—oh, dear. I would never want *you* to…well, this isn't going to come out right, no matter how I say it."

"So just say it."

"Okay. I wasn't talking about *you* kissing me." She sat on the edge of her desk. "But the thing is, I've made a list of potential, um…participants. So I was thinking maybe you could help by looking it over and making some suggestions?"

"You have a list?" Why was he surprised? Kelly made

lists for everything. It was just one of the ways she stayed so organized.

"Of course I have a list." She jumped up, ran around the desk and pulled a pad and pen out of her drawer. "I'm good at making lists."

"Let me get this straight," he said, absently slapping the file folder against his pants leg. "You've made a list of men you're thinking of approaching to ask for help with—what? Kissing lessons?"

She flipped a page over and studied it. "That's right."

"But I'm not on the list?" he asked warily.

"What? No, absolutely not." She shook her head as she held up her hand in a pledge. "Of course you're not on the list. You're my boss."

"Good. As long as we've got that settled." He should've felt nothing but relief. So why was he getting more annoyed by the minute? She considered him good enough to judge her damn panties but not good enough to kiss?

Okay, that might be the most ridiculous thought he'd had all day. This entire situation was getting out of hand. With a heavy exhalation of breath, he shoved away his own ludicrous reactions and tried to empathize with Kelly's bizarre quandary.

"So who's on the list?" he asked, almost afraid to hear her answers.

She glanced up. "What do you think about Jean Pierre?"

"The hotel chef?" She couldn't be serious.

"He's French," she explained. "They invented the sport, right?"

"No way in hell. Not Jean Pierre. You'd probably start an international incident. Absolutely not."

"Okay, okay." She crossed Jean Pierre's name off her list. "What about Jeremy?"

"The guy who mows the lawns?"

"He's a landscape designer," she said pointedly. "Practically an artist. He might know a thing or two about the art of *l'amour*."

"He's gay."

"Really? Why don't I know these things?" She blew out a frustrated breath as she drew a line through Jeremy's name. "Nicholas the winemaker? He's German, right? He might be—"

"Let me see that list." He snatched the pad from her and gazed at the names. "Paulo, the cabana boy?"

"He's cute," she insisted, a little too desperately.

"Forget it. Who's Rocco?"

"One of the limo drivers."

"Which one?"

"The big guy with the—"

"Never mind." He shook his head. "No."

"But—"

"No," he said, handing the list back. "Throw that away. I don't want you going around kissing the staff, for God's sake."

"Fine." Glaring at Brandon, she ripped the page out, crumpled it up and tossed it in the waste bin. "I suppose you're right. It might send the wrong message."

"You think?" he said, his voice tinged with sarcasm.

She folded her arms tightly across her chest, which only served to emphasize her world-class breasts, damn it.

"So who can I ask for help?" she wondered, leaning her hip against her desk. "I've got a full week before Roger gets here. I could do a lot of practicing in that time. Do you have any friends you could recommend?"

"No."

"Too bad." She pursed her lips in thought. "Maybe there's someone in town who—"

"Not a good idea," he said in a tone that cut off all

discussion. *Not a good idea?* Talk about an understatement. Hell, it was one of the worst ideas Brandon had ever heard. He didn't want her kissing the staff *or* any poor, unsuspecting Napa Valley residents. All he needed was to have the locals talking about the crazy kissing woman from the Mansion on Silverado Trail.

But he could tell by the tension building along Kelly's soft jawline that she was determined to carry out this cockeyed plan of hers. And if she went behind his back and enlisted one of the pool attendants…

Brandon stared at those pouty, glossy lips and realized the only man who could help her improve her kissing technique was him. Mainly because he suddenly couldn't stand the thought of her kissing anyone else.

"Fine," he said brusquely. "I'll help you."

She pushed away from the desk. "But you're not on the list."

"Doesn't matter. I'm going to help you myself because I don't want you scaring away the staff."

She placed her hands on her hips and tilted her head at him. "I know you meant that in the nicest way."

"Sorry. Yes." He shook his head as if to erase the comment. "Of course I did."

She continued staring at him. "I don't think it's a good idea."

"It's the only way I'll know for sure that you're not getting into trouble around here."

"I won't get into trouble."

"I know, because I'll be the one helping you."

Inhaling a deep breath, Kelly let it out slowly, then seemed to brace herself for impact. "Okay. I appreciate this, Brandon." She took a hesitant step toward him, but he held up his hand to stop her.

"Wait. We need to set some ground rules first."

"Ground rules? Why?"

"Because there's no way I'm having you fall for me."

"Fall for you?" She blinked, then began to laugh. "Are you kidding?"

"Something funny?" he asked, insulted.

"Yes," she said, giggling like a schoolgirl. "The idea that I would ever be dumb enough to fall for you is pretty funny."

"*Dumb* enough?"

"Yes, dumb enough. Let me count the ways." She held up one hand and began ticking off fingers. "You're a grouch in the morning. You leave newspapers lying around everywhere. You date a woman once and then never call back. You're a big baby when you're sick."

"Wait a minute," he protested.

But she was on a roll now and seemed to be enjoying herself. "And all your weird superstitions left over from when you played in the NFL? My gosh, wearing the same socks for every game was bad enough, but I also heard that you ate only sardines and blueberries the night before every game. Do you still do that before big negotiations? Who does that?"

Brandon had heard enough. He placed the file on the chair in front of her desk and stalked closer. "The socks were washed between games."

"Oh, really?"

"Yeah, really." He brushed against her, then slipped his hand around her nape and urged her closer. "And sardines and blueberries are both excellent sources of omega-three fatty acids."

"Fascinating," she whispered, as she stared wide-eyed at him.

"Helps the brain function better," he added as he caressed her cheek.

"G-good to know." She sounded wary now, probably smart of her.

He bent to kiss her neck, then murmured in her ear, "The quarterback's the brains of the team, did you know that?"

She moaned. "What are you doing?"

"What do you think I'm doing?"

"I'm not sure."

"I am." And he kissed her. She tasted as sweet and hot as he somehow knew she would. Even more so. He had to work to keep the contact light and simple, because it wouldn't do to get carried away. But that didn't stop him from wishing he could lay her down on the desk, run his hands up her thighs, spread her legs and bury himself inside her.

He had to stop. This was wrong in too many ways to count. If he stepped away from her right now, they could both forget this kiss ever happened.

Then she groaned in surrender and he knew she wanted the same things he did. And he was helpless to stop. He used his tongue to gently pry her lips open, plunging inside her sexy mouth. Her tongue met his in a sensual play of thrust and parry.

He wanted to cup her breasts and flick his thumbs across her peaked nipples, but that was a sure road to madness. So with every ounce of will inside him, he forced himself to end the kiss, reluctantly pulling himself away from her warmth.

"Oh," she whispered, licking her lips as she slowly opened her eyes.

Brandon's insides clenched at the sight of her pink tongue tasting him on her mouth.

"Oh, that was good," she said with a note of surprise. "That was really good."

"Yeah," he said, brooding. "It was."

"I liked it a lot."

So did he, but he remained silent. Otherwise, he might've been tempted to follow through on his desire to have her naked under him. But that would never happen and right now, he needed to regain some degree of control over whatever strange emotions were still churning inside him.

"Roger never kissed like that," she said, watching him thoughtfully.

"Did I mention the guy was an idiot?" he muttered.

"No wonder he didn't think I was sexy," she reasoned. "It's because he didn't make me *feel* sexy."

"I rest my case."

"But *you* did," she declared and smiled up at him. "And now…wow. You know, I really think Roger was the problem, not me. But I can't be sure."

"Yeah, you can," he said gruffly. "Roger was the problem. End of story."

She touched his arm. "Thank you, Brandon."

"You're welcome." He started to head for his office, still trying to steady his breathing.

"Wait," she said.

He turned and looked at her. A slight line of concern marred the smooth surface of her forehead. Her lips were pink and tender and about the sexiest thing he'd ever seen. The fact that he wanted more than anything to kiss her again, made him forge ahead into his office.

"I think I could get really good at this and blow Roger's mind, but I need to practice," she said, following him. She had her notepad in hand again, probably hoping she could make another damn list of all the different ways they could kiss each other. If she only knew.

"Not a good idea," he said, sliding the Montclair file into his briefcase.

"But you said that before and it turned out to be a really good idea."

He pierced her with a look. "No more practicing. Ground rules, remember?"

"I remember, don't worry." After scrutinizing him for a moment, she nodded her agreement. "Okay, I guess you're right."

"I know I'm right," he said, and snapped his briefcase closed.

"Thank you for your help," she said. "It was wonderful. On a purely educational level, I mean."

"You're welcome," he said and led the way out of his office. "Now let's call it a night."

"Oh, I'm going to stay for a while," she said, flipping to a clean page, all business now. "I need to make some notes while everything is still fresh in my mind. I'll need to remember everything later."

"You're going to make notes on that kiss?"

"Yes, for future reference." She'd already begun scribbling what looked like mathematical calculations. "If I write everything down—what you did and what I felt, I'll be able to recall each sensation the next time, and I'll know I'm doing it right."

"The next time," he echoed hazily.

"Yes. I tend to remember tactile experiences more clearly if I make a record of it immediately. Then later, I'll study my notes in anticipation of the next occurrence." She beamed at him. "I'm quite confident I can achieve an exponential jump in my skill level and understanding."

"Really?"

"It makes perfect sense on paper."

"On paper. Good."

Tapping her pen against the pad, she murmured, half to herself, "Of course, an actual kiss would give me a lot more insight...."

She looked up and studied Brandon closely. He wasn't liking the look in her eyes. "Don't even think about it."

"Think about what?" she asked, her eyelashes fluttering innocently. If she were any other woman, Brandon would know she was playing a dangerous game of seduction. But this was Kelly, who didn't seem to have a clue about feminine wiles and whose every emotion was evident on her face.

That made it Brandon's responsibility to set her straight.

"Forget it, Kelly. I am not going to kiss you again."

"Oh, I know," she murmured, her moist, glimmering lips pursed in thought.

He lost all memory of what they were talking about. He only knew that right now, his throbbing body parts wanted to put those lips of hers to the best use possible. Maybe after that, he would be able to carry on an intelligent conversation with her.

In the meantime, however, it appeared that he had created a monster.

# Three

*"I am not going to kiss you again."*

Every time Kelly played the words over in her head, she could feel her cheeks heat up in embarrassment. And since she was incapable of putting a halt to the mental words and images, she wouldn't be surprised if, any minute now, her head spontaneously combusted.

"So stop thinking about it," she demanded aloud as she popped a frozen dinner in the microwave oven and slammed the door shut. Now she had four minutes with nothing to do but wait. And think. And remember. She glanced around her comfortable mini-suite with its corner kitchen nook and figured she could use the time to straighten up, but there was nothing out of place. Her room was pristine, as usual.

The Mansion had a world-class housekeeping service and even though Kelly was part of the corporate staff, the housekeepers kindly insisted on stopping by every day to clean and straighten up and make sure everything was perfectly comfortable for her.

So, lucky her, she had plenty of time to dwell on all those damning thoughts that wouldn't stop circling through her mind.

"The fact that you practically begged your boss to kiss you," she berated herself, "in the office, in broad daylight, wasn't bad enough. No, you also had to dangle your panties in his face. So classy. And why couldn't you keep that silly list of kissing candidates to yourself?"

A small sigh escaped as she slid miserably onto the stool at her kitchen counter. Reaching for the bottle of sparkling water she'd opened, she filled her glass and took a sip. And pondered her next move.

There were a few ways she could remedy the situation. One was to go in tomorrow morning and simply apologize to Brandon. She could explain, somewhat truthfully, that she'd ingested nothing but spa cuisine for ten days straight and it had left her brain incapable of clear thought.

He probably wouldn't believe that story since everyone in the entire company knew that Kelly's mind was a steel trap. She could recall the minor details of a telephone conference from three years ago or the specifications of a particular construction job from months back. She had the dates of every birthday, anniversary and important occasion in Brandon's life memorized, along with phone numbers, credit card accounts and travel preferences for him and every member of his family.

There was no way he'd believe she'd suddenly lost the ability to think straight. So her only other solution was to simply move away, somewhere remote, like Duluth, leaving no forwarding address. She was fairly certain Brandon's memory of the outlandish panty-dangling incident would fade within months, a year at the most.

"Oh, God." She leaned her elbows on the counter and buried her face in her hands. The fact that Brandon had obligingly recommended the black thong really didn't help matters right now.

The microwave buzzed and she removed her small dinner. She was proud of herself for continuing to eat lighter portions since leaving the spa, but she could feel a serious ice cream binge coming on.

It was because of the kiss.

She'd vowed not to think about it and had been semisuccessful, deliberately switching tracks whenever her train of thought veered too close to the memory of Brandon's touch, the feel of his mouth on hers. But now, just for a moment or two, she let herself go and thought about it.

She'd never experienced anything like it. It was just one kiss, but she'd felt more passion and excitement in those few seconds than she'd known in the entire two years and seven months she'd dated Roger.

Now, she closed her eyes and gave in to temptation, reliving the exquisite pressure of Brandon's hands, the warm smoothness of his mouth…

After a moment, her eyes flashed open and she stared down at her rapidly cooling dinner. She'd completely lost her appetite. For dinner, anyway.

"You need to snap out of it, right now," she reprimanded herself. Brandon Duke was her employer. Her job was important to her. She couldn't afford to get dreamy-eyed and moony about the man who signed her paychecks. Especially not *that* man.

Once upon a time, Kelly had envisioned a fairy-tale romance and a happily-ever-after with Roger. He had been her handsome prince and she'd considered herself the luckiest girl in the world. But her prince had turned out to be a frog, and not very charming at all. He'd made promises he never intended to keep and had busted her dream of love and marriage flat. The breakup had not been pretty and Kelly had to admit she hadn't handled it well.

Before she met Roger, she had been upbeat and open to every possibility. She knew she was smart and reasonably attractive, knew she wanted to fall in love, get married and have children some day. But after Roger dumped her so cruelly, she'd felt broken, cynical, awkward and unsure of herself, especially around men. She had lost her confidence and she couldn't think about dating for a long time after the breakup.

Ironically, working in the office with Brandon had been the best antidote for her fears and insecurities. He'd made it clear early on that he considered her an indispensible member of his team. He relied on her intelligence and organizational skills to help him run his projects.

Her self-confidence blossomed and grew until she finally decided she was ready to start dating again. She still wanted to fall in love, get married and raise a family some day. And the only way to achieve that goal was to find the right man.

Being her organized self, she began by calling on her friends and coworkers. Then she'd compiled a list of online dating services as well as a number of local organizations she could join and activities in which she could participate in hopes of meeting eligible men.

She was convinced that she was ready to hit the dating scene—until the day she saw Roger's name on the hotel's upcoming conference list. Her throat tightened and her stomach churned. She couldn't catch her breath. The old insecurities rushed back with a vengeance. That's when she realized she would never be able to love another man until she came to terms with Roger and the damage she'd allowed him to inflict on her life.

If that meant confrontation, then so be it. The only problem with confronting Roger was that his ego was so overblown, he might get defensive and lash out at her. She wasn't sure she could endure another unpleasant war of words with him. But how else could she get around his ego? she wondered. And in that moment, Kelly had devised her life-saving plan.

If she could somehow lure Roger back, then reject him, it would help her recapture some of her old optimism and enjoyment of life. She would be free to move forward and love again. In other words, she would get her mojo back.

She also knew for a fact that Roger wouldn't be hurt by her rejection. Thank goodness, because Kelly could never hurt him on purpose, no matter how unkind he'd been to her. No, the fact was, Roger's ego was much too healthy to allow himself to be wounded by a woman. He would brush off the insult as easily as he would a speck of lint on one of his impeccably tailored suits.

As far as Kelly was concerned, Roger could make up any story he wanted to about why she'd refused him. The point was, *she* would be healed and ready to live again, to open her heart to the possibility of finding love and happiness. Right now, that was all that mattered.

The makeover would certainly help her cause. Kissing lessons couldn't hurt, either, especially from a master of the art. And that brought her back to her current predicament.

"Brandon," she said aloud, moving her fork around on her plate.

The problem was, she wasn't sure she had the experience to lure Roger in after just one kiss from Brandon, even though it had been a potent one, for sure. That's why, on the one hand, she wished she could continue learning the secrets of kissing from Brandon. On the other hand, she knew better. He was her boss! How many times did she have to remind herself? And worse than that—if anything could be worse—was that Brandon could jeopardize her plans for Roger's payback. After all, if Brandon continued to help her with her kissing, it might lead to something more. Kissing often did.

It was useless to deny that she was susceptible. All she had to do was think back to a few hours earlier when Brandon had kissed her. If he'd wanted to take things further, she would've gone right along with him. That's how good his kiss had been.

"Okay, fine, the man can kiss." She tossed her fork on the plate and stood, too antsy to eat.

Even if he kissed her again and it led to something more, she would never be so stupid as to fall for Brandon Duke.

She strode around the room, picking up her jacket and hanging it in the small closet, then sorting through her clothes for tomorrow's outfit.

Yes, she'd laughed at his ground rules earlier that day, but now that she'd kissed him, was she still willing to guarantee that she could remain resistant to his charms?

"Yes," she said firmly, and shoved the closet door shut. She wasn't a complete dummy. She knew Brandon's reputation with women, knew his habit of dating one woman for a brief period of time, then moving on to the next. It would be insane for any woman to expect Brandon Duke to reciprocate her tender feelings. So why would Kelly ever fall for him? She simply wouldn't.

Brandon wasn't the "settle down and get married" kind of guy Kelly wanted to meet and fall in love with. He didn't fit in with her life plan at all.

"And that makes him perfect for *this* plan," she said, as comprehension dawned. Since she would never fall for him, Brandon Duke was the perfect man to teach her how to kiss!

Now, if she could just convince him to continue helping her. After all, look how much she'd learned with just one try. Her eyes were now opened to the fact that Roger had been the problem all along. It was obvious now. He had never kissed her the way Brandon had kissed her. She would've remembered.

"Oh yes," she said with another sigh as she forced herself to take another bite of her dinner. She would've remembered a kiss like that.

So how could she convince her boss to let her practice her kissing with him some more? Roger would be here next week so it wasn't as if he would be forced to keep kissing her forever. It would only be for a few days. She needed to make it clear that lessons in romance and seduction would be all she needed. The more skilled she became at romance and seduction, the better her chances would be of putting Roger in his place.

Brandon could appreciate that, right?

Still, it was a dilemma. Brandon was her boss. If she was smart—and she *was*—she'd just forget about Brandon and use her own best instincts to attract Roger.

*What instincts?* she wondered, and grimaced. When it came to romance, she had none!

As she took another bite of chicken and rice, she realized there had to be a website somewhere with instructions she could follow. There was a website for everything else, so why not seduction?

Oh, but it would be so much better to learn from a real live expert. And Brandon was indeed an expert. She couldn't help thinking that if mere kissing had given her this much perspective into her problems with Roger, then having sex with Brandon would be absolutely revelatory.

"What?" She jumped off her chair and wrapped her arms around herself. Where had that thought come from?

"You stop thinking about that right now," she admonished herself as she grabbed her plate and glass and carried them to the sink. "You'll just embarrass yourself." *Again.*

But now that she'd thought it, she couldn't get the image out of her mind. What in the world would happen if she and Brandon ever had sex?

"Oh, no," she said, gasping. What if they had sex and she found out she really *was* bad at it? How could she face Brandon at work? She would have to quit.

But wait. What if she was really *good* at it? Would he think she'd been lying about her lack of experience? Would he assume she'd been having sex all along, with every guy in town? How could she face him at work? She would have to quit.

And oh, dear Lord. What if Brandon was no good at sex? Would she have to lie and tell him it was wonderful? He was her boss, after all. She couldn't exactly tell him he was a loser in bed. She would have to quit.

She moaned and took another sip of water.

"Okay, that's it," she said, as she tapped her fingers on the counter anxiously. "Just forget the whole thing."

This whole kissing thing was too much to think about. She had to figure out some other way to deal with Roger. She would explain to Brandon tomorrow that she'd been wrong. He would have to forgive her. And she was certain that he would. After all, before today, she'd never done anything to cause her employer the least bit of consternation. Tomorrow, after she explained to Brandon that her brief lapse into lunacy was over, everything would be fine. They'd go back to normal. She would assure Brandon that he would never have to worry about inappropriate behavior from her again.

And a year from now, she would look back and be able to laugh over this momentary ripple in her otherwise unblemished record.

The doorbell chimed and she jumped.

Checking her wristwatch, she wondered if it might be Housekeeping at the door. She'd asked them not to stop by with those yummy evening chocolates anymore. But tonight, maybe she'd take one. Anything to provide a diversion from her disconcerting thoughts. She ran to open the door and her resolutions of a moment ago flitted away.

"Brandon," she whispered.

"We need to talk."

Brandon stared at Kelly and could no longer remember why he'd thought it would be a good idea to come by her room.

After a long run around the hotel grounds after work, then another brief conference call with his brothers to finalize arrangements for their family's arrival to attend the resort's grand opening, followed by a quick taste of the chef's latest creations for the harvest festival menu, Brandon had retired to his suite to watch Dallas eviscerate Denver on TV. But he hadn't been able to concentrate on the football game, and that was a first.

He blamed it on Kelly.

The fact was, he couldn't get her out of his mind. Not in a sexual way, he hastened to tell himself, despite the vivid memory of her warm mouth and sweet tongue and an explicit picture of exactly what he'd like to do with... but he wasn't going to go there. No way. Not with Kelly. Not in this lifetime.

In the first place, she worked for him. How big a fool would he be if he jeopardized his working relationship with the best assistant he'd ever had? And even if he was willing to overlook that little fact, Kelly just wasn't his type. She wasn't sophisticated and worldly like the women he usually dated. She wasn't the kind of woman Brandon would ever think of calling on the spur of the moment for a night on the town, followed by a rousing round of sex, followed by no commitment to call again.

No, Kelly was more like the girl next door, the one who was meant to find a nice guy and get married. As far as Brandon was concerned, she might as well have worn a banner that said Hands Off. And he would be wise to heed that invisible warning.

He'd had some pretty awful role models early in his childhood, before Sally Duke adopted him. He'd seen all the ways people could hurt each other in the name of love and marriage, so he wasn't about to go that route. With that in mind, he had decided not to touch Kelly again.

But she'd looked so pensive and uncertain when he'd left the office earlier this evening. He'd never seen Kelly less than one hundred percent confident in herself and her abilities, so this change in attitude worried him.

And then there was that kiss. Which he wasn't going to think about again, damn it.

So why was he standing here at her door, holding a bottle of wine? Oh, yeah.

"We need to talk," he repeated. He'd used the same stupid line in the office much earlier today. It sounded somehow lamer now, even if it was the truth. When she stepped aside, he strolled into her mini-suite. "I hope I'm not interrupting your dinner."

"No, I'm finished," she said, and rushed to dispose of the remnants.

He held out the bottle of wine, a Duke Vineyards pinot noir. "Will you have a glass of this if I open it?"

She stared at the bottle, then up at him. "Sure. I'll find an opener."

He could tell she was nervous as she rattled around in one of the kitchen drawers. And why shouldn't she be? It wasn't every day a woman kissed her employer. And it wasn't every night that said employer showed up at her hotel room carrying a bottle of wine. He just hoped she wouldn't get the wrong idea. All he wanted to do was clear the air so their working relationship could go back to being as exceptional as it had been before the kiss. It was a simple problem and it wouldn't take him long to explain his feelings, but he had to admit that a quick glass of wine would probably help them both relax.

"Here you go," she said, and handed him a corkscrew.

"Glasses?"

"Oh." She swallowed anxiously. "Right."

As he worked to remove the cork, he took a moment to study his longtime assistant—and wondered how he'd ever thought he'd be able to relax in her hotel room.

She wore cutoff shorts and a T-shirt, an outfit that a jury of his peers would consider thoroughly appropriate for spending a balmy night alone in her room. But as she reached for the wineglasses on the second shelf of the cupboard, he watched her T-shirt inch up to reveal the leanness of her stomach. On her tiptoes now, her shorts stretched just enough to show the soft, pale skin above her tan line where the curve of her bottom met her perfectly toned thighs.

"Here you go," she said, placing two glasses on the counter.

Brandon let go of the breath he hadn't realized he was

holding. "Thanks." He took his time pouring wine into the glasses and handed her one. "Kelly, I—"

"Look, Brandon—"

"Sorry. What were you going to say?"

She blinked, then said in a rush, "No, you go first."

"Fine. I just think—"

"Okay, I'll go first." She glanced briefly toward the ceiling as if she were looking for guidance from above. Brandon watched her chest move up and down as she inhaled, then exhaled. She was clearly edgy. She picked up her wineglass and took a gulp, paced a few steps back and forth across the small kitchen, then stopped and met his gaze, her face a mask of regret.

"I want to apologize for the way I behaved today," she said. "I don't know what got into me. I've been going crazy ever since I learned that Roger would be coming here and I guess I…I lost my head. I'm mortified about what happened. I just hope you'll accept my apology and trust that it'll never happen again."

She looked exhausted when she finished and he felt a twinge of sympathy for her.

"Why don't we sit down?" he said, and he led the way to the cozy sitting area of the mini-suite. They each sat at one end of the small couch, leaving barely two feet of space between them.

He should've been relieved that she'd apologized, but for some unfathomable reason, it didn't sit well with him. "So what, exactly, will never happen again?"

She opened her mouth, then closed it. Frowning, she placed her wineglass down on the end table and shifted against the plush sofa cushions until she was facing him more directly. "You know what I'm talking about."

"Tell me."

"Fine." She exhaled heavily and Brandon was once

again mesmerized by the movement of her breasts. "I backed you into a corner. I practically propositioned you." With a groan of disgust, she lifted her arms and waved them for emphasis. "I threw myself at you." She shot him a quick glance. "Figuratively speaking, of course."

"Of course," he said cautiously.

"I left you no choice but to kiss me, Brandon. It was horrible of me." She grabbed her wineglass. "Don't get me wrong, I appreciate what you did. It was wonderful, really. It was so…well, anyway, you helped me confirm a few important things I'd been confused about. But it was still wrong of me to ask it of you, and I'm sorry. I took complete advantage of you."

"Did you?" He stifled a grin. She didn't honestly think any woman had ever taken advantage of him, did she?

"Yes." She pressed two fingers against her eyelids as though she were getting a headache. "I practically begged you to kiss me."

"Well, you didn't exactly beg." Now Brandon had to smile. He was starting to enjoy this. "But go on."

"I'll understand if you can't forgive me, but I hope you will. All I can do is promise it will absolutely never happen again."

"Never?"

"Never, I swear. In fact, if you could just wipe the entire experience from your memory that would be very helpful."

"You're saying I should just forget it ever happened."

"Exactly! I would be so grateful. You know I've never been a problem employee, so if you could just take this day off the books, I promise it'll never happen again."

He rubbed his jaw, considering. "You've always been above reproach."

"I like to think so," she said, clearly relieved. "Honestly, it was just some kind of momentary aberration. We can chalk it up to vacation-induced insanity or something."

"Or something," he murmured.

Beaming, she said, "You've been really understanding. Thank you so much." She picked up her wineglass and took another sip. "I'm so glad we had this little talk. I feel so much better."

"That's what I'm here for."

She gazed at him, her smile tentative. "I was afraid you came here tonight to fire me."

The words stopped him. "I would never fire you for what happened today. I only came by to talk to you and assure you everything was fine. I knew you'd be too hard on yourself."

"Well, the fact is, I behaved inappropriately and I'm sorry for that."

"Yeah, I got it." It was exactly what he'd hoped to hear her say, but something was still bugging him. "There's one thing I'm concerned about, Kelly."

"What's that?"

"Why the hell do you want to get this Roger clown back?"

"It's something I have to do. And I will," she added with quiet intent. "But honestly, Brandon, please don't give it another thought. I shouldn't have dragged you into my personal issues in the first place."

"Kelly, stop apologizing. I'm the one who insisted that you tell me what was bothering you. If you want to know the truth, I'm glad I'm the one you confided in."

"You are? Why?"

"Because it tells me you trust me, and I appreciate that. You're very important to me."

Her eyes grew soft. "Thank you, Brandon. It means a lot to hear you say that."

"I guess I don't say it often enough." He frowned again. "But that's why it bugs me that you'd want to get this guy back. He hurt you."

"He won't ever hurt me again."

"Good to hear," Brandon said. But he didn't believe it. Kelly was too naïve to know how guys like this Roger creep operated. And Brandon was very much afraid the man knew exactly how to hurt her again. He sipped his wine and considered his next move. "So when does Roger arrive?"

"Not until Monday."

"But he'll still be here for many of the opening week events."

"Yes."

Brandon scowled. Somehow, the thought of watching Kelly coming on to the guy for a whole damn week, pissed him off all over again. To distract himself, he swirled his glass and studied the rich color of the pinot. "Would you like me to talk to him?"

"No!" She bolted straight up. "Thank you for offering, but no. You wouldn't, would you?"

"Yeah," he said matter-of-factly. "If I thought it would help, I would. But it's pretty obvious you'd rather I didn't, so I'll honor your wishes. But I'm warning you, if he makes one wrong move…"

She held up her hand to stop him. "He won't. I won't let him."

"I'm glad." He went back to staring at his wine. "But you're still planning on kissing him?"

Kelly froze. "Um…"

Brandon leaned forward and casually rested his elbows on his knees. "I don't mean to pry, Kelly, but we've got a full agenda for opening week and I'm going to need your undivided attention. So if you're planning on kissing the guy or, you know, getting involved, that could present a problem."

"Brandon, whatever I do with Roger will have no effect whatsoever on my attention to my job."

"I'm not sure I want to take that chance."

She shifted uneasily. "We're just talking about a kiss or two. No big deal."

"It's a big deal if it's done right."

"Oh." She bit her lower lip, considering. "Of course. But Roger won't…well."

He studied her. "Roger won't do it right. Is that what you were going to say?"

"Yes, but what I meant was…" Jittery now, she jumped up from the couch and folded her arms across her chest. "Everything will turn out fine."

"You think?"

She smiled through clenched teeth. "Yes. Absolutely. I know what I'm doing now."

"Oh, I see," he drawled. "Now that I've kissed you, you think you'll be able to show Roger how it's done."

Her jaw tensed up even more as she met his gaze defiantly. "Maybe."

"He won't be here for almost a week," Brandon said. "You sure you'll remember how to do it?"

"Of course," she said, then licked her lips nervously, almost bringing Brandon to his knees. Good thing he was sitting down. And now that he thought about it, why the hell was he sitting here when she was halfway across the room, looking more beautiful than anything he'd seen in a long time, if ever?

Damn, he wanted her. He didn't care if it was stupid. He knew what he wanted. And he always went after what he wanted.

Giving in to the inevitable, he pushed himself up from

the couch and moved toward her. "You weren't thinking of practicing with someone else, were you?"

Her shoulders sagged as if she'd been caught plotting to do just that. "No, of course not."

"Good." Brandon approached slowly, his gaze never leaving hers. "Because I wouldn't want to hear any rumors of unbridled kissing going on."

"You won't, I promise," she murmured as she inched backward.

"I hope not."

"Nothing unbridled, anyway," she said, biting back a smile.

"You think that's funny?" he asked, inches away now. "There's nothing funny about unbridled kissing."

"I'm sure you're right," she said, nodding slowly.

"Oh, believe me, I am." From this close, he could see a dusting of freckles across her cheeks and nose that he'd never noticed before.

"Brandon?" She chewed on her lower lip, nearly driving him crazy. "What are you…"

"Shh," he said, watching her delectable mouth. When it curved into a smile aimed directly at him, he couldn't see any possible way to resist temptation. So he did what any other man would do in his position. He kissed her.

And wondered if he'd ever feasted on anything half as sweet.

Her taste was even more incredible than he remembered and he wanted all of her. He angled his head and deepened the kiss, feeling an urgent need to touch her, to bury himself in her. Enveloping her in his arms, he breathed in her delicious scent as he planted light kisses along her neck, forcing himself to go slowly.

"Brandon, I know you didn't want—"

"Shh." He pushed aside the neckline of her T-shirt and kissed the skin of her shoulder. "I want."

"Are you sure?" she whispered.

"That's my line, sweetheart," he said with a sideways glance.

"Oh." She stared at him, her bright eyes sparkling in the soft light. "Well, I'm sure. I'm really, really sure."

"That's all I wanted to hear."

"Please," she murmured.

"That, too." He slid his hand up her side until he reached the swell of her breast. With his thumb, he did what he'd wanted to do all day, teasing her nipple through the material until he felt it stiffen.

"Please don't stop," she moaned.

"I wouldn't dream of it." He lowered his head and covered her mouth with his. The pleasure was instant, intense. How had he waited all day to do this?

She was eager and opened her mouth to welcome him into her warmth, wrapping her arms around his neck to bring them closer.

"I want my hands on you, Kelly," he muttered.

"Mmm, I want that, too."

It was all the encouragement he needed. He swept her into his arms in an effortless move and walked toward the bed.

"Oh, I like that," she said, her lips curved in a sweet smile.

"Babe, you ain't seen nothing yet."

She cuddled in his arms and rained little kisses along his neck and shoulder. When they reached the bed, he placed her gently on top of the covers, then knelt and straddled her. Reaching for the hem of her T-shirt, he lifted it up and off in one swift move. With her arms raised languidly above her head and her lustrous hair spread over the pillow, she looked like the stuff of Brandon's dreams. He had to force himself to take it slow and easy as he slid his hand under her back and unclipped her bra in one smooth move.

"You are gorgeous," he whispered reverently.

She smiled as she reached up and caressed his cheek, almost as though she couldn't quite believe he was real, either. Brandon wasn't sure he'd ever felt quite so alive as he did in this moment. He bent his head to her breasts and took first one nipple, then the other into his mouth. She gasped and arched off the bed, pushing herself into him, straining his control. Had there ever been a woman so responsive to his touch?

His hands continued to move over her breasts as his mouth carried on his sensual exploration, moving down her taut stomach, stopping here and there to kiss and taste her soft skin. When he reached her heated feminine core, she writhed in anticipation and he rushed to satisfy her and appease his own desperate need as well. He might've lost track of time, aware only of her soft moans of delight and his own heady satisfaction. Through the haze of pleasure, he heard her utter his name.

"Please, Brandon," she said. "I need you, now."

With those words, Brandon moved. He stood and quickly tore off his clothing, tossing his things on the chair nearby. Then he pulled a condom from his pocket and slipped it on. As he made his way back to her, Kelly licked her lips in expectation and Brandon's knees nearly buckled. In that moment, he wanted her more than any woman he'd ever known. The thought meant nothing, he assured himself. It was all the heat of the moment.

Joining her, stretched out beside her, he urged her onto him, gripping her lush bottom with both hands as he guided her sweet center toward his rigid length. As his mouth devoured hers, he plunged himself into her heat and filled her completely.

Their bodies moved in perfect rhythm, as though both had been created for just this moment. The passion was explosive. Brandon had never felt more powerful, more driven by one singular need: her ultimate pleasure.

Her body strained to get closer to his, so close that he could feel her heart pounding against his chest. Her lips found his and molded themselves tenderly to his mouth in a gesture so sweet, it caused a shudder to spread through his body. With a desperation he'd never known, he again thrust himself into her, then again and again. She cried out his name and trembled uncontrollably. He tightened his hold on her, pushing himself to the limit until he answered her with his own deep cry and followed her over the edge.

# Four

"So that's what all the fuss is about," Kelly said finally, her soft voice full of wonder.

It had taken a while, but Brandon's head had eventually stopped spinning and his breathing had returned to normal. Now he turned onto his side and, despite being more shaken than he'd like to admit, he flashed a confident smile at her. "Yeah, that's what it's all about. Why do you sound so surprised? I know you've done this before."

"Not like that," she murmured, then quickly looked away and fiddled with the pillow beneath her head.

He reached over and placed his fingers under her chin, urging her to meet his gaze. "Are you telling me your dumb-ass ex-boyfriend never satisfied you?"

She met his gaze warily. "Roger told me I wasn't very good in bed."

Maybe his ears were still ringing from the exertion of a

few minutes ago, because he couldn't have heard her right. So he leaned in close and said, "What did you say?"

"The actual term he used was 'lousy,'" she admitted softly. "According to him, I was *lousy* in bed." She sighed. "When he broke up with me, I made the mistake of asking him why, and that's what he told me."

Brandon wondered if Kelly could see the smoke coming out of his ears because right now he was so angry, he was ready to kill that jackass Roger at the earliest opportunity. This wasn't the time to rant about that, but soon. Very soon. He went up on one elbow and peered at her intently. "He's dead wrong, sweetheart. You know that, right?"

"I do now. Back then, I wasn't so sure."

He shook his head, unwilling to think about that dumb-ass anymore tonight. "Well, that was then and this is now. And I'm sure."

"Really?"

Her smile was tenuous and it almost broke his heart. He touched her soft shoulder with his fingers and said, "Damn it, Kelly, can't you see how tempting you are? Forget what that fool told you. He obviously blamed you for his own inadequacies."

Brandon sat up and leaned against the headboard and pulled her into his arms. "He was wrong, do you hear me? You're amazing. You're hot. I've never…" He stopped and took a deep breath. "Let's just say my brains are still bouncing around my head from your hotness."

She smiled brightly and he was suddenly mesmerized all over again by her mouth.

"Okay," she said, nodding slowly. "I believe you."

"Good," he growled. "You should also believe me when I say that guy needs to be taught a serious lesson."

Her smile dimmed. "That's exactly what I plan to do."

She touched his chest and gazed up at him. "Would you do me a favor?"

"Another one?" he said, and chuckled when she smacked his chest lightly. He grabbed her hand before she pulled it back and held it pressed against his skin where it seemed to belong. "Of course I'll do you a favor, sweetheart. What is it?"

"I don't want to hear any words of remorse or blame or embarrassment tomorrow," she said. "Please, Brandon. This was wonderful and I'm so happy. I don't want a shadow to fall on what happened tonight."

He stared at her for a moment, then nodded. "It's a deal. No shadows."

"Thank you." Her smile was sexy as she added, "And by 'thank you,' I mean it in every possible way."

He smoothed a strand of lustrous hair off her cheek. "Now it's your turn to do me a favor. I don't want to hear any more words of thanks. No more undying gratitude from you, do you hear me?"

"But—"

"No." He pressed his finger to her lips. "I didn't do you any favors, believe me. We both made the decision to do what we did, we both had a good time, and that's all there is to it."

She nodded. "You're right. Okay, fine, no more thank yous."

"Thank you." They both laughed and he leaned in to kiss her.

"I really like the way you kiss," Kelly confessed. She moved closer and touched her lips to his and he felt himself spring to life against her.

"In case you couldn't tell, I think it's pretty clear that I really like everything about you." And he proceeded to show her just how much.

* * *

Much later that night, after the second time they'd made love—or was it the third?—Brandon pulled Kelly into his arms and fitted her warm backside against his body.

"Mmm," she said. "That's nice."

"Yeah, it is," he agreed. But part of him questioned what he was doing. Everything felt way too good. That could be a problem. Maybe he should leave now and go to his own room. It had to be after midnight. He could still get a decent night's sleep.

Kelly chose that moment to stretch her muscles, pushing herself even closer against him. On a soft moan, she said, "Oh, I feel so good."

Brandon's head reeled. Was he really thinking of leaving her now? Was he out of his mind?

Not yet. But he would be if he walked out while she was pressed up against him like this.

But if he was going to stay any longer, he knew they needed to talk. So he wrapped his arm around her waist and with his last ounce of brainpower, he murmured, "Hey, you're not falling for me, are you?"

"What?" She managed to twist and roll around until she was facing him and he was glad to see her smiling lightheartedly. "I should ask you the same question."

"Am I falling for you?" he asked, grinning.

She pressed her finger against his chest. "Well, are you?"

He chuckled. "Hey, I know the rules."

"Good," she said in mock seriousness, "because I'm a busy woman and I don't want to have to deal with you mooning all over me in the office."

Smirking, he said, "I'll try to contain myself."

She laughed softly. "I certainly hope so." Her smile

faded as she added, "But since we're talking about it, we should probably decide on a few things."

"Like what?"

"Like the fact that I really don't want the staff discussing our private affair."

"I don't want that, either," he said. "So we'll be discreet."

"Okay, good." Then she grimaced. "Oh dear, what about your family? They'll be here in a few days and I would rather they didn't find out that I'm sleeping with my boss."

Brandon touched her cheek. "I understand." And he did, because even though he had the utmost respect for her, he realized that others might consider their intimate relationship inappropriate.

"So once your family arrives," she said, "we should stop seeing each other."

"Much as I hate to admit it, that's probably a good idea," he said grudgingly, then he ran his hand down her side and stroked her thigh. "But until then…"

Her eyes lit up as she smiled and moved closer. "Mmm, yes. Until then, maybe you could show me again what all the fuss is about."


"Where did you disappear to last night?" Cameron Duke asked when Brandon answered his office phone the next morning. "I tried to call you a few times and finally gave up."

Brandon thought fast for a way to respond to his brother. "I might've been out on a run. What time did you call?"

"First call was around seven, then I tried twice more until about eight."

"Sorry, bro. I guess I plugged my phone in to recharge and forgot all about it. What did you need?"

"Mom was bugging me to call you and confirm the reservations for everything. I finally decided I'd rather talk to Kelly than you, so I gave her a call, but she didn't answer her phone either."

"Huh. Maybe she went into town for dinner."

"Without her phone? Not our Kelly."

"That's weird all right." Brandon rolled his eyes. He hated lying to his brothers but there was no way he could tell them he was sleeping with his assistant. He didn't need the grief they would give him. The fact was, he and Kelly were wrapped up in each other almost from the time they left the office until early this morning. And thinking about it now, he wished he was back in bed with her still, holding her. Inside her. Her soft, naked skin against his.

"So we'll have the use of two golf carts for the wine and vineyard tour?"

"What?" Brandon shook his head to clear his mind of the erotic images he'd conjured up. Damn. "Uh, yeah."

"You okay, bro? Sounds like you've got something else on your mind."

"Yeah, you know how it is. I've got a whole list of stuff." He scratched his jaw, wondering what the hell was going on with his brain. He'd never been distracted by a woman during business hours. Especially when things were so busy. He really needed to shape up and concentrate on the business at hand.

"I definitely know how it is," Cameron said. "I just hope you're ready for the onslaught."

Brandon dragged a hand through his hair and forced himself to swipe another picture of a gorgeous, naked Kelly from his mind. Hell, it wasn't like him to be preoccupied once he was in the office working.

Like his brothers, Brandon left nothing about the business up to chance. He'd held countless management meetings with his hotel and restaurant managers and had brought the entire staff on full-time in the past few weeks before the official opening. Every day, managers would assign different staff members to play guest while those serving meals or cleaning rooms or arranging sightseeing tours or serving wines on the patio could practice their job skills with the same professionalism they would show any true, paying guest. The management team reviewed any problems or difficulties they encountered, then they repeated the process the next day. It was the tried and true way of working out any kinks before they went "live."

The head chef and kitchen staff in the restaurant had worked out the new menu and Brandon knew the reviews would be fantastic. The Mansion on Silverado Trail would soon be the hottest new wine country destination on the map.

His brothers and their wives would arrive on Thursday for a final pre-opening meeting. Then Mom and her friends would arrive Friday morning. Was he ready?

"I'm as ready as I'll ever be," Brandon said, chuckling at the picture of his mom and her girlfriends living it up at the Mansion.

"Glad to hear it," Cameron said, then took a moment to entertain him with the latest stories about baby Jake before they finished the call. As Brandon hung up the phone, he thought about his family and how much they'd all changed over the past year. Who would've guessed how quickly Sally Duke's sons would go from being sworn bachelors to happy family men? Well, two out of three sons, anyway. Cameron and Adam had both succumbed to the charms of two beautiful women, but Brandon wasn't about to follow in their footsteps. No how, no way.

He flashed a determined grin as he vowed, once again, never to fall victim to his mother's matchmaking skills. Sally had denied up and down that she'd had anything to do with Cameron and Adam meeting and falling in love with their respective spouses, but none of the men believed her. Brandon and his brothers still didn't know how she'd managed it, but there was no doubt in their minds that their mother had had something to do with their eventual fall into matrimony.

But not Brandon. It wasn't going to happen to him. Hey, she was welcome to take her best shot. And he had no doubt she would continue to try. Now that he thought about it, he realized he would have to be extra vigilant this weekend.

It wasn't that he didn't love Sally Duke like crazy. On the contrary, he owed her his very life. From the day she'd rescued him from an imminent sentence to juvenile hall, he'd been indebted to her. Brandon had been the worst kind of bad risk, but that hadn't deterred Sally from taking a chance on him.

Sally was a young, wealthy and generous widow whose beloved husband, William, had been a foster kid, too. She'd wanted to give back to the system that had produced such a wonderful guy as William, so she'd adopted three boys all around the same age: Brandon, Adam and Cameron.

Once the three eight-year-olds had learned to trust each other, they'd sworn an oath of allegiance to themselves and Sally. They were blood brothers and nothing would ever split them apart. As part of their pact, they'd vowed never to marry or bring children into this world because they knew that married people hurt each other, and parents—except for Sally—hurt their kids.

Sally had raised them well and they'd grown up to be good, strong, smart men. Well, smart most of the time, Brandon thought. He'd warned his brothers that Sally was out to get them all married, but did they listen? No. Adam met Trish and fell in love. Months later, Cameron reunited with his old flame Julia and discovered he had a son with her, little Jake. Both couples had married recently and were ridiculously happy. Adam and Trish were expecting a little one any day now.

So Adam and Cameron had both fallen flat on the brotherly pledge, but that was okay. Brandon had already explained to them both that he understood they were weak, so he'd sworn to uphold their blood pact all on his own. They'd laughed and given him a hard time. But the fact was, Brandon had been determined long before he met his new brothers, that he would never marry and have kids. Not if it meant carrying on his own son-of-a-bitch father's legacy. And in case he forgot, he just had to recall the hundreds of brutal beatings delivered by his old man after his drug-addicted mother hit the road. He would never forget the lessons those poundings had taught him.

It's not that he begrudged his brothers any happiness. Hell, he was half in love with Trish and Julia himself. But Brandon had seen the worst kind of human behavior and he didn't want his parents' weaknesses rubbing off on any children he might've ever dreamed of having.

For that reason, he kept his relationships with women on a strictly superficial level. He never stayed in a relationship longer than a few weeks, a month or two at the most. Another thing Brandon rarely allowed himself to do was spend the entire night with a woman. He didn't believe in leading them on, giving them hope that an affair with him would be anything more than a momentary fling.

That practice had fallen by the wayside last night with Kelly. He'd planned to leave her room and sleep in his own bed, but he hadn't been able to tear himself away from her sweetness. He'd awakened several times during the night with an urgent need to be inside her. And this morning, they'd showered together and made love again.

The thought of Kelly and the way she'd looked, with her

body glistening in the soap-scented water, almost made him groan out loud.

It stunned him to think that he'd actually had sex with Kelly. She was a fascinating woman and he'd known that for years, but now he'd seen a completely different side of her. And he wanted more. She'd been so uninhibited and sweet, so unlike any other woman he'd been involved with in the past.

It was a good thing they'd reaffirmed their ground rules last night. The absolute last thing he wanted was to hurt Kelly, so he was glad they'd talked things over. It was good to see her smile as she reassured him that it wouldn't be a problem for her if they kept seeing each other. She insisted they were just having a good time and she was happy to be learning so much about the art of seduction. But, she'd said, there was no way in the world she would ever be dumb enough to fall in love with him.

His mind deep in thought, he didn't notice when Kelly walked into his office until she placed a hot cup of coffee on his desk blotter.

Looking up at her, he murmured "Hey there, stranger," and was about to grab her hand and pull her into his lap when she cut him off brusquely with a sharp look of warning.

"Good morning, Brandon." She said it loudly and followed it with an overly obvious nudge of her chin, just as their concierge manager rushed in behind her. "Serge has a matter of some urgency he'd like to discuss with you."

Serge paced in front of his desk. "Do you have a moment, Brandon? A problem has arisen with the new tour company."

"Sure." He gave Kelly a brief but meaningful nod, then turned to Serge. "What can I do for you?"

* * *

Kelly poured water into the coffeepot and stifled a yawn. It was no wonder she was tired. Besides attending to all the general preparations and last-minute emergencies that went with the grand opening of the hotel, she'd also spent the entire night making love with Brandon. That meant she had gotten almost no sleep and now her body ached in all sorts of places she never even knew she had. Not that she was complaining. No way. And she refused to feel guilty. In fact, she felt wonderful.

She still couldn't quite believe that Brandon had simply appeared at her hotel room door. She was even more incredulous over the fact that she'd spent hours after that having spectacular sex with him. It was so much more fun when you did it right, she thought.

But then this morning as she got dressed, she began to worry about how Brandon would react to seeing her in the office. Even though they'd made a pact that neither of them would feel remorseful or embarrassed, she couldn't be sure. Maybe she'd made a huge mistake by sleeping with him.

Or maybe not. After all, it was sex, nothing more. There were no emotions involved. She was just having a little affair with a man millions of other women would kill for. No pressure.

By the time she walked into the office, she'd worked herself into a state of anxiety, wondering over and over again what in the world she'd been thinking the night before. Had she lost her mind? Why had she slept with him?

But then she'd walked into Brandon's office and he'd smiled broadly and reached for her. And she knew why.

It had been wonderful and totally worth it.

She should've known Brandon would do it right. Besides

being tall, gorgeous, utterly captivating and totally sexy, he'd lived a charmed life ever since he'd been adopted by Sally Duke at the age of eight.

Sally had once given Kelly a thumbnail sketch of Brandon's life, starting with him being a high school honors student and an All-American football player in college. He was drafted into the NFL where he played quarterback for many years before becoming a sports commentator for the premier sports news station in the country. But he'd grown weary of the limelight and had joined his brothers' hotel and real estate development team a few years ago.

Sally had also confided that the man attracted women like flies. Kelly was already well aware of that. For the past four years, she'd been charged with the job of keeper of the keys to the inner sanctum. In other words, she screened every woman who called or came by to speak with Brandon. Depending on his instructions, she would either put them through or put them off.

Never in her wildest dreams did she think she would end up as one of those women. The thought didn't appeal to her as she sat down at her desk and powered up her computer.

"I'm not one of those women," she argued with herself, recalling their conversation late last night. "We've got an arrangement. This is a temporary situation only."

But now she could see why all those women had had such stars in their eyes. Brandon's touch had put a twinkle in her eye, too. The thought made her smile as she gathered the mail and began to open each envelope, sorting the enclosed documents and letters into several different piles, depending on priority. When she caught herself humming off key, she giggled. Then she froze.

"What in the world was that?"

Kelly never giggled. What was wrong with her? Was she coming down with something? She held her hand against her forehead to check her temperature, but her skin was perfectly cool and dry. She was pretty sure there was only one answer to the question. She was…happy?

Okay, happy was a good word to describe how she felt. She couldn't believe her good luck and even though Brandon had warned her not to say the words out loud, she couldn't help but be grateful. She wished she could thank him for his…what? His *assistance?* No, that made it sound like he was helping her bake a cake. Grateful for his *special friendship?* Kelly shivered. No, that sounded vaguely icky.

"For his expertise," she said aloud, and nodded at the description. "I'm in training." She smiled again. It sounded much better, more subtle, than the other choices. After all, she often went for training on new computer systems and software programs, so why not sexual expertise? It made perfect sense and besides, it was true. She really was in training to improve her sexual proficiency. She was the student and Brandon was the master.

She could only imagine the syllabus.

She giggled again. Okay, maybe she was getting a little carried away.

"Kelly, do you have the Redmond file?"

"It's right here, Brandon." She managed to refrain from calling him *Obi-Wan,* then stifled another giggle.

"What's the smile for?" Brandon asked genially.

"I'm just in a good mood," she said. "Coffee'll be ready in a few minutes."

"Thanks," he said, and strolled into his office, closing the door behind him.

She knew Brandon had a conference call starting momentarily that would last an hour or more. She planned to use that time to check on Roger's conference agenda. He and the employees of his small, high-powered hedge-fund company would arrive on Monday. They had reserved two mid-sized conference rooms each day as well as one of the small banquet rooms each evening for dinners and a special event or two. But Kelly remembered that the schedule showed that Thursday night was a free night, during which the attendees could dine at their choice of any one of Napa's world-class restaurants or go off to sample wines at any number of local wineries.

Kelly planned to lure Roger to her room Thursday night, get him all hot and bothered, then kick him out. That would teach him a thing or two. And Kelly looked forward to being the one to teach him. In fact, she was eager for the chance to show her ex-boyfriend a few of the incredible moves Brandon had showed her. She already felt more sure of herself and more sure of her sensuality and attractiveness, thanks to Brandon. Ever since yesterday morning when he got all tongue-tied while gawking at her and her new look, she'd felt her confidence soar. She really appreciated that his gawking turned out to be good in all the right ways.

The telephone rang, startling her. She grabbed the receiver quickly so the ringing wouldn't disturb Brandon's conference call. "Mr. Duke's office, Kelly Meredith speaking."

"It's Bianca Stephens," a breathless voice said. "Let me speak with Brandon immediately."

"I'm sorry, Ms. Stephens, Brandon is on a conference call and can't be disturbed."

The woman gasped. "What? Well, interrupt him. Tell him I'm waiting. I know he'll want to talk to me."

"I'm sure you're right," Kelly said, trying not to roll her eyes, "but he's on a long-distance call with several business clients and his partners. I'll have to take a message and have him get back to you."

"Kathy, do you know who I am?"

"Yes, I do, Ms. Stephens, and it's Kelly."

"Whatever," she said. "Look, just slip a note under his nose. I know he'll take my call."

"Except he gave me instructions not to interrupt him, and since he signs my paycheck, I generally do as he asks. I'm terribly sorry, but I will give him your message."

"What did you say your name was?"

"Kelly," she said distinctly. "Kelly Meredith."

"Well, Kelly," Bianca said with a tone that implied that she was talking down to a particularly stupid first grader. "I'll be sure to tell Brandon how uncooperative you have been."

"Yes, ma'am. And I'll be sure to give him your message."

"You'd better," she said imperiously. "He won't be happy to find out he missed my call."

"I'm sure that's true," Kelly said. "I—"

But the line was already dead.

Shaken, Kelly stared at the phone. "Gosh, I hope I don't forget to give him that message."

After hanging up the phone, she had to get up and walk around the office. She stretched her arms and rolled her neck around, just to get rid of some of the anger she was feeling. Of course she knew who Bianca Stephens was. She was the daughter of a former secretary of defense who hosted a national morning talk show. She was model-thin and Playmate gorgeous, and she was probably really smart, too. Damn her.

Walking into the kitchenette to pour a soda, Kelly gave herself a stern lecture. She understood that there had always been women like Bianca Stephens in Brandon's life and there always would be. They were supermodels, heiresses, actresses and designers. Some were nice and some were awful, like Bianca Stephens. It didn't matter to Brandon. He dated them because they looked good on his arm and probably in his bed, although she didn't want to dwell too closely on that possibility. The plain fact was that Kelly was disappointed by the fact that Brandon would ever want to be with anyone as rude as Bianca Stephens.

Kelly took a moment to thank her lucky stars that she wasn't so emotionally involved with Brandon that she cared one way or the other, but she had to admit it was upsetting to be treated as though she were nothing but the hired help.

That thought stopped Kelly in her tracks. She took a few deep breaths, shook her hair back, did some more shoulder rolls, then headed for her desk feeling cranky and restless.

"Not to put too fine a point on it," she muttered as she sat in her chair. "But *hired help* is exactly what you are."

Fine. Didn't mean she had to dwell on it. She grabbed her knifelike letter opener and pulled out another short stack of mail. Being the hired help wasn't the issue, she insisted to herself. It was having to deal with rude people like Bianca who looked down her nose at someone like Kelly just because she was hired to answer the phone. The fact was, Bianca thought she was better than everyone else, not just Kelly.

But that wasn't the real problem, Kelly realized as she slashed open another letter. She'd fielded these sorts of phone calls from petulant women in the past and she'd always let them roll off her back. So what was different about Bianca's call?

"You wouldn't care so much if you hadn't slept with him," she whispered aloud as she tossed several letters into a file for Brandon's review. With a frown, she ripped open a small parcel and tried to deny the words.

Was that why she was so upset? Did she suddenly care too much for Brandon? She didn't think so. She *cared* for him, of course, but she certainly didn't, well, *love* him, God forbid. There was no way she would ever let that happen. Not only had they talked about it and she'd assured him that she'd never fall for him, but also, she knew better!

But, thinking about it now, she was willing to admit to feeling a little sensitive. After all, they had spent last night doing the most intimate things a man and a woman could do together. So of course she was a bit distressed. Who wouldn't be? But she'd snap out of it, quick. Because if she didn't, she'd wind up with black and blue marks from kicking herself in the behind. No way would she ever allow herself to be that much of a twit.

The telephone rang and she jumped. "Now what?"

Hoping it wasn't Bianca calling back, she grabbed it and answered in her most officious voice.

"Hello, Kelly dear. It's Sally Duke."

"Oh, Mrs. Duke, hello," Kelly said, and relaxed. Brandon's mother was always so lovely and kind. "How are you?"

"Fine, sweetie. I'm looking forward to seeing you this weekend."

"I'm looking forward to seeing you, too." She opened one of the folders on her desk. "I've got your itinerary right here and I see you'll be arriving around two o'clock Friday afternoon. The limousine will be waiting for you at the airport. Did Brandon make dinner reservations for you?"

"I hope so. Would you mind checking for me?"

"Not at all. I don't see anything noted in the file, but I'll ask Brandon as soon as he's off his conference call. We'll make sure you're taken care of."

"I know you will and I must admit I'm excited," Sally

said. "There are hundreds of fabulous restaurants in Napa I'd love to try."

"Oh, me, too."

Sally paused, then said, "Kelly, dear, is something wrong? You don't sound like yourself."

It was not a good thing when the boss's mother could tell you were in a blue mood.

"No, I'm fine," Kelly insisted. "Or I will be. I just had to deal with something unpleasant."

"Something or someone?"

Kelly sighed, knowing she'd already said too much. "Really, it's nothing I can't handle."

"Ah," Sally said. "Some*one.*"

Kelly laughed ruefully. "You're good at that."

"I raised three boys. I've learned to read nuance."

Kelly laughed again as her mind raced to change the subject. It wouldn't do to involve Mrs. Duke in her problems. "I see Brandon's taking you and your friends on a private tour of the winery on Saturday. That'll be fun."

"Oh, we'll have a ball," Sally said jovially. "Now Kelly, we're having a family dinner Saturday night at the hotel restaurant. Adam and Cameron and their wives will be there and it would be wonderful if you could join us. That is, if you're free. You always do so much for all of us. We feel like you're a member of the family."

Sudden tears sprang to her eyes and Kelly quickly brushed them away. Her own mother had died when she was twelve and she still missed her every day. Her father was very much alive, but he lived back in Vermont near her two sisters and their families. She missed them, too, but she could always pick up the phone and say hello. She couldn't do that with her mom.

"As far as I know, I'm free," she said. "And I would love to join you, Mrs. Duke. Thank you so much for asking me." She had the sudden thought that Brandon might bring a date to the dinner, but told herself it didn't matter. The invitation had come from his mother.

"Wonderful," Sally exclaimed. "Oh, by the way, how was your trip to the spa? Did they do everything they promised?"

"It was amazing," Kelly said. "Thank you so much for recommending it."

"I had a fabulous time when I was there last year," Sally said. "So when you mentioned you wanted a bit of a makeover, I thought it would be the perfect place for you."

"It was."

"I'm so glad. I can't wait to see all the fun changes in you."

They hung up from the call, and Kelly spent the rest of the morning answering emails and scheduling conference calls for future projects. She almost wished she wasn't so organized because she could've used a few more hours concentrating on something other than her thoughts. Anything would be preferable to being completely distracted by memories of Brandon and everything they'd done together the night before and early this morning. It was impossible to think straight when she remembered the way he'd touched her, the way his body had quickened inside her, the way his breath had lingered hot on her skin. She thought of the words he'd used, the pleasure he'd shown her, the urgency of their needs, and almost moaned out loud.

"Oh, God." She gulped in air and grabbed her soda to soothe her parched throat. She needed to concentrate on her job, but it wasn't working. She continued to daydream about the way he made her feel, the places he'd touched her, the words he'd whispered in her ear, the heights he'd driven her to.

She stared at the red light on the phone. Thank goodness Brandon was still on the conference call because if he were to walk out and take one look at her, he would know what she'd been thinking. And if he knew she was obsessing over their lovemaking, he would probably accuse her of falling for him. But nothing could be further from the truth. There was no way she would ever fall for Brandon Duke. She'd never been that big of a fool.

Forcing herself to concentrate on work, she got a lot done in the next hour. Still, every few minutes or so, she caught herself imagining his arms around her. The man had a gift, that was for sure.

She spent part of her lunch hour at her desk, eating a sandwich and paying some bills. Brandon left for a meeting outside of the office, so after lunch, Kelly placed all his messages—including Bianca's—on his desk and took the opportunity to go for a short walk along the brick path that skirted the vineyards. It was a beautiful fall day and the leaves on the vines were every shade of orange, red and burnt sienna. She waved to a few of the winery staff who stood a few rows away, testing the vines for ripeness.

She glanced up at the six floors of terraced balcony suites that graced the hillside, with their French doors and elegant patio furniture, then looked over at the many sophisticated, private two-bedroom *maisons* that swept across the length of the hill. She couldn't help but feel a glow of pride whenever she thought of the small but important role she'd played in the development of the luxurious Mansion at Silverado Trail.

With its ivy-covered stucco walls and Mediterranean style, the resort was a first-class mix of old-world charm and modern elegance. The restaurant had already earned a rare three stars from an international travel guide. No wonder she was so justifiably proud of the company she worked for.

In three days, the first guests would arrive, anxious to take part in the grand opening weekend that included full participation in the grape harvest and autumn festival that followed. There would be lovely dinners and wine tastings and a gala celebration Saturday night.

Kelly had worked on the opening events for months. She considered the project her baby. She had sweated out every last detail, down to the color of the ribbon for the cutting ceremony in the lobby that would take place Friday afternoon when the first guests checked in.

But since the project had started, several major changes had occurred in her life. She needed to be at the top of her game in order to focus her energies on the week ahead. First, she hadn't counted on ever having to see Roger again. Now, within days, he would be here and her plan would swing into action.

But a more important change was her involvement with Brandon. Never in her wildest dreams had she imagined she'd be caught up in a lovely affair with Brandon Duke. It was a major distraction and she knew she would require every last ounce of brainpower, discretion and good judgment in her arsenal to make it through the week working so closely with him. Not only that, but she would have to be especially careful that the hotel staff and Brandon's family never suspected a thing.

She was certain it wouldn't be a problem. They'd already decided to end their affair once Brandon's family arrived. And, then she'd have Roger to deal with.

But for the moment, she just breathed in the crisp air and looked around at the welcome signs of autumn. Growing up in Vermont, she'd always been able to recognize the telltale signs of each new season. But here in California, where the hillsides seemed a permanent shade of green and the weather was distressingly mild even in winter, the hints were much more subtle: the dappled hue of the falling leaves, a trace of mesquite in the air, the delicate play of shadows and light on the mountains at sunset.

She loved it here in Napa, but she had to admit she'd be happy to return home to Dunsmuir Bay in a few weeks. She had a charming duplex apartment with a view of the bay and a number of good friends she would be glad to see again. And of course she loved her job and her spacious office at Duke headquarters.

Once she was home, she would be long finished with the Roger Project. She planned to start dating again as soon as possible and would have no reason to ever sleep with Brandon again. Especially since she had no intention of jeopardizing her position at Duke Development, it was absolutely imperative that she go back to being the practical, professional, well-organized assistant Brandon deserved.

And that meant no more sex with Brandon, ever again.

She would use those words as a mantra because within a few days, they would become reality. *No more sex with Brandon,* she repeated and emphasized the words with a firm nod of her head as she turned and walked back to the office.

# Five

The lunch meeting took longer than Brandon had expected and now he wasn't looking forward to playing catch-up. He stalked down the hall toward his suite of offices and braced himself for the onslaught of urgent messages he knew Kelly would hand him as soon as he walked in. He had half a mind to toss every last message in the trash, grab Kelly and go for a drive into the hills where they could hide out for the rest of the day.

He chuckled, figuring he was lucky he still had that half of his mind left, considering the things he and Kelly had done the night before. An erotic image of her gorgeous, naked body spread across the bed flashed in his mind and he gritted his teeth to keep from embarrassing himself in the middle of the hotel. Damn. If that wasn't enough to make him crazed, the fact that he planned to stay with her again tonight was almost enough to drive him the rest of the way to madness. But what a way to go.

Back in his office, he sorted through his message slips, crumpling one from Bianca, a woman he dated once in a while, and tossing it into the trash can. One thing he didn't need right now was another distraction.

He forced himself to concentrate on work, but stimulating thoughts of Kelly kept circling his mind whenever his vigilance slipped. He needed to keep his mind on business. And there was plenty of business to think about.

His brothers would arrive Thursday, two days from now, and things would really start cooking. No doubt, there would be several last-minute meetings, emergency conference calls, inspections and tests of various departments before the festivities began Friday. His mother and her friends would be arriving then, along with the first official guests of the Mansion.

The guest list included numerous wealthy wine lovers, a reviewer from a prestigious travel magazine, several old friends of the Duke brothers and a well-heeled state official they'd done business with. And, lest he forgot, Kelly's idiot ex-boyfriend. Roger and company wouldn't arrive until Monday, but that was still too soon as far as he was concerned.

Part of him still couldn't believe he'd succumbed to Kelly's pleas for help in luring the jerk back. Not that he minded helping her, he thought, his blood pumping faster as he once again pictured her beneath him. No, he didn't mind that at all. But if she truly had the intention of taking Roger to bed, Brandon wouldn't hesitate to obstruct her at every turn.

Hell. Brandon knew if he was smart, he would cancel his plans for Kelly tonight and call last night's passionate activities a one-time-only deal. He knew they were playing with fire and shouldn't continue sleeping with each other.

And he knew he should be the one to call it quits, right now, before they got involved any further. Kelly would understand. They'd already had that discussion.

But every time he thought about cutting her loose, he changed his mind. He couldn't bring himself to do it. He just wanted her too damn much. He also knew those feelings would subside. They always did. He made sure of it. And when that happened, Kelly and he would go back to being companionable working partners and bring the sexual side of their relationship to a civil, friendly end. No mess, no fuss.

Their affair was a strictly temporary arrangement and they were both consenting adults. Once this whole ugly Roger situation passed, Brandon and Kelly would settle down and get back to work and everything would be fine. Fine as wine. No problem.

The following evening, Brandon coaxed Kelly to come to dinner with him at a charming trattoria in downtown Napa. They dressed casually, both glad to escape from the hotel for a few hours. They spent the meal having a good time, chatting about business and family matters. Kelly told Brandon about her sisters and their families and Brandon mentioned his mother's new project to track down her deceased husband's brother.

"Sally's husband, William Duke, had a brother, Tom," Brandon explained as they shared an antipasto platter. "When their parents died, the boys were sent to an orphanage in San Francisco."

Kelly nodded as she filled her small plate with a delicious mixture of baby artichokes, roasted peppers and grilled zucchini. "Sally told me her husband was the reason she wanted to adopt you three boys."

"That's right. Bill's dream was to symbolically give

back to other kids he'd met in the system by adopting children of his own, but he passed away before he could do it."

"It was good of Sally to carry out his dream."

Brandon grinned as he sipped his wine. "I thank my lucky stars every day that she did."

"Has she had any luck finding Bill's brother?"

"Not yet. Apparently the orphanage was a pretty grim place and the boys ran away a few times. Bill told Sally that he was finally adopted, but his brother was still stuck there. Years later, when he was old enough to conduct a search, he found that the orphanage had burned to the ground and all the records were destroyed."

"Oh, that's terrible. Does Sally know if Bill's brother survived?"

"Yeah, Tom would've turned eighteen by the time the fire happened, so he'd be out on his own. But Bill tried to track him down and couldn't find him. His best hope was that Tom was adopted and his adoptive parents changed his name."

"I hope so," Kelly said. "That place sounds awful."

"Yeah. Anyway, Sally's got her work cut out for her."

Kelly reached for an olive. "Please tell her I'll be glad to help if she needs someone to do research. You know I love a challenge."

He smiled at her. "Thanks, Kelly, I appreciate that. I'll let her know."

"That was fun," Kelly said as they strolled back to her hotel room. "And the pasta was delicious. I'm so full."

"Yeah, me too," Brandon said. "I'm glad we could get away for a while. We won't have much of a chance to leave from here on out."

"I know." Kelly stared up at the cloudless night sky.

Countless stars stretched from one horizon to the other and the full moon lit the way along the terrace path.

"It's a beautiful evening," she said.

"Still warm out," Brandon remarked. "It's a perfect night for a swim."

She raised her eyebrows. "I'm not sure it's that warm."

"It is for what I have in mind," he said, grabbing hold of her hand. "Come with me."

Puzzled but willing, Kelly allowed him to change direction and he led her to the owner's *maison* where he was staying. The sleekly comfortable bungalow had been built into the hillside beyond the main building. It was large, with two bedrooms and a vaulted ceiling and a fireplace in the living room. Shuttered French doors opened on to a cozy patio.

Brandon led her through the doors to a lovely space surrounded by a wall of shrubs and flowers and weeping olive trees. A rustic flagstone patio encircled a small hot tub built for two.

Kelly glanced around, intrigued. The thick, lush vegetation grew high around the patio and assured her that they had complete privacy out here.

"It's beautiful," she said, gazing at Brandon.

"I think so." He pressed a button on the wall by the doorway and Kelly watched, smiling, as bubbles began to rise in the water.

Then Brandon reached for Kelly's jacket, slipped it off, folded it and laid it on the chaise. Kelly did the same for him, and together they made quick work of removing their clothes before stepping into the warm bubbling water.

"Oh, it's heaven," she said, and slid down until the water covered her shoulders.

Brandon followed her into the spa and sat on the step, then pulled her onto his lap, facing him.

"Yes, this is definitely heaven." Touching her cheeks with both hands, he leaned forward and kissed her. As his lips touched hers, Kelly's mind emptied of all thought and everything within her focused on this one man and his thrilling touch.

He took his time with her, working his magic, kissing her, touching her, his tongue gently stroking hers. She floated on a sea of pleasure, weightless in his arms.

He cupped her breasts in his hands and bent his head to taste one, then the other. "You're so beautiful."

"Brandon," she whispered.

"I want to make love with you."

"Yes," she said.

He stood up in the water with her in his arms and she wrapped her legs around his waist. He eased her down onto his length and she drew him in so deeply, so fully, she wondered if she would ever feel this complete again. Then he grabbed hold of her bottom and squeezed gently, causing a jolt of rapture to rush through her. She cried out her pleasure as he moved inside her, stroking her faster and harder, plunging deeper, then deeper still. She moved with him as pure sensation pulsated and radiated from her center outward, stirring every part of her body and soul.

She ran her hands over the taut, rippling muscles of his back, relishing his strength as his powerful hips thrust into her, urging her toward completion. She felt her body melt into his and with a guttural groan of release, he let himself join her, flying headlong into an abyss of pure ecstasy.

The next day, Kelly finally began to see that there were flaws in her Roger Plan. As the days had passed and the weekend loomed, her original plot to seek revenge against Roger was becoming less and less important to her. That was fine, of course; she really needed to get over Roger once and for all.

But now she couldn't quite recall the hurt and emptiness anymore. The truth was, in the last few days, whenever she searched her mind, heart and soul for traces of the sadness she'd felt since Roger broke up with her, she couldn't find any painful remnants. That was truly amazing, and she knew she had Brandon to thank for her new acceptance. He'd helped her see that Roger had been wrong; she was perfectly capable of attracting a man. She wasn't lousy in bed. On the contrary, she thought with a happy smile, she was pretty darn good in bed. And she was a good kisser, too. Brandon didn't seem to have any complaints, and he would know, wouldn't he?

But now, since Brandon was in her bed every night, he was also beginning to show up in her daydreams during office hours. If she wasn't ruthlessly diligent, she would find herself sighing like a teenager whenever he walked by her desk.

She'd managed to cover up her reaction the few times it had happened, going so far as to fake a coughing fit one time, then making a quick reference to a missing invoice another time. She needed to get a grip. Not just for Brandon, but for herself.

For goodness sake, where was that practical-minded girl who wouldn't be caught dead giggling or mooning over anyone, *especially* her boss? The last thing she wanted was for him to see her pining over him!

She would drive herself crazy if she didn't nip these feelings in the bud right now. They had ground rules, had she forgotten? She was absolutely forbidden to fall for Brandon Duke. Not only would it never work out, but she'd wind up losing the job she loved.

Any time she caught herself wondering, hoping, or

wishing that she and Brandon could be together for real, all she had to do was log on to his personal address list and count the number of women he'd so nicely dumped over the past year or two, with nothing but a lovely parting gift to remember him by. Kelly should know; she'd been the one to purchase and send out most of those lovely gifts on his behalf.

It didn't help her cause that Brandon had come to her room every night this week and stayed until morning. He would always leave well before Housekeeping came on duty, knowing it wouldn't be appropriate for the rest of the staff to know they were sleeping together. He was an amazing lover, and every night they laughed and talked and…played. And recently, during the day, he had taken to piercing her with long, intense looks that could easily drive her to sin.

What was a girl to do?

She gave herself a mental shake and told herself to get back to work. There was plenty to get done today and it was about time she concentrated on earning her paycheck.

"It is dreck!" head chef Jean Pierre exclaimed, his lips curved in revulsion.

"Are you insane? It's the finest Montepulciano produced in Tuscany in fifty years," Antonio Stellini, the wine steward, countered.

"Italian," Jean Pierre muttered in disdain. "It figures, no?"

"What's that supposed to mean, you French fruitcake?"

Jean Pierre turned on Brandon. "*Qu'est-ce que c'est* fruitcake?"

It was Thursday morning and Brandon had spent the last hour running interference between his autocratic head chef, Jean Pierre, and Antonio, the brilliant sommelier he'd recently hired. The two were in a power struggle over the choice of wine pairings for Saturday night's special tasting menu. Brandon walked out of the meeting feeling a special kinship to King Solomon for effectively negotiating a reasonable solution to an impossible problem. Of course, they'd now added three new premium wines to the elaborate menu, that would have to be reprinted immediately.

Later that afternoon, Cameron and Adam and their wives arrived. Brandon had arranged for each couple to stay in their own private *maison* complete with fireplace, private spa patio and stunning views of the valley. Trish and Julia were able to indulge in soothing massages and facials while he and his brothers held meetings with their key managers.

That night, Brandon hosted dinner for his brothers and their wives in the hotel dining room. He'd tried to convince Kelly to join them, but she'd demurred, saying she had some personal matters to attend to. He couldn't tell if she was telling the truth, but he'd finally let it go. Then, throughout the superb meal, he struggled to avoid thinking about her and the fact that he missed her.

As the main dishes were cleared away and dessert orders were taken, Adam's wife, Trish, turned to Brandon. "I wish Kelly could've joined us. You're not making her work late, are you?"

"No way," Brandon said. "I invited her, but she said she had some personal stuff to take care of."

Cameron shrugged. "Can't blame her. After all, who really wants to have dinner with their boss?"

Brandon said nothing as he made a point of keeping a vigilant watch on the wait staff.

"She looks wonderful," Julia said after finishing the last sip of her wine. "What did she do to herself?"

Baffled, Brandon shook his head. "Some kind of makeover. Not sure why. Who can figure these things out?"

Trish laughed. "Women love to get themselves made over. It's fun."

Brandon shot her a skeptical look. "If you say so. I've got to tell you, though. I love women, but I'll never understand what makes them tick."

Adam chuckled. "Whereas, we men are an open book."

"Exactly," Brandon said, jabbing the air with his finger. "No games. No subterfuge. No *makeovers*." He used air quotes to emphasize the last word.

With a laugh, Julia turned to Trish. "Kelly went to Orchids, didn't she?"

"That's right," Trish said. "It's supposed to be fabulous. Didn't Sally go there last year? I think I remember her raving about the seaweed massage one day when we were sitting around her pool."

"Wait, Mom went to a spa?" Brandon asked, incredulous.

"Yes," Trish said easily. "Just last summer, with Bea and Marjorie."

Brandon felt a chill cross his shoulders. "To the same place Kelly went to?"

"I think so. You should ask her."

Brandon watched as Adam's wife rubbed her ever-expanding stomach. He thought of the eight-month-old baby waiting inside there, all set to emerge and be spoiled silly by its aunts and uncles and one doting grandmother.

"God," Trish said, "I would love to spend an entire weekend getting pampered and rubbed and polished and primped."

"Sounds like heaven," Julia agreed with a happy sigh.

Brandon had worked in hotels and resorts long enough to recognize the allure of an elegant spa for female guests.

And hell, after having spent ten years in the NFL, he could readily admit to the restorative benefits of being pummeled by a physical therapist. He even enjoyed relaxing in a hot tub once in a while. But that had little to do with therapy, he thought, as the vivid memory of a naked Kelly in his own spa almost made him double over.

He gritted his teeth and continued to listen to his sisters-in-law wax poetic over this fabulous spa his mother had recommended to Kelly. They made it sound like some magical realm where dreams came true. His eyes narrowed. "What was the big deal about that place?"

"Oh, there's every type of wonderful massage, of course," Julia said. "You feature several of them here, along with your mud baths and yoga classes. But this place Sally found is designed for women only, and even though they offer more rigorous activities like hiking and horseback riding, they also concentrate on every aspect of a woman's body and mind. You're pampered from the minute you walk into the lobby. But that's not the best part."

Brandon exchanged glances with his brothers, who both looked clueless. "Go on."

"It offers total makeovers," Trish explained. "They do hairstyling and give makeup tips and even offer clothing advice, with suggestions for colors and shapes that will better suit one's body type and season palette."

"Season palette?" Brandon said. It was like they were speaking in a foreign language.

"Oh, and don't forget the meals," Julia added. "They serve these artfully designed portions that look beautiful on the plate but contain maybe fifty calories total."

"That's why I wouldn't last more than one weekend," Trish said, laughing.

"You and me both," Julia said.

Brandon had heard enough. Why hadn't he known that his own mother had been giving Kelly advice on this makeover nonsense? Of course, now that he was aware of the reality of the situation, he had to admit he shouldn't have been completely surprised that his mother had taken Kelly on as her latest matchmaking project.

Didn't it just figure? Sally had made no secret of the fact that she wanted all three of her sons married with children, and she'd accomplished two-thirds of her goal. Now there was just Brandon left to fall.

He knew his mother, knew how sneaky she could be, so he'd been hypervigilant for months now. But Kelly had no idea about Sally's nefarious plotting and had innocently played along with her to such an extent that she'd actually taken two weeks of vacation to the very place his mother had recommended.

Kelly had returned from her holiday a completely new woman. And, lo and behold, her return to the office had signaled the beginning of an affair that he—against his better judgment—didn't want to end.

Brandon scowled. If his mother thought Kelly could lure him to the altar with a change of hairstyle and a few wardrobe modifications, she was sadly mistaken.

And how much did Kelly really know about his mother's desire to marry him off? Frankly, he hesitated to lay any blame at Kelly's feet. This situation had Sally's fingerprints all over it. And, yes, Kelly had told him that the makeover was all about getting Roger back. But had she been telling him the truth?

"I don't like that look at all," Adam said, studying him carefully.

Brandon picked up his wineglass and swirled it thoughtfully. "Tough."

"What's going on in that bizarre head of yours?"

Cameron said. "You look like you're about ready to chew on some nails."

"I'm about ready to chew on something," he muttered.

There was a knock on her door and Kelly's stomach tingled. She couldn't help it. She'd spent a quiet evening catching up on reading and watching television, secure in the knowledge that now that his family was on the scene, Brandon would no longer be spending his nights with her. She'd accepted it and insisted to herself that the only emotion she felt was gratitude. She would be grateful for the rest of her life for the past few wonderful nights with Brandon.

But now he was here and she was bubbling with happiness. That was absurd. Okay, yes, she liked him and all, but she really needed to calm down. It wouldn't do to behave like a giddy schoolgirl every time she saw him. Besides, he probably just wanted to assure her once and for all that they would no longer be spending their nights together. She was okay with that.

She took a few quick, deep breaths and forced herself to walk calmly to the door instead of racing like the wind to greet him.

"Brandon," she said. "I didn't think I'd see you tonight."

"I need to ask you something," he said as he walked in, immediately filling the room with his masculine presence and his faint but intoxicating scent of leather and spice.

"Of course, anything," she said. "Did you enjoy your dinner?"

"What? Oh, yeah. Dinner was fantastic. Jean Pierre outdid himself."

"I'm so glad. It was nice to see Trish and Julia again. They both look so beautiful, and your brothers look so happy."

"Yeah. Nice. Beautiful. Happy."

"Is something wrong?"

He stared at her and frowned. "You're beautiful, too."

"Thank you, I think."

"No, you are," he assured her, studying her features. "You always were, but I guess I didn't realize it before. But you are beautiful, Kelly."

"Brandon, what's wrong? What happened tonight?"

"Nothing." He paced a few steps, then returned to stand directly in front of her. "Let me ask you something. Did my mother suggest that you get a makeover?"

"Your mother? Heavens, no."

"She didn't give you the idea?"

"No." It was Kelly's turn to frown. "Why?"

"Didn't you go to the same place where she went a year or so ago?"

"Well, yes, I did." She led him over to the kitchen area and grabbed her water glass. After taking a long sip, she said, "Your mother only recommended Orchids after I told her I was interested in finding a spa where I could…" She stopped and glanced up at Brandon's expression. "Brandon, what's this all about?"

He stared at her for a moment before looking away. He stalked slowly in one direction, then another, like a caged animal, then stopped and met her gaze again. "You're sure my mother didn't suggest that you needed to get a makeover?"

Kelly blinked. "My goodness, Brandon. Your mother is the sweetest woman in the world. She would never say anything like that to me."

"You're sure?"

"Of course I'm sure. She simply recommended a place after I asked her for suggestions."

His eyes continued to focus on her, then he nodded briefly. "Okay, good."

"I'm surprised you would think so poorly of your mother."

"Whoa." He held up his hand to stop her. "Believe me, I love my mother and don't think poorly of her at all. It's just that she's been known to manipulate a situation or two, and I was just concerned that she might've given you some unsolicited advice."

"Well, please don't be concerned on my account. I simply mentioned my interest in, you know, making a few changes to my hair and…well, other things, and your mother gave me the name of the spa she'd visited. I took it from there."

He seemed satisfied with her explanation. "Okay, I'm glad to hear it."

She shook her head, realizing he was in a mood and she wouldn't get much more of an explanation from him. "Would you like a glass of wine or something?"

"Yeah, something. Come here." With that, he reached out to her with both hands, pulled her against him and wrapped his arms tightly around her. He stroked her back slowly, spreading tendrils of heat up and down her spine.

She rested her cheek against his shoulder. "But we weren't going to do this anymore, remember?"

"Yeah, I thought so, too," he muttered, glancing down at her. "But I changed my mind. Just this once. That okay with you?"

"Oh, yes, more than okay," she murmured, feeling at home in his well-muscled, broad-shouldered embrace. "This is nice."

"Yeah, it is," he said. After a moment, he added, "I missed you at dinner."

"Oh, Brandon," she said, blinking rapidly so he wouldn't

notice the sudden sheen of tears in her eyes brought on by his sweet words. "I didn't want to interfere in the time spent with your family."

"You wouldn't be interfering." He touched her chin and angled her face so that he was gazing into her eyes. "My family's great, but it would've been more fun if you'd been there."

Feeling ridiculously pleased, she smiled up at him. "Well, we're together now, so let's make the best of it."

"Babe," he said with a grin as he led her toward the king-size bed. "I thought you'd never ask."

Early the following morning, both Brandon and Kelly hit the ground running. The first guests began arriving at noon, excited to be a part of the highly anticipated grand opening.

The official ceremony was performed and executed with precision, flair and happy celebration. Brandon's knowledgeable sommelier stood by to pour champagne for everyone as they checked in. Wine tasting tours were recommended, hot air balloon reservations were taken and guests were whisked away to their rooms without a snag. As Brandon watched things unfold, he felt a whole new sense of pride in his employees, each of whom was in outstanding form today. So outstanding that Brandon was beginning to feel almost redundant. Strangely enough, it was a great feeling.

What added to the good vibe was the news his reservations manager had shared with him. The resort was already completely booked for the entire season. Brandon knew the Mansion would soon be recognized as the hottest destination spot in Napa Valley. And he was confident that he'd be able to walk away in a few weeks, leaving the duties of running the small, luxurious hotel to the experienced service experts he'd hired.

It was early afternoon when his mother and her two girlfriends finally arrived. Brandon met their limousine outside in the elegant *porte cochère* and ushered them into the lobby.

"Oh, it's beautiful, Brandon," Sally said as she and her friends gazed around in awe. They were all dressed in light, casual clothing and looked ready to vacation in style.

"I love the colors," Marjorie said.

He'd known his mother's two best friends, Beatrice and Marjorie, for well over twenty years. They were like favorite aunts, and Marjorie was also one of his employees. She'd headed Duke Development's human resources department for years. Now as the women strolled around the well-designed lobby, Brandon tried to see the spacious room through their eyes and concluded, not for the first time, that he was justifiably proud of what he'd accomplished here.

Brandon had been in charge of the Mansion on Silverado Trail project from day one and every decision had been his, including the design and overall concept of the place. All the rooms featured the best of California style blended, as their sales brochure stated, "with Tuscan flourishes and Provençal sensibilities."

The guest rooms were light and warm with rounded, Old World-style fireplaces and cozy hearths, terra-cotta tile floors, elegantly rustic furnishings and bold tapestries on the pale stucco walls. At one end of the wide lobby, French doors opened on to a wide terrace where colorful umbrellas shaded teak patio furniture and plush cushions. A stunning view of the vast acres of vineyards and olive groves that spread across the valley completed the picture.

"I can't wait to take the 'vine to barrel' tour," Beatrice exclaimed. "Do we get to taste the grapes as we pick them?"

"Wouldn't you rather taste the final product?" Sally asked her.

Beatrice grinned. "That, too."

"You can do it all," Brandon said. "Let's get you and your luggage settled and then you can take your pick of afternoon activities."

"I'm definitely up for wine tasting," Sally said.

"Oh, me, too," Marjorie agreed and Beatrice nodded enthusiastically.

Brandon grinned. "Then I'll show you to your suite so you can get started."

"I want to stay here forever," Marjorie cried as she turned in a circle to take in every inch of the cleverly designed and furnished two-bedroom *maison*. "All this and champagne on ice? Brandon, it's so beautiful. I'm so proud of you, and you must be proud of yourself, too."

"I'm feeling pretty good," he admitted with a chuckle. "It's nice, isn't it?"

"Nice?" Beatrice said as she opened the glass doors that led out to their private balcony. "It's glorious."

"I'm glad you think so." After showing them the button that would automatically light up the fireplace, then pointing out the secluded walkway that led to the spa facilities, Brandon headed for the door. "I'll leave you to unpack and relax. If you need anything, including me, just dial the front desk and ask."

Sally rushed over and wrapped her arms around him in a hug. "Thank you, Brandon. This is wonderful."

"You're welcome, Mom. I just want you all to relax,

pour yourselves a glass of champagne and have a great time."

His mother laughed. "Believe me, sweetie, that's exactly what we had in mind."

Two hours later, Brandon had finished up a short meeting with his brothers and the restaurant staff. Adam was on his way back to his room to check on Trish, who'd been taking a nap, while Cameron and Julia had decided to pour themselves glasses of wine and stroll through the vineyards to enjoy the sunset.

Brandon headed back to his office, but as he crossed the lobby, he spied Marjorie and Bea in the gift shop located next to the wine bar on the opposite side of the lobby from the front desk. Marjorie clutched a box of expensive chocolates and Bea held a bottle of good red wine and they were deep in conversation with the clerk. He grinned as he imagined them discussing the best wine to drink with chocolate. Glancing around, he looked for his mother, but she wasn't in the shop. A movement caught his eye and he glanced out at the terrace where Sally stood talking animatedly with Kelly.

For a brief moment, he stopped and simply enjoyed the sight of Kelly's short skirt wafting in the soft breeze and let his mind wander to what she might be wearing underneath. Another thong, he hoped, allowing himself to imagine the feel of featherlight lace against her silky—

He snapped back to reality. That was *his mother* talking to Kelly. And knowing his mother and what she was capable of in the name of matchmaking, Brandon's mood shifted immediately into suspicion. His mother and Kelly chatting? This couldn't be a good thing, so he strolled outside to put a stop to whatever mischief Sally Duke was up to.

"Hello, Mother," he said.

Sally whipped around. "Oh! Brandon, dear, you snuck up on me."

That was exactly what he'd meant to do, but he wasn't about to say so. "What were you two talking about?"

"I was just telling Kelly how marvelous she looks," Sally said. "Don't you agree?"

"Yeah, she looks great," Brandon said warily. "So what?"

Sally gave him a perplexed look. "Are you feeling all right, sweetie?"

"He's probably wondering what I'm doing away from the office," Kelly said lightly. "Which means I'd better get going. It was lovely to see you again, Mrs. Duke."

"You, too, Kelly." Sally gave her a quick hug. "I'll see you tomorrow night, if not sooner."

"I'm looking forward to it," Kelly said, then rushed through the lobby toward their offices.

"What's tomorrow night?" Brandon asked cautiously.

"Kelly's joining us for dinner."

His eyes narrowed. "Mom, what are you doing?"

"I'm not sure what you mean," she said, straightening her shoulders and meeting his gaze head-on. "Kelly does so much for all of us, I thought it would be a nice gesture to include her. My goodness, I haven't booked my own travel in over a year, thanks to her, and she helped me track down that fabulous imported baby gym for little Jake's birthday. And that's just the tip of the iceberg. She works wonders, but all that is beside the point. Kelly is simply a delightful woman and I've come to think of her as a member of our extended family. So I invited her to dinner. Frankly, I'm surprised you didn't invite her yourself."

If she only knew, Brandon thought. "Look, Mom,

Kelly's great, but that doesn't mean I want you playing matchmaker between me and her."

"Matchmaker?" She looked truly mystified, but Brandon knew for a fact that his mother was an excellent actress when she wanted to be.

He rolled his eyes at her attempt to play dumb. "You can deny it all you want, but I know you've been trying to get all of us guys married off." He folded his arms across his chest to show her he meant business. "You might've succeeded with Adam and Cameron, but you won't with me. There's no way you'll ever get me to propose to Kelly, so you might as well give up right now."

"Propose?" She blinked. "To Kelly?" She stared at him in shock for a few more seconds, then began to laugh. And she kept laughing until she was doubled over. Finally, she thumped her chest as she tried to catch her breath. "Oh, my goodness, I haven't laughed like that in years."

"And I'm sure you were laughing *with* me."

She choked on another laugh. "Of course."

"What's so damn funny, Mom?"

"Oh, honey, come on. You? Marry Kelly? That's ridiculous."

"Oh, yeah?" he said, his tone challenging as he loomed over her.

She laughed again. "Brandon sweetie, I love you dearly, but I would never do that to Kelly!"

"To *Kelly?*" Now it was Brandon's turn to be surprised. "What about me?"

"You'll survive," she said dryly, and patted his arm. "My point is, you and Kelly would be a horrible match."

"No, we wouldn't," he said, outraged, then shook his head. Damn, she was deliberately trying to trap him. "I mean, yeah, we would. I mean…what are you talking about?"

She smiled at him patiently. "Kelly is a darling girl and I would be thrilled and honored to have her as a daughter-in-law, but it's never going to happen. You two would never work out. She's too much of a romantic at heart."

"I'm not sure I agree," he said carefully. Sally had already tricked him once so he was watching every word he said.

"Yes, darling, she is," Sally said softly. "Kelly's been hurt and her heart is still tender. But that doesn't mean she's given up on love. She's still looking for a man who will truly love her. She wants the dream, Brandon. She wants to live happily ever after."

"Most women want that, I guess," he allowed, with a philosophical shrug.

"Yes, and you've made it abundantly clear that you are completely unwilling to provide any woman with that blissful scenario."

"True," he said with a rueful grin.

"So why in the world would I want to match Kelly up with you?"

His eyes narrowed. "I don't know. Why would you?"

"Exactly, I wouldn't!" she said triumphantly, effectively ending the conversation. She grabbed him in another hug, patting his back as though he were a clever four-year-old. "Now, the girls and I are going to Tra Vigne for an early dinner, so we'll catch up with you in the morning."

He watched her scurry off, wondering how in the world she'd managed to win that conversation.

# Six

The grape harvest began the next morning. Guests were invited to join in as part of the complete "vine to barrel" experience, despite the fact that the Dukes employed plenty of workers to get the job done. It was a tradition for many people who vacationed in Napa Valley to take part in the harvest ritual. There was something essential and gratifying in the physical act of picking the grapes that would some day become the wine served at one's table.

"How do you know when the grapes are ready to pick?" one of the guests asked.

Brandon turned and recognized Mrs. Kingsley, who'd been one of the first to reserve a room for the harvest. This was her and her husband's first trip to Napa. Brandon stepped forward to say something, but hesitated when Kelly spoke up.

"Different winemakers have various ways of judging the readiness of the grapes," she said, reaching for a cluster of plump grapes and severing it from the vine with her shears. She plucked a few grapes off and handed one each to Mr. and Mrs. Kingsley, then popped one into her own mouth. "You can't usually taste the flavor of the finished wine in the fruit."

The elderly woman chewed her grape. "It's very sweet."

"Yes," Kelly said. "All I can taste is the sugar. But an expert will also taste some tannin and acidity in the skin."

Mrs. Kingsley chewed another moment, then nodded slowly. "I see what you mean."

"There are all sorts of instruments and analyses used to gauge the readiness of the grapes," Kelly continued. "But I also think there's quite a lot of art mixed in with the science. And luck, as well. After all, who knows what the weather will bring from one season to the next?"

"So true, my dear," Mr. Kingsley said, patting his wife on the back.

Kelly had impressed Brandon many times in the past with both her business acumen and her social skills, and today was no different. He watched her walking from row to row, greeting guests, passing out bottles of water and offering advice on everything from how to pick the fruit— grab the large clumps of grapes rather than the individual grapes—to counseling on the dangers of sunburn under the warm October sun. For that problem, she would reach into her backpack and hand out individual tubes of suntan lotion provided by the hotel spa, as well as bright burgundy baseball caps with the Mansion's logo emblazoned on the front. One by one, as the guests got a look at the classy, fun caps, everyone wanted one, and Kelly cheerfully obliged them.

Brandon was both impressed and amused by her resourcefulness. And apparently, so was the well-known hotel reviewer from the national trade magazine, if his exuberant announcement offering vineyard photo opportunities was any indication. The man pulled a small but expensive digital camera from his pocket and began shooting photographs of willing and enthusiastic guests in various stages of grape picking.

The wine-colored baseball caps had been designed to be a part of the marketing team's grand opening promotional giveaway package, but nobody had thought about using them in the vineyards to shield guests from the bright sun. Kelly deserved a bonus for that PR coup.

He made a mental note to make sure the signature caps would always be available to any guests who wanted to work or simply wander through the vineyard fields.

"She's really something," a voice said from behind Brandon.

He turned and saw his brother Adam standing nearby, also watching Kelly. "Yeah, she is."

"Maybe we should talk about promoting her to marketing or public relations."

"No way," Brandon groused. "I'm keeping her."

Intrigued, Adam lifted one eyebrow. "Keeping her?"

Brandon waved away his previous comment. "You know what I mean. Keeping her as my assistant."

"Yeah, your assistant." Adam smirked. "Right."

"What's that supposed to mean?"

"It means I don't blame you," he said, watching Kelly with new interest. "If I had someone that special working for me, I wouldn't let her go either."

"No kidding," Brandon said, knowing Trish had been hired as Adam's temporary assistant. They'd fallen in love and had married each other last year. "But we've all accepted the fact that you're a weak man."

Adam threw back his head and laughed. "Weak, huh?" Glancing around, he spied his beautiful pregnant wife sitting under the umbrella of a patio table the crew had set up earlier for guests, drinking from her water bottle. With a satisfied nod, he turned back and gave Brandon a look fraught with meaning. "It takes a strong man to recognize his own weakness."

"Whatever that means."

"I think you know what that means," he said, turning to take another look at Kelly before glancing back at Brandon.

"Nice try, bro," Brandon said, "but you're barking up the wrong tree. It's not going to happen."

"I hope you're convincing yourself because you're not convincing me."

Brandon shrugged. "I'm only convinced that you don't know what the hell you're talking about."

With a grin, Adam whacked Brandon on the back, then walked away to check on Trish, leaving Brandon to gaze over at Kelly who was still laughing and smiling and working her magic with the guests.

He scowled again as he played Adam's words over in his mind. Great. So Adam thought Brandon was falling for Kelly, while his mother had warned him that falling for Kelly was the worst thing he could do.

What was wrong with everyone in his family?

Just because he wanted Kelly as much as he wanted to take another breath, didn't mean he'd be stupid enough to propose marriage to her. Their affair was all about sex. Not marriage. Brandon didn't *do* marriage. Not now, not ever.

He shook off the serious subject matter and accepted that it was no longer just his mother he had to worry about; it was his brothers, too. Now that they were both married, they probably couldn't stand the fact that Brandon was still footloose and having a good time. In other words, he was a bachelor, unattached, single, happy. And he intended to stay that way permanently, so they would all just have to suck it up.

Meanwhile, he couldn't take his eyes off Kelly. He noticed she was wearing that glossy, berry-flavored stuff on her lips again. She'd been wearing it last night when Brandon arrived at her door after dinner. The memory of what she'd done with those sexy lips of hers made him grit his teeth with the effort it took to keep from turning rock-hard and embarrassing himself in front of his guests.

It didn't help that she wore a flimsy, feminine knit shirt that clung to her curves, along with long, dark blue jeans that showed off her world-class bottom to perfection. She'd pulled her thick, shiny hair into a flirtatious ponytail that swung back and forth, teasing him with every move she made.

If things were different, if he and Kelly were a real couple, he wouldn't hesitate to walk right over there right now and kiss her. But they weren't a real couple, and the longer he hung around staring at her, wanting her, the dumber he felt. He had plenty of work to do in his office and if he was smart, he'd leave right now and get something done. But just then, Kelly laughed, and the sweet, lighthearted sound touched and warmed some part deep within his chest, and he knew he wasn't going anywhere.

"Thanks for all your help, Kelly," Mr. Kingsley said, tipping the brim of his baseball cap toward her. "See you at the wine tasting."

"You bet, Mr. Kingsley," Kelly said, waving to the last guest and his wife as they headed out of the vineyard and back to the hotel. They both looked so cute in their matching caps as they walked away holding hands.

Kelly hadn't realized how much she would enjoy

mingling with the hotel guests. She'd never considered herself shy, but she had to admit she'd never been quite as outgoing as she'd been today. She attributed it to the newfound confidence and self-assurance she'd gained in the past week since she and Brandon had started sleeping together. And that reminded her of something else that was different about her today. She should've been utterly exhausted and ready to take a nap, but instead, she felt energized, exhilarated. How weird was that?

"Don't question it," she advised herself. "Just enjoy the feeling for as long as it lasts."

"What did you say?" Brandon said, coming up behind her.

Kelly sucked in a breath and turned around slowly to gaze up at him. He seemed taller and broader somehow, but maybe that was because she'd worn low-heeled boots today instead of high heels. Or maybe it was because he looked so gorgeous and larger than life in his rugged denim shirt and blue jeans instead of a suit and tie. Whatever the reason, she had to stop staring like a fool and answer the simple question he'd asked her.

"I was just talking to myself," she muttered, then forced herself to smile casually. "Wasn't this a fun day? I think everyone enjoyed themselves."

"Thanks to you," he said with a teasing grin. "My brothers want to give you a bonus and promote you to head of marketing for coming up with the idea to pass out suntan lotion and baseball caps to the guests."

"Oh, that was just a spur of the moment thing," she insisted, but her smile broadened at the compliment. "When I saw the weather report and realized how warm it was going to be, I grabbed a few caps on the way out, just in case. Then when everyone seemed to want one, I ran back and got more. Same goes for the suntan lotion."

"Well, thank you for thinking ahead," he said, slinging a friendly arm around her as they walked. "It really paid off."

The praise, together with his touch, made her feel as warm and cozy as a happy cat. She had the strongest urge to wrap herself around his legs and purr contentedly, but she managed to control herself.

"I understand you're joining us for dinner," Brandon said as they left the vineyard and walked along the flower-lined brick path back to the hotel.

She glanced at him sideways. "I hope that's okay with you."

"Of course it's okay. My mother considers you a part of the family. We'll have a good time. Even though we'll have to keep our hands off each other."

"I guess we can manage that for an hour or two," she said, laughing softly. "I really like your mom."

"That makes two of us," he said, squeezing her shoulder companionably.

*Purr,* she thought to herself, and snuggled against him, wanting to be wrapped up in his warmth for as long as it lasted.

"A toast to the Mansion at Silverado Trail," Adam said, raising his wineglass.

The rest of the Duke family, along with Beatrice and Marjorie and Kelly, raised their glasses to meet his.

"To the Mansion," Cameron echoed.

"Long may it reign as the supreme destination among all the Duke properties," Brandon said with a grin.

Adam chuckled. "In Napa Valley anyway."

"Yeah," Cameron said. "Can't compete with Monarch Dunes."

"Or Fantasy Mountain," Adam added.

"They're all fabulous properties," Marjorie said. "You men have done an incredible job. I'm so proud of you."

"Thanks, Marjorie," Adam said. "But it's partly your fault for making sure we hire only the best people."

"Like Kelly and Trish, for instance," Cameron said, grinning as he raised his glass to both women.

"Ah, yes," Marjorie said, winking at Trish. "I'm glad you've finally recognized the true genius behind Duke Development."

"Since you were the one who hired Kelly and Trish, I would have to agree," Brandon said, his gaze sweeping over Kelly.

Kelly felt her cheeks heating and rushed to change the subject. Turning to Julia, she asked, "Did you enjoy your massage today?"

"Oh, it was heavenly." She looked across the table at Brandon. "I hope you're paying Ingrid, the masseuse, a lot of money. She's worth her weight in gold."

"That's what I like to hear," Brandon said with a firm nod.

Trish pursed her lips in thought. "A massage every day is so civilized, don't you agree."

Kelly laughed. "I really do."

"Absolutely," Beatrice chimed in.

Since there were nine of them, Brandon had reserved the small but elegant private room next to the wine cellar for their dinner. When they first arrived, he'd pulled Kelly's chair out for her and as she'd begun to sit down, he'd let his hand glide from the small of her back up to her neck. Shivers ran through her and she almost gasped from the provocative touch. He'd flashed her a very private, very wicked grin as he took his seat.

They'd all chosen to dine off the tasting menu, that meant a different wine with each course. The food was delicious and the pairings were perfect. Kelly savored each delicate bite and every sip of the outstanding wines. Everyone agreed that the kitchen staff had outdone themselves.

She found the conversations that circled the table to be fascinating and enjoyable. Sally and Marjorie teased Beatrice about some of the men she'd met through her online dating service, urging Beatrice to describe a few of her funnier moments.

Julia talked about the trials and tribulations of turning her massive family estate into an art museum and learning center for children, complete with vegetable garden and petting zoo. She regaled them with stories about the monkey that entertained the kids by riding the goat, and the new zookeeper she'd hired who wanted to give falconry lessons.

As Julia spoke, Cameron reached for her hand and tucked it into his. Kelly found herself both captivated and wistful, looking at the way he gazed at Julia. Both of Brandon's brothers were deeply in love with their wives and weren't afraid to let their feelings show. Was it too much for Kelly to hope that, some day, a man would look at her that way?

A few minutes later, as their first course dishes were cleared, she happened to glance at Brandon who was laughing at something his brother Adam had said. As if he sensed her looking his way, Brandon turned his head and his gaze locked on to hers. The heat was instant, powerful and profound. Her breath caught in her throat and her heart fluttered. Her vision fogged, then narrowed to a point where only Kelly and Brandon existed together in the room. Sounds and voices ceased to be anything more than a mild buzzing in her ears.

Seconds later, she blinked, and just as quickly, Brandon

turned away as though he hadn't experienced the same lightning bolt moment. As though nothing monumental had just occurred between the two of them. So why was her heart still beating too fast? Why had her appetite suddenly vanished?

Kelly would've sworn in that moment that Brandon had looked at her with the same level of intensity and love she'd seen in his brothers' eyes when they gazed at their wives. Had she imagined it? Was she going crazy?

She glanced around to see if anyone else had noticed her sudden discomfiture, but everyone, including Brandon, was talking and laughing, carrying on conversations, sipping their wine and reaching for bread as they'd been doing since the meal began.

She'd clearly misconstrued his look, and the realization made her feel like a lovesick idiot. It had just been wishful thinking, probably because only minutes before, she'd been mooning over the soulful way Cameron had been gazing at Julia.

She reached for her water glass and took a long sip. Then she ordered herself to breathe evenly and resolved to forget what she thought she'd just seen, brushing it off as an inane figment of her imagination.

"You didn't eat much at dinner tonight," Brandon said later that night after they'd made love. They were stretched out on her bed, facing each other, and his hand rested on her arm.

"My first course was so much more filling than I thought it would be," Kelly said, and cursed herself for lying. "But everything I tasted was wonderful. Jean Pierre has a megahit on his hands."

"I think so, too. And I received a number of compliments about you today, too."

"Me?"

"Yes, you," he said, moving closer as he began to slide his hand up and down her back in slow, sensual strokes. "The guests appreciated the way you helped out in the vineyards today. You were a regular social director out there, making sure everyone had whatever they needed and showing the guests how to harvest the grapes. Where did you learn how to do that?"

She sighed as his hand grazed her shoulder, causing little tingles of excitement to surge through her system. "Sometimes I walk through the vineyards on my lunch hour, so I've gotten to know some of the guys who work there. They showed me how to do it."

"Really?" He reached over and swept a strand of hair off her forehead. "Well, you're obviously a natural. If you ever want a job in the vineyard, you just let me know."

She smiled. "I'm sure the perks are enticing. All the wine I can drink?"

"That's right. As long as you pick the grapes and crush them, you can drink all the wine you want."

"I'm kind of a lightweight drinker," she said, "so I'm not sure all that hard work would be worth it."

"But wait, you'd get to wear that really cool hat."

She laughed. "Now you're talking my language."

"Yeah?" He tugged her closer and rolled until she was straddling him.

Her laughter faded and she splayed her hands against his firm chest. "Brandon, our ground rules have gone out the window again."

"You noticed that, too?"

"I did," she said, smiling to hide the sadness she felt. "I think we need to accept the fact that this will be our last night together."

He covered her hands with his. "Do you think so?"

"We're both getting so busy," she added lamely, "and your family's here now."

"Yeah," he said. "And we can't forget that the clown-who-shall-not-be-named will be here in a day or two."

Kelly sighed. She'd been so anxious to carry out her Roger plan, but now the thought of seeing him was simply depressing.

"Tell you what," Brandon said, tapping her chin so that she looked up and met his gaze. "Tomorrow is hours away yet, so for now, let's forget about the world outside this room."

She moaned in pleasure as he lifted her up and onto his solid length. "Oh, that feels so good."

"Now you're talking *my* language," he murmured, and proceeded to please her in every way possible.

A long while later, as Brandon held her in his arms, Kelly tried to commit to memory every sensual feeling she'd experienced tonight. This would be the last time they ever made love with each other, and she wanted to remember the heat of his skin against hers, the weight of his leg on her thigh, his manly scent, the taste and pressure of his lips when he'd kissed her so thoroughly.

She thought back to the dinner with his family earlier tonight and the lovely feeling of warmth and inclusiveness she'd felt. She remembered that moment when Brandon looked at her with all the intensity of a man in love. Oh, maybe it wasn't real, maybe she'd imagined it, maybe she was a fool. But she would never forget how, for those few sweet moments, she'd felt like a woman who was loved by Brandon Duke.

The following morning, Brandon left her room before dawn. Kelly found it impossible to drift back to sleep and eventually tossed the covers aside and sat up. Today was the day, she thought, and mustered every last ounce of resolve she had within her. It was time to accept the unhappy fact that she and Brandon had just spent their last night together.

Climbing out of bed, she made her way to the shower. Today was Sunday and Brandon would spend the day with his family. He'd rented a limousine to take them all on a champagne tour of the valley. It would be fun for everyone, but it was partly a business excursion as well, because he and his brothers had discussed going into partnership with one of the champagne vintners. Last night, he'd been sweet enough to ask Kelly to join them, but she'd demurred. Since they'd decided to bring their delicious affair to an end, it would be awkward for her to spend more than the minimum amount of time required around Brandon.

Tomorrow, Monday, was the day Roger and others from his hedge fund company would check into the Mansion. They would be here for five long days. So besides having to deal with the countless other demands of her job, Kelly would have to deal with her ex-boyfriend.

But that was exactly the way she wanted it to be. She had no intention of calling off her plan to get even with Roger. This small act of revenge was all she'd thought about and worked toward for the past few months. It would bring her much needed closure and allow her to move forward in her life with confidence and a new sense of assurance that she was a strong woman in charge of her own life. Strong enough to take those first daunting steps into the dating arena where she hoped to find a good, decent man who would cherish her as much as she would cherish him.

But because of what she hoped to accomplish with the Roger Plan, she and Brandon had agreed to put an end to their romantic evenings together. It was bad enough that they'd vowed to end things when his family arrived—only to handily break that vow in their rush to make love again. Breaking their ground rules simply couldn't happen again.

For one thing, it wasn't fair to Brandon to use him the way she had been using him. In the beginning, she'd begged him for help in the area of romance and seduction and he'd agreed. At this point, he had more than lived up to his end of the bargain.

And for another thing, it couldn't be healthy for her to keep pretending that the two of them had any sort of loving, caring relationship beyond the walls of their office. No, outside of the office, all they had between them was a few long nights of mutually satisfying sex.

*Satisfying?* As she blew her hair dry, Kelly couldn't help but roll her eyes. *Satisfying* was putting it mildly. What they'd had was a firestorm of passionate, hot, wild, electrifying jungle sex. Whew. She was getting hot just thinking about it. She turned off the hair dryer and patted her wrists with a damp towel. As she dried off, she thought about last night, their final evening together. It had been memorable, to say the least.

Despite losing her appetite during dinner, Kelly was glad she'd been able to bounce back after that one odd, surreal moment when she'd thought she'd seen true emotion in Brandon's eyes. She laughed at herself now, recalling that she'd definitely managed to rally when her favorite chocolate soufflé dessert was placed in front of her.

She'd honestly enjoyed herself with Brandon and his family and his mom's friends. They all shared so much love for each other. It was obvious they enjoyed laughing and teasing each other, telling jokes and sharing old family stories with anyone who was new to the group. It was lovely to hear about Sally's latest victories in tracking down her husband's family members.

As they all left the restaurant and walked back to their rooms, Kelly realized she hadn't had that much fun in years.

Brandon's two sisters-in-law, Trish and Julia, were sweet, funny and smart, and they'd generously welcomed her into their small circle. She'd felt an instant camaraderie with both of them.

And she didn't mind admitting that she was already half in love with Sally Duke. There was no one more gracious and friendly than Brandon's mother. She and her girlfriends, Bea and Marjorie, giggled like teenagers and always managed to have the best time together. Kelly had to admire the three women, who'd staunchly maintained such a strong friendship throughout their lives.

Brandon's brothers were officially her employers, but that hadn't kept them from acting like her own big brothers with their good-natured teasing and clever banter.

After she and Brandon returned to her room for the night, their lovemaking had run the gamut of emotions for both of them. By turns he'd been sweet, funny, passionate, tender, erotic and completely breathtaking. Perhaps it was due to the fact that they both knew this would be their last night together, but it seemed as if their lovemaking had reached a new level of passion and heat. The night had been wonderful and she would never forget it. What woman in her right mind wouldn't hold those memories in her heart forever?

On the other hand, what woman in her right mind would look at Brandon Duke's magnificent naked body and tell him their affair was over? Was there a woman in the world who was that strong?

So maybe she was crazy for insisting they end their

affair now. But on the off chance that Brandon showed up at her door tonight, thinking he could break their ground rules once again, she would have no choice but to turn him away. It was the best thing for both of them. This time, she would have to be firm. They had no future together, except in business. Their fleeting love affair was over.

"He won't care," she whispered. Why was she making such a big deal about it? Brandon attracted women like flies to honey. For goodness' sake, the man had his own gravitational pull! He would have some new woman in his bed in the time it took Kelly to say "Bye-bye."

As she brushed her teeth, she forced herself to recall the many women Brandon had dated and broken up with in the past. She thought of the numerous diamond bracelets she'd purchased, just so he could give his date of the month a lovely parting gift before he kissed her goodbye for the last time.

The last thing Kelly wanted was her very own diamond bracelet from Brandon. Dear God, she would die of humiliation if he tried to give her one as he held the door open for her to leave.

That settled it. There was no way she would ever allow herself to remain in a relationship that was guaranteed to end in such a pathetic, clichéd fashion.

No, her long-range plans to fall in love and get married had to be her overriding single focus from now on.

"He'll follow the rules this time," she murmured as she slipped on a pair of yoga pants and a sleeveless T-shirt. After all, Brandon had been reluctant to get involved with her from the beginning. Oh, he'd been more than reluctant; he had absolutely refused to help her. Of course, he'd obviously changed his mind and she had to admit he'd definitely warmed up to the task. *In more ways than one,* she thought, as a sudden image of his clever hands and mouth on her most intimate parts flashed through her mind.

"Oh, God." With a shake of her head, she calculated that she would only have to suffer from these erotic flashbacks for the next few decades or so. Forcing the images away, she quickly tied her sneakers, grabbed her purse and a light jacket and left the room to do her weekly shopping and errands.

Monday morning, Kelly was seated at her desk bright and early, determined to be the proficient and talented assistant Brandon had hired in the first place—and nothing more. She felt fully rested for the first time in a week and as she made a second pot of coffee, she marveled that she'd actually been able to sleep through the night. She'd worried at first that she'd become so used to sleeping curled up next to Brandon's warmth that she would no longer be able to sleep on her own. But as soon as her head hit the pillow, she'd fallen into an exhausted slumber and when she woke up this morning, she was surprised to realize she'd slept straight through the night.

It helped that Brandon had stayed out late with his brothers and a potential new partner the night before. When he called her on his way back to the hotel, just to say good-night, she'd cut the conversation short, claiming to be half asleep.

Another reason she was grateful for a good's night sleep was because today was the day that Roger would arrive. Kelly would need every ounce of her brainpower to concentrate on him. Earlier, in her room, she'd spent way too long on her hair and makeup and wardrobe choices. But she was glad she'd taken the time, glad she'd chosen the elegant blue-and-white swirly wrap dress that accentuated her narrow waist and curves, because when

Brandon walked into the office this morning and saw her, his eyes had lit up and he'd grinned wolfishly. That was exactly the reaction she'd been hoping for, and it made her feel all warm and glowing inside. Brandon's appreciative gaze had infused her with all the confidence she would need to stand up to Roger this afternoon.

The telephone rang and Kelly answered it immediately.

"Let me speak to Brandon," an imperious female voice demanded.

Kelly's lips twisted in a grimace. Bianca Stephens again. She'd grudgingly given Brandon the woman's message last week, but she had no idea if he'd returned the call.

"Just a moment, please," she murmured, and put the woman on hold. Pressing the intercom button, she announced the call to Brandon.

There was a pause, then Brandon said, "Take a message, would you please, Kelly? I don't have time to talk to her right now."

"All right." Kelly stared at the telephone, knowing the woman wouldn't take the news well. She composed herself, then muttered, "Ah well, here goes nothing," and pressed another button. "I'm sorry, Ms. Stephens, but Brandon is unable to take your call right now. May I give him a message?"

"You must be kidding."

"No, ma'am, I'm not. He's unavailable, so I'll have to take a message for him."

"Fine, I have a message for him," she said heatedly. "Tell him he needs to fire his receptionist, or whoever the hell you are, because you are simply incompetent."

Kelly gasped. "I…I beg your pardon?"

"You didn't hear me? So now you're deaf, too?"

"No, I'm not deaf, but—"

"Then put me through to Brandon now."

"I don't think so," Kelly said, and quickly disconnected the call. Shaking, she jumped up from her desk and paced back and forth, pressing her hands to her cheeks as she shook her head in numb disbelief. Had she actually hung up on someone her boss considered a friend? Yes, she had! On the other hand, she couldn't believe Brandon was actually friends with such a horrible person.

Was it too soon to take another vacation? She must be under more pressure than she'd realized if she'd actually hung up on someone.

How would she explain her actions to Brandon? She had to say something. He would hear about it eventually from the rude queen bee herself. With one last shake of her head, she slid back into her chair and tried to dream up a reasonable explanation.

Brandon breathed deeply in relief as he watched the red light on the phone disappear, signaling that the call was disconnected.

Bianca had phoned last week and he'd never returned her call, and now he'd just refused to talk to her again. He'd never been someone who avoided confrontation, and, hell, Bianca had always been good for some laughs. She'd also made herself available to him countless times and was always up for a hearty round of purely casual sex whenever they were in the same part of the country. So why hadn't he taken the call? What was his problem?

He dug his fingers through his hair, trying to figure it out. Bianca rarely made demands on his time, only calling when she was on the West Coast and wanted to get together for the aforementioned casual sex.

But unfortunately, he reasoned, right now wasn't a good time for him to see her. No, right now, it was important that Brandon make himself available for Kelly and help her get through this difficult time with that idiot Roger. So yeah, that's why he couldn't see Bianca. That was his excuse. He was being Mr. Helpful. That was just the kind of guy he was.

His intercom rang and he picked up the phone. "Yes, Kelly?"

She spoke in a rush. "I wanted to let you know that I accidentally dropped Ms. Stephens's call and she might be a bit angry with me. I know you don't have time to speak with her right now, but would you like me to get her back on the line and explain what happened?"

"Don't bother, she'll get over it," he said. "I'll call her next week."

"All right," she said, sounding relieved. "Thank you."

He hung up the phone, sat back in his chair and stared out the window. Maybe he would call Bianca next week and maybe he wouldn't. To be honest, Bianca had never been someone he'd call "fun." Her world revolved around herself, her job, her problems, her triumphs, her own importance. In other words, she talked about herself all the time. Yes, he'd always found her mildly amusing when she bitched about the people who ran her television network, the people she worked with, the people who came on her show. She was always complaining about something or other.

He didn't need that kind of aggravation right now. He had to concentrate his energy on watching—and possibly "helping"—Kelly complete her warped plan to get Roger back.

And he had to focus on keeping his hands to himself. She'd made it clear two nights ago that he wasn't allowed to break their ground rules again. He might have to revisit that decision sometime in the near future, but not while Roger was here. That didn't mean he would leave Kelly alone, though. He wasn't about to let her get hurt implementing her crazy plan.

Today was the day Roger the schmuck would be arriving. Brandon smacked his hands together in anticipation of finally meeting face to face the jerk who'd made Kelly's life so miserable.

Let the games begin.

# Seven

"Perhaps you don't understand just who you're dealing with," said a cool blonde woman standing at the registration desk. An elegantly dressed man stood nearby, tapping his well-shod foot impatiently.

Kelly would know that foot tapper anywhere, even with his back to her. It was Roger, of course. Watching him now, she recalled that any small inconvenience often sent him into an emotional tailspin. The first warning sign was the foot tapping.

Gathered around the lobby were the rest of Roger's group, ten or twelve businessmen and several women, all waiting to check in.

Sharon, the front desk clerk, smiled warmly. "We're all well aware of Mr. Hempstead, and we're happy and honored to welcome him and his associates to the Mansion on Silverado Trail. We're so pleased that your company has chosen our resort for your retreat. We've arranged for

Mr. Hempstead to stay in *Sauvignon,* our most deluxe and private *maison* suite. I'm just finishing up with his paperwork and I'll take care of the rest of your people right away."

"I certainly hope so."

Sharon's smile never faded as she slid two plastic suite cards inside a sturdy cardboard case and touched the shiny brass bell on the counter. A clear chime rang out. "One of our bellmen will be here momentarily to accompany Mr. Hempstead to his suite. I can show you where it is on our map."

"Don't bother," the woman said frostily. "Just book me into the room nearest Mr. Hempstead's."

Kelly studied the woman curiously and assumed she was Roger's assistant or an associate of some kind. She was attractive in a cold-blooded sort of way. Her black pinstriped designer suit and gray silk shirt seemed overly businesslike and out of place in the casually elegant lobby, but Kelly had to admit that the look suited the woman. She didn't come across as the casual type.

The thought suddenly occurred to Kelly that this woman and Roger might be sleeping together. That could pose a problem, one Kelly hadn't even considered.

She shifted her gaze back to Roger. He was still very good-looking, naturally, but she noticed that his dark blond hair was beginning to thin on top. He looked unnaturally tan and she wondered if he'd taken to visiting a tanning salon. His brown suit was impeccable, of course, but slightly dated, at least by West Coast standards. His striped tie showed off his beloved burgundy and gold college colors. He looked exactly like what he was: the spoiled, privileged scion of a venerable East Coast family.

At that moment, Sharon glanced around with a mildly anxious expression on her face, and Kelly knew it was time to defuse the situation. But just as she started to approach Roger, Brandon entered the lobby from the opposite doorway. He walked right up to Roger as Kelly watched in fear and horror.

"Hello, Mr. Hempstead," Brandon said spiritedly, grabbing Roger's hand, shaking it with enthusiasm. "It's a pleasure to meet you. We've been looking forward to your visit for quite some time. I'm Brandon Duke. Welcome to the Mansion on Silverado Trail."

"Thanks," Roger said, clearly impressed that the former NFL quarterback and billionaire hotel mogul had singled him out. "We've heard good buzz about the place, but there must've been a mix-up because our rooms…"

"Not a mix-up," Brandon said quickly, shaking his finger for emphasis. "An upgrade."

Kelly frowned. What in the world was he up to?

The differences between the two men were blatantly clear to Kelly now, and she couldn't believe she'd ever told Brandon they were similar. Yes, they were both wealthy, Type A and driven to succeed. But she had also called Brandon arrogant. Yes, he was bossy and wanted to have things his way, but now, as she watched him converse with Roger, she could see that Brandon didn't have one iota of the haughty arrogance that her former boyfriend had.

As the men continued to talk, the cool blonde turned around and eyed Brandon from head to toe as if he were a succulent steak and she a hungry lioness.

She'd seen enough. Kelly straightened her shoulders and shook her hair back, then walked briskly toward the front desk.

"Hello, Roger," she said.

Roger looked at her with mild disinterest, then did a double take and his eyes goggled. "Kelly?"

"Yes, Roger, it's me." She circled around to the other

side of the counter. "Now, let's get you registered and off to your rooms, shall we?"

"You work here?" Roger said, unblinking.

"I certainly do," she said, and accompanied the words with what she hoped was an alluring smile. "Welcome to the Mansion on Silverado Trail. Let me see what I can do to speed up the registration process."

Just then, Michael, the other registration clerk, came rushing over. "Thanks, Kelly. I can take over now." He leaned closer and whispered, "I had to change all their restaurant reservations. They brought two extra people with no notice."

It figured that Roger would do something to botch up the works, Kelly thought, but she said nothing as she rounded the counter.

Brandon stepped up beside her and smiled genially to the crowd. "Ladies and gentlemen, Michael and Sharon will have you settled as quickly as possible. I'd like to extend my wishes for a pleasant stay, and hope you'll all enjoy the complimentary champagne basket our catering staff will be delivering to your rooms within the next half hour."

There were smiles and a chorus of thanks from several in the group, but Roger ignored all of it.

"Kelly?" He took hold of her arm and pulled her aside. "I hardly recognized you. It's been a long time. How have you been?"

"I've been wonderful, Roger. How about you?"

He ignored the question and continued to stare. "You look fantastic. What have you done with yourself?"

"Oh, nothing special," she said nonchalantly as she fluffed her hair. "I cut my hair."

"It's more than that," he said, frowning. "There's something else…"

"Oh, you know, I work out, eat right, drink great wine."
She beamed a confident smile at him. "Life is good."

"Well, whatever you're doing, it's working," he said
raptly, and leaned in close. "Listen, are you free tonight?
We could have dinner."

"Tonight? No, I'm afraid—"

"She's busy," Brandon said abruptly, looming directly
behind her. "She has to work late."

Kelly turned and stabbed him with a pointed look that
clearly said *buzz off.* Then she turned back to Roger and
smiled tightly. "Yes, unfortunately, I'm working tonight,
but I'm free Thursday night. Are you?"

"Yes," he said immediately. "We'll have dinner."

"Wait a minute," Brandon muttered.

Kelly elbowed him in the stomach discreetly.

"Oww," he said under his breath.

She ignored him and continued to focus her energy on
her ex-boyfriend. "I've got to get back to my office, Roger,
but I'm sure I'll run into you around the resort between
now and Thursday. I hope you all have a wonderful visit."

Roger raised one eyebrow rakishly. "Oh, I'll definitely
see you around."

"So that's Roger," Brandon said as they strolled back
to the office together.

Kelly stopped and planted her hands on her hips. "And
what did you think you were doing, butting in like that?"

"Hey, I did you a favor."

"You said you wouldn't say anything to him."

"I was being my charming hotelier self. Extending an
open hand to one of our *important* guests."

"Open fist, you mean."

He snorted. "Don't tempt me. Guy's a real snake oil
salesman, isn't he?"

She shook her head as they continued walking. "He's not that bad."

"Yeah, he is," Brandon countered. "And who's the ice queen?"

"That woman with him?" Kelly frowned. "I just assumed she was his assistant, but she was awfully pushy, wasn't she?"

He glanced at her sideways. "Yeah, kind of like you."

"I'm not pushy," she said in mock outrage.

"Yeah, you are," he said as he led her into their office suite and closed and locked the door.

"Well, I guess I can be pushy once in a while, but I'm nothing like—"

Without warning, he spun her around. She let out a tiny shriek as he urged her back against the wall.

"Just look at the way you push me around," Brandon said. "The way you force me to do this…" He lowered his head and began to nibble her neck. Kelly felt the electric sensation all the way down to her toes.

It had only been two days. But oh, how she had missed him.

"And this…" Brandon used both hands to flip her short jacket off her shoulders, trapping her arms behind her and causing her breasts to be thrust forward.

"But…oh, yes."

"So damn pushy." He quickly unknotted the thin ties that held her dress together and reached for her breasts.

"Brandon," she whispered, then moaned when he swiftly maneuvered her bra out of the way and used his fingers to tease and excite her nipples. But through the thick haze of pleasure, she remembered something important and grabbed his hand. "Brandon, wait. We weren't going to do this anymore. We should stop. We should…"

"We'll stop after this, I swear," he muttered. "But I can't stop. I've got to have you now."

"Yes, please," she said, straining to remove her jacket as he bent to lick her breasts. "Hurry."

"Pushy," he murmured again as he kissed and nibbled his way back and forth between her breasts.

"Oh, shut up and kiss me," she grumbled as she reached up and whipped his jacket off.

His laugh was deep and full. "I do love a pushy woman."

Then his lips covered hers in an openmouthed kiss and his tongue swept inside to tangle with hers. Through the mindless haze of passion, Kelly's hands fumbled with his belt, finally undoing it and pulling it loose. She unbuttoned his pants, then started on his zipper, easing it down over his burgeoning erection.

In the back of her brain, she registered the words he'd said, *I do love a pushy woman,* but knew he didn't mean anything by it. It was just something he'd said in the heat of the moment. She wouldn't make more of him using the word "love" than that. Otherwise, she'd go crazy overthinking every word he'd ever said.

Seconds later, Brandon made her forget to think at all as he took first one nipple, then the other, into his mouth, sucking and licking until she thought she would die of sheer pleasure.

He yanked her dress off her shoulders and watched it fall to the floor, revealing the black thong she wore.

"Whoa."

She boldly kicked the dress away, then leaned back against the wall. "Do you like it?"

He simply stared at her for several long moments, taking in every inch of her, from her hair down to her feet. "I recall telling you it was my personal choice."

"I do recall you mentioning it."

His smile was slow and wicked. "The heels are a nice touch, too."

"Why, thank you."

"Damn, you're incredible," he whispered, skimming his hands down the outside of her thighs as he knelt in front of her.

"Brandon, what…"

"Shh, let me have you," he said, gently moving her legs apart to allow him to kiss the inside skin of her thighs, starting above her knee and moving up, up, until he reached her heated core.

"So beautiful," he murmured.

She was incapable of speech as he cupped his hands around her bottom, angled her toward him and feasted. He took his time, lavishing kisses and strokes of his clever tongue everywhere, touching her, urging her up, closer and closer to the peak of oblivion, only to ease back, teasing her, playing her until she was ready to scream.

"Brandon, please," she cried.

"Soon, love," he promised.

"Now." It had to be now or she would die from need.

He moved then, his mouth trailing kisses across her stomach, then up and over her breasts as he stood once again.

She opened her eyes and looked into his, saw the tender passion reflected there and knew in that moment that he felt the same way she did. It was more than simple need or wanting. She couldn't name it, could only feel it, deep in her bones. It flowed through her bloodstream, filling her with an age-old understanding, warming her down into her soul. He felt it, too. She knew it, saw it in his eyes. That stunning awareness filled her with joy as he kissed her lips and met her need with his own.

With no effort at all, he lifted her up and turned so that

he now leaned against the wall with her in his arms. She wrapped her legs around his waist and moaned as he eased her onto his firm erection, filling her completely.

"Yes," he uttered, kissing her, his mouth taking hold of hers in an explosion of heat and pleasure. Together they pushed each other to the limit, then slowed, unwilling to bring an end to the ecstasy. They moved together in a deliberate, unhurried rhythm, until the passion built again and he pumped into her until she couldn't catch her breath. But she didn't care, it didn't matter. He was all she wanted, all she'd been waiting for. He moved with an urgency that matched her own, bringing them back to that edge where they teetered for an instant, then drove themselves over in a climax so all-consuming, so shattering, she wondered if they would survive the fall.

"What just happened here?" Kelly asked, her voice betraying her dazed and confused state.

Brandon nudged her with his foot. "You forced me to have my way with you, remember?"

She tried to work up the energy to smack his leg, but there was no power behind it and she ended up merely grazing his skin with her fingertips.

"So much for ground rules," she said under her breath as she took in the unbelievable scene. Somehow, they'd staggered over to the office couch where they were now sprawled at either end in various stages of undress. Clothing was scattered across the floor. Kelly had grabbed the colorful shawl that was draped over the back of the couch to cover herself, but it didn't do much good. Brandon was gloriously naked. The sight reminded her of some decadent tableau painting.

"Come here," Brandon said, grabbing her ankle and tugging her closer, then pulling her up to sit on his lap.

Kelly wrapped her arms around his middle and allowed herself a moment to cuddle with him and feel cherished.

"Now what were you saying about ground rules?" he said.

"Oh, nothing."

"Well then," he said, taking her at her word as he combed his fingers lazily through her hair. "How about if we get dressed and go grab some dinner?"

But she knew what she had to do.

It was now or never. Breathing in deeply, filling her lungs with fortifying air, she let it all out slowly as she gathered her wits. Then, before she could change her mind, she blurted, "Brandon, we have to stop doing that."

He leaned his head over to meet her gaze. "Stop doing what? Eating dinner?"

"I'm serious."

"About eating?" he asked, stroking her back. "Me, too. I'm starving."

"Brandon."

She could feel his lips curve in a smile as he kissed the top of her head. Then he said, "Yes, Kelly?"

"You know what I'm talking about." She reached to take hold of his hand for strength. "We have to stop, you know, breaking the rules, having sex."

"Do we?"

"You know we do." She stared solemnly into his eyes as she squeezed his firm hand. "We talked about it before. We were supposed to stop when your family got here."

"That didn't work," he said.

"No kidding."

He chuckled and kissed her shoulder.

"Then we said we'd stop when Roger arrived," Kelly said, stretching her neck to allow his mouth to roam her skin. "And now he's here, and look at us."

"Yes, just look at us," he said, and lifted her hair to run more kisses along her neckline.

She could barely speak, but knew she had to say what was on her mind. "You've been so generous to help me with all of this. We've been together almost every night for a week and it's been wonderful. I'm having the most amazing time of my life." Her eyelashes fluttered and she looked away, not wanting him to see the confusion and pain she knew was so close to the surface. "But now we should stop before we get…"

He tipped her chin up gently to get a better look at her. "Before we get…what, Kelly?"

*Before we get involved. Before you get tired of me,* she thought, but didn't say aloud. Instead, she ruffled his hair lightly with her hands and said, "Before we get caught by the housekeeping staff."

Brandon knew he should be glad that she was calling him out on breaking the ground rules—again. He knew they had to finally end their affair.

So why was he so eager to change her mind?

She was right, they definitely needed to pull back—to stop. After all, he knew their affair had been temporary to begin with, and the last thing he wanted to do was jeopardize their working relationship.

But gazing at Kelly now, he also knew there was something else happening here that he wasn't ready to give up on. It was hard to explain, but she touched him on a level that he hadn't known existed before. It wasn't just the sex, although sex with Kelly was incendiary, to put it mildly. No, it was more than just sex. He *liked* her, damn it, and he wanted to be with her. When they weren't together, he missed her. The feeling wouldn't last; it never did. He knew that much. But as long as they were having a good time now, why should they call it quits and be miserable when they could keep seeing each other and be happy?

Ultimately, Brandon knew he would never be the man she needed him to be. His mother had been right about that. Kelly was the type of woman who was made for love and marriage. For family. Real family. The kind of family he knew nothing about.

Yes, it was true that Sally had saved him all those years ago, and together with Adam and Cameron, the four of them had formed a strong family bond. But until Sally came along, all Brandon had ever known of family life was misery. And that kind of memory stayed with a man. Haunted him. Reminded him that he would never be able to live up to the ideal man he saw reflected in Kelly's eyes.

But that didn't mean they couldn't enjoy each other for as long as it lasted.

"Look," he said, stroking the hair back from her face and resting his hand on her neck. "Maybe it's crazy, but I don't want to stop seeing you. I'm having a great time. And you're enjoying yourself, too, aren't you?"

She smiled and reached over to touch his cheek. "Yes, of course. You know I am."

"Then for now, that's all that matters." And to settle it, he pulled her close and met her lips with his.

# Eight

Kelly poked her head inside Brandon's office the next morning. "I'm running these invoices over to the concierge desk. Do you need anything while I'm out?"

"No, thanks," Brandon mouthed and waved her off as he was still wrapped up in a phone call with the lawyers.

As she strolled along the sun-kissed terrace that led toward the lobby, Kelly thought about the night before. She and Brandon had snuck out of the hotel together and driven into St. Helena for the best cheeseburger and French fries she'd ever tasted in her life. Maybe it was the company, but she couldn't remember ever having a better time. They'd laughed and shared stories as though they were a real couple out on a real date. But it hadn't been a real date and they weren't a real couple. They were just enjoying sex and the occasional dinner out.

"But isn't that what dating is all about?" Kelly murmured aloud. "Sex and dinner?" After all, if someone were watching them, they would've thought she and Brandon were a normal young couple in love.

But they weren't in love. Far from it.

But so what? Last night, Brandon had said he was having a great time with her, so why not keep it going? Where was the harm in that?

"We're having fun," Kelly insisted to herself as she turned onto the flower-lined brick walkway that circled the main building housing the lobby, then added to her own conscience, "So back off."

"Kelly?"

"Oh." She'd been wrapped up in her thoughts, paying no attention to where she was going and suddenly, Roger stood a mere three feet in front of her. "Hello, Roger. What are you up to this morning?"

He pointed in the direction of the spa. "We've taken over the Pavilion for the day to conduct some team-building exercises."

The Pavilion was a large, open-beamed cottage used for special occasions, weddings, dinners and small conferences. Secluded, private, it was situated beyond the spa in the midst of old growth olive trees and towering oaks. It was one of Kelly's favorite secret places on the property.

"Oh, how interesting," she said politely. "I hope it's a successful exercise."

He stepped a few inches closer and took hold of her elbow in an intimate gesture. "Listen, Kelly, I've been thinking about you all night. I've really missed you. Do you think we could—"

"Roger?" a female voice called out. "Are you coming?"

Kelly turned and saw the ice queen approaching. Today she wore a severe black suit with a crisp gray blouse and five-inch, patent-leather black heels. She looked like Della the Dominatrix, minus the leather whip.

"Hello, Ariel," Roger said. He didn't sound thrilled to see her.

"We can't start without you," she said, shielding her eyes from the sunshine.

She was pretty, Kelly thought, except for two unfortunate vertical lines between her eyebrows that dug in deep when she was aggravated, which seemed to be her permanent state. The lines pulled on her eyebrows, causing them to arch almost comically, giving her the look of a demented cartoon witch.

Kelly felt instantly ashamed for thinking such bad thoughts about a woman she didn't even know. After all, if Ariel really was interested in Roger, she deserved nothing but Kelly's sympathy.

"Go ahead and get started," Roger said, dismissing her with a wave of his hand. "I'll be along shortly."

He watched her stomp away, then turned back to Kelly. "Kelly, what I'm trying to say is that I think you and I could really be—"

"There you are," Brandon said pleasantly as he strolled up from the opposite direction. "Morning, Hempstead. Hope you slept well."

Roger didn't take his eyes off Kelly as he said, "I plan to sleep even better tonight."

"Good luck with that," Brandon said, and gave him a fraternal slap on the back. "I recommend a cold beer right before bed. Works wonders. Come on, Kelly, weren't you headed over to the concierge desk?"

With that, he maneuvered himself between Kelly and Roger and extracted her arm from the other man's grip. "See you around, Hempstead."

"Are you insane?" she whispered when they were a discreet distance away.

"Did you hear what he said?" Brandon griped. "The guy's delusional. He's got it in his head that you're going to wind up in his bed tonight."

"Yes, I know. And I don't mind letting him think it will happen."

He stopped and glared at her. "Why?"

"Because it'll feel so good to tell him no," she said, her eyes narrowed with rock-solid purpose.

"No?" he repeated.

She glowered at him. "Do you honestly think I would sleep with that man?"

"No," he said slowly, as though it were just occurring to him. "But he doesn't know that."

"Right, and we'll just keep it that way, won't we?"

Brandon frowned in puzzlement, but Kelly merely smiled and said, "Let's please not talk about Roger anymore. I need to get these invoices delivered."

The following night, Brandon wondered for the hundredth time why he hadn't punched Roger in the face when he'd first met him.

Brandon's lead bartender in the wine bar had called in sick, so one of the restaurant waiters was filling in. The hotel was filled to capacity and Brandon was concerned that everything should continue running smoothly. He'd decided to oversee things in the bar until they closed at ten o'clock. If anyone wanted to continue socializing, the restaurant bar would stay open until midnight.

Naturally, Roger the Jerk had chosen this night to tie one on. It was more than clear that the man was a pompous ass who couldn't hold his liquor, but because he was the boss, there was no one around to tell him no, to call it a night and drag him off to his room. If that wasn't bad enough, the more Roger drank, the more impressed with himself he became. At this point, he must've thought he was a regular Fred Astaire, because he'd just grabbed hold of Sherry, the cocktail waitress, and spun her around. Sherry, a consummate professional, had barely managed to keep her tray of drinks from upending.

Personally, Brandon would've loved to have seen Sherry empty all those drinks onto Roger's head, but Brandon knew that wouldn't be good for business. So, with great reluctance, he stepped between them, grabbed hold of Roger's shoulders and turned him in the other direction. "You've had enough, pal."

"You again," Roger slurred. "Back off, will ya? She wants me."

"I'm sure she does," Brandon said, easing his arm around Roger and walking him in the opposite direction. "But I'm doing this for your own good. She's got a wicked right hook, along with a husband who has no sense of humor. He's a big, mean guy. You don't want to piss him off."

"But I can tell she likes me. And she's hot."

"Yeah, pal, I'm sure they all like you," Brandon muttered, leading him toward the door. "Come on, time to call it a night."

The ice queen suddenly appeared at Roger's other side and slipped her arm around his back. "I can take care of him from here."

"Hey, you," Roger exclaimed, pointing a wobbly finger at her. "I know you."

She patted his chest. "Yes, and I know you, too."

"You sure you're okay here?" Brandon asked, concerned that Roger could overpower this thin woman with one careless swipe of his arm.

"Been here, done that," she said, with a brief nod of her head. "I've got it covered."

Roger threw his arm around her shoulders and stared into her face. "How 'bout you and me go back to my room? I've got a hot tub."

"Sounds irresistible," she said, and walked away with him.

Brandon watched them stumble out the door and shook his head in disgust. The man was truly a jackass, but the woman with him seemed okay with that. Guess it took all types. And watching Roger's antics here in the bar tonight, Brandon had clearly recognized Roger's type. He'd seen it before and he didn't like it.

Roger was the type of man who thought he could do whatever he wanted, with whomever he chose, anytime at all. He could drink to excess and order people around with impunity, simply because he had wealth and power. He'd been born with it, grown up knowing it, and now he wielded it like a club.

Brandon had been around plenty of other men like that when he worked in the NFL. Big men who'd always gotten what they wanted by virtue of their size and salary.

Brandon's father had been like that, too, minus the wealth. He'd been a big hulk of a man and he'd used his strength to make others cower. It had been like a game to him, and Brandon and his mother had been his favorite objects of contempt. He'd shown it with his fists.

His father and guys like Roger had a lot in common. Brandon could just imagine what kind of damage a man like that could inflict on someone as gentle and sweet as Kelly. And it made his fists clench and his jaw tighten to know that Kelly had made a date to have dinner with Roger tomorrow night.

Brandon also knew that she'd been putting Roger off

for the last few days, that had the effect of making the guy want her more than ever. The reason Brandon knew this was because he'd been watching her every move. And when Brandon couldn't be around, he'd had others watch her and report back to him. He didn't like Roger, but more than that, he didn't trust him as far as he could kick him.

And while he'd promised Kelly not to do anything that would interfere with her dinner plans with her ex-boyfriend, Brandon had no intention of leaving her truly alone with the guy for a minute. He would remain close by, waiting, watching, making sure that nothing Roger did could ever hurt Kelly again.

The next evening was Kelly's big night. She dressed for her dinner with Roger in a seductive black dress she'd been saving for the occasion. It fit her like a soft, silky glove, with subtle ruching along the sides that accentuated her best curves. Before her makeover, she hadn't even known what ruching was. But now she knew its power, and she liked it. The sleeves of the dress were barely there and the neckline dipped into a heart-shaped curve, nicely showing off just the right amount of cleavage.

She stared at herself in the mirror as she fastened her faux diamond necklace and matching earrings, pleased by her reflection. She'd come a long way and every step had been worth it.

She had decided to join Roger in his elegant suite instead of having dinner in the hotel restaurant. That way, their discussion would be private. In other words, Brandon wouldn't be able to overhear everything and interrupt them for no good reason.

Even though Kelly had known Roger for years and felt perfectly safe with him, she'd gone ahead and checked with the kitchen, just to make sure he had actually ordered dinner. She didn't want him to think he could simply invite her to his room and try to seduce her on an empty stomach. It was a big relief to find out that Roger had, in fact, ordered a lovely dinner for the two of them.

They were to start the evening off with a nice bottle of champagne and a small platter of hors d'oeuvres, then proceed to the entrée of prime rib for two, with chocolate soufflés for dessert. Kelly approved, especially because back when they were dating, Roger had begun to show a touch of cheapness when they dined out. But tonight, he'd pulled out all the stops. Kelly figured he wanted to impress her, and that was exactly what she'd been hoping for.

Now, if she could only get him to beg her to come back to him, her plan would be a success. She would gently refuse him, of course. And if he asked why, she would tell him. He would probably protest and he might even be reduced to insulting her. He excelled at that. But she didn't care. She just wanted the satisfaction of knowing he still found her attractive and wanted her back. Then she could walk out of his life forever and straight into a rosy future.

She had gone over the plan in her mind and even though a part of her knew the whole thing was somewhat petty, she also knew it was something she needed to carry through to the end. Closure. That was her goal. That was all she wanted tonight.

And maybe it was a tiny bit selfish, but she'd been much too nervous to eat lunch earlier, so if she could just arrange to walk out on him *after* she finished that delectable chocolate soufflé, the evening would be a total success.

She never should've come for dinner. The past three hours were a wasted chunk of time she could never get back.

The good news was, the prime rib was cooked to perfection

and the chocolate soufflé was divine. The bad news was, it all sat in her stomach like a brick.

Roger had greeted her at his door looking handsome and debonair in his Armani jacket with his Brooks Brothers pinstriped shirt collar standing up jauntily. She thought the gold ascot was a bit much, but she had to confess that he'd been a perfect gentleman all evening. He'd complimented her and asked her all about life in California. They chatted about mutual friends back East and he shared confidences with her about the people who worked for him.

She was bored stiff.

They'd sipped champagne, nibbled on appetizers, then enjoyed dinner and dessert. And he hadn't made a move on her. What was wrong with him? There simply *must* be something wrong with him tonight. After all, since he'd first checked into the hotel on Monday, he'd been approaching her, seeking her out at least twice a day with an urgency she'd obviously mistaken for desire. Because tonight, there was nothing coming from him. No attraction, no interest, just politeness. A regular snooze-fest.

Maybe it was just as well. After all, she was well and truly *over* Roger. She knew that now. Finally and completely over him. And she had Brandon to thank for it.

"It was such fun catching up with you, Roger," she said, pushing back from the table and standing. "Dinner was wonderful, but I should be going now."

"Kelly, wait," he said, jumping up abruptly and grabbing hold of her hand. "Don't go. We need to talk. About us."

Taken aback, she glanced down at his hand on hers, then up at him. "We've been talking all night, Roger."

He tightened his grip and moved closer. "I know, I know, but I've been holding off saying what needed to be said. Look, Kelly, I want to apologize."

"You do?"

"Yes. God, you look great." He ran his fingers across her shoulder. She shivered, but not in a good way.

"What's this all about, Roger?"

He gritted his teeth, then frowned. He looked vaguely embarrassed. "I've been trying all night to...well, look, I know I said some things I shouldn't have said back when we were together. I was wrong. I was...stupid. But seeing you this week and remembering what we had together, I miss that. I miss you. I want another chance with you. Come back to me, Kelly."

Kelly just stared at him. Now that he was finally saying everything she'd hoped he would say, she didn't believe a single word of it. "I...Roger, I don't know what to say."

"Say yes. Pack your bags and come home with me."

"Roger, I..."

"Wait, don't say a word yet. Just...feel." He made his move, bending his head to kiss her. Actually, it was more of a smashing of his lips against hers.

Maybe it was wrong, but she let him do it. Then he kissed her again with slightly more finesse and Kelly tried really hard to work up some sort of yearning, something, anything. But there was nothing. And she realized it had always been that way. She'd never felt the slightest attraction to Roger. But she'd always thought it was her problem, not his.

Where were the lightning flashes? Where were the fireworks? The rainbows? Sunbursts? She always felt them when Brandon kissed her.

Roger pulled her close and kissed her neck. "Oh, Kelly, we were so good together."

She frowned at that. "We were?"

"You remember." He breathed in her ear. "Don't you feel it all over again when we touch?"

She leaned away to avoid his heavy breath. "I really don't. I'm sorry, Roger. I don't feel anything."

He grabbed her close again. "Yes, you do. I can tell."

"Roger, please don't."

"Now you're just being difficult," he said, trying to angle his head to kiss her again as she tried to push away from him. "Fine, I suppose I deserve some of this after saying the things I said to you five years ago. But you've had your fun. Just admit that you want to come back, and we'll put the past behind us."

With that, he pressed his mouth against hers again and her stomach roiled in protest. She smacked his arm hard enough that he broke off the kiss, giving her a chance to back away from him.

"Don't touch me again," she said when he started walking toward her. "I told you I don't feel the same way about you anymore. I'm leaving now."

He continued to approach her stealthily. "Come on now, Kelly. You're not going to leave after I've spent over three hundred dollars on dinner, are you? You're just nervous because you still don't know how to make love to a man. But don't worry. This time, I'll teach you."

She held up her hand to stop him. "Oh no, you won't. You're the one who doesn't know what you're doing. I know what a really good kiss feels like, Roger. And I just don't feel it from you."

As she stopped to snatch her clutch off the sideboard, Roger grabbed her again. Just then there was a sudden pounding on the door.

Kelly jumped. "What in the world?"

Roger swore loudly. "What is wrong with this damn place?"

"There's nothing wrong with this place!" Kelly said, more insulted by his affront to the hotel than by his disgusting kisses. "There must be something wrong. An emergency."

Someone shouted, "Open up, Hempstead!"

Her eyes widened in shock and she ran to open the door. "Brandon?"

"Duke?" Roger said, scowling at him. "What the hell do you want?"

Brandon walked in and pulled Kelly into his arms. "Are you all right, sweetheart?"

"Take your hands off her, Duke," Roger said in a threatening tone.

"I don't think so," Brandon said, holding her closer.

She took a brief moment to absorb his presence, his scent, his warmth. Then she eased back and gazed up at him. "Brandon, what are you doing here?"

He held Kelly at arm's length and looked her in the eyes. "I know you wanted to get him back, babe. But trust me, he's not the man for you."

Kelly stared at him in bewilderment. "Don't you think I know that?"

"Wait," Roger said. "You want to get me back? Then why aren't you—"

"No," she said immediately, turning to face him. "I didn't want to *get you back*. I wanted to *get back at you*. Big difference."

"I'll say," Brandon said, as his gaze flipped back and forth from Kelly to Roger.

Roger shook his head. "I'm confused."

"Let's get out of here, Kelly," Brandon said, slipping his arm through hers.

"Wait a minute," Roger demanded. "You're leaving with him?"

"Yes, I am."

He snorted. "You think this guy wants you? You really are a fool."

"That's enough, Hempstead," Brandon said quietly.

"Oh, wait. I get it." Roger's laugh was scornful. "You think you're in love with him, don't you? What a load of crap. He just wants you for sex, Kelly. Though God knows why. I'm sure you're still just as lousy in bed as you ever were."

She cringed, but ignored him and kept walking. But Brandon wasn't about to let that go. He turned and said with deceptive calm, "Don't make me hurt you, Hempstead."

But Roger persisted, his eyes wild and desperate. "You can't seriously believe he actually wants you, Kelly. He dates the most beautiful women in the world. Do you really think you can compete with that? You're nothing to him."

She gripped Brandon's arm and forced him to keep walking.

"I mean it, Kelly," Roger said loudly. "You know you'd be better off with me."

At that, Kelly whirled around and shook her finger at him. "No, I wouldn't. I don't mean to be unkind, but you just don't do it for me, Roger. I feel nothing when you kiss me. No spark. No excitement. Nothing. And you know what? It's not my fault. You just don't know how to kiss a woman."

"Fine! Who needs you? Just go," he shouted. As soon as they were out the door, he slammed it behind them.

The night air was crisp and cool as they walked along the wide brick path in silence.

"Well, that was unpleasant," she said finally.

Brandon stopped and studied her in the moonlight. "Are you okay? Did he hurt you?"

"His words were hurtful, but they're nothing I haven't heard before."

He wrapped his arm around her shoulder and pulled her closer. "You managed to get in a few digs."

She nodded. "But it wasn't as satisfying as I thought it would be."

"I'm sorry, sweetheart," Brandon said, as he leaned in close and touched his forehead to hers. "But he's not worth losing sleep over. Especially since he was totally wrong about everything."

"What do you mean?"

"You're fantastic in bed."

She laughed. "You're right."

As they continued walking, she slipped her arm around his waist. "Well, dinner was great anyway. Jean Pierre came through with flying colors."

He chuckled. "Glad to hear it."

After a few more moments, Kelly said, "Roger was right about one thing."

Brandon frowned at her. "No, he wasn't."

"Yes, he was," she said solemnly, and looked up at him. "You only want me for sex."

"You say that like it's a bad thing."

She laughed lightly.

"Come on," he said, squeezing her closer. "Let's go home."

Brandon knew he should've put her to bed and then left her alone. She'd been through a lot with Roger and he could still see remnants of the pain the guy had caused her. But the last thing he wanted to do was leave her with the slightest worry in her mind that anything that schmuck had said was correct.

Tonight, he simply wanted her to feel cherished. Instead of her room, he led her over to his spacious master suite. Once they were inside and the door was closed and

locked, he lifted her into his arms and carried her into
the bedroom, then eased her down until she was standing
beside the bed.

"You look beautiful tonight," he said.

"Thank you," she whispered, gazing up at him.

"Sexy dress." He reached behind her back, found the
zipper and maneuvered it down slowly. "But your skin is
even sexier."

He slipped her sleeves off and inched the dress down
her body, first revealing her luscious full breasts.

"Beautiful." He bent and took first one nipple, then the
other into his mouth, licking, nibbling, sucking until she
was moaning with delight and Brandon felt her fingers
thread through his hair, holding him in place.

Minutes later, he continued removing her dress, baring
her skin inch by soft, gorgeous inch until it dropped to the
floor. He held her hand as she stepped out of the dress,
leaving her wearing a tiny scrap of red lace and her black
heels.

"I can never get enough of you in this wardrobe
combination," he said, moving his hands over her skin,
then dipping his finger between the elastic band of her
panties.

"Brandon…"

"I want to feel you surrender."

She hummed with pleasure. "Yes, please."

In one swift move, he tugged the lace free. Then he
touched her heat and felt her body arch into his.

Unable to resist, he took two seconds to rip his own shirt
off so he could feel her skin against his, then returned his
full attention to her hot, wet core.

As he listened to her sighs and whispers of encouragement, he felt his own body harden and burn with the
anticipation of filling her completely. He moved to cover

her mouth with his, parting her lips with his tongue and sliding inside to taste her essence.

As her breathy groans grew more frantic, his own body tightened with unbearable need. Then she screamed and collapsed against him. He quickly gathered her in his arms and placed her onto the bed. He stripped completely and joined her, wondering if he might expire from the agony of need that had built up inside him.

Blood roared in his ears and he felt himself tremble as he angled his hips and filled her to the hilt. She gasped and lifted herself to allow him to fill her even more, then wrapped her legs around him. They moved in harmony, as though they'd been lovers for years and not just a couple of weeks. He lost himself inside her, lost control, lost sense of everything except the exquisite joining of their bodies as their heartbeats thundered in unison.

He opened his eyes and looked directly into hers and saw the raw desire reflected back at him. As he plunged and thrust to meet her need with his own, he watched as her mouth rounded and she whispered sweet moans of pleasure. The craving for her was so strong, he couldn't resist the pull and he kissed her, swallowing her cries of joy as he followed her to the peak and emptied himself inside her.

# Nine

Roger and his group checked out the next day, and Kelly couldn't have been happier or more relieved to see the last of him. As she strolled back to the office along the pretty, flower-lined path, she thought about the night before. Brandon had been right; Roger really was a jackass and seeing him again made her wonder what she'd ever seen in him in the first place. But that didn't matter anymore.

The only thing that mattered was that before he started insulting her last night, Roger had made it clear that he wanted her back in his life. And Kelly had turned him down flat. Everything had gone according to plan. She had to admit it had been painful to see his true colors, but she finally had closure and that felt really good.

But now she had a much bigger problem to deal with. Brandon. She knew she had to be strong and end things with him, for good. They couldn't continue sleeping together, because even though she'd been teasing him the night before, what she'd said was true. He really did only want her for sex!

Well, of course he also wanted to keep her as his office assistant. He'd told her over and over that she was indispensible to their business. That was nice to hear, and she certainly didn't want to lose that part of her life.

But as far as playing the role of his girlfriend? She couldn't do it anymore.

Facts were facts. Brandon never stayed with one woman longer than a month or so, and he'd already spent almost two weeks with Kelly. Two wonderful weeks. She'd much rather have the happy memories contained in those two weeks than suffer through a painful breakup and be left with nothing but sad memories. And no job.

But above and beyond all of those worries, there was one more thorny issue that Kelly hadn't been willing to face until now.

She was in love with Brandon Duke.

"Oh God," she whispered, and sucked in a breath. How foolish could she get?

She'd finally realized it last night when Brandon came rushing into Roger's room to defend her. He'd been her shining knight, willing to break down doors to protect her, and she'd just about melted at the sight of him. That's when it had dawned on her that she'd lost her heart.

So that was it. She was a fool. She'd broken all the rules and fallen in love.

She would never be able to tell Brandon the truth because she knew it would make him uncomfortable. And if he was uncomfortable, it meant that ultimately, she would have to leave her job and then she would never see him again. So she had already decided to say nothing, to brave it out. She would break up with him, and then get back to doing the job he was paying her to do.

It would have to be strictly business between them from now on. And somehow, some way, she would eventually figure out how to get Brandon Duke out of her heart.

Kelly turned on to the highway and headed south.

Instead of facing Brandon with the truth, Kelly had returned to the office, taken one look at her handsome boss and completely chickened out. She'd claimed exhaustion and begged to take the rest of Friday and all day Monday off. Brandon was gracious enough to give her the time, surmising that she had to be wiped out from her unpleasant run-in with Roger.

She hated lying to Brandon, but she wasn't ready to face the truth and do what she had to do. Now she would use the long weekend to gather her thoughts and figure out the best way to deal with her new reality.

She'd packed a small bag and chosen to drive down the coast and home, to Dunsmuir Bay. Less than four hours later, she pulled her car into the driveway of her marina duplex apartment and turned off the engine. Climbing out of the car, she stretched her limbs and breathed deeply, filling her senses with the pungent scent of cool, salty ocean air. It was good to be home.

She spent what was left of the afternoon dusting the living room and bedroom. Then she poured herself a glass of wine and sat on her terrace, trying to think of nothing at all as she stared at the dark blue water and the movement of boats in the marina.

The next morning, she woke up early and went for a long walk along the waterfront. On her way back, she detoured through the charming block-long section of shops and restaurants known as Old Town Dunsmuir. The intoxicating scent of baked goods lured her into CUPCAKE, Julia Duke's bakery.

She was cheered by the bright blue and white décor and attractive bistro-style tables and chairs that lined the wide, bay windows on either side of the door. She stepped up to the counter and began to drool over the view of so many delicate pastries stacked neatly inside the case.

"Kelly?" someone said.

She glanced over at a small table at the opposite end of the room and saw Julia, Trish and Sally Duke sitting together, enjoying lattes and freshly baked scones.

"Come join us," Sally said.

"Oh, I don't want to intrude on your breakfast."

"You're kidding, right?" Julia teased, and pulled a chair over from a nearby table. "Come sit down. What are you doing here?"

She sat down and smiled gratefully. "I decided to take a few days off and drive down to open up my apartment. We'll be moving back to headquarters in another week or so and I wanted to be prepared."

"Oh, I'll be so glad to have you both back in town," Sally said.

"I'll be glad, too."

Julia stood. "Let me get you a latte."

"Oh, please don't go to any trouble."

"It's no trouble, it's my job," she said with a grin. Just then, Lynnie, the counter girl, came over to take her order and refill Trish's teacup, so Julia sat down again.

"It was great to see you all up in Napa," Kelly said.

"We had a wonderful time," Trish said. "I still dream about Ingrid's magical massages and wake up moaning. I'm sure Adam's getting all sorts of strange ideas."

They all laughed.

"Your husbands are both so wonderful," Kelly said to Trish and Julia. "I probably shouldn't say anything because they're my bosses, after all, but it's so nice to see how much in love they are with both of you."

"It's lovely, isn't it?" Sally said, smiling fondly at her daughters-in-law. "But what about you, Kelly? Wasn't this the week you were going to see a special visitor from your past?"

"Sounds intriguing," Julia said, pulling her chair closer. "Tell us everything."

Kelly laughed. "Oh, it all amounted to a bunch of nothing, really."

"But that's why you wanted the makeover, wasn't it?"

"Yes." Kelly felt herself blush and was glad that Lynnie brought her latte just then. She took a few sips to hide the awkwardness she felt.

"Oh, come on, don't stop now, tell us what happened," Trish said.

Julia patted Kelly's hand. "We promise it won't leave this room, if you're worried that Brandon will find out."

"I'm not worried about that," Kelly said with a frown. "He was right in the middle of it."

"Curiouser and curiouser," Julia said.

They all laughed again, and Kelly went ahead and spilled the story of Roger breaking up with her years ago and her wanting to get back at him.

"He sounds vile," Julia said.

"I'm just happy you got to eat a full dinner," Trish said, rubbing her stomach as the Duke women commiserated with her.

Kelly laughed again. "Yeah, I was happy about that, too." She took another sip of her latte, glad that she'd decided to stop by the bakery. She really liked these women and felt a bond with them, even though she didn't really fit in. Yes, she was sleeping with one of the Duke men, too. But they didn't know about that. And it was over anyway.

That thought was too depressing, so she swept it out of her mind for now.

"This back pain is getting worse," Trish said, arching and twisting to find a more comfortable position. "I hope it doesn't last much longer."

"How long has it been bothering you?" Sally asked.

"All morning."

"Any contractions?"

"Yes, but they don't mean anything. I'm not due for three more days."

Sally and Julia exchanged looks.

"Should we call Adam?" Kelly asked.

"No, no," Trish said, her voice sounding a bit weaker as she stretched her shoulders. "He's at the office today. They've got another big closing this week. I guess you all know that."

"I'll drive you home," Sally offered.

"Or to the hospital," Kelly said.

Trish waved them away. "I'm fine. It'll pass. I'd much rather hear more dirt on Roger. It'll distract me from my aches and pains."

Sally's smile was strained. "Yes, Kelly, and tell us how in the world Brandon got in the middle of this mess."

Kelly willingly explained what happened when Brandon pounded on the door and everyone was impressed by his heroics.

"Uh-oh," Trish said, trying to stand up. "I hate to interrupt the story, but I think my water just broke."

"Don't move," Kelly said, and helped Trish ease back down in the chair. Kelly grabbed her phone and called the office to alert Adam, telling him to meet Trish at the hospital and offering to alert his brothers. That wasn't necessary, since Adam was on a conference call with both men at that moment.

Julia ran into the kitchen and brought back clean dish-cloths.

Sally rubbed Trish's back. "Oh, honey, I'm sorry you're in pain, but I'm so excited. We're going to have a baby!"

At the hospital, Kelly kept trying to leave but Sally wouldn't let her.

"But I'm not part of the family," she protested.

"Yes, you are," Sally insisted. "Besides, you're so cool and calm under pressure, much better than any of us. So if you don't mind, I'd appreciate it if you'd stay."

"Okay, maybe for a little while."

Adam came racing down the hall. "Where is she?"

"She's right inside that room," Sally said, and grabbed Adam's arm. "Take a deep breath first and relax. And fix your hair or you're likely to scare her to death."

"Right." Adam sucked in some air and let it out. His hair looked like he'd been grabbing it to keep from going crazy on the drive from his office to the hospital, so now he smoothed it back with his fingers. Then he grabbed Sally and planted a big kiss on her cheek. "I love you, Mom."

Kelly smiled as happy tears sprang to Sally's eyes.

Cameron jogged down the hall a moment later and greeted Julia with a kiss, then turned to Sally and Kelly. "Brandon's taking the jet down so he should be here in an hour or so."

"Good," Sally said after pulling Cameron close for a hug. "I know Adam will want you all to be here."

Hearing that Brandon would be arriving soon, Kelly touched Sally's arm. "I really should go."

"Please don't," Sally said, then paused and took a long

look at Kelly. "Sweetie, did you want to leave because Brandon is coming?"

"No," she said too quickly, causing Sally's eyebrows to arch.

"Let's have a seat over here," Sally suggested. "I want to ask you something."

Kelly didn't dare refuse or Sally would be even more suspicious, so she followed the older woman over to a quiet corner seating arrangement.

"Now Kelly," Sally began, "I don't mean to pry, but I'm concerned. Do you have feelings for Brandon?"

"Well, of course," she said, trying for a casual tone. "We've worked together for years and he's a great guy. I like him."

Sally folded her arms across her chest. "I think you know what I mean."

Kelly couldn't exactly lie to Brandon's mother so she came clean. "Yes, I know what you mean, and yes, I do like Brandon. A lot. But I also know him really well, and I know that a relationship between us would never work out. He's got women lined up from here all the way to New York City, Mrs. Duke."

"Yes, I know."

"Gorgeous, sophisticated women," she continued with a note of resignation she couldn't disguise. "I can't deal with that kind of competition."

"Oh, I think you can," Sally said.

Kelly shook her head and tried to smile. "Thank you, but I really can't. And even if I could, Brandon just isn't a one-woman man. He goes through them like…well…" She stopped and frowned. It wouldn't be polite to give Sally too many details about her son and all the women in his life.

"Oh, don't bother trying to sugarcoat it, sweetie," Sally

said with a shake of her head. "I know my sons have always been popular with women."

"To say the least," Kelly muttered.

Sally took hold of her hand. "I also know that Brandon is a good, good man, and he's so worthy of love."

"I think so, too," Kelly whispered. "I really do. I just wish, well, I wish I was the one he wanted."

Sally hugged her. "If it means anything at all, I would love it if you were."

Kelly felt tears spring to the surface and she brushed them away. "That's so sweet of you. Thank you."

Sally's eyes narrowed in steely resolve and she murmured something Kelly wasn't sure she heard correctly. But it sounded something like, "We'll just see how sweet I can be."

Brandon walked swiftly down the hospital hall and into the large waiting room. Glancing around, he spied his mother sitting with Julia and Cameron. His brother held a sleepy little Jake against his shoulder.

"What's going on?" Brandon asked.

"Oh sweetie, I'm so glad you're here." Sally jumped up and gave him a hug, then walked with him out into the hall.

Brandon took another visual sweep of the room but didn't see Kelly anywhere. Adam had said that she was the one who had called him earlier to say that Trish was going into labor. So for the last two hours, Brandon had been wondering what the hell Kelly was doing back in Dunsmuir Bay. He'd tried calling her when the plane landed, but she wasn't answering her cell phone. And that rarely happened.

He'd known she was upset about Roger, but now he was

worried that there might be something else bothering her. Otherwise, she would've answered her cell phone.

He glanced up and down the hall. Maybe she'd just gone off to the ladies' room for a minute.

"Are you looking for someone?" his mother asked.

"Yeah, I thought Kelly would be here. Adam said she was on her way to the hospital with all of you."

"She was here for a while, but she left."

"Oh. Is she coming back?"

"I don't know," Sally said, looking a little puzzled. "She seemed to be concerned about not being here when you showed up."

"Not being here?" Now it was Brandon's turn to be puzzled. "Why wouldn't she want to be here when I got here?"

"She said that she wasn't part of the family, so she thought it best if she left."

"What?" he said in disbelief, then muttered, "Well, that's dumb."

"Is it?" she asked.

"Okay, Mom, what are you getting at?"

"We talked about this before, Brandon," she said. "I thought we were in agreement. But now I have to ask you, are you involved with Kelly?"

"Why? What did she say?"

Sally rolled her eyes. "She didn't say a word, but she seemed uncomfortable sticking around. And you didn't answer the question."

"Come on, Mom, let it go."

But his mother gave him "the look," and he capitulated.

"Okay, fine, but it's not like we're really involved. We're just having a good time."

"Oh, sweetie." Sally shook her head. "I don't think Kelly is that kind of girl."

"You've said that before," he said, rubbing his jaw in frustration. "I'm not even sure I know what you mean."

"Yes, you do. She's not as sophisticated as most of the women you date. She doesn't know the rules of the game like those women do. Kelly's sensitive and sweet. She wants to meet a nice guy and fall in love and settle down. And we both know that's not you."

"Hey, I'm a nice guy."

She patted his arm. "Yes, you are, and I know you wouldn't hurt her deliberately. But if you don't stop seeing her, you're going to break her heart."

Trish gave birth to an eight-pound baby boy at two o'clock the following morning. They named the baby Tyler Jackson Duke. Despite the late hour, Adam passed out cigars to his brothers and the whole family celebrated with champagne and apple juice for Trish. Brandon snapped a picture with his phone and sent it along with a text message to Kelly, announcing the birth. A few hours later, he received a two-word message back from her. "Congratulations, Uncle!"

So at least she was communicating with him again, Brandon thought with relief. He decided not to press her any further, knowing he would see her on Tuesday, less than two days from now. By then, she would be long over Roger and back to being her old self. Then she and Brandon could talk about a few things. Meanwhile, as long as he was in Dunsmuir Bay, he'd planned a busy day for himself that centered on finding new and creative ways to spoil his brand-new bouncing baby nephew.

# Ten

Tuesday morning, Brandon walked across the wide terrace toward his office, amused to find he had a spring in his step. He knew where it had come from.

Kelly would be back in the office today and he was really looking forward to seeing her again.

But when he walked into the office, she wasn't at her desk, and he felt a trickle of panic seep down his spine. He ruthlessly shoved the feeling away. It was no big deal. In fact, it was still early. She would be here any minute.

He walked into his inner office, took off his jacket and hung it on the back of his door. Sitting at his desk, he pulled up his calendar to study what was in store for the week. Meetings, conference calls and the start of organizing the move back to headquarters in Dunsmuir Bay. The brief visit home over the weekend had reminded him just how much he missed his family and all the amazing advantages there were to living on the California coast.

It was a full ten minutes later when he finally heard Kelly walk in. A part of him he hadn't even realized was tense began to relax.

"Morning, Kelly," he called. "Come on in when you're settled."

"Okay."

A few minutes later, after starting the coffee and powering up her computer, she walked in.

Brandon looked up and started to grin, then felt his mouth drop open. She was dressed in an old, dull gray pantsuit with a black turtleneck underneath. Her hair was pulled back in a ponytail and she wore the thick horned-rim glasses he thought she'd destroyed.

"What happened to you?" he asked before he could stop himself, then quickly shook his head. "I mean, did you lose your contact lenses?"

"No, the glasses are just easier," she explained. "Now that Roger's gone, I thought I'd go back to wearing some of my more comfortable outfits. This looks okay, doesn't it?"

"Yeah, sure," he said, stymied by her decision.

"Good." She hesitated, then sat down in the chair in front of his desk. "We need to talk, Brandon."

"Okay, let's talk," he said, and watched her take her glasses off and fiddle with them nervously.

Studying her, he realized she looked even better than ever, without any makeup on. True, those pants she wore were too damned baggy and the color did nothing to complement her complexion, but Brandon knew that underneath all that material was a stunning pair of world-class legs. The sudden image of her naked thighs caused his groin to stiffen instantly. With a silent groan, he wheeled his chair closer to his desk to mask the problem.

She took a deep breath and finally started talking. "Don't be angry, but I have to thank you."

He scowled at her. "I thought we'd agreed you wouldn't do that."

"I'm sorry, but I can't help it," she said. "Just let me get through this, okay?"

"Of course. Go ahead."

"Okay." After another deep breath, she said, "First, I have to thank you for helping me prepare for Roger's visit. I think you know what I mean by that. And second, thank you for coming to his hotel room door when you did. Your timing was perfect and it was nice to know that you had my back while I was in there sparring with Roger."

He grinned. "Right. You're welcome."

"Good," she said with a nod of her head. "I'm happy to say that I've kept my original bargain not to fall for you, and now I'm ready to go back to life as we knew it before my ex-boyfriend's name was ever mentioned in this office."

"And what does that mean, exactly, Kelly?"

She refused to meet his gaze as she clutched her hands together in her lap. "It means, you know, we'll no longer be sleeping together."

"Sleeping together."

"Oh, you know." She looked up and her smile was shaky. "Not that I didn't enjoy every moment, I really did. You know I did. But…I'm sorry, Brandon, it's time to end things, once and for all. It was wonderful, but I'm…so sorry." With that, she bolted out of the chair and walked briskly out of his office, closing the door behind her.

As he watched her go, he pondered her words. Part of him was highly dissatisfied with her decision not to continue with their sexual arrangement.

On second thought, *all* of him was dissatisfied. Hell, he

wanted her right now. Even in that ugly suit of hers, she was hotter than any woman he'd known in a long time.

Leaning his elbows on the desk, he thought about his next move. Maybe he would let her stew for a few hours, then ask her to have dinner with him tonight. A great meal, a few glasses of wine, and he was confident they'd end up back in his bed again.

His mother's words suddenly echoed in his brain. Damn, that was the problem with having a conscience. He knew Sally was right. Kelly was sweet and sensitive and deserved to find love some day. If Brandon had his way and their affair continued, Kelly would wind up being hurt eventually. If he wasn't careful, he might just break her heart.

But what about Brandon's heart?

He sat back in his chair and rubbed his chest thoughtfully. Maybe he'd pulled a muscle because for some strange reason, he felt an aching twinge that felt almost like grief.

Brandon asked her out to dinner that night and she politely refused.

The next day, he asked her to join him for lunch and she said she had other plans.

Finally, he asked her if she'd like to come to his room later that evening.

"You know I can't do that, Brandon," she said and tried to smile.

"I figured it was worth a shot," he said.

"I'm sorry," she said, staring up at him from her desk chair. "This whole situation is my fault."

"How's that?"

"It was completely unprofessional of me to drag you into my problems in the first place. But now I'm just anxious for everything to return to business as usual. I hope you can help me do that."

"Right. Okay. Sure." He nodded and walked back into his office, and Kelly had to take great gulping breaths to keep from bursting into tears.

She wasn't sure she could continue working in the same office with him every day. But the alternative was to never see him again and there's no way she could go through that.

She simply had to stop thinking about kissing him and touching him. She had to stop thinking about the way he had touched her and made her laugh. She just had to stop thinking! And she would.

It might take another thirty or forty years, but she was absolutely positive she would get over him.

"It's your mother on line two," Kelly announced over the intercom line.

"Thanks, Kelly," he said, and pressed the button. "Hi, Mom."

"Hi, sweetie, I haven't heard from you all week so I'm calling to make sure you're all right."

"I'm fine. How are you doing?"

"Oh, everything is wonderful. The baby is so beautiful." She went on for five minutes about the joy of baby Tyler. When she finally exhausted that subject, she said, "How's Kelly?"

"She's fine," he said. "Why do you ask?"

"You sound a little irritated. Is everything all right?"

"Sure, why wouldn't it be?" Brandon snapped. "Kelly seems to have forgotten that we ever had sex with each other in the first place, so things are just dandy."

"Ah," she said.

What the hell? Did he really just say that out loud?

Great. Now if only he could kick himself in the ass, everything would be fan-freaking-tastic. "Sorry, Mom, I'm just a little busy right now."

But she wasn't buying that line. "Brandon, are you in love with Kelly?"

"What?" he shouted.

"No need to yell," she said softly. "Sweetie, why else would you be so upset that she doesn't want to sleep with you?"

"Who said I was upset?"

She started laughing, which just annoyed him more.

"Look, Mom, I really don't have time for—"

"Now you listen to me, Brandon Duke. It's as clear as the nose on your face that you're in love with that girl, and I expect you to marry her."

"Mom, what've you been smoking?"

"Very funny, Brandon," she said drily. "You can deny it all you want but I know you better than you know yourself."

He sighed. "I really have to go. I love you, Mom."

"I love you too, son. Call me later and tell me how it went. Bye-bye."

He hung up the phone and rubbed his neck. Damn, between his mother's wild assumptions and Kelly's stiff-shirted business competence, he was likely to go insane.

For the past three days, he'd managed to put up with Kelly's firm need to work professionally and reliably in his office. She was the ultimate assistant, always answering his phones, making his coffee, transcribing his calls, typing his letters, being polite and businesslike at all times.

It was enough to make him spit nails.

He'd made it clear when she returned from Dunsmuir Bay that he would be more than happy to continue their sexual relationship. But Kelly had refused him. He might've asked her again once or twice, maybe three times more during the week. Okay, maybe four times, max.

All of a sudden, she'd turned on him and accused him of being attracted to her only because she'd gotten her makeover!

He'd attempted to deny it, but she'd seen right through him. She'd asked him point-blank, how could she trust his feelings for her now if that was the only reason he'd originally been interested in her?

It seemed an unfair question given his almost constant state of arousal these past few days. Because the irony was, even though she'd gone back to wearing her drab and dowdy pantsuits, he was still getting turned on whenever she walked into the room. But now that he could safely admit that her getting a makeover had nothing to do with his attraction to her, she didn't want to hear him out.

And ever since she'd asked the question, Brandon had seriously wondered why he'd never realized how sexy she was before. Because now it was so damned obvious.

She was a beautiful woman in every way and he couldn't keep his eyes off her whenever she walked into a room. And if he didn't see her right away, he would catch a whiff of her scent, and it drove him wild with desire. But when he accused her of wearing too much perfume, she had the audacity to claim that she never wore perfume.

So maybe he really was going crazy. Maybe he needed a vacation. But where would he go? He already lived in a beautiful part of California and that was pretty close to paradise. He didn't know where to go or what to do and he didn't care. All he knew was that he couldn't keep seeing Kelly every hour of every day and not hold her in his arms again.

"I'll be back in a while," he said to her and rushed out of the office. He headed for his room and once he was there, he decided to go for a run. It would be good to work off some of this insanity. Maybe he'd eaten some bad mushrooms and his brain was filled with toxins. It could happen. Exercise was the answer.

As he ran, he contemplated the situation objectively. He had to admit that breaking up with Kelly had been the best for both of them. She was his employee, after all, and he shouldn't have taken advantage of her in the first place. Of course, that wasn't really fair because, after all, the whole affair had been her idea.

He smiled at the thought, then chuckled. Okay, he was willing to admit that maybe he'd nudged her in the right direction. But nothing changed the fact that it was still best if they didn't sleep together again. But damn, he missed her, and not just in bed. She had a savvy business mind and it was fun to bounce ideas back and forth with her. She made him laugh. How many women had ever made him laugh?

But that didn't matter, because his mother was right about one thing, much as he hated to admit it. Kelly had "white picket fence" practically tattooed across her forehead. She deserved a good man who would love her and treat her right, give her a couple of kids, plus a dog, a couple of hamsters and a fish bowl.

The fact that he hated to picture another man in her bed was something he didn't dwell on too deeply.

Somewhere during his fifth mile, as his breath wheezed out and he had to sweep the sweat from his eyes, Brandon figured out the solution to his problem. It was so simple. He just needed to get laid.

Tonight he would make a few calls to some women he knew, arrange a date or two for the weekend, and participate in some mind-blowing sex. And maybe then this out-of-control desire for Kelly would disappear.

* * *

Kelly adjusted her glasses and continued typing the letter Brandon had dictated. She hated these old eyeglasses but she knew it was better to wear them and look drab, if only to keep Brandon at a distance.

Today, she wore the dark purple pantsuit she'd owned forever. It was so old, it still had lumpy shoulder pads sewn into the jacket. With her sensible brown shoes and her hair pulled back, she looked like someone's maiden aunt. But she could live with that.

It helped to stare at herself in the mirror each morning after she was dressed and ready to go and realize she truly had no business falling in love with her handsome boss. *You are a total cliché,* she would repeat to herself daily. But no matter how many times she had scolded herself, she still hadn't been able to keep from rushing right toward that cliff.

Every time she saw him, she had to fight to ignore her feelings. After all, it wasn't as if he would ever ask her to marry him, for God's sake. So who was she trying to fool? He would never settle down, certainly not with her. A woman would have to be a blithering idiot to think that he would, and Kelly had never been an idiot. Well, not until recently, anyway.

The door swung open and an absolutely beautiful woman walked into the office. She was tall and willowy, with long flowing blond hair and the bluest eyes Kelly had ever seen. Were those contact lenses? No, they had to be real. She was too perfect, too ethereal, not to be completely real.

Kelly shook her head in defeat as she recognized the woman. This was Bianca Stephens, the beautiful wicked witch of her nightmares. Live and in person. And she was the most stunning woman Kelly had ever seen.

"You must be Karen," she said haughtily. "I'm here to see Brandon. He's expecting me."

Kelly didn't have the strength or interest to correct her name again, nor did she care to have the unpleasant woman standing around glaring at her while she checked with Brandon.

"Go right in," Kelly said, and swept her hand toward Brandon's closed door.

"I certainly will."

Bianca closed the door behind her and Kelly felt as though the wind had been knocked out of her. She slumped forward and laid her head on her desk. This was the last straw. She couldn't take it anymore.

When she realized she was crying, she knew she had to act immediately. She couldn't continue living like this. She was hopelessly in love with the big jerk in the next room and she could no longer sit by and watch him play his games with other women.

She was finished making romantic dinner reservations for him and his flavor of the week. She was finished buying diamond tennis bracelets for his civilized breakups.

She was finished.

With all the energy she could muster, she sat up and wiped the tears away, then quickly typed a letter of resignation and emailed it to him. Pulling her purse from the bottom drawer, she stood up and walked out of the office.

"Hello, Brandon darling," Bianca said, closing the door behind her.

"Bianca," he said, unable to disguise his shock.

"Aren't you happy to see me?"

"Uh, yeah, sure," he said, pushing away from his desk and standing to greet her. "But what are you doing here?"

"It was just so good to hear from you the other night," she said, kissing his cheek, then using her little finger to smooth her lipstick. It was a move meant to entice and he'd seen her do it a dozen times before. He watched as she strolled over to the floor-to-ceiling window and gazed nonchalantly at the view. "I didn't feel like waiting for the weekend, so I had Gregory drive me out here to you."

"I see."

She spread her arms in invitation. "And here I am. Are you happy to see me?"

"Happy? Yeah, sure." He looked beyond Bianca over to the closed door. "Did you see my assistant out there?"

"Yes, and honestly, Brandon, I can't believe you still have that rude woman working for you."

"Rude? Kelly?"

"I shouldn't criticize," she said, staring at her fingernails, "but she was very unpleasant to me on the phone the other day."

"Kelly?" Distracted now, Brandon checked his telephone. There was no red light to indicate that his trusted assistant was on the phone. So why hadn't she buzzed him to warn him about Bianca? Where the hell was she? "I'm a little busy today, Bianca."

"Too busy for me?" she said, pouting.

Okay, that might've come across a little harsh. "Uh, no, of course not. It's nice to see you."

"I certainly hope so," she said. "I've come all this way."

He stared at her for a moment. He'd forgotten how beautiful she was, and how self-centered. "Yeah. What a surprise. I just need to handle a few things…"

"You're going to keep working?"

"Just for a minute," he said, folding up the files that were spread on his desk. "Then I guess we can go have a drink or something."

"Sounds yummy." She sat in his visitor's chair and pulled out her smartphone. "I'll just sit here and check my messages until you're ready."

"Fine."

A soft ding came from his computer and he rushed to check his email. It was from Kelly. Good. Maybe she was going to explain exactly how in the hell Bianca had gotten in here.

He opened the message, skimmed the words, but couldn't believe them. *Two weeks' notice...Resignation... Thank you for the opportunity...*

"What?" He stood up. "No, no, no."

"No?" Bianca said.

He stared at her again, wondering why she was here. But he knew why. He was the one who'd called her and told her he wanted to see her. What the hell was wrong with him? He shook his head and muttered, "I'm an idiot."

"Brandon?" Bianca said. "Are you ill?"

He'd made a huge mistake.

"Sorry, Bianca," he said, pulling her gently from the chair and walking her to the door. "You'll have to tell Gregory to drive you back to the city. Something's come up."

He raced out the door.

Kelly had just pulled her suitcase out of the closet when the pounding began. She sighed as she walked across the room to answer the door.

Brandon stood there, looking so handsome, so tall and rugged. And so concerned. "You can't just leave me."

"I'm not just leaving you," she said, leading him into her room. "I'm giving you two weeks' notice."

"But why? Did Bianca say something to make you angry? Is that what this is about?"

"No, of course not." She opened a drawer, grabbed a neatly stacked pile of shirts and put them in her suitcase.

"She did. She said something. I knew it." He paced across the floor. "I've sent her away. I didn't ask her to come to the office, Kelly. She's gone and you'll never see her again. You can't quit."

"Yes, I can. And it's not about Bianca." Kelly shook her head, still a little horrified that Brandon could enjoy spending time with someone as awful as Bianca. But that was none of her business. Not anymore.

"Then why are you leaving? We work really well together."

"We do. Or we did." She smiled sadly at him as she stacked a few pairs of jeans into her suitcase. "But then I broke the rules."

"What rules?" he asked as he walked back and forth behind her. "What are you talking about?"

"The ground rules, remember?" She took a deep breath and turned to gaze up at him. "I fell in love with you, Brandon."

He was stunned into silence.

"I know," she said lightly, reaching for her lingerie and tossing it all onto the bed. "It was a shock to me, too."

"What?" He grabbed her and whipped her around to face him. "No. No, you didn't. I'm a jerk, remember? A big baby when I'm sick. I'm…I'm superstitious. You'd be crazy to fall for me, remember? That's what you said. And you promised you wouldn't…"

"I know what I promised," she said. "And I'm really sorry, but it looks like I wasn't able to keep my word."

"I don't believe it."

"It's true." She patted his arm and stepped back. "I'm sorry."

He blew out a heavy breath, then said slowly, "It had to

be Bianca's fault. When she walked in, you got mad and left."

"I'm not mad," she insisted, shaking her head.

"Then why did you leave? She's gone. I don't want her around. I realized that as soon as I saw her. Was she rude to you? She can be a little abrasive."

"Oh, Brandon." Kelly smiled sadly. "Don't you see? If it's not Bianca, it'll be someone else. My point is, there will always be other women in your life."

"But I want *you* in my life."

"I want you, too, but not in the way you're talking about. Look, I know you're not in love with me. And that's okay. You're not the sort of man to settle down with one woman and I've always known that. This isn't your fault. I'm the one who broke the rules."

"I forgive you."

She laughed. "Thank you. But today I realized that I can't sit outside your office and watch women come and go. Call me a weakling, but I can no longer go shopping for gifts for the women you're sleeping with. I'm sorry."

He grabbed her hands. "This is all my fault."

"How do you figure?" she asked, forcing herself to look into his deep blue eyes.

"We were just too good together. But that's not love, Kelly," he hastened to explain. "That's just good sex."

She laughed again, then realized she'd begun to cry and ruthlessly swiped away the tears. "Yes, the sex was good, really good. But I know my own heart, Brandon. I know that what I feel for you is love, and I know you don't feel the same. I'm okay with that."

"Well, maybe I'm not."

"I'm sorry. But you must understand, I can't work for you anymore."

"Damn, Kelly." He raked his fingers through his hair in frustration. "I don't know what to do to make this right."

"There's nothing you can do to make it right. I'll stay on for two weeks and hire my replacement. Then I'll leave."

The two weeks went by too quickly, and before Brandon was ready to deal with the change, Kelly was gone. Her replacement was Sarah, an older woman so amazingly well organized that she scared Brandon a little. Kelly had trained the woman so well that in no time at all, she could do almost everything as well as her predecessor had.

But she wasn't Kelly.

Sarah organized the major office move back to Dunsmuir Bay, and it went flawlessly from start to finish. Brandon was back in his office without a wrinkle in his schedule. Sarah was an organizational genius.

But she wasn't Kelly.

Brandon knew he would snap out of this funk any day now. After all, it wasn't like he was in love with Kelly. He wasn't in love with anyone. He didn't *do* love. It was just that he missed her. And why not? They'd worked together for over four years. That was all. They'd gotten to know each other well and it was weird that she wasn't around. That was all it was.

And he'd get over it. As usual, he knew exactly what he needed to do to wipe her out of his mind. He would have to make some more phone calls. He had to find another woman to take her place. Not Bianca of course, remembering her visit. Why had he ever wanted to spend time with that vacuous, vain woman? There were plenty of other women out there.

But frankly, he couldn't quite imagine himself having a romantic conversation with another woman. He couldn't picture himself sitting across a dinner table, asking another woman about herself, sharing a bottle of wine, spending an entire evening with her, whoever she might be. He tried to picture the sort of woman he'd dated in the past, tried to remember what he'd talked about with them. But he couldn't remember. They had all faded into the fog and now all he could recall were the fun times with Kelly, when they'd talked and laughed and shared secrets for hours. Whenever he tried to imagine spending time with someone else, he found himself bored to death.

So he buried himself in work, knowing he would snap out of it any day now.

The following Saturday, Adam and Trish invited everyone over to see the baby. Brandon pulled up in front of their sprawling Craftsman home and parked his car, then sat with his hands on the wheel and contemplated whether he should even go inside the house. It had been an effort to get out of bed that morning and he wondered if he'd caught some kind of flu. He didn't want to be around the baby if he was sick.

But his head and sinuses were perfectly clear and he wasn't coughing or anything. His stomach was fine, although he hadn't given a lot of thought to fine dining lately. And he was feeling kind of run-down. He chalked it up to the big move back home and climbed out of the car.

Cameron stood on the front porch. "Hey, did you forget the beer?"

"Nope, got it right here," he said, and jogged back around to the trunk of his car. He shook his head as he grabbed the case of beer he'd bought ten minutes ago on the way over to Adam's house. Where was his brain today?

He found himself asking that same question all afternoon. Whenever his mother or brothers asked him a question, he'd realize halfway through his answer that he'd wandered off on some tangent or another.

They were gathered around the wide bar that separated the kitchen from the family room when his mother finally reached up and pressed the back of her hand to his forehead. "Are you feeling all right, sweetie?"

"Yeah, I'm fine," he said, and grabbed a tortilla chip. "Just a little distracted."

"I hope you're not coming down with something."

"Nope, just working too hard. I might need a vacation."

"Oh, speaking of vacation, I ran into Kelly yesterday," Julia said as she crossed the kitchen with a bowl of salsa. "She just got back from visiting her family. She looks wonderful."

Brandon's ears perked up. "She was back east?"

"That's right," Sally said, dragging a chip through the fresh salsa. "You know her family lives in Vermont."

"Yeah." He studied his beer bottle.

Julia sipped her lemonade. "Roger lives in her hometown, doesn't he?"

"Roger?" Brandon felt the sudden, bitter taste of bile in his throat. "She saw Roger when she went home?"

Trish shut the refrigerator door and turned. "Well, they're both in the same town."

There was no way Kelly had gone back east to see Roger. Brandon knew that in his gut. She wouldn't waste a minute of her time with him. But if Roger was from her hometown, maybe he knew her family. Maybe Kelly's father knew Roger's father. Had her family wanted her to marry Roger? Hell. Brandon knew all about family pressure.

"Sweetie, you do look pale," Sally said, clutching his arm.

Brandon swallowed the last of his beer. "I just need a damn vacation."

He decided to spend a few days back at the Napa resort, but he didn't go there as the boss. Instead, he brought along his oldest boots, his rattiest blue jeans, some tattered shirts, and put himself to work in the vineyards.

As teenagers, Brandon and his brothers had spent a few summers on construction sites around Dunsmuir Bay, so he knew what hard labor was good for. It was basic and tough and real. Sweat and hard work helped a man think about his life, what was authentic and what was fantasy, what was important and what was crap. At the end of a long day, a man could look around and see what he'd accomplished.

As Brandon walked across the fields past the newly weeded and raked rows of grapevines, whose leaves were dry and brittle in the autumn twilight, he looked around and saw what he'd accomplished.

And he knew exactly what was missing.

Kelly had been back from Vermont for over a week now and knew it was time to start compiling her list of social organizations. She'd been putting the task off for long enough. She had a goal, remember? It was time to dive into the dating pool before she grew too old to swim.

There was a knock on her door and Kelly's heart fluttered in her chest.

"Oh, stop it," she scolded herself as she glanced up at the wall clock. It had to be the mailman, that was all. Brandon didn't even know where she lived! What earthly reason would he have for being here? Would she always flip out every time the doorbell chimed or the telephone rang? She put the last dish away in the cabinet and hung up the damp dish towel, then walked over to open the front door.

And forgot how to breathe.

"B-Brandon?"

"Hey, Kelly," he said. "Listen, I need some help."

She blinked, not quite believing her eyes. He stood leaning against her doorjamb looking better than she remembered, and she remembered him looking pretty darn good.

"You gonna let me come in?" he asked.

"Oh, sure." She swung the door open wider for him. "Did Sarah quit?"

"No." He walked into her home, filling the space. "Sarah's fine. She does good work."

"Oh. Okay." She closed the door and stared at him. It had been four long weeks since she'd last seen him and she'd spent all that time trying to stay busy, trying not to think about him, trying to get on with her life. She'd traveled back east for a week to see her father and sisters and their families. It had been a lovely visit, but the trip had cemented in her the understanding that Dunsmuir Bay was truly her home. Now she just had to put the pieces of her life back together. She'd started her list of dating possibilities. And she'd spent all day yesterday on her computer, searching the various employment sites, looking for a new job. She had a list of promising prospects and she planned to send résumés tomorrow.

But now, seeing Brandon, she couldn't remember exactly what any of those job prospects were.

"This is a nice place," he said, glancing around, then walking over to the wide picture window. "Great view."

"Thank you." Was he even taller than she remembered?

Maybe it was seeing him in her house for the first time that made her think so. She licked her lips nervously. "You said you needed my help with something?"

"Yeah." He seemed to consider something for a moment, then walked up close and took hold of her hand. Kelly tried not to focus on the fact that her hand fit so perfectly in his.

He gazed down, then back at her. "You know, this is a little embarrassing. I wonder if maybe we could sit and talk for a few minutes."

"Okay." She led the way to her comfortable sofa and he sat down way too close to her. "What is it, Brandon?"

"The thing is, Kelly, I need some help with my kissing. I'm not sure if I'm doing it right anymore."

She tried to swallow around her suddenly dry throat. "You're kidding, right?"

"Nope. I'm desperate."

She shook her head. "Brandon, you're the last man on earth who needs help with his kissing."

"See, that's where you're wrong," he said, clutching her hand more tightly.

"Okay, fine. But you could get any woman in the world to help you out. Why are you here?"

"Well, that's the thing." He touched her cheek, then ran his fingers through her hair. "I found out it only works right when I'm kissing the person I love."

"Oh Brandon," she said on a sigh.

"I'm in love with you, Kelly."

"No," she whispered.

"I don't blame you for questioning me, because I've been an idiot. I convinced myself that there was no way you could really love me."

"But that's—"

She stopped when he pressed his finger to her lips. "Just

let me get this out because it's not easy for me to admit some things."

With a nod, she said, "Okay."

He clenched his jaw, then began. "My parents were really bad people, really bad. They taught me some hard lessons early on. I'd rather not get into the specifics, but one of the luckiest days of my life was when Sally took me in. But even though she's a fantastic mother and I owe her everything, those first ugly memories lingered."

She put her hand on his knee for her own comfort as well as his, but didn't say anything.

"Because of those old memories," he continued, "I decided a long time ago that I would never really matter to anyone, you know? So I just made up my mind that I would never fall in love. That way, nobody could ever get close enough to hurt me."

"Oh, Brandon."

"It took your leaving for me to realize just how much I wanted to matter to you," he said. "I was blown away when you told me you were in love with me. At first, I couldn't make myself believe it. It was too...*important*, you know?"

"Yes, I know."

He covered her hand with his. "To be honest, it scared the hell out of me. But I want to be important to you, Kelly. I want you to love me, because I'm so in love with you. My heart is empty when you're not around. I can't really live without you in my life."

A tear fell from her eye and Brandon ran his thumb along her cheek to catch the next one. "Please, Kelly. Please put me out of my misery and tell me you still love me."

"Of course I still love you, Brandon," she said. "I love you with all my heart."

"Marry me?" he asked, as he touched her face with both

of his hands. "I want to spend the rest of my life showing you how much I love you."

"Yes, I'll marry you."

"I love you so much."

"Then will you kiss me, please?"

Holding back a smile, he said, "I'm not sure I remember how. Maybe you'd better show me."

She laughed and wrapped her arms around him. "Practice makes perfect."

His laughter joined hers. "Then we'd better get started."

Joy swept through her as he enfolded her in his arms and kissed her with all the love that was overflowing in his heart for her alone. And it was perfect.

# Epilogue

*Two years later*

Midsummer along the central California coast meant warm days and balmy nights and Brandon Duke couldn't think of a better reason to throw a party. Unless it was also a surprise party celebrating his mother's birthday.

As he walked the perimeter of the backyard where family and friends were gathered, Brandon soaked up the sights and sounds of the party. He couldn't help smiling as he realized just how different his and his brothers' lives were now than they had been just a few short years ago.

Back then, this would've been a stylish cocktail party with subdued conversations. Instead, there were sudden bursts of laughter and splashing around the pool. He grinned as he caught a flash of his mom's shocking pink Capri pants that made her look like a teenager. The scents of an ocean breeze and suntan lotion blended with barbecued chicken and ice-cold lemonade.

At that moment, from across the patio, he caught Kelly's eye and felt the fierce punch of joy he always experienced when he gazed upon his beautiful wife. He watched with pride and love as she stroked her stomach where their unborn child, a baby boy, waited patiently to be born. Kelly had changed everything in his life for the better and was just days away from making him a father. Brandon knew without a doubt that with Kelly by his side, he could face any obstacle, conquer any fear. Their future was rosy indeed.

And even though his mother had denied it a thousand times, Brandon was positive she'd had something to do with bringing the two of them together. He would have to thank her some day.

Cameron came up behind him and slapped Brandon on the shoulder. "Great party, man. I think Mom was really surprised."

"For a minute there, I thought she stopped breathing," Brandon admitted, shaking his head.

"Yeah, then she burst into tears." Cameron laughed. "It was perfect."

They both glanced over and Cameron grinned as his son Jake loudly explained to his baby sister Samantha how to race a dump truck on the brick path surrounding the house. In the pool, their little cousin T.J. bobbed confidently in his proud father Adam's arms. Adam continued to insist to whoever would listen that his boy would be competing as an Olympic swimmer any day now.

"Hey, thanks for the invite, Brandon."

Brandon whirled around and saw his cousin, Aidan, popping open a bottle of beer.

"Glad you could make it," Brandon said. "It's about time

we all finally met. And it was a perfect way to surprise Mom on her birthday."

Aidan's identical twin brother, Logan, grabbed his own bottle and the two men joined Brandon and Cameron to survey the activity.

"You have a terrific family," Logan said, smiling his approval.

"Thanks," Cameron said jovially. "We're happy you guys are a part of it."

"It's all because of your mom," Aidan said, chuckling. "She shocked the hell out of Dad when she first called him. He'd been trying to track down his brother Bill for years, but when their orphanage burned down, the records were lost and he finally gave up trying."

Brandon shook his head as he thought of that fateful fire. Sally's husband Bill and his brother Tom were adopted by different families and lost touch with each other. If not for Sally Duke and her stubborn refusal to give up, the Duke brothers might never have met their cousins.

"It almost broke Sally's heart when she heard about the fire," Cameron said. "But Mom is nothing if not tenacious. Once she got the hang of Google and started searching through every bit of information she could find, it was inevitable that she would track you guys down."

"We're thankful that she did," Logan said. "Dad was over the moon about finally getting to meet all of you."

The four cousins stared across the covered patio at Sally and the tall, good-looking older man standing next to her. This was Tom, her deceased husband Bill's brother.

Brandon peered more closely and couldn't help but notice the goofy grin on Tom's face as he gazed down at Sally. He turned and frowned at Logan. "Your father's a widower, right?"

"Yeah, and your mom is a widow," Logan said with a speculative look. "What the hell?"

Adam wrapped a towel around his waist and walked over to grab a bottle of beer before joining his brothers and cousins. After taking a healthy sip of his drink, he jutted his chin in the direction of Sally and Tom, then looked at Brandon and Cameron. "They seem to be enjoying themselves."

"Yeah, we were just noticing that," Aidan said.

Cameron scratched at his beard thoughtfully. "Not sure what to think yet."

Brandon took a long, reflective pull of his beer. "Maybe this family isn't quite finished with matchmaking after all."

\* \* \* \* \*

A sneaky peek at next month...

# Desire™

**PASSIONATE AND DRAMATIC LOVE STORIES**

*My wish list for next month's titles...*

> 2 stories in each book - only **£5.49!**

In stores from 16th March 2012:

☐ Enticed by His Forgotten Lover — Maya Banks

& The Billionaire's Borrowed Baby — Janice Maynard

☐ Reclaiming His Pregnant Widow — Tessa Radley

& To Touch a Sheikh — Olivia Gates

☐ An After-Hours Affair — Barbara Dunlop

& Millionaire Playboy, Maverick Heiress — Robyn Grady

☐ Much More Than a Mistress — Michelle Celmer

& Bachelor Untamed — Brenda Jackson

**Available at WHSmith, Tesco, Asda, Eason, Amazon and Apple**

*Just can't wait?*

*Visit us Online*

You can buy our books online a month before they hit the shops! **www.millsandboon.co.uk**

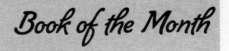

# Special Offers

Every month we put together collections and longer reads written by your favourite authors.

Here are some of next month's highlights— and don't miss our fabulous discount online!

**DIANA PALMER**
**LINDA LAEL MILLER**
*Untameable*

On sale 16th March

*Escape for Easter*

TRISH MOREY · KIM LAWRENCE · AMY ANDREWS

On sale 16th March

Over 400 Million of her books in print worldwide
**NORA ROBERTS**
*Considering Kate*

On sale 6th April

*Save 20%*
*on all Special Releases*

Find out more at
**www.millsandboon.co.uk/specialreleases**

*Visit us Online*

# Have Your Say

## You've just finished your book. So what did you think?

We'd love to hear your thoughts on our 'Have your say' online panel
**www.millsandboon.co.uk/haveyoursay**

- Easy to use
- Short questionnaire
- Chance to win Mills & Boon® goodies

## The World of Mills & Boon®

There's a Mills & Boon® series that's perfect for you. We publish ten series and with new titles every month, you never have to wait long for your favourite to come along.

**Blaze**
Scorching hot, sexy reads

**By Request**
Relive the romance with the best of the best

**Cherish**
Romance to melt the heart every time

**Desire**
Passionate and dramatic love stories